# RUN FOR THE SHADOWS

Ella Drummond

Published by Green Shutter Books Ltd 2018

Copyright © Ella Drummond 2018

The right of Ella Drummond to be identified as the author of this work has been asserted by the author in accordance with the Copyright, Designs and Patents Act 1988.

The story contained within this book is a work of fiction. Names and characters are the product of the author's imagination and any resemblance to actual persons, living or dead, is entirely coincidental.

All rights reserved. No part of this book may be reproduced, stored in a retrieval system, or transmitted in any form or by any means, electronic, electrostatic, magnetic tape, mechanical, photocopying, recording or otherwise, without the written permission of the publishers: Green Shutter Books Ltd, Greenacres, St Ouen, Jersey, JE3 2DA

www.GreenShutterBooks.com

To my husband Rob.

For his endless support and belief in me.

# Acknowledgements

Without the continued support and patience of my husband Rob, son James and daughter Saskia, as well as the rest of my family, I'm sure this book would not have been finished.

I'm eternally grateful to my Beta Readers: Andrea Harrison, Rachael Troy and Julie Collins for taking time out of their busy days to read and comment on this book.

Also, to everyone at Green Shutter Books, my reader at the Hilary Johnson Authors' Advisory Service for her edits and invaluable suggestions, and Helen Baggott for proofreading this book.

# Chapter One

## 2003 – Epernay, Northern France

## Sera

The bathroom door crashed open against the tiled wall startling me from my sleep.

"Sera," Mum shouted, through my half-awake state. "Quick, come here."

I groaned and threw back the covers. Mum was an actress and had a tendency toward the dramatic. "It's the middle of the night," I whispered straining to hear if her theatrics had woken my four-year-old daughter, Katie.

"Never mind that," she said, ignoring my irritation and waving me towards her bedroom. I followed her to the large window overlooking the back of the house. "Look. Over there, towards the woods."

We peered out towards the orangey glow where usually there was nothing but blackness. I had grown up in this house and looked out almost daily across the fields at the end of the garden. They led to the dense woods behind our village, Hautvillers, a couple of kilometres from Epernay.

Until tonight, there had been little excitement in our lives since I'd returned with Katie after my husband Marcus' unexpected death three years previously.

"I've never noticed that light before," Mum said, a tremor in her voice. I was about to ask why she watched the farm at night, when she added, "What do you think it could be?"

I peered towards the light once again, rubbing my eyes to see more clearly. A heavy foreboding gripped my stomach, as I realised that what we were looking at was a fire.

"*Merde*," I gasped, receiving a slap on the forearm for swearing. I winced and rubbed my arm. "That's Hazel's old farm."

A shadow passed over her face, as it usually did if I mentioned Hazel's name in front of her.

"I'm going to see if there's anything I can do to help," I said, prepared for her to argue.

"Don't be ridiculous. It could be dangerous," she said through clenched teeth.

"Be quiet, Mum; you'll wake Katie." I lowered my voice. "I have to go. The new farmer lives alone."

"Do you even know the man?" A fearful glint appeared in her eyes. It was one I recognised, having spent my life being warned about people's true natures by her. "There's a darkness about him, Sera. You mark my words."

"Mum, not everyone is a serial killer," I groaned, too tired to listen to her prophecies of doom.

"It's not a joke," she snapped. "I don't like the way he stares at people when they think they're not looking. I saw him at the shops recently and he unnerved me."

Mum always overreacted to people's behaviour. "You said that about Marcus, remember?" I reminded her, thinking of my kind and affectionate late husband. "Anyway, maybe this bloke is just people watching," I said, attempting to calm her.

"Fine, I admit I was wrong about Marcus. But what this man does is different." She folded her arms across her chest. "Please, stay away from him. There's something about him I don't trust."

"Mum, I'm thirty." I placed a hand on her shoulder. "I know you're only trying to protect me, but I'm old enough to judge people for myself." She opened her mouth to argue, but I added. "And I'm going to the farm, now."

"Fine, but you're not going alone. I'll wake Paul, he can come with you."

I hurried towards my room, stopping when I heard muffled complaints coming from my mother's boyfriend as they argued in her bedroom. Within a minute, a tousle-haired man emerged and scowled at me from my open doorway. Desperate to get a move on, I ignored him.

"I'd only just got off to sleep," he grumbled, partially dressed, a pullover in one hand and a pair of leather shoes in the other.

"Just go with Sera," Mum said, pushing past him. "I've called the fire brigade, so hopefully they won't be long."

Pulling on jeans over my bed shorts and a hoodie over the T-shirt, I ran down the stairs. I pushed my feet into my worn trainers, grabbed the car keys and left, only vaguely aware that Paul was following.

As we drew closer to the farm the smell of smoke increased until I could taste it. My heart pounded. I wasn't feeling nearly as brave as I had done watching from the safety of my mother's bathroom. Paul was more alive by this time, probably from shock at the height of the darting flames. I had never seen a fire this size before. I squinted as the flames lit up the area like a massive orange spotlight. I wasn't sure how much help we would be, but some help was better than none.

I raced through the high stone pillars either side of the farm entrance. From what I could tell, the ancient barn was on fire. It was devastating seeing a beloved place from my childhood going up in flames. I parked on a grassy area and we got out of the car. The intensity of the heat slammed into us as we ran into the yard.

"Shit," Paul shouted his eyes wide with the shock of the scene close-up.

"Monsieur?" I called above the sound of screaming timbers being consumed by the flames. I couldn't see him anywhere.

"Over there," shouted Paul, pointing at the farmer who limped badly as he stepped backwards and forwards focusing on spraying water from an almost useless hose at the burning building.

"The animals? Do you have any?" I asked running up to him

Startled, he stared at Paul and me, his tanned face damaged on one side by a previous injury. I suspected he was in his mid-thirties. "*Non*," he replied, wiping his forehead with the back of one hand brushing sweat across his soot-smeared face. The tension in his expression relaxed a little. I knew we'd done the right thing coming here. He nodded his head in the direction of the field to the side of the house. "I manage to get the animals out, I think. My dog, Patti, she is up there also."

I stared up at the inferno. If there were any unfortunate beasts inside they would be beyond our help now anyway. "What can we do to help?"

"I have one more hose at the back of the house, you can attach it there." He indicated a standpipe. "I must control the fire."

Paul hurried to do as he'd been asked. I took the farmer's hose from him and pointed it at the flame-engulfed timbers doing my best to avoid the devastated expression.

"My mother phoned the fire brigade," I said, hoping this information would comfort him. "They should be here soon."

"*Merci.*" He limped to the side of the barn.

Aware I was doing very little to help, I carried on pointing the hose at the flames. Paul joined me, dragging the second hose around the side of the farmhouse and spraying water against the barn walls.

Henri came back and gazed across the yard, confusion and misery etched on his distorted face. I couldn't help wondering what had happened to him to damage him so cruelly. I presumed it must have been an incident when he was in the army, if the village gossip about him was true.

I pushed the thought away and concentrated on what I

was doing. He grabbed a metal bucket and filled it from the standpipe in the yard. Running as close to the barn as he could, he threw the water onto the fire. Our pathetic efforts to quell the flames were pointless, but I supposed it made him feel as if he was doing something.

As I gazed at the flames darting up into the night sky, I spotted the paint on the shutters of his farmhouse bubbling in places. Desperate, I turned my hose to the side of the house nearest the barn and sprayed it with water to cool it before that too began burning. He didn't need to lose his home as well as his livelihood.

"Oh, hell," I groaned spotting that the window I was aiming near was open. "Shall I go and close those windows?" I shouted, coughing when the wind changed direction and I breathed in too much woody smoke.

He looked horrified at my request. "Non, it is much too dangerous. I will go."

He dropped his bucket and hurried as quickly as he could into the house. Within a short time, the windows were slammed shut and he came back out to join me. He gave me a strange look before continuing to throw water onto the burning barn. It would have been far quicker to let me run inside and do it, but I sensed he was more concerned about what I might see inside his house rather than my safety. I kept my suspicions to myself. It was his house after all and he could play this whichever way he chose.

"They're coming," Paul bellowed, pointing out towards the main road. He looked as relieved as I felt to hear the clanging bells from the fire truck.

Thankfully, it hadn't taken them long to get from Epernay. "Thank you for coming here tonight, and to your mother for her help," he said, hurrying to greet the firemen.

Paul and I stepped back to let them do their job. We stood silently by the gnarled lilac and apple trees that had grown entwined with each other over the years, and watched as the large engine slowly drew into the middle of the yard. The *pompiers* leapt out and immediately began unrolling hoses. Soon gallons of water coursed down onto the flames slowly bringing them under control.

I yawned and turned to get Paul's attention so that we could go home. I shrieked as the farmer grabbed hold of me, jerking me backwards, just as the ancient timbers screeched and crashed to the ground nearby. Stunned, I watched as first one and then all the barn walls followed suit. It was obvious even to me that there wasn't much left to save of this once beautiful building. He let go of me and went to join the firemen. I watched him limp painfully away, sad that he should be going through such a dreadful experience.

I watched Henri. Even slightly stooped on one side, he was still about six feet tall. I realised that all I knew about him was that something terrible had happened in his past. He only ventured into the town when he needed something, which wasn't often as he was quite self-sufficient. Unfortunately, his unwillingness to get to know the villagers only helped exacerbate the gossip about him.

"I heard he killed a man," the woman at the *pâtisserie* told me a couple of weeks before when I was trying to choose some *pain au chocolat*. "Or that he was in the Foreign Legion."

"Non, it was a woman that he murdered," a customer argued.

I paid for my items and left without making any comment. I was dismayed when I'd gone to collect Katie from playgroup days later to hear some of the parents gossiping about Henri. For some reason, they couldn't help making assumptions about why he kept himself to himself.

"You can tell there's something sinister about him," from a grandmother who until then had always been pleasant. I couldn't imagine why and was furious on Henri's behalf, even though I had only seen him once at the garage; I disagreed. "You wait," she retorted. "I will be proved right. And that farm of his, you know better than most, Sera, strange things have happened there."

They had, but that was twenty-four years ago. I suspected my mother had heard similar conversations which was why she had wanted me to stay away from the farm.

He puffed out his cheeks and closed his eyes briefly, relief on his face.

"That was close," Paul said, shaking me from my thoughts. "Poor bastard, I wonder how the fire started?"

I wasn't in the mood to speculate. I could imagine there would be enough people from the village doing that by the morning. I was about to suggest to Paul that we should leave when Henri came up to us.

"Thank you," he said his voice croaky from inhaling smoke. "It took courage to come here with everything they say about me." I must have looked surprised, because he added, "I've heard the stories." He smiled. "Some, although maybe not all. There are villagers who wish me to know how unwelcome I am."

I wasn't sure if I'd picked up the hidden meaning behind his words, but couldn't help asking, "You think someone did this deliberately to force you to move out?"

Paul snorted. "I wouldn't be surprised. Even your mother said…"

I elbowed him to shut him up.

"The locals are a little wary of outsiders, that's all. I had a similar experience when I came back to live here three years ago, and I grew up here before moving away with my husband to Scotland."

He looked confused, which was probably due to me babbling on about my life. This wasn't the time for an introduction.

He moved his hand up near his scarred cheek. "Maybe they, how you say…" he struggled to find the word he wanted in English.

It dawned on me that I had forgotten to speak French. "Speculate?" I suggested.

He nodded. "They speculate how I came to bear my scars."

My insides contracted in embarrassment. I would have loved to assure him that he was wrong.

"You can't blame them for making assumptions though, can you?" Paul asked rolling up one of the garden hoses and hanging it on a hook at the end of the porch.

I closed my eyes for a few seconds wishing I hadn't agreed to let this buffoon come to the farm with me. I shook my head, mortified at my association with him. "I think what he means is…"

Henri held up his hand. "No matter," he said looking very much as if it did.

I changed the subject. "I'm sorry about speaking in English. I forget to speak French sometimes," I explained feeling foolish. "Mum prefers us to speak in English at home. She worries that my daughter, Katie, won't be fluent in her mother tongue if we don't make the effort to ensure she hears it when she's not at school."

"It is a good idea. I am happy for the chance to practise using another language, so please keep on doing this with me."

"Yeah," interrupted Paul, who I could have kicked for being so bloody insensitive earlier. "I only speak one language, too."

I forced a smile. "We'd better go," I said. "Mum is at home with my daughter and I don't want them worrying about us. I hope everything calms down now the fire is almost out."

"It was kind of you both to come to my aid." He walked with us to the car.

I pulled my keys out of my jeans pocket. "I hope they work out how the fire started fairly soon."

He nodded. "*Moi aussi*. I have no idea what could have happened." He gave Paul a pointed look. "There's no electricity in the barn and I didn't see lightning this evening. What else could it have been apart from maybe a misguided vendetta?"

I frowned, horrified at the prospect of someone being that vindictive to a stranger. "Surely not? The animals could have been killed." I lowered my voice. "You could have been killed. You have to tell the gendarmes if you suspect anyone."

He shook his head. "*Non*. The insurance assessors will investigate, and I aim to discover what happened very soon."

"We should be getting back to Mo," Paul said.

"Yes, we'd better let you get on," I said glancing at the *pompiers* working hard to fight the fire.

We returned home to my frantic mother who immediately forgot all about the farm when she saw the state of us.

She pointed Paul in the direction of the bathroom. "You're not coming back to my bed stinking of smoke," she snapped. "You'd better get in your own shower, Seraphina. The entire house is beginning to smell like a bonfire party."

I couldn't imagine my immaculate mother ever deigning to attend a bonfire party, but relieved to have an excuse to return to the peace of my bedroom, I did as she suggested.

The following morning, Henri appeared at my front door with a bag of potatoes and a plait of garlic.

"I want to thank you for aiding me with the fire," he said. "It is only a token, but I wish to thank you."

Stepping back, I waved him in. "Please, come through."

He looked a little unsure then followed me along the tiled corridor. His limp seemed worse than the night before as he navigated the three steps into the pale blue farmhouse kitchen my mother loved so much. Her only concession to modernity being a range she bought at great expense several years before. He stood awkwardly inside the doorway. I motioned for him to take a seat at the bleached pine table that ran most of the length of the room.

"Coffee?" I asked lifting the garlic and hanging it temporarily on the handle of the small window above the bread bin.

He nodded. "*Merci.*"

I poured us both a mug, took an apple pie from the larder that I'd made the day before and sat down opposite him. "So, apart from what happened last night, how are you finding living near Epernay?"

He gave a slow shrug with one shoulder. "It's a beautiful area, much better than some places I've lived. I am not certain how long I will remain here."

I could understand his logic and felt sorry for him. What had he ever done to anyone here? "Where did you live before coming here?"

"Many places. I grew up in Paris." He hesitated frowning thoughtfully, then added, "I moved many times, but lived mainly in Marseille."

I sensed that he didn't often share information about himself and was only doing so to be polite. There was something slightly mysterious about him. However, I still didn't think that excused people's suspicions about him. It infuriated me to think of shoppers in the supermarket whispering behind their hands as he shopped for basics.

At that moment, Katie ran into the room. "Nana Mo said she wants to speak to you in the garden. She needs help tying her beans. Now, Maman."

Sensing someone else was in the room with us, Katie turned and shrunk back into my legs, one arm wrapped around the back of my thighs, the other tugging my skirt.

"This is my daughter, Katie," I said, ruffling her bed hair. "Sorry, I don't know your name."

"Henri." He looked at Katie. "I live on the farm near the woods." Katie murmured a barely coherent greeting and Henri's face softened. It was the first time I'd seen him smile. "*Bonjour*, Katie."

"I'm nearly five," she said letting go of my skirt and edging closer to him. I willed her not to say anything she shouldn't, but she was inquisitive and not at all shy. "Why have you got a hurt on your face?"

I winced.

Henri raised his hand to touch the scarred cheek. "I was bitten by a dragon," he said quietly, bending slightly towards her.

Katie's eyes widened. She glanced at me to gauge if he was telling the truth. "Maman?"

"*Non.*" He shook his head. "It wasn't a dragon, I am teasing. I was hurt in an, er, accident."

"Is it sore?" she asked edging closer to him.

He seemed younger than I'd assumed him to be initially, maybe in his mid-thirties. It was hard to tell. "*Non*, not now. It was for a while though."

"Do you have animals at your farm?" she asked, sitting down on the long bench, bored with his scars.

He nodded. "*Oui.* I 'ave the horses, sheep, hens... and a dog, Patti. Patti is 'aving puppies soon."

Katie jumped up and down clapping her podgy hands gleefully. "Can Maman and I come and see them, please?" she asked.

I hated that she'd put him in such an awkward position; how could anyone say no to an innocent request from a four-year-old.

"But, of course."

"Maman?" She placed her hands, a pleading expression on her face, willing me to agree. It seemed I had an actress in the making living with me.

I nodded, liking the idea of seeing them myself. "Yes, when they've been born," I said, not wishing her to visit when the ruins of the fire were so fresh and probably still smouldering. "Now, run along and tell Nana Mo I'll be up to see her soon."

We watched Katie leave the room. Realising I hadn't got any plates for the pie, I stood to take some from the cupboard and placed them on the table. "Thank you for bringing these," I said, pointing at the garlic. "Did you grow them?"

He nodded. "On my previous farm."

"How lovely, thank you." I held the string of garlic up to my nose and sniffed. Heavenly, I couldn't wait to use them in my cooking.

I served the apple pie and we discussed his animals and the previous night's drama. I did most of the talking as he slowly ate his food.

"Do they know yet if the fire was started deliberately?" I asked, unable to resist from asking,

He looked at me. "It seems an accelerant was discovered at the side of the barn. I didn't put it there."

Fury coursed through me on his behalf. "How could people be so vindictive?"

"There are a lot of evil people in this world, er," he struggled to think of my name.

"Sera. Short for Seraphina," I explained.

"It's an unusual name," he added after a slight pause.

Used to this sort of comment when people learned my name, I said, "My mother wanted a glamorous name for me and came up with this one."

"It suits you." He cleared his throat and glanced at the kitchen wall clock. "I must go. The animals are restless. I don't want to leave them for long." He positioned the palms of his hands against the table and pushed himself up to stand, wincing in pain. I resisted taking his elbow to help him not imagining he would take kindly to my assistance. "I worry that if I am away from the farm they might come back."

Disturbed by this thought, I stood up to show him out. "Call around to see us again if you're in the village. I've only been back here a couple of years myself, so know what it's like to have few friends."

"That is kind of you," he said.

I watched as he walked down the front steps. I went to close the door but saw him stop and turn to look up at the house, a haunted expression on his face. Confused by what I'd seen I closed the front door quietly.

"Has he gone?" my mother asked a second later from the top of the stairs.

"Mum, don't be mean." Her attitude really annoyed me sometimes.

"He's not the sort of man you should get involved with, Sera." There was no mistaking the distaste in her tone.

"What is that supposed to mean?"

She thought for a moment. "There's something about him. I can't quite put my finger on it, but it's as if he's trying to worm his way into our family."

She didn't make any sense. "He brought a thank you gift, that's all," I argued, not admitting what I'd just seen him do outside the house.

Mum closed her eyes and shook her head. "I merely meant you don't know him. You need to be careful not to expose Katie to anyone who… well, who could be dangerous."

I laughed, shocked by her histrionics. "Really, Mum."

"Sera," she said taking hold of my arms. "You don't know anything about him. Where he comes from, or what he's left behind."

Even for my mother this was a little extreme. It opened the festering wound that we both did our best to keep covered most of the time. "I don't know anything about your past either," I reminded her, hating myself when she winced, but unable to resist. "Where do you come from? Why don't you have any family and why did an English girl of, what, seventeen come here alone to have her baby?" I stared at her wondering if I might be about to uncover something of her hidden past.

She looked deflated for a moment, then straightening her

shoulders, said, "I was eighteen, not seventeen. You know I'm from England."

"So why haven't you ever gone back there to see your family? I presume you must have one?"

She shook her head. "No, not anymore."

What did that mean? I opened my mouth to ask, but she held up her hand to stop me.

"I will tell you everything one day. You had a good childhood here in Hautvillers, didn't you?"

"You know I did." I realised today wasn't going to be the day that she shared her secrets.

"Now, going back to Henri. I merely think you should steer clear of the man."

"I'm considering taking Katie to visit his animals on the farm, not marry the man," I shook my head slowly.

"Don't mock me, you know what I mean," she snapped.

I didn't. I was a little irritated that she imagined I would ever put my daughter in any danger. "I know how to protect my daughter," I snapped, unable to contain myself. I walked upstairs to find Katie, my heart pounding with fury. "I'm not involved with anyone," I added as she followed me. "And I don't understand how you think you can tell what sort of man someone is by having a sneaky look at him from a distance."

"I know I'm right about this man," she said from behind me as I entered Katie's room. "But you never did listen to my advice."

Probably because I never thought she knew any better than me, I mused. I thought back over my childhood filled with her rules and regulations, but devoid of affection. I had learnt at an early age that she was a fearful adversary and not to try and stand up to her. If she wasn't away on location somewhere, she was at home insisting on peace as she learnt her lines. It was her reasoning behind the lack of visitors to our home. Today's reaction to Henri exposed her suspicion of people, once again. No wonder he chose to keep to himself if this was how people reacted to him.

"Nana Mo, can we go to the sweet shop today?" my daughter Katie whispered.

"We'll go later when Mummy has gone to work," Mum whispered, grabbing Katie and tickling her. Katie shrieked with laughter.

Katie's giggles made me smile. Their closeness never ceased to amaze me. I thought back to my younger self and how much I craved attention from Mum. We had always lived alone, just the two of us. For some reason, she was able to show her love to Katie in ways that were still surprising to me. I watched them for a moment.

After Dee and Leo had vanished in '89 and I had experienced loss first-hand, it eventually occurred to me that something must have happened in Mum's past to cause her to close off her emotions. It was still surprising to me to see her being so free with her affections for Katie. I loved seeing them together, but it was a bitter sweet experience.

I thought of seeing Leo in town and recalled my heartbreak that hot summer in '89 when my life splintered apart. It hadn't occurred to me back then that time spent with my best friend, Dee, dreaming about our futures, confiding in each other about our latest crush and sharing our secrets was about to end abruptly. I was blissfully ignorant of what was happening around me. I pushed away the negative thoughts.

"How would you like to come to Paris today, Katie?" I asked.

She glanced from Mum to me trying to decide which choice to make.

"You go with Mummy, darling," Mum said smiling at me over Katie's head. "Nana Mo has to learn her lines today."

"Boring lines." Katie pouted, then remembering my offer gave me a beaming smile and grabbed hold of my hand. "Paris, Maman?"

"That little one will go far," Mum said as we all walked back downstairs and into the kitchen where I'd left a short list of items I wanted to find in Paris. "You two go and enjoy yourselves and leave me in peace with this." She pulled a creased script towards her and waved us away.

Ignoring my mother's prophecies of doom and determined to help Henri feel more included in the community, I drove up to Henri's farm moments later. The heat gave the roads a watery sheen. I lowered the sun visor to shield my eyes and turned off the main road onto the dusty dirt track leading to his home. Even the birds seemed quieter in the intense heat. A light breeze did nothing to lessen the temperature, but swept across the heads of corn in a nearby field giving the impression of gently rolling golden waves.

"Henri," I called, not bothering to get out of my battered Citroën 2CV. It was thirty-five degrees and as hot as my car was, it was still cooler than standing in the direct sunshine. "I'm going into Paris; do you want me to pick anything up for you when I'm there?"

I waited outside the rundown farmhouse, its stone walls almost completely covered with rampant ivy. The front door didn't open. I wasn't sure if I'd done the right thing coming here. Tempted to go and knock, the need for a reply was squashed when the weathered, oak door was pulled back and Henri, scowling, looked across his dusty yard at me.

"*Non*," he snapped, hesitating for a moment and then adding, "*Merci.*"

I watched him turn and go back inside his home. His stooped shoulders told me all I needed to know. Not wishing to overstep the boundaries of our fragile acquaintance, I didn't say anything further. I wondered if his limp was always this bad or if maybe he'd been hurt while trying to put out the fire.

I started the ignition. I wasn't certain, but thought I felt him watching me from one of the windows. I wished he would let me in, just a little, but maybe coming here so soon after the visit to Mum's house had unsettled him. We all needed friends and I suspected he needed them more than he let on.

"Maman, do you think Monsieur Henri is sad?" Katie asked from the back seat. "Nana Mo said he isn't nice."

My grip on the steering wheel tightened. I wished my mother would keep her opinions about Henri to herself. She could be ultra-suspicious of people and I didn't want her worrying Katie about someone who hadn't done anything wrong.

"Nana Mo doesn't know Monsieur Henri. He is nice, but sometimes people like to be left alone."

There was a moment's silence as the car drew out of the farmyard, while she contemplated this nugget. "Like you, when you're working?"

"Yes, like me, when I'm working."

I always enjoyed leaving the peace of our village of Hautvillers with its quiet tree-lined lanes and ancient houses. The slow increase in traffic, noise and urgency as we neared Paris gave me a thrill. Katie and I sang her current favourite song countless times during the hour and a half drive south to the city. As we left the River Marne behind to go towards the Seine, my concerns about Henri dissipated. It was another hectic day in Paris. Finding a parking space proved more difficult than I had anticipated although our persistence was eventually paid back when we spotted an elderly gentleman manoeuvring his car out of a space further along the back street where we had driven.

Katie and I were excited to once again be able to explore our favourite places. However, I could not help thinking that the busy boulevards desperately needed a shower of rain to spruce them up a bit. Katie squealed and ducked as drops of water from a recently watered window box dripped on her head. I giggled at her excitement. I loved afternoons like this one when she and I could spend time alone doing something we both enjoyed.

Our first stop was Shakespeare and Company on the Left Bank. I browsed for a couple of books, keeping an eye on Katie who enjoyed sitting in the tiny nooks pretending to read the notes pegged onto cord strung across the width of the booth by previous visitors.

Afterwards, we made our way past a *bouquiniste*. I was looking for any second-hand books that took my fancy. I loved anything by F. Scott Fitzgerald, Ernest Hemingway or Man Ray. Katie studied some colourful postcards, while I took time to choose several books for my ever-growing collection that I assured myself I would one day find the time to read.

Stopping at our favourite café by the pretty René Viviani square, we sat and examined our purchases in silence. I relished these precious moments alone with Katie. Sometimes it was too painful to contemplate life without Marcus. Today, though, I felt strong enough to wonder how it would be for our little family if he was alive and sitting here with us.

The jolly *patron* came over to our table and wiped his chubby hands on his immaculate apron. Greeting us, he nodded in Katie's direction. "You would like your usual drinks, Mademoiselle?"

"*Oui, merci,*" she said.

He gave me a smile and left us, returning moments later. He placed my *café au lait* onto the small circular metal table. Then, with a bow served Katie's frothy milk with sprinkles of cocoa powder on the top that she liked to pretend was coffee.

"*Merci*, monsieur," I said. Katie smiled at him.

"I like it here," she said when he had walked away.

"Me, too." I bent down and kissed the top of her head. "Daddy used to love coming here too, you know?"

I liked to feel as if he was close to us, especially at times like these. By talking about him, I felt that he participated, even if only in some small way, in Katie's life.

Her fair eyebrows lowered in a frown. "With me?"

"Yes, with both of us."

"I wish Daddy was here now," she said blowing on her drink. "Nana Mo liked him, didn't she?"

Eventually, I thought. "Yes, she did."

I washed and dressed Katie the following morning leaving early to take her to playschool. I was relieved that today was one of the three days each week that I drove into Epernay to my workshop renovating old enamelled signs. It was good to get away from the house and Mum repeating her lines, and I needed the peace of my studio after the shocking fire a few nights before. Living at Mum's house meant that I didn't have to pay rent and so Katie and I were able to survive on the small pension we received that Marcus had set up for us about a year before he died.

Sourcing and renovating the signs gave me an interest and added income. It also gave me a reason to drive to different markets looking for stock and kept me from spending too much time at home dwelling on Marcus' untimely death. After a shaky start when my shyness threatened to hold me back, I now enjoyed selling the signs from my market stall in the weekly market in Epernay.

Today, though, I was looking forward to spending a solitary day in the studio. I drove out of our peaceful village along roads flanked by lush green vineyards on my way to Epernay. The day was still and the heat heavy. Determined to lift my mood, I pressed on the car radio. As I turned into the historic town, passing nineteenth century town houses and hinting at the wealth the region had enjoyed from the champagne trade, I sang along to 'Fast Car' by Tracy Chapman. I'd played the song endlessly during the late eighties and it reminded me of my childhood friend Dee. I rounded a corner when I thought I'd spotted someone I hadn't seen for twenty years.

"Leo?" I must be imagining things, and after so little sleep last night it probably wasn't surprising. I shrieked as the car in front stopped at the last minute, when the traffic lights changed to red. It was pure luck I didn't smash into their car. My heart pounded, although whether it was from shock of the near miss, or thinking I had spotted Leo. I wasn't sure. He was my best-friend Dee's younger brother. She and I had been inseparable as teenagers, until their family had disappeared on the hottest night of a heatwave in nineteen eighty-nine.

I could still recall the months I'd waited for a letter from Dee, or any sign that any of the family were still alive and what might have happened to them. I was about to drive on, but what if it was Leo? I couldn't miss a chance to speak to him. I glanced around spotting him again. Excitement bubbling inside me, I looked for a parking space, checking back in his direction unable to see him this time. My stomach churned at the lost opportunity, but then I spotted him walking towards an office along the street.

A car pulled out of a parking space in front of me. Parking my car badly, I stepped out, almost forgetting to lock it before running towards the heavy oak doors of the imposing stone building that was the main bank in the town. I took a deep breath and pushed them open. Running up to him wasn't the way to reintroduce myself; if indeed it was him. I watched the broad-shouldered man speaking to the chic receptionist, willing him to turn his face slightly towards me so that I could get a better look.

The potential humiliation of what I was about to do dawned on me. What was I thinking? Surely, if either Leo or his sister Dee had wanted to get in touch with me since their disappearance, they could have contacted Mum. Why was he back in Epernay? This wasn't a financial district and this man looked the epitome of a financier, if the cut of his suit was anything to go by.

Losing my nerve, I turned away. Walking out of the building the heat of the day hit me. Maybe listening to that eighties song had induced my mind to conjure up one of the people I'd longed to find. Why though would someone that had disappeared without trace in nineteen eighty-nine suddenly return? My tired mind must be playing tricks on me. Embarrassed at getting carried away with my emotions, I hurried to my car. Taking my keys out of my bag, I dropped them when a hand landed heavily on my shoulder.

"Seraphina, is that you?" the man asked, bending down

to retrieve my keys from the gutter.

The voice was much deeper, but the inflection belonged to Leo. A thrill of excitement shot through me.

"Leo," I whispered. "It is you. I thought I was going mad."

He held out my keys and shrugged. "Here I am, back in Epernay."

I took the keys with a shaky hand and couldn't help staring at him as he took a deep breath and smiled. "Where the hell have you been for the past thirteen or fourteen years?"

His smile vanished. After some thought, he said, "Let's not worry about that now, shall we?"

"But…" Why couldn't he tell me? He must know how lost I'd been when his family had vanished?

Taking my shoulders, Leo held me away from him and studied my face. He smiled. "I always suspected you'd grow up and be a beautiful woman," he said, his cornflower blue eyes twinkling with more confidence than I could have ever imagined him having when we were younger. My stomach contracted as I looked up at him. He was taller than my late husband Marcus had been, and he was six feet in height.

Leo frowned, then pulled me into a bear hug. I stiffened for an instant unused to being held by a man since Marcus' death two years before. Despite my best efforts my face reddened. How could this handsome man be the same scruffy boy my best friend Dee and I teased mercilessly when we were teenagers?

"I just can't believe it," I said.

He held me away from him and gave me another wide smile displaying perfect white teeth. He looked wealthy, as if he'd done very well for himself.

Desperate to find out more about his family, but not wishing to give him an excuse to leave, I said, "You don't look dressed for Epernay. More like the London Stock Exchange." Unable to resist, I added, "And Dee? Is she well? She's not here with you, is she?" I asked hopefully.

His smile slipped. "No, Dee's not here."

I waited for him to continue.

His hands dropped. He glanced at his watch. "I have to go. I'm late for a meeting."

I followed his gaze to the large building. "Will I see you again?"

The mystery of their disappearance had plagued me since my teens. I had almost given up hope of ever finding Dee; almost. I needed to know what had happened to her, Leo, their mother Hazel and stepfather Pierre. It looked as if my wait wasn't quite over. I unlocked my car. Glancing back at the majestic bank, it dawned on me that Leo hadn't answered any of my questions.

What *was* Leo doing back here?

# Chapter Two

Hautvillers, near Epernay

1989 – Young Sera

I almost lost my footing on the gnarled branch of the apple tree as I raised one plimsoll-encased foot and reached out to Dee's windowsill, missing by inches.

"*Merde.*" I grimaced, praying silently that I could manage to hold on long enough for her to realise I was there. I could hear her mum Hazel's raucous laughter as she partied with her friends on the other side of the barn where it opened out into the meadow.

Having no siblings of my own and a mum who had long since disconnected with her family back in England, these people at the farm were like my family. Dee was the sister I never had. I could confide in her about anything and she understood how it felt not to know the identity of your father. No one, not even Hazel, was going to stop me seeing her.

I didn't want to insult Mum by letting her know how much I wanted to be a part of Dee's home where everyone chatted openly about their thoughts and dreams. Here, the only dreams were Mum's acting ambitions and the size of the next part she might get. I understood she needed to earn enough money to pay for everything we ate or wore, but did she have to be so intense about every part of our lives? I wondered miserably. Surely Hazel had to find ways to pay for her farm but unlike Mum she was carefree and fun to be with.

I held my breath for a second. I'd never known Dee's mum to ground her before. I couldn't imagine what she must have done to upset Hazel this badly.

Someone put on another record and Hazel began singing. It was safe to carry on. I braced myself ready to propel forward once again. Grabbing hold of the sill with one hand, my nails grazed against one of the wooden shutters. I groaned as two nails broke low down, tearing the skin.

"Dee," I hissed almost, but not quite uncaring if I was overheard by her mum.

I heard something drop onto her wooden floor and Dee's face appeared at her half open window. "What the hell are you doing up here?" she asked, shaking her head, barely able to stop from giggling, her headphones hanging around her neck. No wonder she hadn't heard me.

"Bloody help me," I said through gritted teeth. "I'm stuck."

She pushed the other window wide open and leant out, grabbing me by the elbows, pulling me to her. "Shit, you're heavier than you look."

I didn't have the strength to argue, but pushed my feet hard against the branch, launching myself towards her, and together we fell back heavily onto her floor.

She groaned. "Get off me." She tugged at the wire now wrapped tightly around her neck.

Relieved to be safe, I pushed myself off and lay next to her willing my heart to slow. "I thought I was a goner then."

We stared at each other in silence for a couple of seconds, before she smiled. I could see the amusement wash over her face. "You looked so funny hanging on for dear life," she giggled. "I never knew your eyes could go that wide."

I punched her playfully on the shoulder, wincing as the broken skin under my nails tore further. "Ouch."

"You hit me after nearly strangling me?" She teased, tears of laughter running down her face.

I couldn't help but see the funny side. "It was your headphone wire that nearly strangled you, not me," I argued. "Anyway, I was terrified," I said in between hysterical bouts of laughter. "You know I'm scared of heights."

Dee wiped her wet eyes with the bottom of her T-shirt. "Why did you climb the tree then, moron?"

"To see you."

"You can't use the front door, like everyone else?" She threw her Walkman onto the bed.

"When I saw your mum earlier at the *boulangerie*, she told me I wasn't to come here. She said you were in serious trouble and I wasn't allowed to see you." I sat up and crossed my legs. "What did you do to piss her off?"

She sat up opposite me, frowning. I waited for her to

speak, but she stared at the floor contemplating something. "It's that idiot boyfriend of hers, Pierre."

I didn't like him much either. We'd discussed our thoughts on Hazel's relationship many times, while stuffing our faces with popcorn and watching videos of *St. Elmo's Fire* and *Pretty in Pink*, desperately wanting to be Demi Moore and Molly Ringwald. Our nastiness towards Pierre had mainly been due to boredom on our parts though; the poor man hadn't done anything wrong.

"What did he do?"

She shook her head and swallowed. "He shouted at my brother."

Anger coursed through me. "Why?" Leo was a quiet kid. He never really got into trouble and I couldn't imagine him having the courage to give Pierre any lip.

"Leo said he saw Pierre push Mum, but she denied it."

I thought about how I'd feel if I'd seen someone being rough with my mum. "But why are you grounded if Pierre was the one in the wrong?"

"That's precisely what I said when I walked in on her shouting at Leo." She traced a series of circles in the light dust on her bedroom floor with one finger. "She's been acting a little odd lately." She hesitated. "I think she's doing more than smoking the odd spliff, Sera."

I wasn't sure what to say next.

Dee shrugged. "Never mind that, you know how I never stand up for Leo, so that must tell you how nasty things got earlier."

She was right, she didn't. It must have been a bad row

for her to defend her brother, I realised. "True."

"I couldn't believe it when she turned on the pair of us and sent us to our rooms, so she could be alone with him."

Despite Dee's comments about her mum and what she was getting up to, it still didn't make much sense to me why Hazel had been quite so angry with Dee. I voiced my concerns.

She sighed. "Well, she also caught me cutting up one of her dresses."

"What?" I shrieked. Dee was always braver than me and I could picture her doing something like that.

"She slapped me." She put her palm up against her left cheek.

"Won't do that again then, will you?" I asked, stunned to think of Hazel raising a hand to either of her kids.

She shook her head. "No. I don't know what all the fuss was about; it wasn't as if she'd worn it for years."

"Why did you do it though?" I asked. When she didn't reply, a thought occurred to me. "You were copying Molly Ringwald? Go on, admit it."

"So, what if I was?"

"Can I see your creation?" I had no idea where Dee thought she'd wear a new dress, if she had managed to make one out of her mum's old dress.

"No," she pouted. "She threw it away. Cow."

I hated seeing her cross, she was usually so jolly and cheerful. "At least you have a mum whose clothes you can make into something you'd choose to wear. Imagine me trying to do that with my mum's stuff?" We sat contemplating this amusing notion for a bit. "So," I said, standing up. "Are we going to sit here all night, or are you coming down to the woods for a swim. It's stifling in here."

I was also worried I'd get caught by Hazel, and as much as she could be odd at times, I loved her and didn't want to get into her bad books. Coming to this farm in my free time was what I enjoyed doing most. I wished my mum and Hazel were friends and she could see how lovely this family were, but she would have none of it and didn't really like me spending time here with them.

"Stifling," she said mimicking my voice. "You been listening to your mum talking posh again?"

"Shut up," I pushed her, unable to stop smiling.

She got up and pulled open the middle drawer in the wide chest and lifted out her neon pink bikini. "I think I could do with cooling down a bit," she said stripping off and changing, and I knew she wasn't just referring to the heat in the stuffy bedroom. She was angrier about what had happened between her and her mum than I'd realised.

We stepped out onto the landing, stopping to listen for Hazel's voice, or any one of her cronies who might have come into the house for more drinks. Then we tiptoed down the stairs, covering our mouths with our hands to stop from making a sound. As soon as we were outside, we glanced at one another, and without speaking, tore off, running as fast as we could towards the wood.

Dee shrieked as we neared the coolness of the dense trees circled around the natural pool. When we were younger and first discovered this place, Dee had insisted it was a fairy glade. I didn't believe her, but I was sure that this place had magical properties.

"Remember when we thought time stood still for everyone else when we were in here?" Dee asked. Without waiting for a reply, she dropped her towel, running into the water. She didn't stop until she was in the deepest part of the pool, instantly lowering her head under the water.

I still suspected there was something precious about this place. I imagined it must be spooky at night-time, but right now it was an oasis cooling our hot skin. I followed her, my breath catching as the cold water reached my ribcage.

"This is brill," she shouted, splashing me and cheering as if she hadn't been out here only the day before. "I love it here. One day I'm going to buy this wood. I'll make sure I never leave it."

"You have to leave it sometime, you can't stay here forever." Dee gave me a sad look and I wondered if maybe the situation between her mum and Pierre was worrying her more than she was letting on.

"How come you're here tonight?" she said interrupting my thoughts. "Your mum doesn't usually let you out this late."

"She's away filming, again."

Dee's mouth fell open. "She never leaves you by yourself in the house though?"

"I know." I thought of my controlling mother leaving me alone for several days in the house. "She's got another babysitter from that agency to stay with me while she's away."

"That doesn't explain why you're allowed out," Dee said

lying on her back floating, her arms and legs outstretched. "Where is this babysitter?" she asked, emphasising the word 'baby'. "How did you escape from her?"

I copied what she was doing. I hated my mum treating me like a baby when I was a twelve-year-old. I sulked as I stared up at the dusky sky through the trees.

"Her boyfriend came to the house about half an hour after Mum left. I told her I had loads of homework to be getting on with and needed to be left in peace in my bedroom to do it. I said I'd see her tomorrow morning at breakfast."

Dee turned to look at me, a look of admiration on her tanned face. "And she believed you?"

"Yup."

"Fab."

She rested her head back on the water again and we floated silently in the cool water after our tedious day spent in a humid classroom. I was almost dozing off when she splashed me. The shock made me sink slightly, so that I swallowed a mouthful of water. I frantically attempted to clear my airways.

"What did you do that for?" I eventually managed to splutter.

"Sorry." She grabbed hold of me and helped me swim to the side of the pool. "I had a thought."

We both giggled, amused that her thought had caused me to almost drown. I grabbed my towel and sat on it, patting the space next to me for her to join me. "Go on then, spill."

She raised her shoulders and gave a little squeal. "Why don't we ask your mum if you can come and stay with us every time she goes on location?" She held her hands out, palms up, and grinned. "Brilliant idea, don't you think?"

I shook my head. "She'll never go for it. You know she's odd about your mum."

"So? Just cos my mum's a nutty hippy. We'll just have to work on her and persuade her it's the best option." She thought for a moment. "We could tell her how much money she'd save by not hiring in nannies for you so often."

I grimaced. "Nah, she'd hate anyone to think she didn't have money. No, it'll have to be something else. But what?"

Dee hugged me. "We'll think of something. Imagine you being able to stay at my house night after night, it would be fun. We could have midnight feasts at midnight."

I laughed. "Not at seven-thirty in the evening, you mean?"

"Yes. And we could sneak out and meet boys together."

I pushed her so hard she fell backwards, leaves from the ground getting caught in her damp hair when she landed on the ground. "We don't know any boys, silly," I said, wishing we had the nerve to do as she suggested. "Only the stupid ones from school."

"True, but we could meet some if we sneaked into the village at night." She widened her eyes. "I heard that Francine was caught snogging Stefan the other night, by the bins near the *crêperie*."

"No, really?" I didn't like Francine very much, she was often spiteful and teased me about not having a dad, but I couldn't help being impressed with this news.

"It would be fun. We just have to think of a way to get your mum to agree."

I had to admit I liked this plan of hers. Staying at the farm and sharing Dee's bright bedroom would be far more fun than having to make small talk to an endless round of babysitters. "What about Hazel though? We'd need to ask her permission first."

She shrugged. "You know my mum would love you to stay with us. Especially if it kept me quiet and out of her way."

This was true. "Fine then, we'll make a plan. I'll hint to my mum when she gets back."

Just as I'd expected, my mother's initial reaction had been one of horror. She looked over her shoulder as if expecting to see someone. I was used to this behaviour, she'd always worried about strangers and checking doors were locked even when it was the middle of the day and the house was busy with people. In fact, I was sure that her slightly neurotic way was the reason I pushed myself to be more open and trusting of others.

"Leave you in the care of that mad hippy? I don't think so, Sera."

"Why not," I said, frustrated by my mother's unjustified dislike for Hazel. "I know she's very different to you, but you're both English…"

Mum's eyes widened. "What does that have to do with anything?"

For once I didn't care about her issues with Hazel, whatever they might be, I had never understood this unspoken rule never to mention Hazel's name. It was ridiculous. I'd had enough.

"If you met her and tried to get to know her you'd probably get on well," I said. "She's kind and funny. She's a bit dippy," I laughed, picturing Hazel's silly antics. "And she's an incredible singer…"

"Shut up," Mum screamed. "You don't know her."

"I do," I shouted, hands on my hips as I bent towards her. "Hazel's nicer than you are."

Grabbing me by the shoulders, she shook me so hard my neck hurt.

I cried out, shocked by her violent reaction. The loathing in her face scared me. I pulled away from her. "I hate you," I shrieked, running away from her up to my bedroom.

"Hazel isn't the perfect person you think, Sera," she screamed, as I slammed my door.

# Chapter Three
## 1976 – London
### Mo

The pretty girl, with tiny bells on her brightly coloured maxi skirt, held out her hand. "Hello, I'm Hazel."

I couldn't understand why she looked so pleased with herself. This crummy guesthouse I'd been directed to from the nearby café was even worse than I'd expected. I was relieved my mum and sister couldn't see where I was intending to sleep. I'd dreamt of being an actress ever since the previous summer when I'd accompanied a friend to a garden fete. We'd watched as a sophisticated actress gave a brief speech, her clipped vowels echoing a little over the ancient tannoy system. She'd smiled at the little girl nervously walking up to her before curtseying and presenting her with a bouquet. I had never seen anyone so polished, or sophisticated. From her expertly arranged chignon to her flowery summer dress and the pristine white gloves covering her hands. She was enchanting, and I wanted to be just like her.

The memory of my mortification when my mother shared my secret with my older sister was something I would never forget, or forgive. "You, an actress?" my older sister, Mary, had mocked. "You should be glad Mum's managed to secure you an interview at Salways, there's plenty that would be grateful to be in your shoes."

"Let them have the bloody job then," I'd snapped, receiving a stinging slap across my left cheek for being so rude.

I could picture their amusement if they could see me in this dump. I'd prove them wrong, somehow. I was determined to be signed by a theatrical agent and then the joke would be on them.

"I only got here a month ago," Hazel added snapping my thoughts back to the present. "I don't know many people here yet."

"I'm Mo," I said forcing a smile. I decided that if I was to reinvent myself then this was the time to start. It was my chance to become someone other than Maureen, the girl my mother brought up to work in the local leather factory, just as she and my sister had done. I had other plans. "I'm an actress and I'm eighteen."

"Me, too," she giggled. "Eighteen, that is, not an actress. How exciting," Hazel said. She reminded me of an over-excited puppy. "Where've you come from, lovey?"

"Dalingbrook, it's a small village near Northampton," I said, truthfully. That would be the last time I'd mention where I grew up, I decided. "You?"

"York," she said beaming at me. She whooped in delight,

her wavy blonde hair bouncing around her cherubic face.

I stifled a groan. I'd hoped to escape childish friends, but it looked as if I was going to end up having to spend my nights sharing a room with one.

"I'm a singer," she said. "Have you been in anything I might have seen?"

Not willing to admit that the only stage I'd performed on was in my school hall in an amateur production of the *Nutcracker Suite*. It might have been very basic, but I'd put in a great effort to be a perfect Sugar Plum Fairy. I studied Hazel, deciding that if she had wings then she'd make a colourful fairy. I could picture her flitting about in the sunshine in a wooded glade somewhere. I smiled at the thought. "Nothing much. Not yet anyway. That's why I've come here. I want to audition for bigger parts and make a name for myself."

Hazel clapped her small hands in delight. "Me, too. Oh, I knew we'd be great friends."

I wish I shared her enthusiasm.

The introductions over, she reached out and switched on her transistor radio. David Bowie's dulcet tones crooned out the lyrics to 'Golden Years'. Maybe she wouldn't be such a problem to live with, I mused, at least her taste in music was good. I studied the small back bedroom we were to share.

"Is that my bed?" I asked, looking at the one covered with discarded items of clothing.

Hazel nodded, her face reddening. "Sorry, I've always been a messy bugger. Let me move them." She scraped the clothes together and dumped them onto her creased sheets.

"You don't mind this, do you?" she nodded towards the radio.

I shook my head. "How can anyone dislike Bowie, he's incredible," I said, picturing my chameleon-like hero and my beloved posters of him I'd had to leave behind on my bedroom wall in Dalingbrook.

Hazel beamed at me. "We're going to get along well, I can tell."

Could she? I wasn't so sure. I'd come from sharing a room with my sister and hadn't banked on moving on to sharing with a stranger, and an over-excited one at that.

"Do you have any contacts here yet?" I asked hopefully. I may as well make the most of having to put up with this messy girl.

She pursed her plump lips together. "I might just have," she said conspiratorially. "There's a party at this club in Soho tonight and I've been invited by this really cool guy who runs it. Vince, he's called. He owns a few bars around Soho. He also runs several nightclubs where all the theatrical people hang out."

Excited that I might finally meeting some famous people, I sat heavily on my newly-cleared bed. "Really?"

She nodded, her wild curls bouncing up and down in her enthusiasm to convince me. "Yeah, it's not just actors and singers, but their agents go there too. Someone told me recently that Vince has a back office at the club we're going to tonight where they do deals."

I could barely take in what she was telling me. "Theatrical agents?"

"Yes," she lowered her voice despite no one else being around to overhear our conversation. "I heard recently that he grew up in the East End and until a couple of years ago ran things for this older guy."

"What happened to him?" I asked, fascinated.

"He died," Hazel said looking out of the window briefly.

"How?"

"Look, I don't know alright? It was something mysterious, but no one talks about what exactly happened."

My stomach fluttered nervously. "He sounds a little dangerous."

Hazel pushed my shoulder. "No, nothing like that," she giggled, but it seemed forced. I wondered if maybe she was panicking that I might repeat what she had told me. "He's always immaculately dressed," she added. "If someone upsets him, he fires them but sees to it that none of the other clubs or bars will employ that person."

"That's mean," I said, not sure if he sounded like the sort of person I would like.

Hazel pulled a face. "If they're stupid enough to cross him then serves them right."

I decided that if she was going to help make my dreams come true then I wasn't going to annoy her by arguing.

"Do you think he would mind if I came to the party?"

Anticipating her reply, I reached up to check my shaggy perm was still vaguely presentable, grateful I'd bothered spending the previous week getting my hair trimmed and permed by a school friend's sister. I needed to make the right impression even though it had meant paying her more than I would have liked.

"Yeah, course you can. He said to bring a friend, or ten." She giggled. "He's a real hunk, you'll love him; everyone does." Her pale cheeks reddened. "I think he looks a little like David Essex and to be honest I quite like him, if you know what I mean."

I didn't. The boys I vaguely knew were dull and ordinary. It was probably why I was so fascinated by David Bowie. He was different, magnificent and the caressing quality of his voice lulled me to believe that I had the strength to make something interesting of my life.

"Have you got a boyfriend in Dalingbrook?" Hazel asked.

I shook my head. I wasn't going to admit that I'd never had a boyfriend. One quick snog after a local church dance was all I'd experienced. And that had been short-lived when my mother appeared from the shadows to shout at him. I often wondered if my father would have been more or less strict than her if he hadn't died when I was seven. I'd had enough of being a wimp, this was my time to make something of myself and force that smile off my sister's grinning face.

"What time do we have to be at the party?"

Her dip into seriousness forgotten, she smiled. "Any time after nine, so we've got hours yet. Time for you to unpack."

"Time for me to try and find a job," I said.

I lifted my battered cream case onto the bed and opened it. Staring at the measly collection of clothes I began lifting the only other two outfits I possessed, an orange maxi dress with a halter neck I'd borrowed from a friend and omitted to return before hurriedly leaving home, a jumpsuit I hoped showed off my body in the most flattering way possible, a flowered skirt, and my jeans. I dropped my wedges onto the floor, promising myself I'd replace them with the first pay packet I earned.

Hazel pulled open the bottom drawer of an oak chest of drawers that, like everything else in the room, had seen better days, and separated our two beds. I hurriedly scrunched up my greying underwear and pushed it to the back. Nothing much there to impress, I decided miserably. How was I going to make a decent impression if this was the best I could come up with?

Hazel opened the wardrobe and easily pushed her clothes to one side. "We don't have very much, do we?" she said. Then, looking me up and down, added. "You're taller than me, but I think we're almost the same size. Maybe we could share our clothes. That way it'll look like we have more."

I hadn't liked sharing with my sister, but she did have a point. "Okay, why not?" I took one of the hangers and hung up the orange dress, hoping the creases fell out before it was time to leave for the party. "I need to find work," I said. "I probably only have enough money to pay my rent for the next three weeks."

She thought for a moment. "We can go out and ask around. I'm working as a waitress in Dave's Diner," she laughed. "It's a greasy café down the road and they pay a pittance, but it's a job. I'm hoping to make a contact at this party. Maybe Vince can get me a singing job somewhere at one of the clubs."

Vince was sounding better and better. "Maybe he might know someone who could help me?" I suggested hopefully.

Later, as we sat on the bus on our way to the club, I slipped my feet from my shoes and bent down to rub them. "We must have walked miles," I groaned. "I wouldn't mind if I'd found a job." I tried to quell the rising panic in my stomach. I couldn't bear the thought of returning to my home village, where the most exciting thing to look forward to was the annual flower show in the old Nissen hut that passed for a village hall. "I need to find something soon."

Hazel stopped humming. "Don't panic, you will. I promise." She beamed at me. "This is London. We can't be miserable in this fab city." She stifled a squeal. "If my mum could see me now, all dolled up and on my way to a party, she'd be so proud."

Mine would have a stroke, I thought. "Hmm, mine too."

"I wish I was as tall as you," she said, her buoyant mood dipping slightly.

I needed her to be chirpy and gave her a nudge. "You're very pretty, Hazel. Like a gypsy princess, with all that long black curly hair. You're lucky, mine is nowhere near as lustrous as yours."

"Do you really think so?" She perked up instantly.

"I do. Right, we've got a lot riding on tonight, so you must smile however miserable you feel. If we want to be in the entertainment business, we're going to have to pretend to be confident and happy whenever we're in company."

This agreed, we got off the bus and walked along the narrow pavement down the gloomy road. I was about to say something when a group of sullen-faced people probably no older than me, walked around the corner in our direction. Hazel and I slowed our pace as we neared them. I tried not to stare at their strange make-up, torn clothes and colourful spiky hair as we passed them.

My heart pounded. I tried to look as if this was familiar to me. I could hear the lolloping beat to Donna Summer's song 'Love to Love You Baby'. A shiver of excitement shot through me as I realised how close we were to the club. Looking over my shoulder to check they were far behind us, I bent slightly to whisper to Hazel. "Is there a film studio around here?"

She stopped walking and frowned. "Not that I know of, why?"

I nodded in the direction of the strange looking group now crossing the road to the other side. "Where would they come from, do you think?"

She smiled. "They're punks."

Her knowing smile irritated me. "Why has that guy got nappy pins in his ears?"

"It's all part of their look," Hazel said. "I'm not sure why they try to make themselves look as unattractive as possible. Their music is horrible, too. Sounds like crappy jazz to me."

The thought of my mother's horrified reaction to seeing these punks amused me. "We're going to have to try pretty hard to stand out in this place, aren't we?"

Hazel laughed. "I don't think I'll dye my hair blue though, do you?"

The lively disco beat echoed out of the basement into the

warm night. I looked at the neon sign with its arrow pointing down some steep stone steps and excitement welled up inside me. Smoothing down the front of my dress, I hoped I wouldn't look foolish in front of everyone else in the club. The nearest I'd come to a night life had been one or two discos in the local parish hall. It was difficult to imagine anything about the place we were soon to enter.

I took a deep breath. The anticipation that whatever happened tonight could change my life in some way was almost overwhelming. I'd dreamt of this moment for years. I was determined this party would alter everything for me. I'd make certain it did.

"Come along, dolly daydream," Hazel said waving for me to follow her.

Willing my nerves to steady, I stepped gingerly down the stairs into my future. We entered the club, the dark red walls giving a feel of depth that was impossible to decipher, while the flashing lights from the stage drew my eyes to the glamorous woman singing with the band. The smoke-filled air, mirrored ceiling and walls made it impossible to work out exactly how big this place was.

I stood up as straight as possible, sucking in my non-existent stomach, trying my best to look confident and as if I was born to be there. Hazel seemed to skip rather than walk. I didn't know if it was excitement or nerves, but my legs felt like they were made of cotton wool. I pushed away my shock at seeing those punks for the first time and walked behind Hazel looking from side to side trying to give off an air of indifferent confidence.

Every woman we passed, beautiful or not, was immaculately made up. This was a totally different world to the one we'd just left outside. The smartly dressed men appeared so worldly, like they knew we were naive provincials. Everyone seemed so self-assured and the women achingly glamorous. The random groups of men, some with their hair styled neatly into place with Brylcreem, and others their faces partially hidden by much longer rock star hair, watched us. None of them bothered to conceal their approval of Hazel and me as they smoked their cigarettes and continued drinking. It was as if they were evaluating our worth in some way.

Maybe my dress didn't look as cheap and inexpensive as I'd feared. I smiled to myself as it dawned on me that I could have worn almost any fabric in this dim lighting. It might even be possible that the other women also looked better in this light. I thought of my dad. He would despair seeing people me in this place with these people. He always ranted about how every new phase that began in London eventually found its way to our village. I couldn't imagine these people ever pitching up in our local church though.

Hazel came to a halt in front of a small group of people. One of the women, a tall blonde, threw her head back in laughter. She almost spilled the pink cocktail she was holding in one manicured hand down a man's suit. He flinched, pushing away her other arm, which was loosely draped around his broad shoulders. Then, glaring at her, he bent his head next to hers and whispered something I couldn't make out. She lowered her head briefly, and then raised it, a fixed smile on her made up face. I couldn't miss how her large eyes glistened suspiciously.

He sensed me staring at him and turned to face us. The others in his group stepped back and followed his line of vision. I cleared my throat and stared back at them, determined not to let them see how nervous I was to be there.

Hazel nudged me. "Isn't he heavenly?" she whispered from the side of her mouth.

I hoped he hadn't heard. I gazed at him and assumed this tall man, wearing a tailored steel grey suit must be Vince.

Suddenly breathless, I cleared my throat. I could see why she liked him. My breath caught in my throat as his deep blue eyes connected with mine. He was mesmerising. His dark, almost black hair was shorter than most of the other men in the club; his tanned face set his perfect white teeth off to perfection. It was easy to understand why she liked him. His self-assured air gave him presence that made him stand out among everyone else. He watched me silently. I tried to act unfazed but blushed under his intense scrutiny.

"Mo," Hazel snapped, glaring at me.

I saw him wave us over to him.

"Go on then," I murmured. "Introduce me."

Hazel took me by the arm and pulled me over to stand in front of him. I jerked my arm from her grasp and smiled at him.

"Vince," Hazel said, her panicky smile not reaching her eyes. "This is Mo, she's my flatmate."

Flatmate? We barely shared a room, but, hey, if she

wanted to give them a more up market impression of us then who was I to argue. Blimey, I thought, she was showing off about me. I must look better than I'd thought.

Vince held out his hand without taking his eyes off me. I shook his hand, still holding his gaze and did my best not to feel intimidated by the blonde woman he had pushed away who was glaring at me. She raised her arm, resting it on his. He stepped closer to me and her arm dropped. Flattered, I sensed he was casting her off and taking ownership of me.

"Mo?" he asked, raising a thick eyebrow. "It's good to meet you." His grasp tightened on my hand and pulled me gently into his group. Then, putting an arm around my shoulders and the other around Hazel's, he led us towards the bar. "You, gorgeous ladies, are coming with me. We could do with some fresh faces around this place."

Hazel and I exchanged delighted glances. "I think you both need a drink and proper introduction to this place." Hazel giggled. "Is this your first time in London?" he asked me.

"Yes," I said, desperate to appear sophisticated like the blonde woman. He seemed too worldly to be fooled by any facade though, so I didn't bother trying too hard. I didn't want to make a fool of myself in front of him.

He looked at the barman. "A bottle of champagne and four glasses, Joe." He turned his attention to me again. "So, what have you come to this vibrant capital for, Mo?"

"She's an actress," Hazel chirped before I had time to reply. "She's looking for work and we thought maybe you could help her find something?"

I frowned at her, hoping she'd shut up. I didn't want Vince to think I was too shy to speak for myself.

"Hey, it's okay," he said spotting my warning glare at Hazel. "She's right to tell me. I always do my best to help friends."

"Friends?" I asked laughing a little too loudly. It was partly out of relief that he liked me, but also because I had never received such rapt attention from any man before, let alone one as charismatic as Vince. "But we only met five minutes ago," I added.

He smiled, the tanned skin around his dark blue eyes crinkling in amusement. "Maybe, but we'll soon get to know each other and I'm sure we'll become firm friends."

"Okay," I said, sounding ridiculously grateful.

He winked at me and picking up the bottle of champagne pushed at the cork with his thumb until it flew out. Vince poured the bubbly, golden liquid into the four glasses and passed one each to me and Hazel. He then handed one to the blonde woman, his hand holding the glass mid-air for a few seconds when he spotted her scowling at me. "This is Alice," he said, finally passing over the glass.

I assumed she must be his girlfriend and my mood plummeted. If she wasn't a model, she certainly could pass for one. How could I ever compete with someone as beautifully groomed as her? She wasn't any taller than me, but there was something about her that I ached to duplicate. I resented her immediately.

"So, you're an actress," Vince said, ignoring her and focusing on me.

"Yes," I said.

"Have you done much acting work?" I shook my head. "Never mind, if you're determined and have any talent then you might stand a chance." He narrowed his eyes and drank some of his champagne. "I might be able to help you, at least with an introduction or two."

"That would be perfect," I said, taking a sip but the champagne went down my throat the wrong way. I began coughing, mortified to have made such a fool of myself. Unable to catch my breath I held out my glass trying to place it on the bar so that I could go to the Ladies and gather myself. My eyes streamed. It was all I could do not to cry.

"Here, let me take this," Vince said quietly, taking my glass with one hand and patting my back with the other. "Joe, get the kid a glass of water. Now!"

I fought to draw breath and Vince's hard pats on my back helped a bit.

"Here," he said, his voice gentle. "Take a few sips of this water, it should help."

I did as he said, taking first one sip and then another few. Gradually the coughing ceased, and my breathing began to return to normal.

"I'm just going to the loo," I said forcing a smile. I gave him back the half-empty glass of water and ran to the Ladies. Bursting into the room, I tried to ignore the startled expressions of three women standing eyebrows raised as I hurried into the cubicle. One giggled.

"Bloody hell, what's happened to her do you think?"

I grabbed a tissue and blew my nose, wishing the ground

would swallow me whole. Laughter echoed in the tiled room and an unmistakeable whisper ensured my humiliation was complete.

"Leave her be," another woman snapped. "Can't you see she's upset."

"Yes," I heard Vince say. I gasped, shocked to discover he'd followed me into the lavatories. "You heard what she said. Get lost."

"Oh, Mr, er…"

"In fact, get out of the club," he demanded, his voice low but the threat in his tone unmistakeable. If I come out of here and you three bitches are still around…"

"We won't be," I heard the woman who'd defended me insist. There was a little scuttling and then their hurried footsteps click-clacked on the floor as they left the room.

The door slammed shut behind them. I grabbed at some loo roll, trying not to panic, and blew my nose again.

"You can come out now," Vince said, his voice gentle and kind. When I didn't unlock the door, he added gently, "Come on now, Mo. We've all been caught out by drinking champers too quickly, there's nothing to be embarrassed about."

I wiped under my eyes with my fingers and pinched my cheeks to give them a bit of colour, trying to look presentable.

"Are you coming out, or am I going to have to call the lavatory attendant to unlock this door?" He sighed. "Come on, Mo, we're all friends here. You should see some of the states I've got myself into. Choking on a few bubbles is nothing."

I could tell he was trying to be kind and I didn't feel quite so badly. I took a deep breath, smoothed down my dress and unlocked the door. As I pulled it back I came face to face with him.

Vince's beautiful lips drew back into a smile and his eyes twinkled. "You need a hug?"

He seemed so caring that despite being surprised by his question, I stepped forward into his open arms. He wrapped me in a bear hug and breathed in the smell of his citrus cologne. The combination of the hug and the exquisite smell lifted my mood instantly.

"You alright?"

"Yes," I said quietly not wishing the moment to end. "A little bit mortified, that's all."

His arms dropped away from around me and he took hold of my shoulders. Stepping back, he studied my face for a second. He took a tissue from the decorated box on a nearby shelf, dampened it by patting it under the tap and gently wiped mascara away from under my eyes. The door opened, and a woman walked in. Her eyes widened, and her step faltered before she walked to the sink.

"Do you have a little powder my friend could use?" Vince asked.

She looked at his reflection in the mirror and turned a fixed smile on her perfectly made up face as she opened her bag. "Yes, of course." Rummaging around quickly, she produced a gold-plated compact and handed it to him. "You can keep it if you like?"

I sensed her fear and supposed that she was more shocked

than I had assumed by coming across us in the lavatory this way.

"That won't be necessary," he said. Pressing the tiny clasp, the lid flicked open. Vince lifted the pad and dabbed it onto the pressed pale powder. I couldn't help staring at his face as he leaned closer to me to focus his attention on tidying up my face. I fantasised that he might kiss me, forgetting for a moment that we weren't alone. But having gently tapped the powder onto my face, he stood back and smiled. "Yes, that'll do." He winked at me. "You'll see," he said. "No one will ever notice you were upset."

He snapped the compact closed and turned to the woman, smiling at her. "Thank you."

She gave us another fixed smile, which didn't meet her eyes and nodded. "Not at all."

Vince took me by the hand and led me out of the Ladies and stopped in the hallway.

"Don't ever be ashamed of yourself, Mo," he said. "You're a beautiful and I'll bet talented woman, and one day you'll have the confidence to go with those traits."

He let go of my hand and I followed him back to join the others at the bar. "Grab your glass and come with me," he said as if we were the only ones there. "There's someone I'd like you to meet."

I did as he asked, nervously hoping that this would be my life-changing moment. Vince put an arm around my waist and lowered his head slightly towards me. "The guy I'm taking you to meet puts on shows around the country; he might be able to help you. He's a business contact of mine."

The saliva in my mouth dried instantly. I could barely contain my nerves. "Really?" I said, my voice croaking embarrassingly.

He gave me a little squeeze. "Yes, really."

Hazel had been right, Vince was lovely. He also made me feel more important than I'd ever remotely managed to feel during the previous eighteen years of my life. We drew up next to a short, skinny man with thick glasses. He didn't look very impressive, but the people around him seemed to be in awe of him, so I assumed I should be, too.

"Vinnie," he shouted, raising his arms in the air and waving him over to give him a hug. "Where've you been hiding all night?"

Vince waited for the man to let go of him and placing his palm against the small of my back, propelled me forward. "Jack, this is Mo."

I almost lost my footing; regaining my composure, I came face to face with the second person that evening who had taken more time to study me than I was used to. "Mo," he said in a high-pitched nasally voice. "You are a doll, aren't you?"

His attention unnerved me a little. He had the smallest eyes I'd ever seen on a grown person, but seemed to see right inside me. I was a little unsure how I should react. "Thank you."

"You're an actress." He puffed on a short, fat cigar, removing it to reveal how wet it was at one end and waved it in the air. "You're a pretty little thing, aren't you? Can you actually act though?"

I nodded, my previous confidence vanishing.

"And you want me to find you work?"

I nodded again, a little less sure about how much I wanted his help. I glanced over to Hazel and Alice, but they were watching the introduction with great interest not bothering to hide their jealousy. Maybe, Jack wasn't such a bad person to be introduced to, after all. I forced a smile, wishing to appear a little friendlier and less afraid.

"I think I might be able to do that." He took out his wallet and withdrew a business card. Handing it to me, he said, "Here's the address for my office, be there at ten o'clock sharp on Monday and we'll have a chat. See what I can do for you."

"Thank you," I said breathlessly, grateful for such an easy introduction to the world of entertainment.

Delighted to have passed my first test on my route to stardom, I couldn't help standing a little taller, confident that I'd just experienced the moment I'd been waiting for all my life. It was. Meeting Vince did change my life, but not in the way I'd expected.

# Chapter Four

## 2003 – Epernay

### Sera

After a few unproductive hours in my studio in Epernay, I finally arrived back at the house. I stopped off on the way home to buy a box of fresh cakes from my favourite local *pâtisserie*, La Pâtisserie des Pays. It was another sweltering day. The heat was so intense that everyone felt drained and lacking in energy.

I had spent the morning recalling the countless nights I had fallen into an exhausted, fretful sleep wondering what had happened to Dee and her family and why they had disappeared. The last time I saw them it had been to deliver a letter from my mother. Had she said something to make them leave? Countless times I had woken startled by a nightmare about the family falling into a black, bottomless pit. Today, though, I hoped to finally discover what really happened to them.

Checking the kitchen wall clock yet again, I ground fresh coffee beans and set them to percolate on the range to keep myself busy. I tried not to get too excited and pottered about the house, finally giving up and sitting to wait for Leo's arrival.

I glanced at the clock. What if he changed his mind and wasn't ready to speak to someone from his past? I stood up and wiped down the worktops; then, when he hadn't arrived by two-thirty, I washed the kitchen floor to keep busy, wondering if he was coming.

The doorbell rang just before three; my heart pounded as I hurried to answer it. Could he really be on the other side of that door? Was I about to discover what had happened to my best friend and her family all those years before? I'd imagined this moment many times since their disappearance that hot summer night when Dee and I were barely thirteen and although I wasn't going to see her today, at least I might learn where she was now and how I could contact her.

I turned the brass handle and pulled back the front door. There he was, smiling back at me. I wasn't sure who was more delighted to see the other.

"Come on in," I said, my voice wavering. I waited for him to enter the bright hallway.

He walked in, stopping at the base of the staircase and gazed around the room and up towards the landing.

"I remember coming here with Dee a few times and you two would always make me go and play in the back garden. You never let me join in with whatever it was you were doing."

I walked past him towards the kitchen, laughing at the memory. "That was because we were practically teenagers and always talking about boys. You were what, nine?" He nodded. "We didn't want you spying on us and reporting back to your mum."

"Hah, you think she would have noticed?"

I pictured Hazel, her mind elsewhere whenever she was harvesting her crop of lavender. She seemed perpetually happy as she picked the purple scented flowers, the hem of her colourful, flowing skirt tucked into the elastic waistband and a wicker basket by her feet slowly filling up. Singing as she worked as she later placed the stems into oil-filled bottles, or plaiting hearts with the longer stems of lavender to sell on her occasional market stall in the village.

"True, we could pretty much do whatever we liked at her farm," I said, happy to be able to reminisce about those blissful days when in my mind, it was always a hot summer's day. "As long as we didn't overstep the mark when it came to pinching the odd tot of whatever cocktail someone had made, or sneaking off with a suspicious looking cigarette." I hesitated. "She was besotted with your stepdad, Pierre, wasn't she? Always desperately trying to please him."

I thought I noticed his smile slip slightly.

"They never actually married," Leo, said thoughtfully. "Pierre was okay, but I think he got tired of the constant stream of people visiting the farm."

"It was a bit full on, sometimes, wasn't it?" If she wasn't trying out a new idea to make money, Hazel was entertaining her eccentric friends.

"It was." He hesitated. "Have you been there at all?" He glanced out of the window. "To the farm?"

I picked up the coffee percolator and pointed at it. Leo nodded.

"Oddly enough, yes," I said, pouring us both a mug of coffee.

He seemed surprised by this, though I wasn't sure why. I had lived here most of my life and the farm was only down the road. I pushed the cream cakes towards him, indicating the plates and napkins and told him all about Henri and the fire burning down the barn.

His eyes widened. "Hell, that must have been frightening."

"It was, but I mostly felt very sorry for Henri. He's new to the town and a little, um, reserved. The people around here haven't really taken to him."

"Because he's interesting, you mean?"

I laughed, choking on the mouthful of coffee I'd half swallowed. "Stop it. There's nothing wrong with the people around here. Anyway, neither of our mums are from here and they didn't find it hard to settle in."

He pondered my comment for a moment. "We don't really know that though, do we?"

"No, we don't," I said, surprised that I hadn't considered how little I knew about Mum's early years here when I was tiny.

"They had kids," Leo continued, breaking my reverie. "Us attending the local schools and being born and brought up here would have helped them fit in. He's a stranger with no connections."

That was true. "But he's French, so I'm not sure why they have such an issue with him."

Leo stared at me for a moment. "We were always slight outsiders here, probably because our mothers were quite different in their own ways to the other local mums."

They were. My mum, always flitting here and there, either going to auditions in Paris or filming her latest bit parts somewhere. I think the people around here were slightly in awe of her lifestyle. As for Hazel with her barely concealed ambitions to be a professional singer, she had fewer airs about her and tended to make friends a little more easily.

"Our mums were so English in their own ways," I said thoughtfully. "Despite speaking fluent French. No matter how much they tried not to stick out from the other locals, they never quite fitted in properly, which is probably why we didn't." And, I mused, probably also why the three of us gravitated towards each other.

"Our mums were entertainment for the locals, I always thought?"

I smiled, recalling Hazel's battered Land Rover with coloured beads strung along the windows on the inside of the back windows. "They were probably too stunned by your mother's antics to find the right words to criticise any of us."

Leo laughed. "You're probably right. And as for your friend, Henri, is it?" I nodded. "You say he's quite reserved, maybe they take that as being secretive and untrustworthy."

I could see his point. I didn't pick up any bad vibes from Henri, but Mum certainly did. Unwilling to be negative about Henri, I pushed the plate of pastries towards him. "Please take one."

"They look delicious. I've missed eating these. Are they from that local *pâtisserie* we always used to go to?"

"They are," I said, watching him choose a chocolate covered choux bun and eat half of it before asking the one question I'd been dying to put to him. "So, Dee, is she well?"

He looked up at me, wiping the sides of his mouth with the napkin before lowering his gaze and staring silently at the table.

"I wondered how long it'd take you to ask about my sister," he said quietly. "After all, I'm fully aware that your excitement in finding me today was because you're hoping to see her again." I didn't disagree. "She's okay," he added eventually.

He didn't sound that convincing. "Has something happened to her?"

He seemed to be gathering his thoughts and then looked me in the eye. "To be honest, she's had a rough time of it." I waited for him to continue, not daring to put him off elaborating further. "In fact, I'm rather concerned about her, Sera."

"Why?" I asked, trying not panic. "Is there anything I can do to help?"

He shook his head. "No," he hesitated. "I couldn't ask you. I've only just met up with you again, and you haven't seen Dee for years."

"So, what?" I said, frantic. I wasn't ready to miss the chance of meeting up with her again. "If there's something I can do for her, please promise me you'll let me know."

He looked so sad. Once again, he seemed like a small boy

with a mountain of trouble weighing him down. He'd always been a worrier, but then it had been about his mother's latest boyfriend, lack of money, or an unwanted guest who was refusing to leave their farm.

"I'd want to, Leo. Promise me."

He sighed. "Thanks. I'll bear that in mind. Now," he said, pointing at the cakes, "all right, if I take a second one of these?"

"Of course," I said, irritated that he was changing the subject so soon. "Help yourself."

I could see my questioning was making him uncomfortable. "Be careful though, you don't want to make yourself sick," I teased, trying to raise the sudden dip in the atmosphere.

He pulled a face at me. "I was what, seven, when I ate all my mother's Black Forest gateau?"

I laughed at the memory of how furious Hazel had been to discover that not only had Leo eaten most of her boyfriend's, Pierre's, birthday cake, but that he'd then gone upstairs and thrown up all over his freshly made bed. "I didn't think she'd ever forgive you for that incident."

He shook his head and grimaced. "Nor me."

"I was always envious of you and Dee growing up at the farm with your colourful mum and her floaty friends," I said.

"Floaty?" he asked, confused. "That's a good way to describe them. Most of them were off their faces on something they'd smoked."

It had all seemed so lyrical to me, as if their farm was in an invisible bubble. "It was their long and flowing skirts and scarves I adored. My mum always wanted me to dress conservatively. She was all big hair, massive shoulder pads and power-dressing, but I craved Dee's wardrobe." I smiled, warmed at the memory. "Some of your mum's friends might have been pretty spaced out most of the time, but Hazel was a really cool mum."

"When she took notice of us. Unlike your mum, from what I remember, she was a little over protective of you."

Something I'd battled with most of my life, I mused. "Hazel was always reinventing herself," I said thinking back to the vivacious woman I'd hoped to emulate when I grew up. One day she was a bleached blonde glamorous singer, the next rushing off to an ashram somewhere deep in the French countryside leaving Dee and Leo with whichever boyfriend was living at the farm at that time. "Pierre calmed her down a bit, don't you think?"

Leo drank some of his coffee while he contemplated my comment. "I suppose he did. He certainly lasted longer than most of her boyfriends."

I took a sip of my coffee, relishing the hot, rich liquid. "You can't say we had dull childhoods though, can you?"

"A little normality would have been a treat sometimes."

I agreed. Sitting here with Leo and reminiscing made me aware how different my childhood seemed from an adult's point of view. My past had always been a bit of a mystery to me. Mum would never discuss where she grew up, despite my pleading. All she once said was that she'd spent her childhood planning her escape from her home town. I learnt not to press her from an early age. I did think her airs were probably put on a bit as I got older and mixed with different kinds of people.

"I wish our mothers had been better friends," I said recalling how my mother's dislike of Hazel had been the hardest part of my childhood. It had been a relief that she hadn't minded Dee and Leo, but even though she'd been a pretty good actress she could never fail to show her loathing of Hazel whenever I mistakenly mentioned her name. "Do you think she was jealous of Hazel's carefree ways?" I asked.

"Maybe." A key in the front door and Leo turned instantly to face the hallway. "Could that be your mum?"

"Probably. She'll be amazed to see you here."

The rapid tapping of her heels click-clacked on the tiled flooring as she neared. I waited, anticipating the look of astonishment on her face when she spotted who was with me. I wasn't disappointed. Her initial expression was one of delight to find me talking to a man at the table; she was always nagging me to start dating again, irritated when I tried to insist that I was perfectly happy by myself.

My mother stepped further into the kitchen. She squinted, realisation slowly dawning as Leo turned around to her, a smile on his tanned face. "Leo, is that you?" she asked raising a perfectly threaded eyebrow.

He stood up and gave her a brief hug. "Hello, Maureen. You still look the same."

"I don't, but it's very kind of you to fib," she said smoothing down her immaculate hair. "I think I need a cup of tea, Sera," she said, sitting down at the end of the table, all the time staring in disbelief at him. "You look so different."

"Mum, we'd find it odd if he hadn't grown up at all." I poured hot water into the teapot and added a few spoons of tea leaves, placing the pot in front of her on the table. It was only when I turned back to her having taken a cup and saucer from the dresser that I realised she looked troubled. I decided to ask her why later, after he'd left.

After an awkward silence, she asked, "How are Hazel and Delilah? Are they well?" Taking the silver strainer from the table and placing it on the rim of her cup, she concentrated on pouring her tea, forgetting to leave the teapot to stand for her usual requisite two minutes. "There was much gossip when you disappeared all those years ago, no one knew what had happened to any of you. There was even talk of dredging the pool in the woods at the back of your old farm."

He shuddered slightly. "I always assumed us leaving like that must have been the most exciting event to happen here for years." He didn't smile at his own attempt at humour. "It was a strange time for us, too," he added quietly.

I took a breath wanting to discover more. "Leo…"

He glanced down at his watch. "Hell, is that the time?" he said, interrupting me. "I should go; I was supposed to meet someone ten minutes ago." He got to his feet. "It was good to see you, Maureen."

She nodded and gave him a sad smile. "Will you come and see us again, or will you be disappearing for another twenty years?"

I still hadn't found out what had happened to Dee and wanted to be sure I'd see him at least once more. "I'll see you out," I said, giving Mum a pointed glare as I passed her. She didn't seem at all bothered that she'd been rude to a second person that day. It was very unlike her and I couldn't help wondering if seeing him here brought back her concern for me and the devastation I'd felt after his family had disappeared.

I accompanied him along the hallway, both of us walking to the door in silence. He opened it, stopping and turning once outside.

"It really was wonderful seeing you again, Sera."

"But you haven't told me where you're living, or why you're here," I asked.

He gave me a kiss on the cheek and smiled. "It's work related and I'm afraid I can't talk about it just yet," he explained.

Unsatisfied with his answer and determined not to let him go without trying to find out more about Dee, I placed a hand on one of his arms. "Leo, you still haven't told me where Dee is. Will you give me her contact details, so I can get in touch with her?"

He shook his head. "She doesn't have a mobile and I'm not sure she'd want me to give out her landline right now." He considered his next words. "Tell you what though, I'll speak to her. I can put her in touch with you, if you like?"

I hid my concern that she wouldn't call me. "Okay," I said aware that I didn't have any choice in the matter. "Please tell her I can't wait to catch up with her." I reached out and took one of my business cards from the hall table, handing it to him. "Here are my numbers and an email address. I'll wait to hear from you, or Dee."

He took the card and read it before lowering his head and kissing me on both cheeks. "It really is very good to see you again. I promise I'll be in touch soon."

I watched him walk down the steps to the pavement and out of my life, once again. Aware he hadn't offered to give me his contact details, I hoped he was a man of his word and would get in touch. I sighed, closed the door, and returned to the kitchen.

"What was all that about?" I asked, unable to stop myself.

Mum looked up, her perfectly made up face seeming older than it had this morning. "I'm sorry, I didn't mean to be rude. It was a shock seeing him here after so long. I never thought we'd see them again."

"Nor did I."

Feeling mean for being harsh, I sat down and told her all about spotting Leo that morning on my way to the studio.

"It was the weirdest thing. He looks so different, but I still sensed it was him for some reason. Don't you think that's strange, like it was meant to be?" She didn't reply. "He told me this is the first time he's been back since they left in the eighties."

"Serendipity," she murmured almost to herself. "At least we know he's still alive."

She stared at her cup thoughtfully for a while and I watched noticing a softness in her demeanour for the first time. I wondered why there had been such antagonism between her and Hazel. Mum didn't make friends easily, but she didn't fall out with people either.

She straightened her cup in its saucer. "Whatever happened to the rest of the family?"

"Their lives have probably been pretty much like ours," I said trying to picture Dee as she was now.

"I doubt Dee's husband was killed in a plane crash like Marcus. I can't imagine she's had to cope with the things that have happened to you."

The reference to Marcus stung, as it usually did when I wasn't expecting to hear his name. I'd struggled over the past three years since his plane had crashed into a hillside on the way to a meeting in Wales. "Maybe not, but apart from that difficult time our lives have been ordinary, wouldn't you say?"

Mum sighed heavily. "Not really, no." It dawned on me that her boyfriend Paul wasn't with her. "Where's Paul?"

She took a sip of her tea. "I ended our relationship." She stood up, collected the crockery and carried them over to the sink. Pulling on her rubber washing-up gloves she always wore to do any housework, she turned on the taps to fill the sink. "We're not as well matched as I'd hoped."

I had experienced this before and unlike the occasions when she met someone I thought did suit her, I wasn't sorry to hear Paul wouldn't be coming to stay a third time.

She glanced over her shoulder at me. "It's getting late. Shouldn't you have left to collect Katie by now?"

I noticed for the first time how tense her shoulders appeared. I could tell Leo's visit had unnerved her for some reason. Reminded of her dislike of Hazel, I put it down to that and left her alone in her thoughts. Although I was still unsure why he had come to the house, when he seemed reluctant to share anything much about his family.

# Chapter Five

## 2003 – Hautvillers, near Epernay

## Sera

A few weeks passed by and I'd almost given up ever hearing from Leo again. I still found it strange to picture Leo as the broad-shouldered man he had become. He was such a timid little boy, so skinny and shy, it was difficult to see them as the same person. I couldn't help wondering why he had returned after all this time. Why meet with someone at the main bank in Epernay? Unless he was planning on buying a home here. Soothed by this thought, I decided it made perfect sense. Maybe enough time had passed for him and Dee to return to where they had grown up? Perhaps he didn't want to confide in me until they had bought a place. I hoped so.

I didn't visit Henri either. I was aware that the locals, including Mum, were still very suspicious of him. Doubting any of them would have bothered checking on him after the fire, I drove over to his farm with Katie one afternoon after picking her up from school. We turned the last bend of his dusty driveway and I spotted him leaning on a rake, one hand up to his eyes to shade them from the glare of the sun. He peered towards us trying to see who was coming, uninvited, to his home.

I pulled up by the lilac and apple trees and stepped out of the car. Opening the rear door, I unstrapped Katie's car seat and lifted her down, before he reached us and complained. Then I let her run around in the yard. "I hope you don't mind us coming to see you?" I said, sensing he did, very much.

He stared at Katie as she crouched down to study a couple of chickens and shook his head. Resting the rake against the house wall, he said, "*Non, pas du tout.*"

Feeling a little awkward for my unexpected arrival, I turned my attention to the charred remains of his barn. "Any idea when you'll be allowed to clear this away and start rebuilding?"

"*Non.*"

He must be nervous living here alone if the culprits were still out there somewhere. "I hope they catch whoever did this soon."

Again, a slow shrug of his left shoulder. "I can defend myself if I must."

I believed him. Despite his limp and scarred face, he was muscular, and I didn't doubt that somewhere along the line he'd learnt to look out for himself. There was nothing delicate about Henri. "Good, I'm glad."

He looked confused by my visit. "You want to see the damage to the barn?"

I studied the stakes of blackened wood standing like rotten teeth where the ancient slightly warped walls had once been. The barn was solidly built, the oak beams darkened by decades of use. I pictured the stores of apples collected in the autumn months, next to Hazel's willow boxes containing her lavender harvests. The brown bags filled with sunflower seeds from previous years and the more recent drying heads of flowers hung up along two of the walls. This barn had been majestic and filled with laughter, especially when Dee and I had been sent by Hazel to hang fresh bunting for one of her parties. I recalled the calming scent and flickering glow of the lavender candles resting in elaborate candleholders Hazel favoured for those evenings. Seeing it crushed by the fire was devastating. It wasn't just a building, it was part of my past that I hadn't ever expected to vanish.

"Yes, okay." I followed him, trying to summon up her lyrical voice singing those long-ago songs from Hazel's impromptu parties and wished I could travel back to that time, if only for a few hours. I longed to revisit those magical days with Hazel and her friends dancing around in their flowing, brightly coloured dresses, their hair long with flowers woven in to their tresses, the men with their faded jeans and unfashionably faded T-shirts. Now I could only smell charred wood, but back then the aromas of lavender mixed with the heady scent of patchouli and sandalwood filled this space. I'd loved being a part of the magical world so reminiscent of the sixties and seventies rather than the eighties when they'd inhabited my world.

I thought back to my younger self with Dee, liking the

latest fashions of that decade and teasing me that I should have been Hazel's daughter as I fitted in so much better with her carefree world. I imagined how heartbroken I'd be if Katie went through the same mysterious loss of her closest confidante like I had and hoped her teenage years would be more settled. I'd been such an awkward age when I lost touch with Dee. Had she missed me in the same way after they'd left? Had she managed to find a way to make sense of our odd lives?

It hurt that Leo hadn't been in touch. I couldn't help thinking that maybe it would have been better not to have seen him again because doing so brought back too many memories I'd spent years learning to suppress. I'd missed them so much, and my life at their farm.

I realised at that second why my mother had been so odd with Leo. She'd watched me grieve for the loss of my best friend and a family I wanted as my own. It couldn't have been easy coping with your only child withdrawing instead of turning to you for comfort. Poor Mum, I thought, guiltily. I'd put her through so much back then.

I glanced at Henri and seeing his mouth moving realised he was saying speaking. "Pardon?"

He smiled crookedly, one side of his face not working as well as the other. It gave him an air of danger somehow. "I was asking how you are?" he said, kicking a charred piece of wood out of his way.

I told him about my childhood friend reappearing and then not hearing from him again for several weeks. "I miss not having many friends," I said, thinking of the life I'd left behind in Scotland. I had joined the local book club soon after Marcus and I had moved there and enjoyed getting to know the women. I had considered them friends, but after Marcus' sudden death they had kept away. Their withdrawal from my life was painful and Mum suggested it was because they were unsure what to say to me. "Some of them will feel threatened that you're now a beautiful young widow," she had added. "They'll be concerned you'll look to one of their husbands for comfort." I had been angry by her comment, but looking back it could have been one of the reasons why I was abandoned.

"Friends, what are they really?" he said matter-of-factly. "Only people who talk to you but usually want something you're not willing to give."

I wasn't sure what he meant exactly and didn't ask, but his comment saddened me. "You must have some people you consider friends?"

He looked up at me for the first time since we'd entered the barn. "You are my only friend in Epernay, Sera."

"Really?" I couldn't miss the intensity of his gaze. We barely knew each other. It occurred to me that if anyone else had said that to me I probably would have felt a little claustrophobic. For some reason I didn't mind Henri feeling this way. Maybe it was because I felt defensive of the way he'd been treated. I picked up that rather than not liking people, he simply didn't need the company of others to feel secure.

"You don't think me strange saying this to you?" he asked narrowing his eyes.

"No," I said honestly. "It's a compliment." Again, that intensity as he stared at me. Why didn't it make me uncomfortable?

"*Bien.*" He walked over to the other side of the barn, careful where he placed each step.

I glanced over to the yard to check where Katie had got to and spotted her sitting on the ground playing with Henri's scruffy Collie. She was so sweet. My heart constricted to think that Marcus, so full of hope and ambition when he died, would never get to see her growing up. I swallowed the lump constricting my throat. Now wasn't the time to immerse myself in self-pity. I thought about the stories I had shared with him about my time here with Hazel and her family. Marcus had wanted to visit the farm the next time we travelled to Hautvillers, but we never managed to before he died.

"Sera?"

Henri's voice snapped me out of my reverie. I hurried to the other side of the damaged building wondering what could be so interesting about lumps of burnt wood and earth.

"*Ici*," he said pointing down at the floor. "They think there is a cellar below."

"Seriously?"

He nodded. "You knew this place when you were a child? Do you remember anything being stored down there?"

I didn't recall ever seeing a cellar and told him. "I'm not sure Leo and Dee's family ever knew a cellar existed, I certainly didn't."

"The fire burnt away some of the wooden floor covering it. Maybe it had been covered over for many years," he frowned and bent down to study the area further. "It will be interesting to have a look, no?"

I agreed. "You could find out how large the area is," I suggested, intrigued that I'd thought I knew every inch of this place and here was somewhere I'd never come across before now.

"Storage is useful. A cellar keeps stock cold," he said. "When I rebuild the barn, I will make much use of it."

"Especially in the summer time," I said, sensing he wanted to ask me something but wasn't sure whether to mention it. He walked off. I went to follow him and stepping over a piece of wood, my ankle gave way causing me to slam my hip against part of a brick step as I fell.

"Shit." I winced, mortified, trying not to let on how much it hurt.

"Sera." Henri hurried back to me. I held my hand up to stop him, concerned that he'd end up tripping in his haste and damaging his bad leg further. "You are hurt," he said reaching me and bending down to place his hand on my thigh. "You should check it," he said pointing to my skirt and turning his gaze away.

I gritted my teeth, nervous to discover how badly I'd hurt myself. Then, gently lifting the cotton material until it bared my skin, I grimaced.

"The skin isn't broken," I said seeing a dark bruise already becoming visible. "But I'm going to be pretty sore for the next few days," I said, embarrassed.

"Give me your hand, so you can stand." He took my arm and pulled it around his shoulders, slipping his hand around my waist to slowly lift me.

"Thank you," I said wincing. "How stupid of me." I touched the painful area lightly with the palm of my hand and rubbed carefully. "Damn, that's sore." I could hear Katie giggling and singing to the dog, grateful she hadn't witnessed my antics.

He stepped carefully over the debris in our path and led me out of the barn area. "I have arnica in my house; it will help where you have bruising."

We slowly made our way to his front steps and both limped up to the front door. Not wishing to leave Katie outside alone, I called out for her to come with me.

"Maman, you are hurt?" she asked, her little face crumbling with fear.

"No, I'm fine. I just twisted my ankle, it's nothing. Come inside with me and Henri."

"You want some water to drink?" he asked, as she ran up to him. He looked a little more at ease with her and I couldn't help wondering if he'd ever had his own family at some point.

We reached his kitchen and he motioned for me to sit on an old fabric chair by the fireplace as he went to pull open drawers looking for the cream. Finding it he handed it to me and then crossed the room to pour Katie a glass of water.

"I have old books in another room," he said to her. "Would you like me to find them for you?"

"I'll come with you," she said in a loud whisper. "I can

take them to the porch to read them to your dog."

He glanced at me and shook his head. "You talk with Patti," he said as left the room. I heard her chattering away to the tatty dog telling her how she couldn't read yet, but liked making up stories when she looked at the pictures in books. Henri soon returned laden with a pile of books which he placed just outside the open door. Katie beamed at him and sat down, immediately immersed in the pages of the first book.

Henri returned to sit in the chair at the other side of the cold fireplace. I watched him for a while, not sure why his mood seemed to have changed. "Henri, is there something troubling you?"

He rubbed the palm of his left hand with his right thumb absentmindedly. "I do not wish to offend you."

"You won't," I assured him, a frisson of nerves building in my stomach. "What is it?"

I waited for him to gather his thoughts and squinted at the instructions on the metal tube in my hand to distract myself.

"You said you grew up here and returned three years ago. What made you come back?"

Deciding that if I was hoping for him to open up a little to me then I needed to do the same, replied, "My husband, Marcus, died in a plane crash. I tried to carry on in our home in Scotland, but everything reminded me of him, so I came back to France and moved into my mother's house." I could see the pity on his face. "It meant that Katie and I could start rebuilding our lives somewhere familiar. I could also look after Mum's house whenever she was away working."

"I should not have asked." He shook his head and looked down at the grate.

I hadn't meant to shock him. "It's fine, I'm almost used to not having him around now," I said. It was a half-truth and sometimes the pain of Marcus' absence shot through me. "I still miss him, of course. Marcus was a good husband and a wonderful father to Katie, for the short time he was with her."

"A plane crash?"

I nodded. "He was flying. Marcus always wanted his own plane. He and his business partner shared it. They both died in the crash."

"Do you mind me asking what was his business?"

It made a nice change to speak about my past with someone who didn't have any pre-conceived ideas about it. I thought back to the smart functions Marcus and I had attended, the plans we made together and our dreams of the perfect future for us and our beautiful daughter. It took me a moment to collect my emotions enough to be able to reply.

"I hadn't realised Marcus and his partner had overreached themselves financially," I admitted. Why was I telling him this much detail? "The meeting they were flying to was with prospective buyers for the firm, but naturally the sale fell through after their deaths and everything went to creditors.

"That is terrible."

It was at the time. "I was left with very little. I sold our home, paid off our mortgage, and came back to France." I pushed back the fear of those frightening times when so much seemed lost.

"You have a new life now. You are happy again?"

He looked so guilty asking me such a personal question that I smiled to put him at his ease. "Yes, most of the time."

This last comment of mine made him frown. "I think your husband would be happy that you have taken these choices."

My mother said almost the same thing to me many times and a part of me believed it, too. "I find it difficult sometimes not having him here." A sob caught in my throat and I coughed to be able to continue with what I was saying. "Marcus was a lovely man, funny and kind. It almost doesn't seem right that I'm enjoying seeing our daughter growing up while he's missing out on everything."

"Life is cruel." He spoke as if the pain of his own past weighed heavily on his mind.

"Tell me about you, Henri. What happened to bring you here?"

"Loss, like you." He looked thoughtful. "A different loss, but one I struggle to accept. In that we are the same, I think."

Seeing his mood dipping and not wishing to be the reason his day was made more difficult, I leant forward in the chair and smiled at him. "We're a couple of miseries; we need to do something to cheer ourselves up."

He narrowed his eyes suspiciously unsure whether to take me seriously. "You wish to do something, together?"

I could tell that my suggestion had unnerved him. "Yes, we could go somewhere with Katie. Fishing maybe, or swimming in the large pool in the woods at the back of your farm. Have you ever been there?"

He shook his head slowly. I could see my suggestion disconcerted him, but it was too late to take back the suggestion.

"No. This makes it a little painful to walk far." He tapped his thigh and once again I was intrigued to know what had happened to him.

I recalled my mother's warning about him, but remembered how she also mistrusted Marcus when she had first met him. Turning my attention back to Henri and my intention to encourage him to confide in me at some point, I said, "We can drive part of the way, if you like?"

He considered this suggestion. "It is hot. I do like to swim."

"Then it's decided," I said, happy to have persuaded him.

I asked him to fetch a couple of towels for us and went to put away the books Katie was looking through. Entering the living room across the hallway, I glanced around the room for a bookcase and not seeing one, walked over to a small table in the corner of the large room that already had a pile of papers spread out on it. I straightened them slightly and spotted a framed picture on the wall. Hearing footsteps coming towards the room down the hallway, I waited for Henri to join me.

"You have found something?" he asked, frowning, three rolled up towels under one arm.

I pointed up at the framed poster of David Bowie's Thin White Duke concert. "That was a famous concert, wasn't it? You must be a fan?"

"Of course, and you?"

I loved Bowie's music, but for some reason my mother hated it, always switching off the transistor radio if one of his songs came on. "I am. That concert must have been, what…" I tried to work it out.

"Twenty-seven years ago," he said instantly, before I had time to do my maths. He stared at the poster thoughtfully for a moment.

I wondered what he was thinking, he certainly couldn't be recalling being there himself, he must have been a toddler back then. I looked up at the picture with some of my favourite songs listed on it. "My favourite has to be 'Golden Years'."

He gave a half smile. "Mine, also."

I opened my mouth to say something, but he shook his head. "We must go to swim."

I was aware he'd changed the subject, which I found a little odd, but before I could prod him for further information Katie ran into the room. "Why is Monsieur Henri holding towels?"

She was such a nosy little devil. I walked over to her and picking her up, winced when she landed against my bruised thigh. She spotted my reaction and looked upset, so I tickled her to distract her from fretting about me. She tried to wriggle out of my arms and argued a little, until I told her of our plans to go to the pool for a dip.

We reached the car and I strapped Katie into her car seat and waited for Henri to come and join us. He looked unsure as he stood on the steps in front of the farmhouse. Refusing to allow him to stay behind and ruin my plans to get him to confide in me, I turned on the ignition and motioned for him to come over. "Get in," I said, before he had a chance to change his mind.

We drove to the wood and parked the car. I'd already worked out that my dark underwear could have passed for a bikini, and Katie's pants and vest worked well as a makeshift costume. Henri stood by the car. I could see he was unsure of the situation as he silently watched me remove our outer clothes and step in to the water.

I held Katie in my arms and crouched down so that we were up to our underarms in the cold water. She gasped as it connected with our skin. It was a shock to our systems at first especially after the extreme heat of the day, and Katie squealed in delight, soon becoming accustomed to the cooler temperature. I purposely didn't watch Henri take off his trousers. He was shy and I didn't want to give him reason to not enjoy a swim.

Katie splashed about. I held her under her tummy as she kicked and pretended to swim. I heard Henri's feet step into the water's edge and glanced up, trying to hide my shock at the sight of the deep, vivid scars across and down his right thigh. The angry gashes depicted the pain of what had happened to him. It was obvious that he'd been lucky to have kept his leg, although his shocking scars and limp made me wonder how close he'd come to losing his life.

He sensed me watching and mid-way to removing his T-shirt, letting it drop back down to his waist. Catching my gaze, he held his hands out. "Hideous, no?"

I shook my head. "Your scars are on the outside, mine are inside, but no less terrible." I pulled a stern face. "Now get into the water, it's glorious."

His expression softened, and he stared silently at me. For a moment, I wondered if it was a look like this that had disconcerted my mother but reasoned that his discomfort must come from allowing a relative stranger to come socially close, albeit only for a short swim. I had seen his damaged body and hadn't flinched. I had thought him shy, but now I could see he was ashamed of how he looked. He had no reason to be.

"Come on, what are you waiting for?" I teased.

"You are bossy," he said, hurrying into the dark, cold water, his breath catching for a second as the cold hit him. "*Merde*, it is too cold."

"No, it isn't," Katie giggled. "Monsieur Henri is being a big baby, isn't he Maman?"

"He is, Katie," I mocked, smiling at him over her mop of damp curls. "You're far braver than him."

"Swim," she insisted, bored with our chatter. I held her under her tummy once again and laughed when she kicked and paddled with her hands. She would soon be swimming by herself. We played for a while longer and then she wanted me to help her swim again.

"She is good," he said, before diving under and disappearing for longer than I thought possible. I scanned the water for him and was beginning to wonder if his legs had got tangled in reeds when his head popped up out of the water away from us.

"Don't do that," I shouted. "You frightened us."

"He didn't scare me," Katie said. "Monsieur Henri is a fish. I want to swim like him when I'm big."

"Then you'll have to practise, little one," he said swimming slowly back towards us.

Katie shivered. "Right, that's enough. You're getting cold," I said, taking her over to the side of the pool.

"No," she screamed indignantly kicking her legs in temper. "Swim, now."

"We can come back another day," I assured her.

"I want to swim now." Katie began to cry. I held her close to me and carried her over to the car to dry her. Thankfully, it was so hot out of the water she soon warmed up. Tired from the excitement of the afternoon and being at playschool earlier, she quickly became dozy. Closing her eyes as soon as I placed her in her car seat, I quickly strapped her in.

I turned to pick up my towel where I'd dropped it closer to the water, but Henri reached it first and bent down to grab it. He straightened up and opening the towel draped it around my shoulders, the water from his hair dripping on to my arms. He stood still, so close we almost touched. I wasn't sure how to react.

"Sera," he whispered in his lyrical accent, so different to Marcus' harsh Scottish one that I'd loved so much. "I must tell you…"

He was about to say something else when I heard a deep voice calling my name. Henri and I stared wide-eyed at each other. Who could know we were here? I peered past him through the trees to try and see who it might be.

Twigs cracked underfoot as the person intruding our intimacy strode closer through the undergrowth. "There you are," he said, his smile faltering as he spotted Henri still holding the edges of my towel.

"Leo?" I shouted, stunned to see him so unexpectedly. What was he doing here? I sensed Henri tense. He let go of the soft material. I daren't look at him again, but not wishing to appear rude to Leo, walked a few steps to the pathway to greet him. "What are you doing here?"

"Maureen told me I might find you," he said awkwardly. "I hope it's okay, me coming here, that is?"

I didn't look at the silent man standing by the water's edge. "Yes, why wouldn't it be?"

I wondered momentarily what Henri had been trying to tell me, but Leo's voice dissipated my thoughts.

"Great. I would hate to interrupt your afternoon." Leo gave me a bear hug. "Phew, it's a relief to be in this shade. I don't think I've ever been so hot." He walked over to the water and bent down and scooped up some water in his hands, wiping it over his face and hair to cool down. "I'm sorry I haven't been back to visit you before now, but there's been so much going on at work. Now I'm here, I didn't think I should waste a moment coming to find you and giving you the great news."

My heart pounded with excitement. Henri walked up to stand slightly behind me as if he were guarding me in some way, which I found a little irritating.

"Tell me," I said, forcing a smile and willing away the

tension pervading the air around us. Leo glanced unsmiling over my right shoulder at Henri, still a little unsure of the situation. "Go on then, what news?"

He returned his gaze to me. "Dee is with me. I told her about meeting up with you and she insisted on travelling here as soon as possible."

I hardly dared believe what he was telling me. "Here? But that's amazing." Then remembering Henri, I turned to him. "Dee is Leo's older sister," I explained. "We were best friends when we were teenagers. Did I tell you that? They lived on your farm."

His expression darkened; he watched Leo silently. "*Non*," he said eventually. "You have much to talk about." He backed away. "I will leave you to welcome your friend."

I couldn't understand why he was acting so strangely but supposed he was irritated with Leo for interrupting whatever it was he'd been about to tell me. I thought of his bad leg. "I'll drop you off at the farm."

"It is not necessary," he said shaking his head, droplets of water splashing down on his tanned shoulders. "I will walk."

"No, please," I insisted, touching his arm lightly. "I'll take you home. It's on the way." I turned to Leo. "Your car must be here somewhere?"

"Yes, it's not far. I'll go, and meet you back at your house. "Good to meet you, Henri," he said proffering his right hand towards Henri, who, after a moment's hesitation, shook it.

Leo walked back the way he'd come.

"I suppose we'd better get going," I murmured. I hated how the carefree atmosphere between me and Henri had vanished. Just when I thought I was getting close enough to find out more about him and put my mother's suspicions to rest. I got into the car and turned the key in the ignition, setting off as soon as Henri was seated. He sat resting one arm on the open window as the car exited the wood.

The full force of the sun pierced through the windscreen and I lowered the sun visor to shield the worst of the sun's glare from my eyes. It had been good to spend a little time with him so soon after the drama of the fire. I hoped that despite Leo's interruption his day had been made a little better by leaving the farm for a bit.

"Henri," I said hoping to entice him to finish what he'd begun telling me by the pool. "Was there something you wanted to discuss with me?"

He didn't reply immediately, but eventually said, "*Non*, it is nothing."

By the tone of regret in his voice I suspected it was fairly important, but decided that maybe it was a confidence that needed to be shared when he was in the right frame of mind. I hoped he'd choose to tell me soon.

# Chapter Six

## 2003 – Hautvillers, Near Epernay

## Sera

"Mummy's friend has come to visit us," I explained, wishing I'd managed to find a parking space closer to the house. My skin was so hot and the blissful coolness of our swim now only a memory, as I carried Katie into the house, trying to distract her from her grizzling.

"We're out in the garden," Mum shouted hearing me slam the front door closed with my heel. "Hurry up; you'll never believe who's here."

Barely able to contain myself, I put Katie down to stand on the tiled hall floor, watching as she ran out to the garden, her bad mood forgotten in the thrill of having visitors at the house. I followed her and hurried down the stone stairs to the established oasis I'd created as a subdued teenager needing to escape my inner torment.

I couldn't see Dee anywhere, but a little girl a year or so older than Katie sat quietly opposite my mum. "Dee?" I called, spotting movement behind the largest hydrangea. A slim figure with dark, bobbed hair stepped forward. She looked timid and nothing like the Dee I remembered. "You're all grown up," I laughed, desperate to hide my shock at her tense, sullen appearance. I hurried over to her.

She stood stiffly as I put my arms around her skinny body, barely touching my back as I held her. Not wishing to make her uncomfortable, I cut short my hug. I stepped back, unable to miss the set expression on her pinched face, once so pretty and cheeky, and now so, what? Sad? Haunted? I couldn't decide. She didn't speak.

"It's fantastic to see you again," I said willing my enthusiasm to pass to her, desperate to fill the strained silence. "I couldn't believe it when Leo told me you were here. And," I said motioning towards the fragile looking little girl. "Who's this?"

"I asked her name, but I'm still waiting for her to answer me," Mum teased.

"Her name is, Ashley," Dee said, her voice monotone. "She's shy."

I tried hard to hide my shock at her odd manner. "Would she like to something to eat, or drink?"

Dee shook her head. "No, thanks, we ate before coming here. She'll be happy as long as she's with me."

Katie, oblivious to any nuance of awkwardness must have gone inside to fetch a couple of her teddies and came running out. She handed one to Ashley, who stared at it. Then glancing over to Dee, she waited for her to nod an approval before snatching it from Katie and holding it tightly against her chest.

"She can have that one, Mummy," Katie said looking a little startled by the other child's reaction.

I ruffled her messy hair and bent down to her. "Thank you, Katie, that was very thoughtful of you."

"Can she come and play in my room?" Katie whispered.

"If she wants to, but I think she'll probably want to stay near her mummy for a bit until she gets used to us."

She twisted her teddy's crumpled ear and thought about my comment. "I'll ask her later."

I nodded, and she went back inside the house.

I was dying to ask my once extrovert friend more about her life, but by the look of her Leo had underplayed the difficulties she'd experienced in the years since we'd last seen each other. It was hard to imagine we could be the same age. Her skin was lined and her once full mouth now tight and sullen. What had happened to diminish her enthusiasm for life so completely?

Disappointment welled up inside me. I knew that if I didn't hurry up and distract myself somehow, I wouldn't be able to hold back my tears. I went over to the peach tree and raised my arm gently cupping one, careful not to bruise the round juicy fruit. It came away effortlessly, and I held it out to Dee. She'd always loved this tree and could never get enough of the sweet peaches whenever she had come to see us.

She shook her head. "No. Thank you."

I covered my disappointment and walked with her moving silently next to me. Unsure what to say next, I smiled at her.

She stopped. "You must think me very rude."

"No," I fibbed, assuming she meant her snapped refusal of the peach.

"Because I didn't say goodbye and never contacted you. Now I'm back here again, I can't think of a single thing to say to you."

I laughed, relieved to see a glimmer of the person I'd once known so well. "I'm sure you had your reasons. You're here now; that's all that matters."

"Katie's gorgeous and like you when you were small," she said, glancing over to her silent little girl sitting, eyes closed hugging the teddy bear to her as if her life depended on it.

"Ashley is very sweet," I said. I tried to see some resemblance of the little girl in her mother but assumed she must take after her father. "Katie would love to show her all her toys when she's feeling a bit more at home."

Dee frowned. "She's very timid." We walked on further. "I was sorry to read about your husband's death. Marcus, wasn't it?"

I hadn't expected her to know about his plane crash, and hesitated. "You knew?"

Dee frowned in confusion at my question. "Of course, it was in all the papers."

Why hadn't she bothered to contact me then? I wondered, upset at her lack of concern. Surely it wouldn't have been hard to send a note to Mum's house, or give her a call, Mum's number though only given out to a few people, had never changed. I closed my eyes, gathering my thoughts.

"It was devastating," I said, my voice breaking at recalling those black days twice in one day. "We were very much in love, and Katie wasn't even a year old when he was killed. She doesn't remember anything about him."

"Shit." She stared at me before looking down at the lawn. "Definitely shit."

Dee put her arm around me. "I'm a lousy friend," she whispered. "I know I am, but I'm here now and I promise I'll make it up to you."

My heart ached for her, she had obviously had a hard time. "I'm just glad to have you here now. We've got so much to catch up on and I can't wait for us to spend time together. How long are you going to stay?"

"Well…" She looked over at Leo who was watching us, his arms folded. Poor thing, I suppose he hadn't known how we would react in each other's company, after all this time.

He came over to join us. "What?" He stared at Dee.

"Sera was asking how long we were staying," she said. It sounded like an apology, which seemed odd. "I wasn't sure what to tell her."

I watched them exchange glances and tried to figure out what I was missing. It dawned on me that I hadn't offered to put them up while they were in the area. "You must stay here," I said quickly. "We have the room and it would be the perfect way for us all to catch up properly." I looked over at Mum and before they had time to argue, added. "Mum? Don't you agree? Leo, Dee and Ashley must stay here with us?"

She smiled, looking pleased at my suggestion. "I'd be insulted if they stayed anywhere else."

"That's settled then," I said, taking hold of one each of their hands. "It'll be like old times."

Leo threw his head back and laughed. "You two were horrible to me back then."

"We weren't that bad, Leo," Dee argued, a fragment of her old self escaping. Her mouth pulled back in a tense smile.

"We were pretty vile to him, Dee." I winked at her. "Poor Leo. I'm surprised we didn't put you off girls forever. You can relax though; we've grown up now."

"We have," Dee agreed.

"Yes," I said. "And far nicer than we were." I didn't have a clue how Dee was now, which saddened me. I was sure she was the same Dee I'd loved as a teenager, but it was impossible to dismiss that life had been hard for her, in what way though I didn't know.

We continued chatting and slowly Dee relaxed a little. I could hardly believe I was sitting in the garden with her and Leo after all these years. We'd both been through a lot since that last summer we spent together, but nothing was going to come between us now, I was certain of it.

"How is Hazel, Dee?" Mum asked suddenly.

I recalled Hazel mentioning something about my mother's determination in the seventies when they were both trying to make it in show business. I hadn't missed the sarcasm in Hazel's voice at the time, probably because she was usually so friendly and never had a nasty word to say for anyone. I had gone straight home and asked my mother to tell me about her time in London, but she refused to discuss it, and no amount of begging made any difference. So, it was very strange to hear her asking Dee about Hazel now.

I watched Dee contemplating her answer and my mother's concentration while she waited to hear it. I'd been so curious about anything to do with London when I was growing up in Epernay with such an obviously English mother and friends, but Mum was determined not to discuss anything from that time in her life. All I had ever managed to glean from her had been an innate understanding that something had transpired between Mum and Hazel that had shattered their bond forever. Why then, I wondered, had they both decided to come and live so near to each other in France. It was a strange situation and one that I was going to have to find a way to uncover, somehow.

"Mum?" Dee asked.

Leo glanced at his sister then turned his attention back to Mum. "She's blissfully happy living in a village in Yorkshire. She helps run a donkey sanctuary with her boyfriend."

It made me happy to think of Hazel doing something she loved. "That sounds like something she would enjoy." I thought back to the carefree hours listening to Hazel's angelic voice.

My mother had let it slip once that she and Hazel had come across each other when they'd both been trying to make a name for themselves in the mid-seventies in London. Back then, Mum was desperate to be the next Diane Keaton, and Hazel saw herself more as a dark-haired Stevie Nicks, yearning for a number one single. Hazel also once mentioned living in a run-down flat somewhere in Soho.

I saw them exchange a pointed glance. "Have I said something wrong? I hope she's okay."

"She's fine," my mother interrupted, but I couldn't imagine how she would know. "She always is."

I nudged Mum, willing her not to be mean about Hazel. She closed her eyes briefly probably fighting a need to criticise. Hazel had always been lovely to me and I couldn't imagine her being different to anyone else. I wondered if my mother resented her because I'd chosen to be at the farm most of my free time, rather than spending it at home all those years ago. I changed the subject and suggested I make up a couple of the rooms. When I stood up to go in to the house, Leo came with me.

"Only if you're certain," Leo said. "I'd hate to put either of you to any trouble."

Horrified at the prospect of them changing their minds because of some misinterpreted comment from Mum, I shook my head. "Don't be silly. Mum said she was happy for you all to stay here and she meant it. I want to make the most of you both being here."

"Well, if you're sure," he said looking relieved.

"I am. Anyway, Katie would love to have a friend her own age to play with for a few days. You go and check out of whatever hotel you're booked into and then come back. We can have supper together. Let's enjoy a long evening getting to know each other again?"

"Great," he said, waving Dee and Ashley over. "We'll collect a takeaway on our way back here to save on the cooking. What's your preference with wine?"

"I love rosé," I said. "Any one, as long as it's cool." I joked, delighted to have persuaded him to stay so easily.

I wasn't sure why they all needed to go back to their hotel and pack, but didn't want to force the issue about Dee and Ashley staying behind. They returned about an hour later, bringing bags of the most exquisite Thai food I'd eaten since visiting Thailand with Marcus when we were first together.

"You must tell me where you bought this," I said, wiping my mouth with a paper napkin.

"It was on the Rue Jean Moët, I think," Dee said, looking to Leo for reassurance.

"Yes, it was," he said, tucking in to his meal.

"What's brought you back here after so long?" Mum asked having taken only a few mouthfuls of her food.

Dee and Leo seemed shocked by her question, but I'd been dying to know too, and thought it an obvious question for Mum to have asked.

We waited in silence for them to answer. "We're thrilled you're here," I said as they struggled to reply.

Leo nodded. "Of course, you want to know. I would too, if it was the other way around." Dee cleared her throat and after giving her a quick glance he smiled and added, "The thing is, it's business related, but I'm not allowed to share it with anyone just yet."

"What, until everything's finalised you mean?" I asked trying to work out what it could be. "You did look very official when I met you that day in Epernay."

He nodded and placed a hand on Dee's arm. "Poor Dee, even she doesn't know yet. Do you, Dee?"

She shook her head. "I keep asking but he's been sworn to secrecy."

"Contracts to sign before I can say anything further," he explained. "I don't want to say something and put the entire business deal in jeopardy."

"You'll be moving back here for good then?" Mum asked. "We can help you find a home to rent if you need us to."

Delighted at the prospect of having my old friends back here permanently I smiled. "Yes, you only have to ask."

After dinner, he brought their cases in from the car and I was a little taken aback by the small cabin bag in which Dee and Ashley's clothes were packed. Leo's case wasn't much bigger.

I wondered why Dee hadn't thought to let her daughter bring a few familiar bits with her on holiday. I doubted Katie would go away without her favourite toys packed safely in her case. It was obvious the little girl needed the comfort of something to cuddle. Even Katie had been aware of that as soon as she'd given the teddy to Ashley.

I suggested Ashley share Katie's bedroom, but Dee wanted her daughter to sleep next to her, which was understandable, so they took the larger room in the attic and Leo was happy to have the box room next door to them. After supper, we put the little ones to bed.

Katie came down about an hour after she and Ashley had been put to bed to tell me that Ashley was crying.

"I didn't know what it was, Maman," she said clinging to me. She looked at Dee and then Leo. "I think she's not feeling well."

Dee went up to settle Ashley and I took Katie back to bed. I peered around Dee's bedroom door to check there wasn't anything wrong. Dee was leaning over Ashley and whispering in her ear. Ashley had her eyes closed and was cuddling the bear Katie had given her earlier. I could understand the little girl being unsettled by this big old house and went back downstairs.

The evening had grown a little cooler and we all moved into the living room to enjoy a few bottles of the wine he'd bought earlier.

I was conscious not to mention Hazel again and despite my intense curiosity decided also not to try and push either of them to reveal where they had been and what they'd been doing in the intervening years. I couldn't help staring at them both, picturing us as youngsters and enjoyed simply being with them again, talking mostly about Mum's work and our daughters' funny ways.

The following morning, I got up early, and, not sure when the rest of the household would want to bath, showered and dressed before going downstairs to put on the coffee ready for when anyone else wanted breakfast.

"Morning," Leo said, making me jump when he silently entered the kitchen freshly showered and dressed, this time in chinos and a slightly creased shirt. "That bed is so comfortable I almost didn't get up," he said raking his hands through his blonde hair, pushing it back only for it to flop forward onto his forehead once again.

I laughed relieved he'd had a good night's sleep, noticing

he'd made coffee in the percolator. Pouring him a mug of the hot dark liquid, I handed it to him and picked up my own leading the way out to the garden. "It's a little warm out here, but I love sitting outside enjoying my first cup of the morning while I wake up properly. It's very peaceful."

We sat down opposite each other. He leant back cupping his mug in both hands, closing his eyes and stretching his long legs out in front of him, crossing them casually at the ankles. He breathed in the fresh, morning air, and sighed. "This is very relaxing."

"I love it here. Coming into the garden before Mum and Katie wake up, really sets me up for the rest of the day."

"It's a good way to work through your thoughts, too."

It was. "It was relishing moments like these that gave me back the strength to carry on after Marcus' death," I admitted, wanting to open up to him and hoping he might feel inclined to do the same. "I needed help to look ahead and found it hard to work out how to make a future for myself and Katie."

He widened his eyes and the sadness in them bothered me. He leant forward and took one of my hands in his. "I'm sorry we never contacted you when he had his accident, Sera." He looked guilty and any resentment I'd harboured dissipated. "Looking back now it seems unforgiveable that we didn't at least write to you, or your mum. I think we were embarrassed about leaving without saying goodbye and after that neither of us knew quite how to approach you."

I thought about how it must have been for them. "I was too devastated to care about reproaching anyone back then,"

I said honestly. "It was all I could do to force myself to get out of bed and look after my baby. If I hadn't had Katie to care for, I... well, I don't see how I could have kept going."

He sighed. "But you did, despite your world turning inside out."

"It was only because she was Marcus' baby and he adored her that I forced myself to give her the life he would have wanted for her," I said, not daring to dwell for too long on the past.

Leo let go of my hand and sat back in his chair, studying me silently.

Changing the subject before I got too maudlin, I added. "I'm intrigued about where you and Dee have been though. Something's obviously happened to her. I can't help noticing how troubled she is." I shrugged. "I just want to put everything behind us and be there for her." I realised I'd have more chance of finding out about them without her being here, so added, "I want to do anything I can to help to bring back that spark she used to have."

"You're a good woman, Sera," he said his face expressionless. "Beautiful on the inside, as well as outside."

He seemed sad when he said those words and it dawned on me that maybe Dee wasn't the only one who'd suffered. "We'll work something out," I assured him. "She'll be fine; I'll make sure she is. It's a shame you're here for such a short time though."

He dropped his head, his chin almost resting on his chest, his shoulders stooped. I wasn't sure what I'd said to change his mood and waited for him to speak, busying myself sipping at my hot coffee. He got up quickly, making me jump, and mumbling an apology hurried over to the corner of the garden by an old apple tree. I wasn't sure what had just happened. Then I noticed his shoulders shuddering and with a rush of dread realised he was crying.

I wasn't sure what to do next. I'd never seen a grown man in tears before and he obviously didn't want me to witness him in this state. I had to do something though. Not wishing the children to come down and see him upset, I put down my coffee mug and went to join him. I touched his arm lightly. "Leo? What's the matter?"

He turned away from me, covering his eyes with one hand and gripping my hand with the other. "I'm sorry. Please, you go inside, I'll be fine in a bit."

I put my free hand up to his damp cheek and gently pulled his face towards me. "Leo, look at me."

He groaned, looking away from me. "I'll be fine, really."

I stroked his back. I didn't wish to add to his humiliation, but wanted to help him. "You can tell me. What is it?"

He didn't reply for a while and I could sense he was struggling to get his emotions in check. I was about to move back from him when he gave my hand a squeeze. "It's Dee and Ashley."

"Go on," I said when he hesitated.

He sighed. "It's not my story to tell."

"I understand," I said, wishing I did. "If you tell me, maybe I'll be able to help them in some way." When he didn't say anything, I added, "Has she just got out of an abusive relationship? Or something like that?"

"What?" He faced me, and I couldn't tell if he was shocked or angry by my suggestion.

"Sorry," I said, wincing with embarrassment at my nosiness. "I shouldn't be so inquisitive."

"Don't be silly, you're trying to help. No, it's too difficult to talk about. I'm sure she'll tell you if she can."

I hid my disappointment. "Of course."

"I've got to go back to the UK," he said. "I need to know they're safe when I'm not with them." He sighed. "I know it's a terrible imposition, but would you mind if Dee and Ashley stayed here with you for a few weeks, until I manage to sort somewhere else for them to live?"

I was so relieved he wasn't cross with me for sticking my nose into their personal problems that I agreed. "I'd love that. They can stay as long as they need to."

His shoulders relaxed, and he smiled. "Thank you, Sera." He bent down to kiss me on the cheek. "You've no idea how much I appreciate this."

"Don't be silly." I gave his hand a squeeze. "What are friends for, if not to help each other in times of crisis." He tensed, his smile slipping briefly. I didn't want him to think I was being sarcastic about their lack of contact over Marcus' death and nudged him playfully. "You know what I mean."

We stood in silence, the awkwardness of our lack of conversation evident in the atmosphere between us.

"The farm," I said.

"Sorry?"

I took a sip of my coffee. "Your old farm. Have you ever wanted to go back and pay it a visit?"

He shook his head. "No." He rubbed his unshaven chin with one hand. "I've never considered going back there," he said thoughtfully. Then narrowing his eyes, added, "I don't think I could bear to be reminded of everything we left behind."

Not ready to elaborate about my visits both in the eighties, or more recently, I said. "I always remember how pretty your mum made everything in your home."

He smiled. "I suppose you're right. She loved her lacy bits of material draped in strange places." He laughed at the memory. "Who else have you ever known to hang silk scarves from fence posts, or branches in trees?"

Warming to the change in tone of our conversation I thought back to her love of flowers. "Her pots of geraniums were everywhere. I always loved their bright colours."

He grimaced. "Seeing them always reminds me of trudging through farmers' markets and the endless garden centres she dragged us to on weekends when we were smaller."

I pictured Dee and Leo's boredom at their mother's infatuation with plants. "Remember the field she insisted we help plant up with lavender?"

Leo studied his hands, turning them over as if looking for something. "I was off school for two days with horrendous blisters on my hands. God, that was an endless day, wasn't it?"

I giggled. "My mum went mad when she saw how exhausted I was that night." I bit my lower lip gently at the memory. "I never dared admit to her what I'd really been doing. If she'd realised that I'd been planting a field for Hazel, she would have been furious."

"Thank heavens it was only a small field."

We laughed at the shared memory. I pictured that blissful June and July when the lavender bloomed covering Hazel's small field in an aromatic, purple hue, like something out of a Monet painting I'd later learned to appreciate. I suspected her passion had instilled my love of gardening, something my own mother had always found to be a curious hobby for a teenage girl to enjoy.

"It was glorious to look at," I said wistfully. "Such a shame Hazel never got the chance to harvest the plants and produce the lavender oil she'd planned to sell in the markets."

Leo's face took on a closed-off expression again and I could have kicked myself for referring again to what must have been a traumatic time for them. "Poor Mum, she loved that farm so much," he said thoughtfully.

"Why did you all leave then?" I asked, keeping my tone as gentle as I could. I knew I was pushing my luck by voicing the one question I sensed was out of bounds, but couldn't help myself.

Leo's mood changed instantly. He rose to leave. "It's been wonderful catching up with you, but I really should go and see how my sister and Ashley are settling in."

Aware I'd ruined the moment, I watched him go. Would I ever discover what happened that night when the heat had been at its highest and the dryness in the air made everything, even breathing, much harder work than usual? I was beginning to doubt it.

# Chapter Seven

2003 – Hautvillers, Near Epernay

## Sera

Leo had been gone a few days, back to his job in finance. I assumed the more time Dee and I spent together the closer we'd become. However, after that initial evening when she'd relaxed a little, she reverted to her quiet mouse-like ways and still hadn't opened up further to me. After almost a week I began to give up trying. It was like having a stranger staying in the house. She didn't even look or act like the old Dee. I was beginning to wonder if my memory of those days together as youngsters had been built up into something that wasn't as magical as I recalled.

My initial delight at having her to stay was beginning to wane. I couldn't help wondering if maybe it would have been better to have been left with the memories I'd lived off for so long. She was a stranger, that much was obvious, more so now than ever.

Dee complained that the surrounding fields were causing her hay fever to flare up. Even the little girls didn't play together in the way I'd hoped. Like me, Katie gave up trying so hard to please Ashley. I'd never been around such a solemn child and I wondered if she was like this because of some sort of reaction to Dee's trauma, whatever it had been. I hated to think what this little girl might have witnessed at home.

The temperature was intensifying each day and the longed-for rain to water my garden and save my plants from drying out completely didn't come. Even the pavements felt hot beneath the soles of our shoes whenever we walked to the row of small shops at the end of our street. No one wanted to spend long outside, preferring to wait until after sunset. Even then it was almost too hot to stand. Mum insisted this heatwave was even more unbearable than the one she'd endured in nineteen seventy-six.

"Drama always happens to this family during intense heatwaves," she predicted the previous night before going up to her room for a cooling shower. "You mark my words; it's going to happen again this year, too."

I tried to brush off her ominous words, but they stuck in my head and that night I had nightmares that Dee and Leo were strangers masquerading as my friends.

\*\*\*\*

Mum joined me in the kitchen later that day catching me mid yawn. "Sleepless night?"

"Nightmares," I said.

"Me, too," she said picking up an old copy of *Le Monde* and fanned herself. "I think it's probably hotter than when

Dee and her family disappeared in eighty-nine"

I thought back to those stifling days when the summers seemed to last for months and everything had been easy and enchanted before they'd left.

"Coffee?" I held up the dented percolator from the range.

She nodded. Her face crumpled up and she sniffed the air. "What is that horrible smell?"

"What smell?"

"I'm not sure, but it's been driving me mad for days." She took her cup of coffee from me and placed it on the table in front of her. "It's getting worse, but I can't think what it must be."

I sniffed a few times; there was a definite air of something. I looked around, unsure.

"Look up," Mum said, hands on her slim hips when she figured out what was annoying her.

"What?"

"There." She pointed over my head. I turned to see Henri's plait of garlic still hanging from the window.

"Bugger, I meant to take that down to the cellar to keep cool." I lifted it from the window catch and as I held it closer to my face my eyes watered slightly. "Blimey, it is strong," I said wincing as I carried it out to the hallway to hang in the cellar.

"I think I'll take my bed down there later," I joked to Mum when I returned to the kitchen. "It's lovely and cool."

Mum went out to meet some friends for lunch and I thought I should spend time with Dee after dropping Katie at pre-school. I went to join them, but she barely looked up from the book she was reading, sitting with one arm around Ashley's narrow shoulders as the child sat sucking her thumb. My suggestions for ways to entertain ourselves and the children were met with a sullen sigh, so I decided to leave them in peace.

I washed my hair and without bothering to dry it, grabbed my car keys and left for Henri's farm. With only the remnants of the barn, a few stables and small outbuildings, if there was any breeze at all, the farm was the place to find it.

The three-minute drive couldn't pass quickly enough. I hadn't seen Henri since our swim in the woods and I couldn't help feeling a little guilty that I hadn't been in touch with him. It was a bit of a cheek, especially after inwardly criticising Leo for doing the same thing to me.

"Henri," I called as I stepped out of my car, the punch of the heat hitting me despite my old car's non-existent air conditioning.

There wasn't any sign of him outside, so I walked up to the front door and knocked. No reply. Determined to see him, I jogged around to the back of the house where I found Henri fast asleep. He was lying in the shade on an old wooden bench, earphones in his ears, his feet resting either side on the ground, one foot tapping along to the beat of the bass.

He was only wearing shorts. I watched his tanned chest moving up and down, his breathing calm as he enjoyed the music. I savoured being able to watch him, uninhibited at believing he was alone. I was aware it couldn't last very long and wished he didn't feel so ashamed by his scars. I didn't want to give him a shock to find me there, so slowly moved nearer to him and sat on a large log.

He must have sensed my presence and his eyes opened. Startled to see me there, he sat upright, pulling the earphones out of his ears and hurriedly pressing the music off. "Sera, what are you doing here?" He reached out and grabbed his T-shirt, pulling it over his head.

I raised my eyebrows and pulled an apologetic face. "Sorry," I grimaced. "I didn't mean to give you a fright."

He looked past me. "You are alone?"

I wasn't certain if he was referring to Leo, or Katie. I nodded. "Yes, and I'm sorry I haven't been to visit you before now, but things have been a little chaotic at home recently."

Henri shrugged. "You and Katie are okay?"

"Yes, but I have house guests. They're harder work than I was expecting."

"Leo?" he asked his voice quieter.

"No, he's returned to England, but his sister and her daughter are staying with me for a few weeks." I sighed. "I hope you don't mind, but I wanted to escape for a while, so thought I'd come here."

He gave that slow lazy, one shouldered shrug of his and I was grateful he didn't hold a grudge against me for not bothering with him for two weeks. "Good." He stood up, waving for me to follow him. "I have something I wish to show you."

Intrigued, I did as he asked and walked with him to his

house. It was good to have something to take my mind of Dee and I was glad I'd made the effort to visit him. "What is it?"

"No, you must wait."

"Tell me?" I asked, impatiently.

He walked up the wooden steps to his porch and opened the front door, standing back, waiting for me to walk inside. "To the kitchen," he said, his dark eyes shining with uncontained amusement.

Intrigued by this unusually light mood and unable to wait another second, I hurried in stopping suddenly when I spotted his beautiful Collie bitch, Patti, lying in her basket with five adorable bundles of fluff suckling frantically at her.

"Puppies," I whispered clasping my hands together. "Katie will be desperate for one of these." Me too, I thought. "They are so cute."

"Yes, they are," he smiled. "She was being strange when I went to bed some days ago. The next morning, I find these little ones. I don't know where I'll find homes for them. I hope maybe you will help me and ask people you might know if they want one."

I crouched down slowly so as not to frighten Patti and stroked her glossy head. "You're such a clever girl." She looked up at me and then nuzzled the pup closest to her as if to tell me to take note of her achievement. I stroked the pups in turn. "They're adorable."

"Will you permit me to gift one to Katie?"

"When she sees these, I'll have little choice but to take one home, so yes. Thank you. She'll be thrilled." It would be wonderful to have a dog around the house again. I checked my watch and stood up. "I have half an hour before I need to leave and collect her from school."

"Tea?" he asked, in a mock English accent.

I nodded. "I thought you'd never ask, but I'd rather something cooler, like standing under an ice-cold shower for ten minutes to try and cool off. I'm melting today."

"Melting?" He pulled a face. "Yes, it is too hot for a body."

I laughed again. "It is; far too hot."

He walked over to his large fridge and pulled back the door.

I hurried over to stand slightly back from him lifting my top a few inches and relishing the cold air as it hit my perspiring stomach. "This is bliss."

He took out two icy cold beers and turned before I expected him to, stopping motionless, beers held in the air when he spotted what I was doing.

"Beer?" he asked eventually, without moving to give me one.

"Um, please." Embarrassed, I dropped my top, wondering what I must have been thinking to act in such an abandoned way with someone I'd only recently met.

He cleared his throat and looked me in the eye. "Do you wish to sit outside?"

Glad of his change of subject, I agreed. "That would be great." We went to sit at the back of the house and I was hoping to entice him to carry on telling me whatever it was he'd been about to share when Leo had interrupted us that day by the pool. After half an hour of small talk and many silences I realised Henri wasn't to be rushed to speak about anything other than what he chose to say.

I arrived at Katie's playgroup. Usually she was one of the first to race out to hug me, but today I had to wait. Eventually she was escorted outside by her form teacher. I pulled a sympathetic face at Katie as she hobbled towards me, a large plaster stuck over her pudgy knee.

"What happened?" I asked crouching down to touch the side of her leg lightly.

A large tear rolled down her rosy cheek. "I tripped on my way outside just now," she sniffed.

I gave her a bear hug and held her close, breathing in the hint of strawberry from her favourite shampoo that I used to wash her hair. "Is it a bad cut?" I looked up at the teacher.

She shook her head and smiled. "A little graze, nothing more," she said ruffling Katie's curls. "She will be fine tomorrow."

Katie ignored her teacher's reassurances. "It hurts, Maman."

I knew my daughter well enough to realise that she was hoping for a day off school in case I took Dee and Ashley somewhere.

"We'll see how it is tomorrow, okay?"

"Yes," she said, satisfied.

We arrived home a little later.

"Guess who?" Leo said, greeting us at the door.

"You're here," I said, stating the obvious. "It's good to see you."

He kissed me on both cheeks. "It's great to be back." He looked over my shoulder in the direction of the garden. "How's Dee?" he whispered. I couldn't miss the strain on his face when he mentioned her. "I hope it's not been too difficult for you having them staying here."

I struggled to find the right words to answer him.

"It's okay," he said. "I know it's hard work being with her right now. She's sullen, and doesn't even try to interact most of the time."

I could see he was under no illusion about Dee's mental state. "We haven't seen each other for years. We've both changed so much," I said miserably. "I didn't think we'd be this distant though." I glanced down the hallway to the garden. "Where's Dee and Ashley now?"

All Dee seemed to want to do during the day was sleep and read. She barely let Ashley out of her sight, fretting and needing to know where she was at all times. It stung me to think she didn't trust Mum or me with her daughter.

When he didn't answer, I tried again. "Is there something I can do to encourage Dee to chat more?" I asked. "I wish I could encourage her to relax a bit where Ashley's concerned, Leo. I feel sorry for the little girl. Dee pretty much suffocates her with all that attention."

"She's fine. She might take herself off for a little walk to clear her head sometimes, that's all."

"I have to admit I'm a little concerned about Ashley though."

He studied me for a few seconds, his earlier cheerfulness evaporating. "Don't be, she's fine. Look, if you'd rather we go elsewhere, you only have to say."

"That wasn't what I meant," I said, shocked by his defensiveness.

"Really, I don't want to cause you any problems."

He had totally misunderstood what I was trying to say. It was as if he was determined to be insulted for some reason. I could see I wasn't going to get through to him today. "It's fine," I assured him not wishing to make things worse.

"If you're sure?" he asked, frowning.

I nodded. I wasn't sure at all, but Dee was my oldest friend and the least I could do was offer them somewhere to stay, at least for the time being.

Later that night, Leo barbequed king prawns and scallops. He had placed them in a marinade of oil with a little crushed garlic and lemon for a couple of hours and was in much better spirits.

"That was delicious," I said honestly. "You're a fantastic cook." I pushed away my plate leaving nothing but a couple of scraps of lettuce. I watched as he concentrated on opening a second bottle of wine before topping up my glass.

"Thanks," he said, smiling at me. "I wanted to impress you. I'm glad that I did."

I wasn't sure, but suspected he might be flirting with me. It was an odd sensation, but not an altogether unpleasant one. He was very handsome, after all.

I cleared my throat. "There's somewhere I want to take you tomorrow morning," I said. If we had to spend time together I wanted us to go out occasionally. There was so much beautiful countryside to see around Hautvillers and Epernay, it seemed a waste to spend most of our time at the house.

"I'm intrigued," he laughed.

"You used to go there years ago," I said giving him a clue. "I thought it would be fun to revisit."

"I'm not going to the farm," Dee snapped standing up and knocking over an empty bottle of wine. It was the first time all evening that she'd interacted with us in any way.

"I didn't mean that," I said, horrified. "I'd never expect you to do something that made you uncomfortable." I shook my head. "It's somewhere else. We'll need to leave straight after breakfast and I promise you'll enjoy it there."

"We'd love to," Leo said quickly before Dee had time to argue.

He opened another bottle of wine and went to pour some into Dee's glass. "No," she said, placing her hand over the top. "I'm going to go to bed." Her mouth drew back in a tight, forced smile. "I need an early night if I we're going out early tomorrow." She hesitated. "Thank you for a lovely meal."

She sounded so formal. I stood to give her frail body a hug and watched as she walked silently into the house to join her daughter in their room.

Sitting down, I lifted my glass and took a sip. "I don't want you to make her come tomorrow if she doesn't want to."

"It'll do her good to get out." He looked up at Dee's bedroom window. "She'll come around soon," he said.

I doubted it. "I hate seeing her troubled."

"So do I. She'll be much better staying here though, I'm sure." He looked at me. "Thank you for being such a good friend, Sera, it means a lot. I've enjoyed meeting up with you and getting to know the adult you." He lowered his voice. "I know I'm only three years younger than you and Dee, but you two were way above me in the maturity stakes when we lived here in the eighties. I always secretly liked you."

I couldn't help grinning at the thought of Dee's little brother having a crush on me all those years ago. I felt guilty that we'd been so mean to him. "Really? I never suspected a thing."

He raised an eyebrow. "You weren't supposed to."

Enjoying the moment, I settled back into my chair, my heart rate calming slightly. "I like having you around, too," I said, realising it for the first time. "It's good to be able to reminisce about when we were teenagers messing around at your mum's farm. I've missed not being able to do that."

"Dee doesn't like to talk about it."

I couldn't understand why. "That's a shame," I said. "I wished many times we could go back to how it was then. I had a fantastic life until your family disappeared." I didn't add that I'd battled for the following decade trying to find them; willing Dee to come back.

"Yes, well sometimes things happen that you'd rather forget." He took a large gulp of his wine and stared out towards the woods at the back of the garden.

"What things?" I said, eager to discover more about their past.

He closed his eyes. "Leave it, Sera." Then opening them, he gazed at me as if lost in thought. "Some things are best left in the past."

"But…"

His expression changed. "What's the story with Henri?"

"What do you mean?" I asked, taken aback by the sudden change in topic.

"He seems a little insidious, that's all."

I thought back to the noisy days at the farm and how different it seemed now. "Mysterious, maybe," I said trying not to sound defensive.

"You seemed close to him when I met him that time in the woods."

I stared at him not used to being questioned by anyone apart from Mum. I could feel my hackles rising. "I haven't known him long at all."

"Look, it's nothing to do with me, but how well do you know him?" he asked.

I didn't like being interrogated in this way. "Henri is a friend." I looked away from him. "I don't know everything about him, that's true. In fact, I know very little," I admitted to myself as much as Leo. "But I go by my instinct and he's been kind to me and Katie, and I'm happy with that."

"I didn't mean to offend you." He smiled apologetically. "I suppose I just want to look out for you."

"I'm not your sister, Leo." I could tell he meant well. "It's very gentlemanly of you, but I'm used to looking after myself. Just be my friend, I don't need a protector." I smiled to soften my words. I didn't want us to fall out and had been honest when I said how much I'd enjoyed having him around. "Let's talk about what we're doing tomorrow instead, shall we?"

That night I lay in my bed mesmerised by the shadows swaying gently on the ceiling. The large pine tree outside my window was barely moving, but it lulled me and allowed my mind to wander back to being with Marcus. I had missed him for so long that I wasn't sure if I could ever truly feel deep love for anyone else. Leo was familiar to me; it was easy to trust him. I could hardly believe I was even contemplating how it might feel to become close to a man. I pulled the covers over my shoulders and closed my eyes. When sleep evaded me yet again, I let my thoughts wander.

Could I finally be reaching the end of my grieving process for Marcus? Was that possible? I would always miss him and what might have been, but I was beginning to think that it might be time to take a chance and see how it felt to share experiences with someone else. Could Leo be that man? I didn't think so, but how could I be sure?

\*\*\*\*

"Maman," Katie chirped from the end of my bed. I pushed myself up onto my elbows squinting when a shard of light streaming through a gap in my curtains blinded me. How long had she been sitting there playing with her dolls? I must have slept deeply not to have noticed her earlier. "You didn't wake up," she said frowning, her fair hair sticking out all around her face like a halo.

I smiled at the golden-haired child so precious to me and wished for the umpteenth time that her father was here to enjoy her funny ways and strong personality.

"Yes, poppet, I was very tired." I glanced at my bedside

clock and gasped, throwing back my duvet and jumping out of bed almost in one movement. "Come on, Katie," I said pulling on my dressing gown over my bed shorts and vest. "You're going to be late to playgroup if we don't get a wriggle on." I lifted her up, tickling her under her ribs and making her giggle.

Pushing my feet into my flip-flops, I carried her downstairs and sat her at the kitchen table. "What do you want today? Toast with an egg on top, or porridge?"

She stuck her tongue out and shook her head. "Yuck. I hate porridge. Want egg and soldiers."

I put a couple of eggs in a pan of water and poured her a glass of milk and made me a cup of coffee. "Do you think you'll finish the rabbit painting at school today?"

"You've been painting a rabbit?" Leo asked from the doorway.

"Yes." Katie smiled at him, proud of her accomplishment. Her smile faltered when she noticed Ashley standing silently behind him. Katie glanced up at me. "Ashley wants an egg?"

"Would you?" I asked the silent child. She nodded slowly. She barely seemed to eat anything, so I was happy she was joining Katie for breakfast. I walked over to her and took her hand. "Come and sit down with Katie and I'll make you both a lovely runny egg with soldiers."

Katie watched Ashley take a seat and lowering her voice, explained. "I don't go to school, it's playgroup and they're not really soldiers; they're pieces of toast and butter that we dip in our eggs. It's yummy."

"You slept well?" Leo asked, coming to stand next to me by the range.

"Eventually," I said checking the eggs. "Then rather too well, I'm now running a bit late."

"This is such a peaceful house. Even though it's on the edge of the town and cars drive past most of the time, I go into a deep sleep as soon as my head touches those pillows."

I was happy to hear he was so relaxed. "Good, and Dee? Have you seen her yet this morning?" I did my best to sound upbeat.

"Not yet, but I'm sure we will do soon. She's not one to get up late usually, although I think she's struggling to settle in here. I'm afraid us all being together again feels a little foreign to her, too."

I served the little girls with their breakfast, and then leaving Leo to watch over them, I ran upstairs to have a quick shower and change, giving Dee a reminder that we would have to leave soon.

I asked Katie if she would like a day off from playgroup to come out with Ashley, Dee, Leo and I.

"*Non*, thank you, Maman," she whispered, I presumed not to offend Ashley. "My knee is much better and I remembered we're making a big painting this week. You will be able to come and see it soon."

"That sounds exciting," I said happy that she enjoyed her playgroup so much. "I'll look forward to coming and seeing it."

I dropped Katie off and then drove into town with Ashley to buy some fruit and pastries. It was another sweltering day, so I treated her to a cool drink. We were walking out of the *supermarché* hand-in-hand, when one of the bags broke and several tins of tuna rolled away from me towards the parking area. I bent to salvage a bag of oranges and some tea, but it was difficult doing it with only one free hand. "Damn."

"I will bring them to you," I heard Henri say when I struggled to put what I had retrieved into the other bag hoping that wouldn't break too.

I did my best but ended up dropping other bits. "For pity's sake."

I could hear his deep laugh as he grabbed the shopping I kept dropping. "Stop," he said, smiling broadly at me. "One minute."

I watched him limp into the shop and come out seconds later with two new bags. "*Ici*, these are better."

"Thank you," I said, relieved to be able to stop making an idiot of myself. I helped him finish packing everything with Ashley clasping tightly onto my hand. "I didn't think you shopped here?"

"On occasion." He gave Ashley a crooked smile. He raised the bags and indicated my car. "I will carry these. You are well?"

I walked next to him towards the car. "Yes, thanks. I'm taking my guests to a market today, to have a look around. Any news on how the fire was started yet?"

"*Non*. They have found nothing, but I am hoping there will be soon. I am working on the barn this afternoon." He waited for me to open the boot of my car, and lowered the shopping into it, closing it for me. He checked his watch, although I couldn't imagine why if he didn't have anything planned today. "I will leave you to your day."

"I'll bring Katie to see the puppies soon," I said. "Maybe your mummy will let you come with us," I added to Ashley.

I arrived home to collect the others and walked into the house to hear screaming and crying coming from the kitchen. I had barely closed the door, when Dee raced through the hall and kneeling on the hard tiles, grabbing Ashley and clinging on to her.

"Where have you been?" she screamed at me, spittle at the sides of her mouth. "How dare you take my child without asking my permission first?"

I couldn't believe her reaction. "We only popped out to the shops. We can't have been gone more than half an hour."

"Don't do it again, do you hear me?" Her wide eyes blazed with fury. I nodded, not daring to upset her further by arguing.

I left her to take Ashley to their room and hoped she'd soon calm down. Frustrated with Dee's dramatics, I went to find Mum, confiding in her about my plans for the day and hoping she'd join us.

"I've got lines to learn today."

I looked at her out of the corner of my eye and suspected she was telling an untruth.

I didn't blame her; she must be desperate for time alone in her own house, especially after this latest bout of hysteria. Making the most of the others being out of the way, we sat down to enjoy a cup of tea.

Mum looked at me. "You do know she's insane, don't you?"

"I knew she was a little odd," I whispered. "I didn't realise her walls should be padded."

"We're ready now," Leo shouted from the upstairs landing. Coming down the stairs with Ashley in his arms, I saw Dee following close behind them, her face puffy from crying. I couldn't help feeling a little guilty about instigating her upset but kept quiet. "We're going on an adventure," he said to Ashley.

The child didn't react, but looked at him as if she might cry. I couldn't understand it. If I'd told Katie what we were doing today, she would have been jumping up and down and giggling. She wouldn't mind what we were doing; it was the anticipation of going out in the car to do anything remotely fun.

Leo saw me watching Ashley and pulled a face. "We're all different, I suppose."

It saddened me to see so little joy in the child's face. "Come along then, let's go."

Leo made small talk during the forty-minute journey. We wound the windows right down, but the heat in the air did little to cool us in the car. The roads were dusty, which added to our discomfort, but I hoped that once we arrived at the market they would agree that it had been worthwhile.

Dee and Ashley sat in silence in the back of the car for the entire time, while Leo and I made small talk about the usually lush plantation on either side of the road looking dull due to the coating of dust.

"We need some rain desperately," I said thinking of the farmers and growers who were contending with this unprecedented heat.

Ashley started to cough and I reached back to the basket

I'd placed behind my seat until I felt the neck of a bottle of water. Lifting it, I said, "Dee, can you pass this to Ashley." She took it from my hand and undid the top, passing it to the little girl. "Sorry, Ashley," I said, wishing I had decent air con in my car and could close the windows. We'll be there very soon."

Moments later I spotted the *tourelle* of the rundown castle that I'd been looking out for and pointed at it.

"There we are," I said. "That's where we're going today."

"It doesn't look very inviting," Dee said as I slowed before the ivy-clad entrance.

I checked that there wasn't a car behind me in my rear-view mirror and stopped. "What do you think, Ashley?" I asked as all of us stared at the huge stone building. The ornate gates were now rusted open and the enamelled family crest above the metal archway mostly worn away.

"It looks sad," Ashley said in a timid voice.

"I thought so too," I agreed turning to smile at her.

I put the car in gear and drove through the tall gateposts. Some of the stones were missing and I wondered how long it would be until they completely collapsed.

Leo smiled thoughtfully. "This place looks familiar," he said, as the chatter and shouts from the stallholders trying to grab the attention of passing shoppers became louder the closer we got to the marketplace.

"We haven't got there yet," I teased, relieved one of them was being positive. I turned right and took the short bumpy lane, past old tenants' cottages, and turned into a stony car park. We eventually spotted a space between two other cars under the shelter of a large walnut tree.

"This is the market," Dee said, hurriedly stepping out of the car, forgetting about Ashley. It was so out of character I wasn't sure how to react.

Leo followed her. I went to Ashley, taking her hand in mine. "Here, you'd better put this on," I suggested, picking up the peaked cap from the car seat and putting it on the little girl's head. "We don't want you to get sunburnt, do we?"

I slipped on my sunglasses, grabbed my purse and locked the car. At least Dee seemed cheerful, for once. "What do you think of this place?" I bent to ask the little girl. She stared up at me and gave a little shrug. It was a reaction of sorts, I supposed.

Leo stopped to let us catch up with him by the entrance of the yard where two rows of tightly packed stalls were set up.

"I remember Mum bringing us here when we were small." He stepped back to avoid two elderly ladies who were marching towards a nearby second-hand clothes stall. "You take your life in your hands coming here, don't you?" he said watching them shuffling on their way.

"You do. There are a lot of determined people here," I said quietly when we were next to him. "I couldn't wait to come again when I returned from Scotland."

He nodded towards my favourite stall that had also been one of his mother's chosen shopping spots. "I can almost picture Mum standing over there," he said, his voice catching.

"She loved the skirts and tops that girl used to bring from her buying trips to India. Do you remember?"

He nodded. "I do. I seem to recall you always banging on about this place, too."

I breathed in the heady scents of the market. A mixture of lavender and geraniums took me back to when I was small and did the same thing at this very spot. In fact the wizened little man serving at the stall was the same one from my childhood. I watched him deftly counting change for a customer. He didn't look all that different to when I'd first come here.

We walked through the crowds looking at everything from brightly painted pottery to straw baskets with colourful ribbons threaded through the weaving. I breathed in the patchouli and sandalwood from the clothes I liked to buy and was about to pick a material bag to check it, when Ashley pulled me towards the second-hand book store.

Happy to see her enjoying her visit to the market, I willingly went with her and watched her looking through the books. She moved several. Picking them up, she breathed in the familiar smell of an old book, closing her eyes in recognition; it was a strange thing for someone as young as her to do. She checked the front and back covers of other books, unsatisfied with them, putting them down again. Eventually, she found one I recognised from my own childhood and held it up to me. I took it from her and smiled.

"*What Katy Did* by Susan Coolidge. I remember my mum reading this to me many times." I couldn't picture Dee taking the time to do the same and wondered if maybe it had been a book she'd enjoyed at school. "Do you want me to buy it for you?"

She nodded, so shy compared to Katie's usual exuberance. Her lips drew back slightly giving the hint of a smile. I was so delighted to see her reaction that I hugged her. "All right then." I was finally getting somewhere with this child and it thrilled me.

I left her slowly turning the pages and looked for one I might want to read. I chose a battered copy of *Jane Eyre* and a couple of Georgette Heyer books I recalled reading when I lived in Scotland. After haggling briefly with the stallholder, I paid him and gratefully accepted the plastic bag with my books inside. I looked forward to reading those over the next couple of weeks. I couldn't see Leo anywhere, so took Ashley's hand and went to look at the next stall.

"Having fun?" he asked about fifteen minutes later. "That's new, isn't it?" He lifted the bottom of the striped material shoulder bag I'd treated myself to. "It's already filled with stuff," he teased. "It weighs a ton."

"Rubbish, we've only bought a few things," I joked. "Anyway, I've wanted one similar to this for ages."

"And it suits you," he said. "You're a bit of a hippy at heart, aren't you?"

Thinking about it, he had a point. "Come along, we'd better see where Dee's got to."

We found her holding up a thirties vase with a yellow and black geometrical pattern on the front. "That's gorgeous," I said.

She stared at me and handing the vase to Leo, took Ashley's hand from mine.

"Dee," Leo didn't bother to hide the determination in his voice. "Sera bought Ashley a lovely book."

Dee closed her eyes in irritation for a few seconds, then opened them and smiled at him. She pointed at the vase. "Will you buy this for me please?"

I couldn't help being taken aback by her odd reaction, or that she didn't have money of her own. There was no point in arguing with her, so I moved away and focused my attention on a delicate, silver-plated toast rack. Ashley picked up an elephant-shaped egg cup with her free hand.

"That would be perfect for your breakfast egg and soldiers," I said. She nodded shyly. "Shall we ask Mummy if you can have it?"

She glanced at Dee out of the corner of her eye, seeing her deep in conversation with Leo. Ashley shook her head.

"I don't think she'd mind," I whispered, not very convinced by my assurances.

"No, thank you."

I was so unused to hearing her voice that I hesitated before replying. "Um, okay, then," I said, saddened by her refusal. "If you're sure?"

We looked at a few more stalls, but the intensity of the heat was becoming overbearing. I noticed Ashley wiping her forehead and becoming fretful. I was more concerned about the child than offending Dee, so asked if I could take Ashley to buy a drink.

Dee nodded and let go of the child's hand. "Don't go far, will you?"

"No," I assured her and quickly led Ashley to the shade under a tree at the other end of the market. "What would you like to drink?" I asked her, aware she would need to keep hydrated on such a hot day. She stared up at me silently. "I'll get us some water."

I took her to a stall and bought us a bottle of chilled water each. "Make sure you drink all of that today," I said, pulling the top off and downing half my own bottle. I poured a little into my hand and wiped my face and the back of my neck.

I checked my watch. I needed to start for home soon. I was hoping to spend a few hours working on several signs that I was holding on consignment at my studio. I caught Leo's eye and held up my car keys. He nodded and scanned the market for Dee. Eventually, they came over to us, Dee, smiling and holding up two bags.

"That's a beautiful vase," I said, happy that she had enjoyed our outing.

"I've also found a couple of cushions for our beds," she said, indicating the larger bag. "They're a wonderful burnt orange colour."

We had been there nearly an hour and were all hot and sticky. I didn't relish the uncomfortable drive home again, but hoped they had all enjoyed their outing.

"Ready to go?" I asked fanning my face with my hand. She didn't argue so we loaded the car and got in. The sun had moved, and the car was no longer in the shade. "Sorry about the car," I winced sitting on my hot seat."

The drive home seemed to take much longer in the strong heat of the midday sun. None of us spoke and Dee and Ashley dozed off as I drove. I was relieved Katie hadn't wanted to come too because she would have had to cram in the back seat along with the other two.

Leo and I each had an arm out of our respective windows, doing our best to cool down as much as possible. "It's at times like these I wouldn't mind having a pool in the garden."

"A paddling pool would do for me right now," Leo said, turning my paltry air conditioning up full blast.

"Or a bottle of water."

"Anything at all," he laughed.

"We'll have to settle for a cold shower and a glass of something."

Freshly showered and changed into a thin cotton top and shorts, I left them with Mum at home and drove to my studio. The concrete walls kept the temperature low. It could be too cold at times, especially in the winter. Today, though, the space gave a welcome relief from the heat of the market earlier. Seeing all the stalls had inspired me and I couldn't wait for the next time I was at my stall in the village square later that week.

I completed a small job and then collected Katie from playgroup, going home to join the others who were enjoying a drink with Mum in the shade in the garden.

Dee seemed a little more focused tonight and was beginning to relax a little. Even her demeanour seemed calmer. I hoped she'd enjoyed our trip to the market and was feeling a little more at home here.

"I was wondering if we could arrange to take the girls out

somewhere together this weekend," she suggested, taking me by surprise.

"I'd love that," I said. "We could maybe go for a walk in the wood near your old farm. If it's still this hot, we could swim in the pool there. Do you remember it?" I asked hopefully.

She frowned, her eyes glazing over. Then, after a moment's hesitation Dee smiled. "I do. I was going to buy it and live there with my husband."

"Yes," I shrieked unable to contain my excitement that she was finally reminiscing with me. "And I was going to be the only person you invited to visit."

She giggled. "I remember." She stared down at the space in front of her. "I remember," she whispered, lost in her own thoughts again.

I could see Leo tense as he watched her mood changing. "It's lovely and shady," I said, not wishing the atmosphere to drop yet again. "So we won't get sunburnt."

"Would you like that, Ashley?" Dee asked, with enthusiasm. "I could show you where I grew up." The little girl stared at her, her expression uncertain. Dee turned back to me and smiled tightly. "She'd love to, but she'll probably have to borrow a swimming costume from Katie."

I willed Dee to be a little less intense with her daughter, but at least she was happy now. I didn't know what had brought about her unexpected change of mood, but I wasn't going to chance ruining it by asking her. I was relieved to experience a hint of how my old friend used to be.

"We could make some sandwiches and take a little picnic

with us," she suggested. "You'd like that, girls, wouldn't you?"

Katie nodded enthusiastically. Ashley sucked her thumb and gave Katie a sideways glance. I couldn't fathom the little girl out.

"I've bought some ice creams if you girls want one later," I said.

Katie jumped up and down. "Yes, please, Maman. Can me and Ashley go and get them?"

I laughed. "You can't reach the freezer compartment, you know that." I tickled her. I smiled at Ashley. "Do you like ice cream?" For a second I thought she was about to cry, but was relieved when she simply nodded. "Good, I'll get you both one."

I could hear Katie's excited voice. "You'll love them, Ashley. Maman buys strawberry and chocolate ice creams and they taste yummy."

# Chapter Eight
## 1976 – London

## Mo

My meeting in the Soho backstreet office went well. At least I hoped it had. Mr Collins, or Jack, as he'd insisted I call him, assured me he could find me work.

"It won't be as exciting as you might think," he said, eyeing me up and down after I'd finished my brief audition for him. "And I want you to have a few photos taken to, you know, show off different aspects of your, um, personality. I'm certain I'll find you something." He hesitated. "In the meantime, you'll need to find a job to tide you over."

"Oh." I couldn't hide my disappointment. I'd foolishly expected him to send me off to one of the impressive theatres in London with a note in my hand to start work immediately. Fool. I recalled my mother's high-pitched voice mocking me about the lacklustre future she swore would be mine, as I insisted for the hundredth time that I would become a successful actress.

"You'll end up back here within a month," she'd warned.

"Then you can get yourself down to the leather factory, like your sister and me. You can't earn a living on dreams, my girl."

Jack shook his head. "You girls, you're all the same; dreamers, the lot of you." He wrote a few notes on the pad on his heavy oak desk. Picking up a business card from a small holder, he turned it over and scribbled a name and address. Handing it to me, he said, "A friend of mine runs this club, she'll give you work, but she'll expect you to turn up looking immaculate at all times."

I forced a smile, relieved not to have to resort to waitressing in the grubby café where Hazel spent so much of her time working for a pittance. "Thank you."

He picked up a fat cigar, clipped one end off and rolled it between his index finger and thumb as he held it up to his ear. Satisfied, he placed it in his mouth and flicked on a gold lighter, puffing away on the cigar to light it. "You haven't seen the place yet." He laughed. "I'll get word to you if anything comes up here, but if you don't hear from me before, pop back to see me next Monday morning. We'll chat again then."

"Thank you," I said, hypnotised by the swirling thick smoke above his desk.

He rubbed his jowly chin. "If I do get you some acting work, you're going to have to change your name. Mo just isn't a professional enough sounding name for an actress."

"My real name is Maureen," I said. "Will that do? I'm willing to change it to anything you like though."

"Good. I'll give it some thought." He looked me up and down. "How tall are you?"

"Five feet seven inches, I think."

He nodded and made a note on the pad in front of him. "You could certainly play the cool blonde to perfection, if your acting skills are as good as I hope. You might even be able to play Swedish birds with your looks. Since Britt Ekland played a Bond girl, there's been a liking for others with Nordic looks. You'll fit the part well."

I couldn't hide my delight. "I'd love that."

"Fine." He waved me away. "I'll do my best."

I thanked him and hurried out. Relieved to be away from the smoky atmosphere, I leant against the office door to inspect his scrawl. I vaguely recognized the name of the club. Whatever this job was, it would be better than dragging myself back home. This might be small steps, I decided, but it was infinitely better than working in the factory. Whatever my mother professed about my future, I had no intention of ever going back, however desperate things got in London.

"He must really like you," Hazel said, when I called in quickly for a cup of tea during her short break. "Vince never even introduced me to Mr Collins." She stuck out her lower lip. "I can't help being a teeny bit jealous of you. You've only just arrived and already you're on your way."

"I am, aren't I?" I said not feeling as positive as I was making out. "And it's all down to you, Hazel. If you hadn't taken me with you to meet Vince I wouldn't be about to go and get a job in a glamorous club."

She gave me a smile that bordered on a grimace. "Yeah, cool."

****

"But that's nothing more than a bathing suit," moaned a tall girl next to me in the dingy room that only had one mirror and a couple of working bulbs either side of it that was supposed to be our dressing room. She glowered at me when I didn't back her up to the blousy manageress. "We're supposed to be cocktail waitresses."

"Some of you are." The manageress studied the prospective employees lined up in front of her, the black painted sweep above her large eyes adding to her menacing gaze. It was hard to know what she really looked like under all her make-up. She was terrifying, but I was certain her elaborate dress must have cost a fortune. However much this wasn't what I'd hoped for, I decided I couldn't afford to knock back the only job I'd been offered.

I smiled at her. "Do we all have to wear the costumes?" I asked indicating two other girls in bright cocktail dresses.

"Not everyone," she said, sizing me up. "Everyone starts the same though, as a waitress. If I see something in you I like, a spark, you'll soon be promoted." She nodded sagely. "You'll be allowed to mix with the clientele if that happens, and yes, you'll be given a cocktail dress to wear."

In my naivety I assumed this promotion would make all the difference. I'd heard about Hollywood producers coming to these nightspots and meeting waitresses they then turned in to the 'next big thing'. If I wanted to look the part when I met this miraculous person, I was going to need the right dress. This was the only way I could think of where I'd get the chance to do both. Hazel would be so envious.

After two nights doing my best to be sparkly and glamorous at the club, I wasn't sure if Hazel could ever be persuaded to swap places with me. The hours were long, and it was a constant battle to avoid the sweaty hands that seemed to grab whatever part of me they could reach. I was beginning to think maybe I wasn't going to stick it out when on the third night just as I was giving a particularly revolting customer a pinch on his flabby hand, I looked up and saw Vince leaning against the bar watching me. He smiled, his amusement at my retaliation to the 'hand' obvious on his handsome face.

I stuck my nose in the air and walked up to the bar, placing my tray down near him ready for the barman to reload it with fresh cocktails. "I didn't know you frequented this place," I said trying my best to sound as mature as possible.

"I don't very often, but I thought I'd better check up on my protégée."

I couldn't help beaming at him, all thoughts of acting cool in front of him vanishing at his words. It felt good to belong even in a tiny way to someone other than my family. I was about to say something, when I noticed someone else had drawn his attention away from me. I turned to see who it could be, jealous. It was a man, the shadows under his eyes dark and his expression wretched. He averted his eyes and stared at the floor.

I glanced at Vince. He was still, like a cat deciding whether to pounce on its prey. His eyes narrowed. A chill ran down my spine at the force of his fleeting glare. Sobered by his reaction, I realised then that Vince wasn't a man to cross. Which was just as well, I thought, because I would be heartbroken to be on the receiving end of such cold distaste. I determined never to give him cause to be angry with me.

The power Vince exuded and people's reverent reactions to him somehow made him more appealing to me. Sexier, too. I wanted to be with him. For him to want me as much as I wanted him. I pictured the two of us posing for photos on a red carpet at my first movie premiere, him with his arm around my shoulders, me with a ten-carat diamond solitaire on my engagement finger.

"You okay?" he asked his back resting against the bar.

I realised I'd been daydreaming. "Sorry." I blushed, hoping he couldn't guess what had been going through my mind. "Who was that man?"

"No one you need to worry about." He raised his right hand and moved his thumb lightly over my heavily made up cheek. "You look much older with this slap on your face."

"You don't approve?" I asked, panic surging through me.

"Of you looking older?" He scanned the room. "I couldn't care." My heart plummeted. I had angered him, and I wanted to cry. "Of you wearing this gunk on your face?" He studied me briefly. "You're far prettier without it."

I was barely able to hide my relief. I beamed at him. "Really?"

Soothed by his assurances, I put my shoulders back, standing proud. I wanted him to approve of me. I tilted my head in what I hoped was a coquettish way, and smiled at him.

He smiled. "You're gorgeous, do you know that?"

"Yes," I fibbed.

He lowered his voice and leaned closer to me. "Good girl not letting that creep touch you up. You must look out for yourself. I wasn't sure if the clientele at this place might be a little too full-on for you."

"I'll be fine," I insisted, loving him being protective of me.

"You get any problems," he lifted my chin with his finger. "Any mind, you tell me, and I'll have a word with them."

"Okay, Vince."

"Promise me, Mo," he said, his beautiful eyes seemingly boring into my soul.

"I promise," I said, my stomach contracting under his focus. My heart pounded, when he leaned closer grazing his lips against my cheek.

"Good girl. You're special and I've got big plans for your future. How about coming out with me tomorrow afternoon. I'm testing out my new E-Type Jag. Have you ever been in one?"

I shook my head.

"Good, then you can come with me to the country and maybe I can buy you a little treat of some kind."

I couldn't believe someone as handsome as Vince was taking me out. I pictured us together in his flash sports car, a silk scarf tied around my hair as we raced along the lanes. I didn't own a scarf, but it was enough to dream. Maybe I could ask him to buy one for me.

My heart pounded with excitement, but before I could think of a response the manageress came over. She gave me a withering look before kissing him firmly on the lips. She made her point only too clearly. I took a breath to speak, when I saw him watching me over her shoulder. He winked at me, soothing my irritation with her slightly.

When she stepped back from him, he said. "Greta, you're looking glorious as ever. I was just telling your waitress here how you make all the difference to this place."

She ignored me, but pouted at him. "You're a liar, Vincent Black, but a charming one." Then giving me a sideways glance, added, "If my waitress doesn't get a bloody move on, she's going to be looking for another job tomorrow morning."

"Sorry, Miss," I said trying to keep the sarcasm out of my voice. I bobbed a curtsey. Vince widened his eyes, but I could see the amusement in them. "I was waiting for my tray to be filled," I explained.

She glared at me through her thick false eyelashes. "Remember, you don't mix with the clientele until you're one of my hostesses."

Vince took her by the arm. "Come along, Greta, stop worrying about your girls for once. Join me for a drink. We haven't caught up with each other for months and I've missed you."

I watched them walk away, her rounded hips swaying from side to side as Vince whispered something in her ear. She threw her head back and shrieked with laughter. My chest constricted. It was all I could do not to grab a nearby glass and aim it at her head. Her hand stroked his lower back and rested on his buttocks. I wondered if they had ever been lovers.

"You can cut that crap out for a start."

I immediately turned my attention to the middle-aged barman. "What did you say?"

Wiping a glass with his tea towel, he motioned towards Vince and Greta. "You shouldn't get on the wrong side of either of those two," he whispered, shaking his head. "You'd live to regret it if you do."

I looked back at the pair of them deep in conversation at a burgundy velvet booth to one side of the club. I was sick of everyone treating me like some country kid who barely knew how to tie her own shoelaces. I was tougher than I looked and one day I would prove it to them all. I glowered at the barman in silence, watching him make a couple of cocktails. He pulled the lid off the cocktail shaker and poured the pink liquid into two glasses.

"Just be careful." He wiped the bottom of one of the glasses where he'd spilt a few drops before loading them onto my tray. "You're new around here. You don't know the ropes. Take it a little easy until you do." He held up a glass to one of the mounted optic dispensers at the side of the bar. "Don't look now, but Greta's watching you," he warned, his lips barely moving. "Get a bloody move on, or she'll have you out that door. I mean it, kid. Watch out for yourself. Do your job, bugger off home and you'll be okay."

I picked up my tray carefully. I might be irritated, but I didn't fancy having to pay for a round of expensive, spilt cocktails. "I'm not as soft as I look," I said glaring at him briefly before walking away. "That old cow doesn't scare me."

"Well she bloody well should, and what's more, so should he."

# Chapter Nine

2003 – Hautvillers, Near Epernay

## Sera

"Maybe Dee doesn't want to talk about Hazel," I whispered, when Mum and I were on our way up to bed later.

She didn't look convinced. "Well, something's amiss between them if you ask me."

I had the same suspicions, but I didn't want to add to the tension between them so kept my thoughts to myself. "You've never been interested in what Hazel was doing before. Why would you want to know now?"

"Before, she was nearby on that damn farm, now she's gone. I can't help being curious to know what's become of her."

That didn't make sense. The mother I knew would have been only too pleased that Hazel wasn't about to come and visit her son and daughter. "You're not happy Dee's come to stay here, are you?"

She put a finger up to her lips and pulled me into her bathroom, closing the door quietly behind us. "There's something about that girl." She shook her head slowly. "She was always such a bubbly young thing; I can't make her out at all now. It's as if she's a completely different person, although we know she's not. What could have possibly happened to change her so radically?" She glanced at herself in the mirror as if she was expecting her reflection to have the answer. "How long will she be staying here, do you think?"

I would like an answer to that question myself. All I knew was she'd had an especially difficult time of it lately, whatever 'it' was. "No idea."

"I know you were a little lonely before they came here, darling," my mother said. "But I think I preferred it that way."

I couldn't blame her. It was her house and it did feel a bit like Dee's life was taking over our once peaceful home. I agreed. "I think I did too, but Leo's a good man and he's doing his best to keep everyone happy. Even if I could turn Dee away, I couldn't do that to her little girl, or Leo. I feel sorry for them both. I think they're struggling as much as Dee is, in their own way."

"You're probably right," she said thoughtfully. "Leo's turned into a delicious looking young chap, especially when you think how gawky he used to be. It's a shame he couldn't stay here without them." She raised a perfectly waxed eyebrow. "I remember when he was younger and came here with his sister, he was always mooning about over you then."

Her comment surprised me. "I never noticed."

"No, because you were oblivious to the poor boy's

feelings," she said. "And always day dreaming about some pop star or other."

"He was three years younger than me, Mum. When you're a teenager, three years is a big difference in age."

"True." She smiled. "Thank heavens those couple of years don't matter when we're grown-ups."

I winced. "You're impossible, do you know that?" I teased, pecking her on the cheek before leaving the bathroom, only to find Leo outside on the landing, staring out of the window across the fields behind the house. I hoped he hadn't overheard Mum and me chatting.

"I love this house," he said, his hands pushed into his shorts pockets.

As he turned, he stared at me with a look of such intensity it almost took my breath away.

"Sera," he said, his voice barely above a whisper. "I enjoy being with you very much."

This isn't what I wanted to hear and I hoped Mum would not choose this moment to come out of the bathroom. I realised my mouth had dropped open, so closed it.

He crossed his arms in front of his chest looking awkward. "You know what I mean."

I didn't know how to react but not wishing to cause further problems in the house, I replied, "I'm glad you're feeling at home here." I was aware it wasn't what he'd been hoping I'd say. He was such a caring guy and I didn't want to drag his embarrassment out any further, but I couldn't lie to him. "I've really enjoyed getting to know you again."

He went to say something then seemed to think better of it and said, "Thank you. I know being in Epernay is doing Dee, Ashley and me the power of good."

"I'm glad being here is helping them."

\*\*\*\*

"Wake up, Sera." Mum knocked quietly on my bedroom door, her voice just above a whisper, but the shrill tone of it woke me. "Hurry up, I need you to come and see something."

"I'm coming," I groaned, flinging back the duvet and getting out of bed. "What…" I started to shout as I opened the door, but she put her hand over my mouth to shut me up.

"Shhh." She motioned over her shoulder to the attic stairs. "Let me in."

I did as she asked, not that I had much choice. "What's the matter?" I asked as soon as she closed the door, leaning against it and rolling her eyes heavenward. Mum had a tendency towards the melodramatic, she was an actress after all, but this was a little over the top even for her.

"This really has to stop, Sera," she said in a way that didn't invite argument. "That mad girl was ranting outside in the garden first thing this morning. I'm amazed it didn't wake you; it bloody well woke me up. I've got lines to learn and it doesn't get easier as I'm getting a tiny bit older. I need my sleep, darling."

My mother never swore. "Mum, my room overlooks the road at the front; I wouldn't hear anything from the garden from in here. Did you work out what was upsetting her?"

She shook her head, "No, but Leo manhandled her out of the back gate pretty soon afterwards. I think the child is still sleeping upstairs, though I can't imagine how. What do you think happened?"

I rubbed my eyes. "How would I know? I was sleeping when it all kicked off, remember?"

"Get showered and dressed, so you're ready for when they come back; if they come back." I could hear by the tone of her voice she would rather they didn't. She flounced off before I could say another word.

I went into the bathroom and undressing, stepped into the shower cubicle. I turned on the water, not caring that it was freezing cold after the initial shock of it hitting my skin. The water slowly warmed and my brain cleared. Another drama with Dee, this was becoming a habit. I poured a little shampoo into the palm of my hand, lathered it up and washed my hair. What was happening to my once peaceful life? I washed and stepped out of the shower, drying myself hurriedly before, still damp, dressing in fresh underwear, shorts and a T-shirt.

It was hotter than it had been this time last year but I always enjoyed this weather. It was so like the summers I recalled growing up here with Mum. Even when she was away on location and left me with a temporary nanny, I never wanted to leave this area. I loved living in Epernay and coming back here after Marcus' death had definitely been the right thing for me and Katie to do. Had inviting Leo and Dee back into our lives been a change I wasn't ready for?

I could hear voices and a commotion outside the back of

the house. I didn't want Katie to get a fright so kicked my damp towel out of the way and ran onto the landing. "Katie?" I called. "Where are you?"

"Mummy, Mummy," she shouted from downstairs. She was up earlier than usual. I hoped my mother was down there with her, but could tell by the panic in her voice Katie was frightened.

"I'm coming down now." I ran down to find her. She was waiting by the kitchen door, sucking her thumb. She'd picked that up from Ashley, I thought with irritation, wondering why I'd seen fit to invite them into our home to cause so much disruption. I bent to lift Katie.

"It's all right," I whispered, kissing her tanned cheek. "Let's go and see what's going on, shall we?"

Leo was holding Dee by the shoulder and shaking her. "That's enough. You have to stop this, now. Getting hysterical isn't going to help anyone, is it?"

"What's happened?" I asked, not sure I wanted to hear the answer. He tilted his head and smiled at Katie.

"I'm sorry if we scared you." He bent down so his face was level with hers. She immediately turned away from him, burying her face in my shoulder. "Silly Dee found a lizard in the garden," he added, stroking her arm.

I frowned at him in confusion and he shrugged. It was a silly comment and obviously not the reason behind her hysterics, but it had the desired effect with Katie.

She looked at him, eyes wide with curiosity. "Was it big, or small?"

He held his index fingers about four inches apart. "I

don't know, but it was about this size."

She didn't seem very impressed. "That's only small," she said with distain.

"Yes," he replied. "But Ashley hasn't ever seen a lizard, so if you go and find her, we can show her one together."

Katie smiled and wriggled to get down. "Okay." She ran off up the stairs and confident that she wasn't within earshot, I turned to him and Dee. She was hugging herself tightly and sniffing noisily in between sobs by the back door.

"What the hell happened?" I demanded. I wasn't going to let the atmosphere in my home be ruined. "Quickly, tell me before Katie and Ashley come down."

Leo rubbed his face with both hands. "They've found a body."

What did he say? I stared at him. "Who has? Where?"

Dee cried out. Leo glared at her and she blew her nose on a soggy looking tissue. "Our old farm, that's where," he said.

"A body at the farm?" I repeated like an idiot. I couldn't focus for a second. "Henri?"

Leo shook his head. "He's the one who found the body."

I closed my eyes, relieved. For a moment there I'd thought the arsonist had returned and finished off his intended victim. I tried to gather myself. "How do you know all this?"

Dee sobbed again, and Leo pulled her into a hug. I suspected he was trying to shut her up. "You've got to get a grip on your emotions, Dee." He looked over her head at me. "I went to the *pâtisserie* to buy us croissants for breakfast and the woman serving in there told me. There were a few people in the queue gossiping about the chap you know who lives there."

"I can imagine," I said, unable to keep the irritation from my voice. If any of those miseries had bothered to try and get to know him, I was certain they wouldn't be so quick to judge.

He shook his head slowly. "They don't like him much around here, do they?"

No, they didn't. "I think they're only suspicious about him because he doesn't mix with them."

"Silly bugger. He should make the effort if he hopes to settle here permanently."

He was right. It wasn't the best way to integrate in any town. This was a tight knit community and a stranger who obviously had a traumatic past and kept to himself was asking for interest, if not suspicion. Even Leo was already back in the fold, having made an effort to shop at the local market and be friendly to people. He always bought meat from the *boulangerie* rather than driving a little way to the *supermarché*, and it was noted and appreciated by the locals.

"It's easier for us," I said, wanting to defend Henri's actions. "We lived here years ago. Some people still remember us from when we were kids." Although, I had to admit Henri didn't seem to care how the town people were towards him, if they left him well alone.

"True."

"Does anyone know who the dead person is?" I asked.

"No," Leo said, raking his right hand through his hair.

"No one can work out who it could be."

I tried to imagine how horrifying it must have been for Henri to make such a grim discovery at his farm. However, I couldn't see what reason Dee had for being so upset.

"I need to make sure Henri is coping with all the attention this must be bringing him," I said, ignoring Leo's disapproving glare at me. Not wishing to discuss the matter with Mum and have to put up with her declarations about her suspicions of Henri, I added, "Can I leave you to look after Katie for a bit while I pay him a visit?"

For a moment, I was sure he'd refuse. "Of course. Please ask him to let me know if there's anything I can do to help."

His reply confused me, but not wishing to give him an opportunity to change his mind, I hurried away. "I will," I said, feeling mean for snapping at him earlier. "I'm sure he'll be grateful to have your support."

"I wouldn't be so sure," Leo laughed, his arm still around Dee's shaking shoulders.

"You're probably right," I shouted running up the stairs to the kitchen door, grabbing my keys as I ran through the hallway.

I hurried to the farm, racing through the stone pillars and pulled up in front of the lilac and apple trees causing a small dust cloud to rise around my car. There were voices coming from the direction of the barn, and as I neared the ruins I noticed a white van parked the other side of the hedge with two people dressed in white paper suits. I presumed they must be the forensics team, so stopped and watched them for a few minutes hoping Henri was about somewhere and would come over and speak to me.

When he didn't appear, I decided to go and find him. I checked around the back of his house, spotting the old weathered tree trunk that I realised had probably been there as a makeshift seat since Hazel's time. Then retracing my steps to the front, I hurried up the porch stairs. I knocked a couple of times on the door frame of the open doorway and called his name. Nothing.

Determined not to leave without checking he was okay, I went through to the kitchen giving Patti and the puppies a quick cuddle, and hurried down the long dark passageway to the back of the house where I remembered Hazel used to have a small snug room. I pulled open the door and went to speak.

My breath caught in my throat at the sight of him standing by a bookcase wearing nothing but shorts, as he flicked through the pages of an open book. Livid red welts covered the right side of his muscled back, down his side and over most of his right leg. I had assumed the damage to his leg that I'd seen when we'd gone swimming was the only other scarring apart from the slightly puckered skin on his right cheek. I had no idea his body had been this badly damaged.

He looked across the room at me, horror in his eyes to discover me in there with him. Neither of us spoke. I tried not to react, but didn't know whether to state the obvious, or not. "I came to see if you were all right," I stammered.

He sighed and held his hands out as if to say, this is me. "I'm not a pretty sight, am I?" He looked away from me, slamming the book closed and replacing it onto the bookcase shelf.

"Don't be silly," I said, desperate to find something to say to put him at his ease, but failing dismally. I hesitated, searching for the right words, hating myself when I couldn't manage it, asked. "What happened to you?"

He caught my eye again. "I'd feel better talking about this with my clothes on."

"Of course, sorry." I stepped back to let him pass, unable to help staring at his retreating figure. The broad, muscular back so cruelly damaged. Why the hell hadn't I thought to knock on this door before barging in? Stupid, stupid idiot.

I went outside to wait for him in the shade of the porch recalling how pretty the area had always been with Hazel's beloved geraniums lining the steps up to the porch. He was back downstairs before I had time to clear my head and figure out what to say next. I chewed the skin around one of my thumbnails.

"Sera, it's okay."

Furious with myself for being so tongue-tied, I grimaced. "Sorry, I shouldn't have said anything." How could I have made him feel so awkward? "It was rude of me to barge in without knocking."

"It is okay," he said, even though it clearly wasn't.

I struggled to think of something else to say then remembered why I'd hurried over here in the first place. Relieved to have something to focus on, I said, "I heard they've found a body."

He looked troubled as he glanced in the direction of the

barn. "I don't know how no one saw it there before. How could I have missed it?"

He sounded so guilty, as if it was his fault somehow. "How were you to know there was a body in there. Could it have been the person who started the fire do you suppose?"

He shook his head. "No, this poor soul has been there for a long time. It was in a shallow grave and barely covered."

"Who spotted it?"

"Me," he sighed. "This morning." He lowered himself painfully to sit on a low wall next to me. "The insurance assessors finished working at the barn a few days ago. I wanted to tidy up and began moving charred planks of wood that fell from the walls and ceiling." He shook his head. "I put my hand into the soil to pull up what I thought was a piece of wood; it was a charred bone from a finger."

I shivered at the thought. "How horrible."

"I have seen much worse, but not at my home, of course." He stared over at the remains of the collapsed barn. "It gave me a shock. I called the gendarmes and the forensics team have been here for a few hours."

"I wonder who it could be?" I sat next to him and thought back to the elderly couple who took on the farm after Hazel's departure. "I can't imagine it would have anything to do with the old people who've lived here for the past twenty years," I said. "I never took much notice of them, but they seemed very ordinary and not the sort of people you'd imagine burying a body on their farm." Then again, what did murderers look like? "This place lay empty for about a year after Leo and Dee's family disappeared.

Maybe it happened when the house was empty?"

"They don't know yet," he said. "I hope they discover the person's identity soon."

"Hmm, me too."

He turned to look at me. "How did you hear about this? In the village?"

I nodded. "Naturally. Leo went in to town buy breakfast and they were gossiping about the body in the *pâtisserie*."

He shook his head slowly. After a few seconds he asked, "What did they waste their time gossiping about before I lived at the farm?"

"No idea." I rocked to one side and nudged him lightly. "Don't take any notice, it's only because you're new and rather mysterious."

He pulled a puzzled expression. "I cannot imagine what is so mysterious about me."

I could see he was lying, but didn't push the point. I was as curious as the villagers about him, but now was not the time for answers about his past. It was none of my business where he'd come from and why he was so determined to guard his privacy. "If you want company, you're more than welcome to join the rest of us for dinner at Mum's house. Katie would love to see you again."

He smiled. "She is a sweet child. Thank you, but I'll remain here at the farm. The animals remain nervous after the fire. I still don't know how it started…"

"That's fine, I understand." I wished I could stay with him and be some sort of support. It must be hard to be so alone, especially at an uncertain time like this. I checked my watch. "I should return home. Leo said to offer his support to you though."

He narrowed his eyes. "That is kind," he said quietly.

I sighed, wanting to keep him company for a little longer. "I left Katie with Leo. I think they've had enough of Dee's hysteria, so I really better go back."

"She is upset? Why?" He frowned. I imagined he must think my friends very odd and over-emotional.

"I'm not sure. It could be because they lived here, maybe? Although I'm not sure why it would bother her so much."

"Perhaps she is sickened at the thought of playing in the barn as a child when a body could have been lying below her feet. Some people have a problem with death that way. Spirits worry them."

I hadn't thought of that. I wasn't enthralled with the notion of Dee and me spending hours terrifying each other at night by telling ghost stories. We'd given Leo many nightmares after evenings in that barn.

"Maybe, but I think there's more to it where Dee's concerned. Something happened to her recently to make her this frail, but I can't seem to discover what it was."

"She has her child and her family," he scowled. "To me she's very self-indulgent."

To me, too, I thought. "We don't know what's happened to her though. Maybe she's got a good reason to be like she is?" And maybe she's being self-indulgent, I reasoned, but refrained from adding. I thought back to what I'd learned about him just before. "Everyone is different. Some people cope with tragedy better than others."

He stared at me silently for a moment weighing up whether to say something. "And you, Sera?"

"Sorry?" My heart pounded in anticipation of what he was about to say next.

"Your husband's death; how did you cope with it?"

I blinked, shocked by the force of his comment. "Badly," I admitted. "For a long time, it was as if my life had ended, which it had in a way."

He moved to place his hand on my wrist but lowered his hand instead. "I should not ask. It is cruel."

"It's okay. You have your own demons, I assume," I said averting my gaze from him and staring up at the apple tree.

"You mean after my accident." He removed his hand and stared at the barn. "I wish you hadn't seen my scars."

I wasn't sure whether or not to continue the conversation, but took a chance. "I'm your friend. The only thing that bothers me about them is thinking what you might have suffered when you got them."

"You have seen them though." He sounded utterly miserable. "I worry that to some people these scars define who I am." When I didn't speak, he added, "I believe the people in the town make up their own minds about me once they've seen me."

"They don't," I said, hoping I was right and wishing I'd made more of an effort to announce my arrival earlier avoiding the need of having this conversation. "Do you want to tell me what happened? You don't have to."

He raked his hands back through his short black hair. "I hate it, it's true. These… burns have ruined my life."

"It must have been incredibly painful."

He swallowed. "Agony, for a time. The hardest part was no longer being able to do the job I loved." He stood up and began walking up the stairs back into the house.

"Which was?" I asked, following him into the kitchen where he took two bottles of cider from the fridge and held them up. I took one and opened it. "I shouldn't, I really do have to get back."

"This, and that." He opened one bottle lifting it to his lips taking a mouthful of the cool liquid. "I lived in Paris."

I noticed he had avoided answering my question. "But why couldn't you carry on doing your job?"

"Because my leg was so badly burnt it pulled the skin and I now limp. You've seen how slowly I move sometimes." He stared at me. "Do not feel pity for me. That gives me more pain than my damaged skin."

"I don't pity you," I lied. "I'm just sad happened, that's all."

He shrugged nonchalantly. "*Et moi, aussi.*"

We stood in silence, both drinking every now and then from our bottles enjoying the refreshing cider and the fact that he seemed to be relaxing a little. I stared out of the back window in the direction of the wood.

"You want to know how it happened," he said. It was a statement rather than a question, his matter-of-fact tone filling the silence.

I chewed my lower lip sensing that this was probably the only time he'd offer the information. "You don't have to tell me if you don't want to," I said not wanting him to feel forced into confiding in me despite my desperation to learn the facts.

"I will tell you." His embarrassment forgotten, or at least well hidden, he said, "It was Bastille Day and the people in Paris were celebrating." He glanced up at the kitchen clock and frowned. "You said you needed to hurry home."

"Bugger," I said noticing the time, the responsibility of returning to Katie tugging at my need to know his story.

He gave me a crooked smile that just for a moment lit up his scarred face. "You must wait then."

I frowned, not bothering to hide my irritation. "You did that on purpose." I didn't blame him, I supposed. "Be prepared to tell me when you next see me though, because I will ask you about it."

"You are like an English schoolteacher," he said as I handed him my bottle.

I assumed he meant that I was bossy. "Actually, I was born in France," I said getting up to leave. He wasn't the only one with secrets.

# Chapter Ten

## 2003 – Hautvillers, Near Epernay

### Sera

I wasn't looking forward to going home and wondered if Leo had managed to calm Dee a little. It would have been nice to be able to tell her something more definite about the body they'd discovered at the farm and I hoped she didn't take what I'd discovered too badly.

I found them out in the garden drinking coffee.

"Did you find anything out at the farm?"

I relayed everything Henri had told me.

She burst into tears. "Oh, Leo."

He put his arm around her narrow shoulders. "Shush, calm down." He pulled an apologetic face at me. "Sorry, Sera. I think the thought of us playing in that barn as children with a body lying there is upsetting for Dee right now."

"I thought the same thing. It's a little unnerving, isn't it?"

"I'm just finding this a bit much, I'm afraid," Dee said sniffing. Leo handed her a tissue and she blew her nose. "Sorry."

It was enough having to deal with Mum's annoyance having them in the house, but I wasn't prepared to watch everything I said about the farm in front of them.

"Maybe you should go back home to the UK," I suggested willing her to agree. "The gossip and intrigue is only going to get worse over the coming days and probably weeks. The investigation will probably not be solved for some time." I could only guess, but it made sense to me. "I think it might be traumatic for you to be so close to everything."

She pushed Leo roughly away and glared at me. "You. It's always all about you and what you think, isn't it Sera? It always has been."

I couldn't believe the viciousness of her accusations. "What do you mean?" As far as I could remember, Dee had always been the bossy, dramatic one out of us. Had I remembered things so differently to her?

"Hey, that's enough," Leo snapped. "Cut it out. Sera has been a good friend to you. To us both."

She stood up, knocking her coffee all over her flowered skirt. "Now look what you made me do." She marched over to me, stopping almost nose to nose with me. "We all know why he's so fucking defensive of you, don't we, Sera?" Her right shoulder crashed into my left one as she slammed past me and stormed into the house.

Shocked by what had just happened, I rubbed the point of impact trying to make sense of her reaction. "I didn't realise she resented me." I turned to Leo. "Is that why she's been so surly since she arrived? Have you forced her to come and stay here?"

"Not at all," he said, looking mortified at the suggestion. "I'm sorry. It's not your fault. You've only done as I've asked. You've been a good friend to her. Please don't take any notice of her outbursts."

It was easier in theory not to take notice of someone, but by the look on her face she resented me, and badly. I knew she relied heavily on him for most of her emotional support. I couldn't understand her feeling threatened by me though. Could it be because she and I had always been the inseparable ones and now the balance of our relationship had altered? I needed to be careful to stay out of her and Leo's odd relationship and remember that I was an outsider here, not her.

"It's fine," I said, wanting to make him feel better. "I'll try to be more sensitive towards her." I lowered my voice, conscious that if I didn't she would be able to hear me from her attic bedroom. "We both should."

He stood up and came over to me. "No. I won't have her ruining our friendship." He faltered momentarily. "Meeting up with you has been the best thing that's happened to me in a long time, and as much as I love my sister and care about her, I'm not going to allow her insecurities to come between us."

"However things seem now, Leo," I said, "ultimately my loyalty, and yours, has always been to Dee. Now isn't the time to change that. It's pretty obvious she needs us both, and we can't let her feel pushed out, it would be cruel."

He didn't reply, but stared into space, looking at something only he could see. I looked over my shoulder to check she wasn't nearby, before carrying on talking, willing him to understand.

"I don't think she can take much more right now." Was he even listening to me? I tapped him on the shoulder. "Leo, did you hear what I said?"

He snapped out of his reverie, looking stunned as if he hadn't even realised I was there never mind talking to him. "What? Sorry."

I closed my eyes to concentrate all my efforts on not losing my temper. "I don't want to have to face the consequences of what Dee might do in her present emotional state." I hoped he was getting the message that if he did harbour feelings for me that they couldn't go any further. I really didn't want to have to spell it out to him and chance hurting his feelings, too. Having Dee upset with me was bad enough.

"I'm going to talk to her," he said. Without waiting for me to answer he went inside the house.

"Bugger," I said. Sitting on the wooden seat, I hugged myself. I really should think before speaking. Mum was always telling me not to react instantly to things and to consider what I wanted to say before opening my mouth. It was about time I started following this particular nugget of advice.

"Mummy," Katie called from the stairs by the back door. "You said a rude word."

I pulled an apologetic face. "I did, and I'm very naughty. You wouldn't do that, would you?"

She shook her head, her blonde curls bouncing around her face. "No." She giggled. "Silly, Mummy."

We went looking for lizards, crouching down near the garden wall behind the flowers in the cool soil until I heard raised voices and stamping feet on the tiled hallway floor. "You keep looking, I'll be back shortly," I said, standing up and brushing earth from my knees.

Mum poked her head out of the back door. "They're leaving," she shouted, looking rather pleased about it. She went back in and immediately after I heard the front door slamming. "They've gone," Mum said rubbing her hands together.

Katie's face crumbled miserably. "Uncle Leo, Auntie Dee and Ashley?" A big tear ran down her pudgy cheek. "Gone?"

I reached her and picked her up to give her a cuddle. "Maybe they were late going somewhere. I don't know." I kissed away her tear and squeezed her close to me hoping that in soothing her, I might be able to comfort myself a little.

Katie wrapped her arms around my neck and rested her chin on my shoulder, the tickling sensation of the pressure of her chin making me giggle involuntarily. She looked at me, trying not to smile. "What, Mummy?"

I shook my head and smiled. "You're funny."

She beamed at me, delighted to have cheered us both up. "And you." She kissed my cheek, pressing her little mouth hard against my cheek and shook her head as if to make a permanent imprint on my face. I tickled her sides with my fingertips and tried to put my houseguests out of my mind.

"I wonder if they're coming back?" I said, almost to myself.

"More than likely," Mum shouted from inside the kitchen. My mother had incredible hearing, when it suited her.

I carried Katie into the kitchen, putting her down near Mum with a cool drink and a biscuit and ran upstairs to the attic room where Dee had been sleeping. Stopping at the doorway, it wasn't necessary to check if their clothes had been taken, every drawer remained open as did the wardrobe doors.

"Bloody hell."

"Well?" my mother shouted from the lower landing.

I went to lean over the banisters to speak to her. "They've moved out."

"Thank heavens for that," she said, going into the bathroom and locking the door.

"Mum, they've left." I went back over my last conversation with Leo, had I offended him? I told my mother what had happened, shouting through the closed door to her.

"Sera, it may have escaped your notice," she said, her voice slightly muffled by the door being in the way. "But I'm in the lavatory. Kindly go away and leave me in peace."

I stepped back. "Sorry." I went downstairs to the kitchen to wait for her, offering Katie the biscuit tin to take another one. I kept going over and over what I'd said to Leo to make him take such drastic action.

I sat down at the table and rested my elbows on the worn pine and lowered my head into my hands. "It's such a mess"

I wiped crumbs from Katie's cheek and watched her go back outside. "Do you think I've become hard since Marcus died?" I asked Mum.

She inspected her scarlet nail polish for a moment before addressing me. "I think you lost the love of your life and it almost destroyed you. You needed to toughen up and become independent, but maybe now it's time to let someone else do things for you for a change."

"You do things for me," I said, taking her hand and giving it a gentle squeeze.

She bent forward and kissed me on the forehead. "Not really. You live here, but you look after the house for me, especially when I'm away. You earn your own money by running your small business and you do everything for Katie. What does anyone else ever really do for you, Sera?"

I thought for a couple of seconds. "I like being independent."

"Aren't you ready for another relationship yet?"

Was I? I did like Leo, but in that way? I wasn't sure. "Marcus controlled everything when we were together," I said. "I'm not ready to give up my independence to someone else yet."

"It doesn't have to be like that with Leo." She studied me. "He's used to taking charge of his sister and, knowing Hazel as I did, needs to keep her organised too. He'd probably relish a relationship with a woman who doesn't need too much pampering."

"It all seems a bit quick and I don't know if I even like him in that way."

"What do you want to do?" She reached out and took my hands in hers. "I can't bear seeing you looking so lost. I'm going away with Paul tomorrow." She raised an eyebrow when I went to argue. "Yes, I'm seeing him again and I hate leaving you in the middle of this mess."

"Then don't," I said frowning. When had she and Paul been in touch? "I thought it was over for good between you two?"

She shrugged. "So did I." She sighed heavily. "Oh, Sera, it's all right for you young things."

I couldn't see how and said so.

"You have so much time ahead of you." She picked up a loose strand of my hair and in an uncharacteristic action tucked it behind my ear. "You're so young and fresh and, well, gorgeous."

I wasn't fooled by her act. "Mum, you know you look stunning, so stop trying to kid me. If you want to spend time with Paul, that's fine by me. I just think you could do far better, that's all."

"I know he can be a tad immature, but he is attractive."

I didn't want to think about Paul any more. "Go on. I'll be fine, I always am."

She gave me a brief hug. "No, darling, you just pretend to be fine."

Did I? I hadn't thought so. "Maybe I'll pop over and visit Henri for a bit, he needs cheering up too."

Mum walked over to the window, staring out at the back garden and across to the woods. "Why do you insist on ignoring me about that man? He's dangerous, I can feel it."

"Mum, you don't even know Henri, how can you say such a thing?"

"Why don't you phone Leo? He's been your friend

forever and you need to make amends. Maybe it's time we stopped being annoyed by Dee and tried to work out why she's behaving so appallingly?"

That was a bit of a turnaround, even for Mum. It made me wonder how strongly she did dislike Henri. "Really? You don't mind her coming back here?"

She shook her head. "She's obviously upset. Even you must be a little spooked by this body business at the farm? I know am."

"It is a bit unnerving," I admitted.

"Well, imagine how that poor girl feels. She's been through something lately and this is probably the thing that could tip her over the edge. I don't think we have much of a choice, not if we consider ourselves to be decent human beings."

She'd unnerved me more about Henri than the body at the farm, but she did have a point about supporting my old friend. "I'll call him then, but I'm going to want some answers this time."

"Good, me too."

I picked up the phone.

\*\*\*\*

"You went without me," Katie said reproaching Leo as he entered the house the following morning.

He bent down to her level. "We needed to go somewhere, but we bought you these." He handed her a large baguette, then opening the bag pointed to a bottle of red wine.

She giggled. "I can't drink wine, Maman said."

"Okay then," he smiled. "What about this?" He lifted out a wheel of Brie.

"Eugh." She shook her head. Taking one side of the bag, Katie peered in and putting her hand in pulled out a punnet of strawberries. "I can have these."

"Katie," I said, not pleased to see her delving into someone else's bag. "You mustn't do that, it's very rude."

He smiled down the hallway to me. "It's fine." He gave me an apologetic smile. "I thought we could all go on a picnic today."

"A picnic, a picnic!" Katie cheered jumping up and down, dropping the punnet spilling the strawberries on to the tiles.

I bent to pick them up, ruffling her hair. "You take Ashley to unpack her things in her bedroom and I'll speak with Leo and Dee about this afternoon."

Happy with this suggestion, she took hold of Ashley's hand, forcing her thumb from her mouth and dragged her upstairs.

I watched the two walk up the stairs. Katie and the silent child complying with whatever anyone wanted from her.

Dee came in behind them looking rather pink cheeked. "Leo said I was unforgivably rude to you yesterday and I'm sorry."

Recalling Mum's words, I walked over and gave her a hug. "It's forgotten. Why don't you take your things up to your room and unpack? There's a brilliant market in the town today and I think it'll be fun to go and have a look." I smiled at Leo.

"We can go after our picnic," he said.

"We might be able to find a few bits for the girls and maybe ourselves," Dee said.

I was delighted she was agreeing to go. Maybe yesterday was the catalyst that would snap us all out of our awkwardness with each other so that we could finally move forward to build up our friendships again.

"Give me an hour to unpack and have a bit of a lie down," she said. "It's so hot out there I'm feeling a little nauseous. I'll be fine in a bit." She looked up at Leo and some unspoken message passed between them. "I'll be here to watch the kids. Why don't the two of you go for a bit of a walk?"

I didn't answer. Her question seemed rather loaded, but I wanted a chance to speak to him, so led the way out of the back door. We walked through the garden and pulling hard at the warped garden gate, opened it with a little difficulty. "Shall we go to the woods?" I asked without waiting for an answer aware that to get any answers meant we needed to be away from earshot of everyone in the house.

We walked silently through the long, dried grasses in the field behind the house. As usual, I stepped this way and that to miss the poppies, their blood red petals so delicate and bright. The heat of the morning sunshine bore down on my neck warming my body further and relaxing me. I loved walking to the woods, with Katie, or by myself. It always soothed me to come this way.

"It's all my fault," he said eventually, the sudden sound of his voice startling me. I stopped and stared at him. "What is?"

"This mess, everything."

I doubted that. "Go on, tell me."

"She'd tried to hint about her difficulties, but I didn't want to face that she was in trouble."

"I understand how that feels," I said, recalling my denial when Mum tried to insist I wasn't coping after Marcus' death. "If you face it you have no excuse not to do something to resolve it."

"Exactly." He reached out and took my hand in his, lifting it and turning it over to kiss my palm. "Thank you."

"What difficulties do you mean though exactly?"

"Drugs."

I snatched my hand away. "Drugs? Is she on them now?" I asked not happy to have left my daughter in her care.

"No." When I didn't look convinced, he took my hand and tried to pull me forward. "I promise you. I wouldn't leave the girls with her if I suspected she was back on that crap again."

I believed him. "Tell me everything."

We carried on walking, not looking at each other as he spoke. "She's never coped well since leaving here. I don't know if it was because I was younger when we left France, but even though I missed Epernay, I settled in quite quickly in the UK. Dee struggled a lot. She hated that Mum insisted we keep to ourselves and became very introverted."

He stopped walking and looked at me. "She missed you very much. I know it probably doesn't seem like it because she's being impossible, but I think she was grieving for you and our lives here for years."

I sighed heavily, I understood that pain. "It must have been very different to everything she'd known all her life."

"It was. We went from the freedom of living in the countryside, with warmer weather and lots of open spaces, to having to live in a small flat on a grey council estate in the north of England. It didn't help that Mum was paranoid about our safety and refused to let us out much for the first year or so."

I could relate to part of what he was saying. "I found the winters very hard to deal with when I went to live with Marcus in Scotland, even though the place itself was incredibly beautiful."

"Yes, I especially hated the winters."

"I wouldn't mind a day there now though." I sighed, wiping away perspiration from my forehead.

He began walking again, picking a piece of lavender and sniffing it. "Eventually, I went away to university and made friends and a new life for myself. No one cared that I'd grown up in France or had an odd dress sense; they accepted me as I was. Dee, on the other hand, was left behind with Mum who was drinking more and more."

He rubbed his face with the palms of his hands and I noticed how exhausted he looked. "Dee got in with a bad crowd and got married on a whim. Her life seemed to spiral downwards after that. Each time I went home she appeared to have disintegrated a little further."

"Poor Dee." I thought of all the dreams she used to share with me about a magical future. It was upsetting to think none of her hopes had amounted to anything.

"She rallied when she discovered she was pregnant and had the baby…"

"Ashley."

"What?" He looked confused and I could have kicked myself for interrupting. "Yes, Ashley." He appeared to be mulling over his words before continuing. "She's damaged, Sera. Something dreadful happened." He cleared his throat. "She reverted to old habits that I hoped she'd mastered." I waited for him to continue. "She fell into debt, selling some of the few items we'd managed to take with us when we left the farm that night." His eyes filled with tears and he closed his eyes briefly. "I'm sorry, but it's hard for me to talk about. I want to trust my sister. She's made many promises to me only to sneak off to her moronic friends as soon as I had to go away on business."

"Oh, Leo. It all sounds too horrible," I said, sympathising but wishing he would be more specific.

"I tried to help her," he puffed out his cheeks and shook his head. "She lied to me. I had no idea how bad things were for her. By the time I figured it out, Dee was in a hospital bed."

I gasped. "But that's terrible." It was hard to imagine Dee's life being so troubled. "Poor thing,"

He nodded. "She swore on Ashley's life that she was finished with her ex, but a few nights after she came home from hospital I spotted him hanging around her flat. I'd had enough and was determined to help her this time. I snuck Dee out the back door and drove through the night to catch the ferry. We didn't have any plans, but I was determined to get them far away from that life."

I stopped walking. I didn't buy his sorry tale, but he looked stricken and I couldn't tell if maybe part of it was true. "It sounds like you've all been through hell." I didn't want to, but felt compelled to add, "You must feel free to stay here for as long as you both need."

He squeezed my hand. "I'm relieved to hear you say that, Sera."

# Chapter Eleven

## 2003 – Hautvillers, Near Epernay

## Sera

Now I had a better understanding about why Dee and Ashley had so few belongings, I was even more determined to get them to come out with me to a nearby weekly market. It didn't take long to drive there. The sight of the town square was filled with stalls covered with bright colours like a chaotic rainbow, didn't let me down.

"This takes me back," he said marching over to the nearest book stall.

"Come along, girls," I said to the others. "Let's go and find some treats." I led them to a favourite stall of mine where two sisters sold their beautifully hand-made children's clothes. "Hello, ladies," I said kissing them both several times on each cheek. "We're looking for a few things for this little girl," I said, raising Ashley's hand slightly.

Unused to me speaking to them in English, the older one widened her eyes. "I forget you are English," she said, smiling. "These are your guests?"

"Yes, they've come to spend the summer with us."

"What is your favourite colour?" she asked Ashley, obviously taken aback when the child didn't seem to know how to answer this simple question.

I knew that if anyone had asked Katie the same thing she'd have bellowed 'pink' back at them without hesitation. "She's shy," I explained. "Show us a few things and Ashley can tell us if she likes them, or not." I was expecting Dee to involve herself in this bit of shopping, but she walked away towards a nearby pottery stall. Maybe she was trying to show me that she trusted me with her daughter. I watched her studying the vases and plates displayed chaotically on the stall and wondered where she was thinking of keeping these new items.

Realizing one of the sisters was waiting for me to answer, I took my cue from Katie's taste and chose two skirts, T-shirts and a jacket I thought would suit Ashley. Katie had similar clothes in her wardrobe and loved them. I then bought three brightly coloured towels for them. If they were going to stay here for the summer, then I was determined to get them out of the house and swimming a few times each week. Who knew how long this heatwave was going to last, or when they would decide to return to England and the probability of another dismal autumn there? I wanted Ashley to have happy memories of her stay with us in France.

The throngs of shoppers made it difficult to see how far Dee had gone and the traffic was busy around the outskirts of the market, so I kept Katie and Ashley with me. I loved seeing families making the most of their Sunday together milling around us, chattering as they bartered for produce. As we stopped at each stall, Katie chattered to Ashley oblivious that their conversation was one-sided.

I waved Leo over. "Take these, will you?" I asked, handing him the basket and two bags I'd been carrying. "We still need to buy fruit and veg."

He pulled a face. "Great." He grimaced theatrically. "What have you been buying, logs?"

I giggled and went to inspect some melons that I'd spotted. I pressed the top lightly and gave them both a sniff. I didn't need to gauge their freshness, I'd never picked up anything here that hadn't come straight from the fields either that morning, or the day before. Breathing in their cool sweetness, I handed them to the stallholder and studied the grapes. Having bought enough fruit to complete our picnic, I sought out the vegetables we needed and paid for everything, refusing Leo's attempts to do so.

Dee ambled ahead of us. I walked up to her when I spotted her checking out a piece of Quimper pottery. "That would look perfect in your bedroom at home," I said.

She frowned. I imagined she was trying to work out to which home I was referring. "The attic has so few pieces in it," she said quietly. "It could do with a pretty plate to brighten it up."

I held back a snappy retort. Spotting a display of Porringer two-handled bowls like the ones Katie and I enjoyed using whenever we ate cereal, soup, or drank *café au lait*, I decided to buy one as a gift for Ashley.

"Look," I said lifting a typically decorated white bowl in

front of her, with its dark blue banding around the rim and over the small handles on each side. "I don't think we'll find one with your name on, but this one says '*petite dejeuner*', which means breakfast. Would you like that?"

"Say yes," Katie squealed. "I've got one."

Ashley treated us to a half-smile and nodded. Delighted with my progress with her, I bought the bowl.

"Hey, you lot, look what I've found," Leo shouted from the other side of the square. I hadn't notice him leaving us and peered over to see what he was so excited about.

"Come along, girls. You too, Dee," I said, urging them to join him. They didn't need any encouragement and after a slight hesitation even Dee's curiosity was roused. I couldn't help being amused by his childlike enthusiasm. "What have you found?" I asked when we reached him.

We watched a man taking a cooked crêpe from the top of a pile next to him and place it on a hot metal plate. Then lavishly spreading chocolate sauce over the top of the crêpe, he deftly flipped the edges over with his spatula until it was folded into a triangle. He gave us a smile before wrapping the lower two thirds in paper and handing it over to the next customer, after a woman took the money.

"Crêpes with chocolate spread," Leo said, holding up a warm crêpe. He closed his eyes and took a large bite. "Delicious," he mumbled his mouth full of the delicious food.

"Please can I have one?" Katie asked her eyes wide with anticipation. "Ashley wants the same."

I wasn't certain she did, so checked. "Do you?"

She nodded frantically. I placed their order and asked for a third one for me.

"Dee?" I indicated the tempting food. She was painfully thin. I willed her to want one. She'd always loved the crêpes we'd eaten as children, most weeks from this very market. Unable to hide my delight when she nodded, I put my arm around her shoulders and gave her a hug.

"I wonder if they're as good as when we were teenagers," I whispered.

"I doubt it," she said, amusement shining through her eyes.

It was such a joy to have her acting like the Dee I remembered.

We held on to our crêpes, munching them as we made our way back to the house. It had been a fraught start to the day, but the afternoon was more enjoyable than I could have hoped.

I left the girls playing in the garden and unwrapped our packages with Leo in the kitchen.

"You've spoilt Ashley with all these gifts," he said, sounding happy.

"It's my pleasure," I said honestly. "She has so little of her own here and I thought it might help her feel more at home to have a few of her own bits and pieces in the house."

"That's very thoughtful of you, thanks."

We put away the shopping. "Now for the picnic," I said, packing a knife, one of the melons and having washed the grapes and strawberries, added them to Mum's well-used wicker hamper. I rolled up the new towels and took two from the airing cupboard for Katie and me. Finally, we were ready. "I know exactly where I'm taking you," I said, excited at the thought of our outing. "If you don't have costumes Leo can borrow one that Paul left behind. Dee and Ashley can use spares from Katie and me."

I wouldn't tell them where we were going because I wanted it to be a surprise. I was going to do what Mum had done with me when I was small, and we had no money to spare. I recalled her olive green Citroën Deux Chevaux, an older version of my own red and white car, and how upset I'd been when she'd replaced it with a Mercedes. Looking back, her new car suited her character far more than the other, more familiar car had done, but it had been so much a part of my childhood that when the opportunity of buying one came along soon after my return to Epernay, I grabbed it.

Mum took me on so many picnics in her old car over the years. There had been many afternoons when she collected me from school and I'd become excited at the sight of her old wicker hamper sitting on the back seat, knowing we were off on a 'mystery tour', as she called them.

We loaded the car and set off, stopping first at the local *boulangerie* on the edge of our village to buy two baguettes for our sandwiches before driving out past Epernay and into the surrounding hilly countryside. Leo watched the scenery as we drove by and pointed out one especially large vineyard, the bright sunshine glowing against the small imperfections in the stone facade and making it glow as if it was on fire.

"How could I forget how beautiful this place is?"

I slowed down spotting a roadside stall with an untidy

sign letting us know that they had bottles of elderflower juice for sale. I'd stopped here many times over the years and the taste of the sweet drink was like nectar. "We must take some of this with us," I insisted, when Dee groaned as I stopped the car and got out.

I dropped several euros into a plastic tube and took two bottles. These would make the perfect accompaniment for the food I'd brought. I handed the bottles across to Leo and got back into the car.

"I'd forgotten Epernay was the champagne capital of France," Leo said. "Why are my memories about this place so vague?"

I wasn't sure. "Maybe you didn't remember the champagne because you were still too young to drink it when you left."

"More likely it's because Mum couldn't ever afford to buy the stuff," Dee said from her seat in the back between the two girls.

I turned off the main road onto a sloping lane that would lead us down to a quiet spot near the river, perfect for setting up our picnic. The tarmac ended. We continued our lazy drive down a dusty dirt track passing bees and butterflies flitting about the heads of the poppies and cornflowers. Finally, I took one sharp turn and there was the river.

"Thank heavens for that," Dee groaned from the back of the car. "I thought we'd never get here."

"It's lovely," Katie said. "Do you love it, Ashley?"

I glanced in the rear-view mirror and smiled when I saw Ashley nodding shyly, looking at Dee out of the corner of her eye.

"We'll have to come here by ourselves, one day," Dee said to Ashley stroking her hair. The young girl looked up at her shyly.

What was it with those two? I couldn't understand why she was so timid around her mother. Maybe she was like that due to the experiences she'd had over her short life. I thought back to what Leo had said about Dee's past issues and was relieved to be giving Ashley a respite from everything back in England.

"Come on," I said, parking the car and getting out. "Help me with this hamper and these swimming things."

Leo went and lifted the hamper out of the small boot. I handed the bags to Dee unclipping the girls from their car seats and gave each of them a towel to carry. There was no need to lock the car I couldn't see anyone else in the area.

"It's almost two o'clock, we want to make the most of the afternoon," I said catching sight of several sunflowers randomly dotted around the parking area.

"It's so hot," Dee said, closing the boot of the car and following. "We'll need to sit in the shade, or we'll fry in no time."

I agreed and spotting a large oak tree pointed to it. "Over there looks shady enough for us and it's close enough to the water."

I followed Leo to the patch under the tree and helped him set out the rug and unpack the hamper. Realising I'd forgotten our baguettes, I walked back to the car to retrieve them. Dee was fretting over Ashley's lack of shade and rummaging around in her bag, I presumed, for sun cream.

"I can't find her cap," she said, glancing at the little girl.

I grabbed the bread and a spare hat of Katie's and handed it to Dee on my way back to the picnic area.

"Have you got everything you need?" I asked, irritated with myself for not thinking to mention applying protection to the little girl's pale skin before we left the house. I always covered Katie with a layer of cream before she went to school each day in the summer months and forgot it wasn't part of Dee's daily routine with Ashley.

I helped Katie change and, happy to bathe in my T-shirt and shorts, didn't bother to put on my swimming costume. I picked her up and carefully stepped into the cool water. There had been so little rainfall for the previous few months and such heat that the water level was very low and the current light. It was a shame for the farmers having to water their animals further downstream, but for us it was perfect for swimming and paddling about.

"This is bliss," Dee said, closing her eyes while clasping tightly hold of Ashley's hand.

"I think I'll join you," Leo called coming over to us. "Why haven't you brought us here before?" he asked lying back and resting one arm on the bank. "I could have done with this every day of our stay here."

Dee laughed. "I'm quite happy not to have to drive all this way every day, thank you."

"It isn't far." He glared at her as if daring her to argue. "And it's worth the drive."

Katie giggled as Leo splashed water in our direction. I held her around her waist, lifting her and swinging her out of the way of the drops of water and then back again for his next gentle onslaught.

"Right, that's enough now," I said lifting her up towards the bank.

Katie wriggled and pleaded to stay in the water. "More, Maman."

I looked to see if Leo minded and he nodded.

"Two minutes, Katie. No more."

Eventually, our skin began wrinkling like mummified bodies, so I lifted Katie out of the water and onto the bank, the sun glinting off her wet shoulders like diamonds on her golden skin. I ignored her insistence that she hadn't finished playing in the water. "We need to eat something," I said. "Come along, you lot, we can always go back in to the water again."

I draped a towel around her shoulders, which she instantly shrugged off, and set to making everyone sandwiches. "Hand out the plates, Katie," I said to give her something to do.

"This is just what I needed," Dee said, coming with Ashley to join us under the shade of the leafy tree. "Thanks, Sera."

Seeing her so relaxed and enjoying herself with her little girl made me slightly emotional. I swallowed the lump forming in my throat and handed her a plate with some baguette on it. "The fillings for the sandwiches are in there." I pointed to the small cool box in the hamper, sitting back on my haunches and watching as she caringly put together a small plate of food for her daughter. Maybe all she needed was the peace and quiet of the French countryside, days out with nothing to think about but taking it easy and relishing the sunshine. I hoped so because these were things I could give to her.

I wished I'd thought to bring a camera with me. I watched Katie eating and lay back, closing my eyes, listening as she laughed, chattering away to Ashley speaking her usual mixture of French and English. One of these days I was going to have to focus on helping her work out the difference in the language. It was all very well me and Mum understanding her, but not everyone did.

Dee hummed tunelessly to herself and watched Ashley picking at her food. Leo lay back on the rug, closed his eyes and dozed off, snoring lightly while the rest of us finished our lunches.

"I don't mean to be as snappy as I am, Sera," Dee said quietly. "I've had a difficult time of it recently and I think I need a little time to distance myself from the pain."

"Then you're in the perfect place," I said stroking her arm. "You take all the time you need."

After we'd digested our food, we all had another swim to cool down, and wash off the stickiness of the melons from the girls' faces, before piling back into the car and setting off for home. Both girls fell asleep during the journey and as I drove over the crest of the hill towards the town Leo asked me to stop so he could get out and take in the view.

"You're lucky to live here, Sera," he said as we stood side by side looking down through rows of dark green vines, to the church steeple standing high above the town.

I murmured an agreement, enjoying the scene ahead of

the sun shining on the river like a silvery ribbon cutting through the countryside. "I am," I admitted. This was the perfect place for me to bring up my daughter and I was grateful Mum had insisted we return here.

"You should come here when the town is shrouded in mist some mornings," I said. "It's magical."

He looked at me, went to say something and then changed his mind. "We'd better get those two sleepyheads home to bed, they're exhausted."

Dee smiled at him when we joined her in the car. "It was a good day," she said before resting a hand on each of our shoulders. "Thanks, Sera."

I looked at Ashley and Katie, two little girls with such different experiences in life and my heart contracted in pain. Whatever Dee's difficulties with the people around her and however she saw fit to treat Ashley, I needed to support her for the little girl's sake. I couldn't help ease Ashley's life if she was in England and we were in France. For now, I needed to hold my tongue and put Ashley's feelings before my own. Let her enjoy some of the things Katie took for granted. Let her be as carefree as she could be. It was the least I could do.

# Chapter Twelve

1989 – Hautvillers, Near Epernay

## Young Sera

"You take this note to Hazel, you hear me?" My mum said on yet another stinking hot day. I was glad of the excuse to get out of the house and go to the farm despite being fed up with always being clammy and sweaty. The heat made my hair go frizzy, but it didn't seem to make any difference to my mum, she always looked immaculate, as if there might be a photographer lurking behind a corner waiting to take her photo at any second. I had no idea how she managed to pull it off especially on days like this one.

She glanced at my nails and shook her head. "Oh, Sera," she grimaced. "Don't you have any taste at all? Acid yellow nail polish, how revolting. Where did you find such a vile colour?"

I didn't like to admit it was one of Hazel's varnishes. "I think it looks sunny."

She gave me a disapproving look and tapped the envelope in my hand.

"What does it say?" I asked, hoping to change the subject before she gave me one of her full-on lectures about being more ladylike. I held it up to the living room window to try and see through the thick cream envelope she'd sealed shut.

"Never you mind," she snapped. "Just make sure you don't forget to hand it to her personally. I want to be certain she's read it."

Intrigued by this out of character friendliness towards Dee's mum, I stared at her open-mouthed. "But Mum, you hate Hazel," I said, confused. "Why are you writing to her?"

"I don't hate her." She frowned, something she didn't often do as the thought of wrinkles horrified her. "And stop looking gormless, the wind will change if you're not careful and you'll end up looking like that for the rest of your life."

I shook my head. "Why won't you tell me what it says?"

She tilted her head to one side and glared at me. "Stop being so nosy. Do as I ask, or you can stay here, and I'll take it over to her and give you chores to do while I'm gone." As expected, she knew her threat would work. I pushed a strand of hair away from my face and walked to the door. "I'll be expecting a reply too, so don't think you can go and read this sneakily with that daughter of hers."

My hackles rose at her nastiness towards my best friend. "Why don't you like her?"

She rubbed her temples with her fingertips. "I do. It's this heat, it's getting me down. Now stop answering me back and get a move on. Make sure you give it to her."

I crammed the envelope into my denim shorts pocket and ran out of the house, through the garden and out of the heavy wooden gate. Sometimes she really got on my nerves. I didn't understand why she was so horrible about that family. What had they ever done to her?

Dee must have been waiting for me to come out of our garden, because as soon as I'd gone through the gateway, I saw her in the field.

"We're going to the pool in the woods," Dee shouted, waving me over to her.

Irritated with Mum, I was in no rush to deliver her letter. I waded through the long grasses to join Dee. I noticed Leo ambling along behind her as if he was trying not to be noticed.

"Hi, Leo," I said guiltily when I saw his scabbed knee through his worn, jeans. "Sorry again for pulling you out of the tree the other day."

"It's okay," he mumbled, shuffling his feet in the dusty ground.

"I should have let Pierre rescue the cat from the apple tree like he suggested." I thought back to the incident and rubbed my arm. "Damn thing clawed me and jumped down by itself anyway."

Leo said something I couldn't hear.

"It wasn't even our cat, you dope." Dee laughed, then glancing at her brother, added, "Come on, ignore him. He's just weird. Do you think of my hair?"

"It's great," I said, envious that she always managed to get her hair bigger than mine. "You're so lucky having curly hair, mine's so flat with just a bit of frizz." I stared enviously at the colourful silk scarf tied around her head. "Is that one of your mum's scarves you've nicked?"

"Yeah." She giggled and punched me playfully on the arm.

"Maybe you could come to my house the next time Mum's away and we can try bleaching our hair?" I said bravely.

Remembering the letter I was supposed to deliver, I added, "I need to take something to your mum."

"Surely it can wait?" Dee asked waving a fly away from her face.

Hazel and Mum were so different, I mused as we walked through the field. I never would have found a collection of *Angelique* books in Mum's bookshelves. Dee's mum never seemed to work. I was sure Mum would be more relaxed if she didn't need to travel away on location so often. She was never carefree enough to dance through the wildflowers outside like I'd spotted Hazel doing a few times in the small field closest to her farmhouse.

Everything about Hazel was light and fun; she even smelt amazing. In fact, the scent of patchouli and sandalwood emanated throughout her untidy farmhouse. She was like a gypsy princess from one of my childhood fairy tales with her wild curly black hair.

She'd never choke me with hairspray, or spend hours making sure everything in the house was exactly in its place. No one cared if the furniture was a bit dusty, or the beds were left unmade for a day at the farm. Nothing was ever done on the spur of the moment at my house, unlike at Hazel's farm where she somehow conjured a party seamlessly with her guests dancing in the field or the barn with candles pushed into makeshift holders nailed onto the walls. Mum's idea of a party was dull people standing around our living room holding cocktails with me having to walk around the room offering canapés from a tray.

"Do you think your mum might have another party soon?" I asked Dee as we ran through the field.

"Tonight maybe," she said stopping for breath. "You know what she's like."

I pictured the sixty or seventy people at her most recent party. Someone lit a bonfire in one of the nearby fields and everyone carried a chair or old piece of tree trunk to sit on. Once organised with drinks the guests sang, danced and smoked suspicious smelling cigarettes and the fun always carried on until mid-morning the following day.

"Do you have that cigarette with you?"

Dee glanced back to make sure Leo wasn't near enough to hear us. "I don't want him splitting on us and telling Pierre I've nicked this," she said, stopping right next to me, slowly pushing her hand inside her front pocket and carefully extracting the rolled-up cigarette we'd pinched from him the night before when he wasn't looking.

"Do you think we should?" I giggled. I liked Hazel's boyfriend, he was fine with us as long as we didn't bug him and Hazel at the parties.

"We'll lose Leo and smoke it in the woods," she whispered.

I'd once heard my mum commenting that Hazel spent her life surrounded by noise to block out her past. I couldn't imagine it being true though. I just assumed Mum was jealous of Hazel and her spontaneous, carefree life.

I touched my pocket lightly feeling the letter underneath

the material. "I need to give something to your mum," I admitted.

"Mum's writing songs again and wants some peace," Dee said. "We have to stay away from the farm for a bit."

"You must be excited that she's writing songs again?"

"None of her other songs have ever done anything," Dee pouted. "She gets really down when something doesn't work out. I wish she wouldn't have these bouts of trying."

"What does Pierre think?"

"He thinks it's a good thing," Leo said. "He says she's got a beautiful voice and should make the most of it."

"Why don't you bugger off," Dee shouted pushing him roughly on his shoulder. "Sera and I've got stuff to talk about." When he didn't change direction, she added. "Private things."

"You bugger off." He glowered at her and stomped off in a different direction.

"Good," she said. "Now we can smoke this and see what it's like."

We ran towards the shade of the wood, jumping over stinging nettles and flowers as they came across our path. I was a bit nervous to see what happened when we did smoke Pierre's strange smelling roll-up, but ran through the trees enjoying being cool for a change.

"I really need to deliver this to your mum," I said pulling the letter out of my back pocket and waving it in front of Dee's face.

"What's in it?" she asked.

"No idea."

She snatched it from me and studied it. "Typical, your mum sealed it. Come on, let's sneak into the house and steam it open."

"We can't," I snapped, reaching to take it. Dee swung away from me and held it high before tugging gently at the top to try and peak inside.

"Typical of your mum to use a fancy thick envelope," Dee moaned.

It was. I squinted up through the trees at the cornflower blue sky. "I don't care if Hazel's writing, my mum will kill me if I don't deliver this letter today."

"Fine. We'll smoke this tomorrow then." She sighed heavily and got up.

We hurried to the farm. Leo was just arriving at the edge of the wood, waving a stick to knock the blood red petals from the poppies standing in his path.

"Don't do that, you moron," Dee shouted, pushing his shoulder, grabbing the stick and throwing it away from him.

"Hey, that's mine."

"Tough," I shouted. Poppies were my favourite flower and he'd annoyed me by being destructive.

We ran as fast as we could to the farm, running up the front steps and into the house. The front door banged loudly against the hall wall to signify our arrival.

"What the hell are you lot doing?" Hazel shouted. "You were supposed to leave me in peace for a few hours."

"It's not her fault." I held the envelope out towards her. "Mum said I had to bring you this. She's waiting for your reply."

"Your mum?" Hazel stared at the envelope in my hand as if I was trying to hand her a lit firework. "What's it about?"

I shook my head wondering why she was acting so odd. "No idea."

She took it from me, slowly turning the envelope over and studying it, "It says '*Hazel*'."

I'm not sure what else she expected to see written on an envelope, it was for her after all. I knew Mum could be a bit of a control freak, but she wasn't that scary, not really.

Hazel took a deep breath and turned to go back into the living room. "I'd better read it then."

Dee and I followed her in silence, glancing at Pierre who was staring out of the window.

"Hello, girls," he said turning to face us.

I spotted the packet with his nicked cigarette sticking out of Dee's shorts pocket and pulled a face at her. She noticed.

"What?" she mouthed frowning.

I looked pointedly at her pocket and she moved behind a chair out of Pierre's line of vision and pushed the pack further inside.

"I thought you were told to stay away for a few hours," he said looking from us to Hazel.

Hazel explained about the letter. She pulled open a small drawer, retrieving a silver paperknife. We watched in anticipation as she slid the blade into the paper and ripped it open in one clean swipe. She carefully took out the single sheet of paper and opened it. She'd only just started reading when she gasped. Clamping a hand to her mouth she reached for the back of the sofa sat down clutching the paper in her hand.

Pierre rushed to her side and crouched down in front of her, trying and failing to take the letter from her grasp.

"Mum, what's the matter?" Dee asked. "What did Maureen say?" She glanced up at me accusatorily and I widened my eyes trying to show that I was innocent of any wrongdoing. I was as ignorant as she about the contents.

"Are you okay?" I asked my voice shaky from fright.

She didn't react.

"Of course she's not, you idiot," Dee shouted.

"Girls, stop." Hazel put her hand out to take mine and gave it a little squeeze. "It's not Sera's fault." She hesitated. "I've just had a bit of a fright. I'll be fine."

I watched her for a bit, summoning up the courage before asking, "What should I tell Mum?"

"Tell her?" She averted her eyes. "Let me think for a minute."

We stood watching her. Pierre stroked her legs and I waited for her to reply. I'd never seen Hazel like this before and couldn't imagine what Mum must have told her. I wasn't sure I wanted to know either, not if this was how much it upset people.

Eventually, she sat upright and forced a smile. "I'm fine. Sera. Please tell your mum I've received her note. I feel the same way she does, and I'll be sure to do as she asked."

What the hell did that mean? I frowned, disappointed not to be any the wiser.

"I'm scared," I heard Leo say quietly from the doorway.

"No, baby, it's nothing for you to worry about." She hugged Pierre tightly, then let go waving Leo over and ruffled his hair. "I just have to think things through for a bit." She looked up at me. "If Mo…" she hesitated. "Your mum needs to speak to me again about this, she can give me a call. She has my number." She smiled at Pierre and stood up. "Tell her, I'll meet her, if she thinks it would be better." She waved me away. "You'd better go home now, Sera. Let Mo know what I've said. She'll be waiting to hear from you."

I hesitated and glanced at Dee. Hazel rarely referred to Mum at all and when she did she didn't mention her by name. To hear her use a shortened version of her name was odd to say the least. She made it sound as if they were real friends at one point. They certainly shared some sort of history, even though it was something neither of them seemed to want to share with the rest of us.

I sensed that something terrible had happened, or was about to happen. I couldn't work out what. I struggled not to panic. "What's wrong, Hazel?" I asked, my voice quivering with fear. Were we in danger? "I don't understand what's happening," I admitted, too frightened to keep quiet. "What has Mum told you?"

"What's happening?" Dee asked starting to cry.

I looked at my friend and then to Hazel, who was staring at her hands, a haunted look in her eyes. There must be something badly wrong. Why else would she react this way and why would our mums, who never bothered with each other, make contact now?

"It's not for me to say," Hazel said eventually. She

grabbed me and pulled me to her holding me tightly for longer than felt necessary. She then kissed the top of my head and taking my wrist pulled me to the front door and pushed me outside. "Hurry home now. Don't stop for anything along the way."

# Chapter Thirteen

## 2003 – Hautvillers, Near Epernay

### Sera

Mum was away on a shoot for a week and Katie went down with a sore throat, so I was tied to the house more than usual. The heat added to her misery and she cried if I left her even if for a short time. I bought several electric fans and plugged them in at various locations in the house in a vain attempt to circulate some of the air. Placing bowls of ice in front of the fans helped but only slightly. I would have given a lot for air conditioning, but it wasn't something we could afford to have installed. I had to stop feeling sorry for myself and Katie and do the best I could. Poor Katie only wanted to eat ice cream and drink orange juice for several days and all of us were thoroughly sick of the heat.

When she was feeling a little better, I rummaged around in the basement and found an old blow-up paddling pool. Leo cleaned it, setting it up for me in the shadiest part of the garden under the large pear tree. After a little encouragement, Ashley nervously stepped in to the water and eventually, having watched Katie pretending to swim for a few minutes, joined her.

Both girls spent hours staying cool despite the heat of the day, by wallowing in the water and it was a relief that Katie had cheered up.

Apart from the occasional topping up from buckets filled at the outside tap to keep the water cool, all we had to do was watch them and fan ourselves and I looked forward to her returning to playgroup, so that I could get on with my work at the studio.

"What are all these tubs you've got dotted around the garden for?" Dee asked one morning.

"They're for Mummy's birds and little animals to have a drink," Katie told her, puffing out her chest in pride that she knew more than an adult about something.

"What a good idea," Dee said, peering into one of the pots. "This one needs refilling." She went to take it into the kitchen. "This heat is exhausting. If we don't get some rain soon I'm going to go mad with this hay fever, it's getting worse by the day." She sneezed as she reached the kitchen door.

Later that day, I left Katie with Dee and Ashley and walked to the small corner shop at the end of our road to buy some sweets for the girls.

"Ahh, Sera," said Madame du Val. "You have heard the news?"

"I don't think so," I said, not sure to what news she was referring.

"It is the tenant. The one at the farm?"

I nodded eager for her to continue, but not wishing her

to see how anxious her comment made me. I picked up two paper bags and using the small plastic scoop, half-filled them with a mixture of sweets for Katie and Ashley.

"He was taken by the gendarmes for questioning at the station," she said.

"When?" I asked unable to hide my panic.

She gave a one-shouldered shrug and pulled a face. "Yesterday morning." Her delight at my reaction exhausted, she eventually added. "They released him in the afternoon."

Old crone, looking so self-satisfied. I'd never liked her and rarely used her shop, but today I was too lazy to walk far in the oppressive heat. Why anyone could glean enjoyment from someone else's misery I could not imagine. She weighed the sweets I'd selected and twisting the tops, handed them to me, holding out her wrinkled hand for payment.

"He's a good man, you know," I said, counting my coins and handing her a couple of euros.

She closed her fingers over the metal and shook her head, pressing the total on the old till and dropping the euros into it. She took out my change, checked it and handed to me. "Too many changes and too many strangers; everything is different in Epernay now."

She turned her attention to the ancient fan above her head and switched it to a higher speed. "There have been fires reported south of here," she added her voice doom-filled and dour.

"Hopefully we'll have rain soon, then we won't have to worry about the fires," I answered as cheerily as I could manage, desperate to cut short this depressing conversation and leave her shop.

I hurried home to deliver their sweets.

Having received Dee's assurance that I could give Ashley the sweets, I called both girls into the kitchen. "Both packets have the same amount of sweets," I told them as I handed out a bag to each of the delighted little girls. They ran to play upstairs.

I went to find Mum to ask her to look after Katie while I paid Henri a visit when the doorbell rang.

"I'll get that," I shouted. I walked up to the front door and pulled it open. Two gendarmes stood, grim-faced on the doorstep. Recovering my shock at seeing them there, I opened my mouth to speak. "Can I help you?" They explained that they wished to ask Leo and Dee some questions. "But, what about?"

"We are unable to discuss this with anyone but the two people mentioned," one snapped. "Now, if you would take us to them?"

"Of course, I'm sorry," I said stepping back to give them space to enter the hallway. "Please, come this way."

I showed them to the living room. It was stifling in there. For some reason neither Mum nor I had remembered to open the double doors onto the balcony overlooking the garden. As I did so, I heard something drop behind me and noticed Dee staring, an open book at her feet.

"What... what are they doing here?" she whispered glaring at me, all colour disappearing from her face.

"Sorry, Dee," I said, wishing I could have warned her.

"They want to speak to you and Leo. Is he in?"

She stared wide-eyed at the gendarmes. "What? Um, outside maybe?" She stepped towards the door. "I'll go and look for him."

"*Non.*" The taller of the two men stepped in front of the open doorway to block it. He nodded in my direction. "You, please go and fetch him."

I gave Dee a reassuring smile. She had been slightly calmer and more relaxed lately and it irked me that these visitors would no doubt change that. "I'll be as quick as I can. Sit down. I'm sure this won't take long."

She sat, her back straight as she picked at the skin on the side of her thumb.

I rushed out of the room, aware that I could have no idea how long their questions would take or even why they wished to ask Leo and Dee any at all. Reaching the back door, I ran down the stairs to the garden.

"Where's Leo?" I asked Mum, who was standing at the far end of the garden facing Paul. She had a script in one hand with the other in the air, her fist clasped as if holding a dagger. Paul was holding his own script and grabbed her by the throat with his free hand. "Two gendarmes are here," I shouted as I neared them. "They want to speak to him and Dee about something."

Mum turned to me, her legs almost giving way. Paul grabbed hold of her and led her to a nearby seat. "You okay, Maureen?" he asked. "Blimey, it's not as if they want to speak to you," he joked.

I did my best not to give him a mouthful. Why was he

always so useless in a crisis? Mum was not someone who liked to cause a scene, or show any weakness, so her reaction confused me. I walked over to her seat and knelt on the grass next to it. "You okay, Mum?"

"Yes, yes," she snapped. "It's the heat. We've been out here too long, and it's got to me, that's all. Stop making a fuss." She waved me away like an annoying wasp.

I stood up, knowing to leave her alone. "Do you know where I can find Leo?" I asked, picturing Dee's anxiety at being left alone with the gendarmes in the living room. "I've left Dee alone long enough already."

The sound of the front door slamming against the hall wall made me and Mum jump. "What the…?"

"Dee," Leo shouted. "Where the hell are you?"

I ran to the back steps and into the house.

"Why are the gendarmes here?" he demanded. "And where's my sister and Ashley?"

"She's in the living room," I said, assuming he must have seen the gendarmes car parked outside the front of the house. I noticed the living room door was closed and was certain I'd left it open earlier. "They're only here to ask you and her a few questions. I think Ashley's upstairs with Katie. I'll keep her away, don't fret."

He took a deep breath. "I don't mean to act like a lunatic, but she's too fragile to be left alone with them."

I watched him go. When he'd closed the door I leant in closer, but was only able to hear muffled voices and the occasional snippet about the dead body at the farm. Why would they be asking Dee and Leo about that? I wondered.

I lived nearby and would have more reason to be involved in any questioning than two people who hadn't lived here for nearly twenty years.

I heard crying and Leo was, as usual, doing his best to comfort his sister. I remembered Ashley and went up to her room to check on her.

Opening the door quietly, I watched as she hummed to the teddy Katie had given her. She seemed fine, so I crept back out and closed the door after me not wishing her to hear the commotion downstairs. I wanted to find out if the gendarmes were intending staying much longer. I didn't think the strained atmosphere was healthy for the little girl. It dawned on me that maybe I should make enquiries at the playgroup to see if Ashley could attend with Katie. It would probably do her good to get out of the house and meet some other little girls.

I went to check on Katie. She was lying on top of her bed brushing her doll's hair. "Ashley wants her mummy," she said when I crouched down to straighten her doll's skirt.

I stroked her face. "She'll be fine, sweetheart, you mustn't worry."

Satisfied they hadn't been disturbed by the latest goings on in the house, I went back outside to see if Mum was feeling better. She and Paul were continuing with their rehearsal as if nothing had happened. It was as if I'd imagined her reaction minutes earlier. Maybe it had been the heat that had caused her to become light-headed, it was another hot and humid day.

I wished she didn't feel the need to always appear strong

in front of me. She had once told me when I had asked where my father was, that she was both mother and father to me. I presumed that she felt it was her duty, therefore, to always hide her fears from me. Unfortunately, it also meant that she kept her innermost thoughts and emotions from me, too. I knew she found my openness difficult to cope with at times and must question why I hadn't absorbed more of the reserved side of her nature. I tried to picture what my father must have been like for me to be so different to her.

I noticed her picking at her thumbnail. "You okay, Mum?" I asked, trying not to let her see how much it upset me to see her get such a fright. "Do you need me to do anything for you?"

She gave me her best actress smile. "Darling, don't I look perfectly fine?"

"That's the point of my question, how do I know when I'm looking at the real 'you'?" I teased.

"That's not funny, Seraphina," she said, glaring at me. Her large eyes darkened. I couldn't think why she was taking my silly joke so badly.

"Hey, relax. I was only messing about," I said. When she didn't look like she was going to calm down, I added. "You know that, surely?"

She stared at me for a little longer. I could almost see her thoughts clambering through her mind. She glanced up at the living room window where Leo and Dee were still ensconced with the two gendarmes and then back at me. Finally, her shoulders lowered slightly. She gave me a half smile.

"Maybe, but it wasn't very funny."

I couldn't see why not, but didn't vocalise my thoughts, she had enough to cope with for one day without an unnecessary quarrel with me. "I really didn't mean to upset you." I changed the subject by telling about my idea for Ashley joining Katie at playgroup.

She leant closer to me and lowered her voice. "She could do with getting away from that nutty mother of hers occasionally. Dee's obsessed with that child."

I couldn't agree more. I nodded my agreement. I made sure Mum was okay and then walked back into the house, stopping in the hallway, but could only make out hushed voices coming from the living room.

A while later, I thought I'd better check on the girls again, so went upstairs to find Katie and Ashley.

"Hey girls," I said opening Katie's door to her completely pink bedroom. "How are you both?"

Katie held up a ragdoll that Mum had bought her when she was very small and said, "Ashley doesn't have any dolls." When I looked concerned at this snippet of information, she nudged Ashley. "Do you, Ashley?"

The little girl stared wide-eyed at me for a second and then shook her head slowly. She almost looked guilty, as if she was betraying a secret.

"Are the gendarmes speaking with Leo and Ashley's mummy?"

I crouched down next to Katie. "Have you been downstairs?"

Ashley looked terrified. Sorry to have frightened her, I

cupped her chin and smiled. "It's okay," I said in what I hoped was a soothing voice. "I won't tell anyone." I looked down at Katie. "You should probably keep this a secret, too. Okay?"

She nodded her head vigorously. "Yes, Maman." She put an arm around Ashley's skinny shoulders. "Are they telling them off?"

"Don't be silly, Katie," I said.

The contrast in these children was incredible, Katie with her bubbly character, golden-tanned skin and pudgy arm, next to Ashley's almost luminescent skin. I would have hugged Ashley if I didn't suspect me doing so would terrify her. I wondered when her birthday might be, and if maybe Katie and I could buy her a doll then without offending Dee.

I waited for Dee and Leo to come out of the living room, but after a while my impatience got the better of me. I decided I could be making better use of my time rather than hovering around in the hallway doing nothing. I needed to prepare my stock for my regular stall in the market and would have loved to pop out to my studio and sort through everything but didn't leave in case Dee needed me to look after Ashley later.

The lack of breeze through the house, despite the fans and all the downstairs windows being opened, left the place with a fuggy air about it. It wasn't simply the tension between us that instilled heaviness about this place. I couldn't help thinking it must be our determination to discover hidden truths about each other that no one was willing to share. Maybe if I opened all the other windows some of this oppressive tension would dissipate?

I walked slowly up the stairs, going from room to room checking all the windows were open. The sun streamed into my bedroom. I ran my hand over the thick layers of white paint on the wooden shutters. These would need to be repainted soon, I thought, aware Mum despised her home to be anything less than immaculate, at least to the eyes of the outside world. I pulled them closed to keep in as much shade as possible before leaving the room and crossing the landing to go up the stairs to the attic to Dee's and Leo's bedrooms.

Entering Leo's room at the front of the house, I opened his window and pulled the small single shutter closed. Nothing was out of place. I could see his rucksack on the top of the wardrobe. There wasn't a crease on his bed sheets or pillow. Next to his bed a single book lay beside a carafe of water, its lid a clean glass resting upside down, both of them joined by a plain lamp on the oak bedside table. I smiled at the simplicity of the room and turned to leave. Leo's beige linen jacket, placed neatly on a wooden hanger was hanging from the hook on the back of the bedroom door moving slowly from side to side from the jolting of me opening the door.

Where had he been all these years? I wondered where the rest of his things must be and what his home would be like back in England. He must miss his personal effects; I know I would if I had to be away from everything for long. I didn't own much, but my photos and books were precious to me, as were an overnight case crammed with Katie's baby clothes, drawings she had done for me at playschool, and little gifts and cards Mum helped her make for me on birthdays and other special occasions.

I entered the larger attic room. This was another sight entirely. Clothes were strewn on every surface, including the floor. I hadn't realised Dee had managed to fit so many items in her bag when she'd been brought here. Ashley's bed, on the other hand, was roughly made, but tidy. It seemed odd for such a little girl to take pride in her bed. The teddy Katie had given her was resting against her pillow. Tears welled in my eyes, blurring the vision in front of me. I wanted to look after her. Teach her to be a little girl and not spend her time worrying so much.

Remembering what I'd come up here for, I hurried over to the two square windows and opened them, pushing them as far out as I could. This room above all the others needed fresh, clean air to waft through it blowing away the tension and the fear. Even though it wasn't my room, I couldn't help hanging up and folding away Dee's T-shirts and straightening her bedclothes. I heard the front door slam downstairs.

Quickly leaving the bedroom, I ran down the stairs. Dee rushed passed me, panic etched on her taut face. "She's in Katie's room," I said before she had time to ask her daughter's whereabouts.

"Thanks," she said giving me a forced smile. "I need to give her a cuddle. She always makes me feel better when she hugs me."

I smiled, understanding her sentiment.

Leo must have gone through to the kitchen, or outside,

because I didn't see him on my way to the cellar. He always seemed to be busy doing nothing much, which I found a little odd. I presumed he wasn't used to having spare time and not quite knowing what to do with himself when he was away from work. I reached up and lifted the small hook that I'd installed far out of Katie's reach and turning on the Bakelite light switch, walked into the huge cavernous room. Looking at the enamel signs I was going to take to the market, I tried to get my head around the recent changes in my life.

I began sorting through the signs, being careful not to allow any of them to chip another. I preferred the distressed signs, but many buyers wanted them to look perfect. My arms ached in the warm dim room after moving so many of them into two rows. It didn't matter how I tried to focus on what I was doing I couldn't stop thinking about how my small family's lives had changed since Dee and Leo's arrival. I rested my hands on my waist and arched my back to try and ease the ache. Spotting the plait of garlic hanging from the hook nearby I was reminded of Henri and realised nothing made sense any more. It hadn't made sense for some time!

# Chapter Fourteen
## 1976 – Paris

## Mo

It was hard to imagine I hadn't known Vince two months ago and now, here I was, relaxing against pale blue leather seats in the back an immaculate Citroen DS. The leather was cool against my skin. I barely contained my excitement. I still couldn't quite believe we were travelling with Jack, Vince, and a group of their friends to see the David Bowie concert in Paris that everyone had been talking about for months. I loved Bowie and his Thin White Duke persona was my favourite so far. When Vince suggested taking Hazel and me with him to Paris two days previously, neither of us could believe our luck and had been ecstatic with excitement.

To be attending this concert was something I couldn't have dreamt about when we had been introduced to Vince that night. So much had changed for me since meeting Hazel and Vince. I was living the life I'd imagined. Well, not quite, but I was getting there and seeing glamour and wealth that I couldn't even imagine before leaving home.

I half listened to Vince chatting to Jean-Paul, our driver for the journey, about some phone calls he needed to make. I gazed out of the window as we passed vibrant fields that looked as if an artist had got carried away with the abundant greens and yellows on his palette. There so few buildings compared to driving in the lush British countryside and the tiny villages were pretty with many of their windowsills graced with tubs of scarlet geraniums.

I couldn't help thinking how glad I was that Alice was unable to come with us. I pushed away a guilty pang at the notion that she'd been called back to her family's estate in Hereford for her grandfather's funeral. It was easy to do; I knew Alice wouldn't give me a second thought if the tables were turned and I'd been the one having to miss out on this trip.

Jack was travelling with his mistress and a couple of his and Vince's other friends in the car behind us. Mistress. What would my parents think if they knew I was mixing with people who openly flaunted their lover in front of friends? The thought thrilled me. I loved my new life. I was eager to make the most of any opportunity that presented itself to me and this had to be the most exciting experience so far.

"Pull over here, Jean-Paul," Vince said as we entered a tiny village which didn't seem to consist of much more than a café and a tobacconist. "If you girls need to use the bathroom, now's the time," Vince said getting out of the car and holding the doors open for us.

Hazel and I stepped out. I stretched, watching her staring

after Vince as he walked with Jack to the tiny shop.

"We'd better get a move on," Hazel said. "We don't want to keep him waiting."

I bit back a retort. I didn't like her assuming she knew best how we should behave around Vince. He had been sitting next to me in the back of the car, while insisting she sat in the front and was certain he fancied me more than he did her. Vince was charming though, I mused as we walked towards the café and asked in schoolgirl French to use the bathroom, maybe he had led her to believe she was the special one. I clenched my teeth at the thought.

"You don't know him nearly as well as you think you do," I whispered as we washed our hands in the small cracked basin on the wall, studying my eyeshadow and mascara to check it still looked pristine.

She gave me a knowing smile. "Maybe, you're the delusional one, Mo. Have you ever considered that?"

I straightened the bodice on my crimson dress that Vince had treated me to before coming away. "No," I said simply satisfied with my reflection.

"What are you both doing in there?" Vince bellowed from outside.

We both hurriedly retouched our lipstick and ran out to join him. "Sorry, Vince," we said in unison, glaring at each other for a split second.

"Get in and let's go."

We had been driving for a few minutes when Vince's hand moved slightly up my thigh. "Glad you came?" he asked, a twinkle in his eyes.

I giggled. "What do you think?" I said enjoying this attention and understanding why he'd insisted Hazel sat in the front with Jean-Paul. "I've never been to France before. It's very different, isn't it?" I asked, relieved that Vince had somehow arranged for me to have a passport at such short notice. I would have been heartbroken if he had left me behind and only brought Hazel.

"Of course, it's different," Hazel sniggered, as if she knew more about the country than me. I tensed, disliking the prospect of her needing to emphasise that my only experience of life had been a mundane life in a rural town outside Manchester.

"We're on the Continent now, Mo, not back in some bucolic village."

I hoped I would have hidden my jealousy of her if she'd been the one Vince chose to sit next to him. She'd never shown this side of her character before. Maybe she wasn't the sweet, innocent girl we all took her for?

"Now, that's not very friendly, is it?" Vince said, resting a large hand heavily on her bare tanned shoulder, while giving my thigh a little squeeze with his other hand.

I snuggled a little closer to him relishing the closeness between us. "It's okay," I said, enjoying her ignorance of his flirtation. I loved it when he stood up for me. One of these days he would be telling people I was his girlfriend, if I had my way. "I'm sure Hazel didn't mean to sound so nasty."

She laughed. I could hear the embarrassment in her voice and couldn't help feeling a little sorry for her. "I didn't mean to sound snappy with you," she admitted. "But you forget,

Mo, it was only a few months ago that you came to London and you've still got a lot to learn about how everything works in the big city."

"Maybe not as much as you think," I said as sweetly as I could manage. Vince nudged me lightly with his elbow and mouthed, 'naughty girl' to me. If only she knew about our two secret meetings when she was working at the café or away at auditions. I pushed away the image of Hazel's disappointment if she ever discovered that some of my auditions had in fact been assignations with the man that filled both of our daydreams.

"I want you girls to enjoy yourselves," he said, his voice a little louder than usual. "I didn't bring you on this trip for you to snipe at each other."

"Sorry, Vince," we said in unison.

"Good. Now, Hazel, I want you to get a sense of the set up when we get to the concert. The stage, sound, lights, atmosphere, that sort of thing."

"Me?" she said in her sweetest voice.

"Yes. Look, I'm not suggesting you'll ever be on the same level as Bowie," he laughed at the thought, "but if you want to eventually tour, it won't hurt for you to see how true genius operates."

"I understand," she said.

"And me?" I asked, unable to hide my envy. "Why have you brought me along?"

He laughed a deep, sexy laugh that brightened everything around him. His beautiful lips drew back in a wide smile; he was so handsome my heart contracted painfully. "I brought you, beautiful Mo, because I know you're his biggest fan and I was hoping I might be able to wangle an introduction with the-god-that-is-Bowie for you."

"Seriously?" When he nodded I squealed, not caring if I was making a show of myself. "Do you really think you can do that?"

He winked at me. "I'll do my best to make it happen."

"Have you met him before?"

He gave me that movie star smile of his again. "Yup, and he's a great guy."

Vince went up even higher in my estimation at this news. "Do you hear that, Hazel? Vince has met Bowie."

"I am in the car with you," she groaned. "And I'm not deaf."

His hand moved higher and eager for his touch, I slid down slightly in my chair, stifling a gasp when his fingers cupped my right breast. "Why don't you close your eyes and have a doze," he said.

"Who, me?" Hazel asked pulling down the sunshade and gazing at him in the mirror.

"Both of you." I watched him smile at her. "It's a long drive to Paris and we've got a late night ahead. I'm going to grab forty winks while I have the chance and it'll be easier if you two stop sniping at each other and give me a bit of peace to have a kip." He tapped Jean-Paul on his shoulder. "Put on some music, will you, mate?"

For a moment I felt disappointed, believing he meant what he'd said. I saw Hazel turning her head to one side and closing her eyes, doing exactly as she was told. Jean-Paul twiddled around with the radio until he found something by Roxy Music. As the first strains of 'Love is the Drug' began to play, Vince closed his eyes, but not before giving me a wink. He was certainly my drug of choice. Then again, I hadn't tried anything stronger than a few timid puffs from his joint.

He bent his head and kissed my shoulder lightly.

"You're so perfect," he whispered.

I opened my eyes to look at him, catching Jean-Paul's gaze through the rear-view mirror. I could tell he was smiling. Horrified, I took my hand from Vince's and wriggled my bottom backward into the seat trying to distance myself from him, hoping the driver didn't work out what had just been going on in the back of his car. He looked away, focusing on the road, but I sensed he was fully aware of what Vince had just done.

I glanced at Vince and nodded towards Jean-Paul. He shrugged. "Don't worry about it."

I hadn't done anything like this before. Did these people do this sort of thing often? I wondered. My mother constantly accused me of wanting to grow up too fast. Leaving home to find some excitement had been my ambition for as long as I could remember, but there were so many aspects of this new life that hadn't occurred to me before I'd moved to London. Maybe it was because I was mixing with sophisticated people? This crowd wouldn't be constricted by old-fashioned, unnecessary morals. I realised I would have to be a little less sensitive if I wanted to be one of them.

He kissed the side of my neck and my resolve vanished. Vince smelt so good. He was nothing like the pasty-faced, spotty boys at home. He spoilt me by treating me like a princess and buying me unexpected gifts, my favourite being the beautiful crimson dress, with matching shoes and bag that I was wearing. I smoothed it down to try and eradicate the slight creases that had formed during the journey and sighed, relieved I'd saved myself for a real man.

The next thing I knew, the car was stopping. "Oh, look," Hazel squealed from her front seat. I woke with a start. Desperate to rub my eyes, I remembered just in time that I was wearing make-up.

"Hurry up, you two," her sing-song voice pierced through my half-asleep brain. "Look at that."

I peered out of the car window and saw the top two stages of the Eiffel Tower. Fuelled with delight, I wound down the window.

"Look, Vince," I said. When he didn't reply, I turned to look at him over my shoulder. "Look, it's the Eiffel Tower. Isn't it incredible?" I reached back to grab his hand.

He took my hand in one of his and gently pushed my cheek so that I was once again looking away from him out of the window. "It's your first view of Paris," he said. "Look at it properly.

I could feel his warm breath on my shoulders, and shivered. I sensed Hazel glaring at us. When she didn't look away, I frowned. "What's the matter with you?"

She stared at me for a bit and then turned her attention to Vince, her face softening almost instantly as she forced a smile back onto her face and turned to stare out of the window. "Nothing," she said sweetly.

Jean-Paul, satisfied we had seen the view, started the car and drove on again. I couldn't help feeling a little guilty; after all she had met Vince before me and never made any secret about her crush on him. I pretended to stare at the beautiful scene in front of us, the beaux arts architecture my dad talked about and Notre Dame in the distance. The wind rushed through my sleep muzzled hair and I tried to fix everything I was feeling at that moment into my mind to remember forever. My anticipation of the next few days gave me a buzz I wanted to savour.

Hazel was the one who told me only the night before in our tiny shared room to make the most of every experience that came our way. We both wanted success, and both wanted Vince. We had little money and only one chance to make our new life in London work for us. I wasn't going to hold back and end up having to return home, not if I could possibly help it.

"Do you want me to keep going into the city, boss?" Jean-Paul asked breaking the tense silence that had taken over the car.

"We can drive along Quai de Montebello and stop off quickly at Shakespeare & Company," Vince said. "I know you've mentioned going there, Hazel." He gave her one of his appealing smiles. She beamed, giving me a sideways glance that contained all the smugness I would have felt if I'd been on the receiving end of his attention. I knew we were acting like children, but the stakes were so high as far as we were concerned.

He squeezed me gently to him. "And as for you, beautiful girl, what can I show you?" He winked at me and my jealousy seeped away.

"I'm sure Mo doesn't know anything about Paris," Hazel said, once again staring out of the window. "Let alone the best places to visit."

"Then maybe we should educate her," he said. "What do you think, Mo?"

I tried to keep the excitement out of my voice. I was in Paris and I was in love. Could life be any better?

"Umm," I tried to picture the famous places I might have heard about, but nothing came to mind. "How about the hunchback of Notre Dame?"

Hazel screamed with hysterical laughter.

"What?" I couldn't understand her amusement.

"That's ridiculous," Hazel mocked. "You do know he wasn't real, don't you?" She laughed hysterically, almost losing her breath in her delight at my faux pas.

"Of course I did," I snapped, mortified by my stupid suggestion. I lowered my head so that my hair covered my flaming cheeks.

Vince stroked my hair. "Never mind that, the cathedral is magnificent and worth visiting." His voice was so seductive, it took the sting out of my humiliation. I could see him staring at her, but he didn't look at all angry. I pushed away a suspicion that he enjoyed our little spats.

Hazel wiped under her eyes; I was delighted to see the backs of her fingers stained with mascara. Serves her right, I thought a little mollified.

"Jean-Paul," Vince said. "Drop us off and leave us for an hour."

"Yes, boss."

Vince directed his attention at me. "Hazel can go and spend time getting familiar with those books, maybe find some old song sheets in there. I'll take Mo across to Notre Dame; see if we can find the hunchback." He winked at me.

"Really?" I couldn't hide my delight. "But you said he wasn't real." It was fun to joke with him.

He laughed, but unlike Hazel's mocking laughter, his laughter was kind and gentle. "Maybe not," he soothed, "but that doesn't have to stop us looking for him, does it?"

"Thanks, Vince," I said, not taking my eyes off Hazel. "I'll enjoy searching the cathedral with you."

"Stop calling me Vince, it makes me feel like I'm at work. Call me Vinnie, we're close friends now."

Without any warning Hazel's arm shot out at me, her fingers stretching out towards my face. I flinched just in time for her to miss clawing my eyes. She clenched hold of my hair and yanked. "You bitch," she screamed.

I could feel her tearing my hair out by the roots and grabbed hold of her fist with both hands and pinched, digging my nails as deep into her skin as I could manage. "Let go, you cow."

"Hey, what the hell is this all about?" Vinnie asked, looking shocked.

Jean-Paul flinched as Hazel's other arm flayed towards me in an attempted punch.

"Right, that's enough," Vinnie shouted, his voice cold and

not inviting argument. "Let go of her hair," he said slowly. "Now."

She locked eyes with him, opened her mouth to say something, closing it immediately. Letting go, she grimaced at the sight of my blond strands entangled in her long fingers. Reaching out of the window, Hazel brushed her hands together to rid them of my tresses.

I rubbed my head vigorously. "That bloody hurt," I whined.

"I said, that's enough," Vinnie said, his tone quiet, yet menacing. He moved slightly away from me, the coolness of the space between us devastating me. "Hazel is right though."

What about? I wondered. Had he known how she felt about him? Did he feel the same way? I sensed what was coming next and willed him not to say it.

"Jean-Paul, pull over," Vinnie ordered.

I chewed my lower lip to stop from arguing. The car slowed and slid over to the side of the road.

"Right, you get out," he said, pushing my bottom away from him. "Hazel, you slide in the back with me. We'll have none of this ridiculous behaviour. I've got business to attend to tonight and I don't need you two acting like a couple of spoilt kids."

I couldn't believe how quickly she launched herself out of the car. Hazel pulled open my door and held her arm out. "Come along then, stop wasting time." She winked at me as if she'd planned this to happen all along.

I slunk out of the car, miserable and wishing I was back at home, without Hazel. I was going to have to find another place to live, I decided. I couldn't spend time with someone who wanted the same things I did, it just wouldn't work. I heard her giggle, hating the thought that he'd replaced me so easily. It was a stark reminder he didn't belong to me at all. So why couldn't I shift the sensation that I somehow belonged to him?

"Are we still stopping in Paris?" Hazel asked.

"No," I heard Vinnie say. "I wanted you girls to have a look at the city in the day time, because when we come back for the concert it'll be dark." He patted Jean-Paul's shoulder and pointed away from the city. "I think you two have had enough excitement for one day though."

"It's exactly how you described it to me the other day," Hazel murmured, enjoying letting me know they had spent time alone together at some point.

My throat hurt with the size of the lump constricting it. I was determined not to show how upset I was. If he wanted to play games then that was fine, but I had a few games of my own I could play.

# Chapter Fifteen

## 2003 – Hautvillers, Near Epernay

### Sera

After a day working on my stall at the village market, I finished packing the remaining enamel signs I hadn't managed to sell and drank the rest of the bottled water I'd taken with me. Grateful to be shaded from the sun, I crouched down and carefully arranged the stock in the box, so none would be damaged on the way back to the studio. It was fine to have them artfully aged, but I didn't need them to be unsaleable. Satisfied with my efforts, I folded the tops of the box over and wove the four cardboard leaves together to hold the top closed.

"Good sales today?"

"Henri." I smiled, not thinking to hide my delight at seeing him standing holding a large baguette and a full shopping bag at the other side of the stall.

He smiled, the damage side of his face pulling back slightly more than the perfect side. "You are happy to see me, *non*?"

I tilted my head to one side, pressing my lips together, hands on my hips and pretended to think. "Yes, I am," I said having forgotten my annoyance with him. "Where have you been the past few weeks? If you had a phone I could have called."

"I am waiting for one to be set up at the farm, but the phone company, it takes many weeks."

"I hope you're getting an answer phone like other people?"

He contemplated this idea briefly. "No need. You are the only person will use the telephone to contact me."

"Or not," I teased.

"Pardon?"

My English sarcasm was lost on him. I studied him. Maybe it wasn't. Maybe he simply chose not to understand me.

He walked around to join me. "I do not understand."

"Hmm, I'm not so sure about that," I said enjoying the cool grassy smell of his clothes. "How come you're out and away from your farm?"

He stepped back, pointing at his watch. "I 'ave something I must do before I can go home. You will meet me at the farm in one hour, yes?"

I was too intrigued to argue, so nodded. "Okay."

He glanced down at the filled box of signs. "I will put this into your car."

"It's fine, I can manage," I argued half-heartedly as he bent down and lifted it up and started to walk to my car. It wasn't such a big box, but it was heavy. "Are you sure you can manage?" I asked before thinking.

He immediately stopped and turned to face me. "I am capable of more than you suppose, Sera. Please, do not assume otherwise."

I couldn't miss the hurt on his face. "Idiot," I mumbled, unable to believe my own thoughtlessness. "Of course," I said quickly. "Sorry." I raced ahead of him and opened the boot of the car, watching as he lowered the box into the awkward space, just about big enough to take it. "Henri," I said, embarrassed. "I…"

He stood upright and stared at me, raising a hand to stop me saying anything further. "Enough." He began walking away, his footsteps laboured where only moments before his whole demeanour had been light.

I ran to catch up with him. Taking him by his arm I held on to him and when he didn't stop. I stepped in front of him, so he would have to move around me to get past. "Look, I know you're capable of whatever you put your mind to. I only asked because I care."

His scowl softened. Then as if remembering why he was so cross, his expression darkened again. "It is good to have a friend." He held his hands out. "I know how I look, but I do not need to be reminded how I am."

I wanted to cry. I had offended him, deeply. "Henri, please."

Before I could utter another word, he put one hand at the back of my head and bending down pressed his lips hard against mine in a kiss. The shock of what he was doing passed instantly as I forgot my surprise and surrendered to the exquisite sensation.

Eventually he stopped, leaving me wanting more. We stared at each other, both getting used to what had just happened between us. "Do not see me as an invalid," he said, his voice catching slightly.

I hadn't expected this. Then again, I hadn't ever thought of us kissing. "Henri, I…"

He exhaled sharply. "It is okay, we are friends, *non*?"

I nodded slowly. I wasn't sure I could be happy having him simply as a friend after that kiss. It ignited something in me that I hadn't experienced since kissing Marcus for the first time. I couldn't find the right words and stared at him silently, thoughts racing through my head. I'd been single by choice since losing Marcus. I was almost used to not having him in my life. This kiss changed everything though, especially the equilibrium of my long dormant emotions. First Leo, spending time at the house getting used to being a part of my small family. I enjoyed his company, more than I'd ever expected to, but Henri was different. He was a friend, but now I realized he could be more than that, to me at least. He was someone I never wanted to lose.

"Shall I still meet you at the farm?" I said eventually.

"Yes."

I sighed with relief. "Good."

He took me by both elbows bent his head down towards me. "I am sensitive, but I am not a fool. You ask me if I am okay because you have concern for me." He kissed the tip of my nose. "I will see you in one hour."

He walked away shaking his head. I wasn't sure if it was because of what I had said, or his reaction to it, but I did know at that moment I would have rather he kissed my mouth. I touched my nose, as I watched Henri walk away. He was certainly complex. I wasn't sure if I'd ever be able to work him out.

Still shaky after my encounter with Henri, I drove to my studio to drop off the unsold signs. It had been another long hot day and I was relieved Mum had offered to look after Katie for me while she learnt her lines. She had yet again split up from Paul and I wondered if this time it would be for good. I loved summery days, but this year the consistently high temperatures and feeling like I was trapped inside a thick blanket got a little wearisome after a while.

I drew up alongside the studio and parked the car. Stepping out, I thought I spotted someone through the window. My heart pounded as I cupped my hand either side of my face on the glass to block out the sun and try to get a better view. Squinting, I stared into the darkened room. The only light was through a small window at the back in the tiny kitchenette. I couldn't see anything. I watched for a little longer, until feeling a little foolish for my paranoia.

Stepping back, I retrieved the front door key from my pocket, unlocked the door. I pulled both sides back to let out some of the dank air and freshen up the space a bit. Opening the boot of the car, I took a deep breath before reaching down to manoeuvre the box out, cursing the depth of the area.

"Need any help?" A familiar voice with an amused tone, asked.

Startled to hear Dee's voice here in Epernay, I stood up

too quickly and cracked my head on the edge of the opened boot.

"Ouch, shit." I rubbed my damaged scalp tentatively. "What are you doing in town?" I looked around to see if she was alone.

"Leo dropped me off a while ago. He's taken Ashley to buy sandals. I thought I'd see how well I remembered the place and try to find your studio."

Irritated to have my peace shattered, I couldn't tell if she was joking, or not. "Help me with this and I'll show you around, if you like?"

We bent down and took a side each. "Blimey, this is heavy," she groaned her face reddening as she walked backwards into the darkness of my studio.

"Let's put it on here," I said, nodding in the direction of the metal table where I carried out most of my work. "I've only really popped in quickly to drop this off," I said, not wanting her to get used to being here.

"I'm sick of this heat," she said fanning her face with one of my small posters. "It's oppressive. I don't remember it being this bad when I was a kid." She wrinkled her nose.

I wiped my forehead with the back of my hand. "They say it's going to reach the low forties tomorrow."

Dee groaned. "I thought about offering to help at your stall today, but it was too hot."

"It's fine," I said, relieved she hadn't come. "You did well to find this place." I knew from the first few times I'd come here how confusing the back streets were to navigate.

"Not sure really," she laughed. "In fact, you could give

me a lift home. I'm shattered. Coming into town wasn't a clever move today, even some of the tarmac on the roads has shifted under the pressure of the heavier vehicles."

I nodded, recalling seeing melting tarmac on my way here. I walked through to the kitchenette and poured a glass of water. "Want one?"

She nodded. "Yes, please."

I handed her my drink and held a second glass under the running tap. I grimaced. "The water's warm, I'm afraid."

"No worries, I'm thirsty as hell, so anything will do."

What had she been doing? I wondered. This wasn't the sort of place you simply walked by. There was nothing else around the area apart from smaller terraced houses and storage units. "Won't Leo be expecting to pick you up from somewhere?"

She looked at me as if I'd asked her when she last exploded in to millions of pieces of glass. "I am capable of finding my own way around, you know. I'm not a complete idiot."

I sipped my drink. "I didn't mean to insinuate you were. It's just that, well." I wasn't exactly sure what to say next. "Didn't he wonder what you wanted to come here for?" There, I'd said it.

She smiled at me. "You want to know, you mean." Without waiting for me to disagree she shrugged. "Is it so strange I might want to find out where my best friend spends so much of her time?"

Put like that, my curiosity did seem a little odd. "No." My head was starting to throb. I rubbed my temples lightly willing the pain to ease.

"So, why ask then?"

I drained the last of the water in my glass. It was too hot for a confrontation. I couldn't wait to get her away from here. This was the only space I had left that she hadn't invaded. I needed her to go. I held out my hand to take her glass.

She passed it over slowly. "You don't like me very much anymore, do you?"

Should I lie? I considered her question for a nanosecond and something snapped. "You haven't given me much reason to be fond of you."

Dee's shoulders slumped. "I suppose not."

I folded my arms across my chest. "When will you tell me why you've come here?" A shadow crossed her face, but she had asked. I wasn't ready to give up trying to discover the truth behind her extended visit. I still wasn't sure if any of Leo's tale was based on truth. "What happened to you that was so bad? You left your home without packing any toys for your little girl?"

She didn't say anything for a bit, then when I was about to have another go at her, she gave me a pointed stare. "Your marriage was perfect, or so your mother insists. Mine wasn't, so you're not in a position to judge me."

"When were you married?" I asked trying to sound a little friendlier to hurry her along. I washed the glasses and put them away in the small cupboard, eager to finish this nonsense and go to be with Henri.

"I was eighteen; desperate to leave home and live my life my way." She puffed out her cheeks and shook her head.

"He thought I was someone to vent his frustrations on. When I decided I'd had enough of his shit, he battered me. I was pregnant at the time."

I closed my eyes at the picture in my head. "Dee, that's horrendous." I leant against the worktop surprised by her bluntness and concentrated on hiding my shock. "What about Leo?"

"He was away," she looked relieved at the thought. "I hate to think what would have happened if he'd come home sooner." She stared at her feet. "Or if he'd stayed away longer."

I didn't quite understand what she meant, but didn't interrupt to delay leaving the studio.

"He came to me on his return to England, wanting to know why I hadn't answered any of his calls." She sighed. "He found me pretty messed up. We spent time by the coast while my bruises faded and then came here."

I imagined Leo's horror to arrive home and find his sister in such a state. It wasn't the same story he had told me, but the main gist I got from them both was that Dee had been physically as well as mentally abused by someone she'd been involved with. It wasn't surprising then that she seemed so different after all the things she must have suffered in the intervening years since we'd last been together at the farm. I suspected her version was probably a little closer to what had really happened than Leo's.

"At least the baby was okay," I said hoping I didn't sound patronising.

"What?" Dee snapped, as if she didn't understand what I'd just said.

"Ashley," I said. "At least she was okay."

She opened her mouth to speak, closing it again without answering. Crossing one ankle over the other, she studied the toes of her trainers. She slammed one hand down on the metal table.

I'd wasted enough time listening to her confusing stories, I grabbed my car keys. "Come on, I thought you wanted to go home?"

She followed me to the door. Although a part of me was curious about Dee's lost years, she had changed so utterly I wasn't sure how to be with her any more, especially considering my stupidly offering to help Henri earlier. Henri. I couldn't wait to deliver Dee back at the house, shower, change and go to see him. He was another mystery, but one I was determined to unravel.

Life must have been very dull here before these people came into my life, I decided. Dull, or simply peaceful? I wasn't certain which.

"Leo's got a soft spot for you, did you know that?" she asked as if she could sense I was thinking about another man.

"Yes."

Her face reddened. "I think you should leave him alone."

I wasn't sure why we were having this conversation. "Why?"

"I don't want my brother getting hurt," she said simply. "He's a good man and has a lot going on."

I pulled the right sliding door closed. Then, standing back waiting for her to leave, I did the same with the other side, locking the door. "I think that's between me and Leo, don't you?"

"He's my younger brother, Sera," she said, a barely concealed threat in her tone as she waited for me to unlock the car. "He may seem like the one in charge of most situations, but not everything is as straight forward as it might appear."

You can say that again, I thought.

We barely spoke to each other during the drive home, each of us knowing the other well enough not to waste time with pointless small-talk. I checked on Katie and, leaving her with Mum, hurried up to my room to shower. Feeling refreshed, I left the house, shouting my goodbyes to everyone. I needed someone sane to talk to.

I barely kept to the speed limit on my way to Henri's, although slowed down as I entered his dusty driveway. Parking the car, I got out and ran up his porch stairs. He must have heard my car, because he pushed open the front door, concern on his tanned face as he grabbed my arms. "Has something happened, Sera? You are okay?"

I smiled, soothed by his touch. "Sorry, I know we said one hour, but I had an unexpected visitor at my studio." Unable to help myself, I leant forward and kissed him. He hesitated and then taking me in his arms held me tightly and kissed me.

Letting go, he stepped back. We stared at each other. Both shocked by the turn of recent events.

Henri laughed. "That was… unexpected. We will sit outside maybe? Where it is cooler."

"Perfect," I said slightly dizzy from the kiss.

"I will get us a cold drink and then we can talk."

He sounded a little odd, but I put it down to my kissing

him. "I hope it's more of that delicious cider," I said, hoping he still had some from his orchard. Hazel's cider had always been heavenly, too. I yearned to taste it again.

"Not today. I have Calvados." He widened his eyes. "You look tense in your shoulders. I prescribe at least two glasses, each."

I grinned. I liked this friendlier version of Henri. "Perfect. I need something to calm me down after spending the last half an hour with Dee." I went to go with him into his kitchen.

"No," he said, a little too harshly I thought. "I will bring your drink to you, outside."

I went to do as he'd said, but first stopped to pet the puppies. Henri took two glasses from the shelf above the sink and caught my eye. I went to smile but he immediately glanced at the table. I followed his gaze noticing the table was covered with papers. Some looked very old, but from my vantage point I couldn't make out what they were about.

"What's that?"

He picked up a tea towel and gave the clean glasses a cursory wipe before dropping the cloth over the papers on the table. "My work. Come," he said, grabbing a bottle of Calvados from the sideboard. He shook his head and smiled as he stood back to let me go in front of him, his determination that I leave obvious.

I was surrounded by too many secrets and didn't like the idea of him being party to more. I walked ahead of him when he didn't reply, not letting myself look back at the table, despite how much I wanted to.

We sat either side of the small rattan table and I recounted my visit to the studio and Dee's unexpected arrival. "I know I sound like a whiny brat, but it's my private space where I go to get away from everyone."

I watched as he poured us both a glass of the amber liquid. He handed me one, held his up and waited for me to do the same.

"*Santé*. To the whiny brat," he said mimicking my French accent that always had a hint of English about it.

"Do you even know what that means?"

He shook his head. "No."

I grinned at him. "*Santé*," I echoed, staring at my glass, entranced. "This is just what I need, thank you."

He stared at me thoughtfully, reaching out and taking my nearest hand to him. "Drink."

I did as I was told this time, enjoying the heat of the apple-brandy drink as it wended its way down my throat and past my chest.

"You're a man of few words," I said, stating the obvious. "I've been trying to figure out what your job used to be."

He tapped the side of his nose. "I will not tell you. You must guess."

"Were you in the army?" I thought for a second and gasped, excited with my idea. "I bet you were in the French Foreign Legion."

He refilled both of our glasses and shook his head, amused. "*Non*. I'm aware you think there is a mystique about me, but I was not in the *Légion Étrangère*."

I pouted thoughtfully. "Shame, I could picture you in

one of those caps, marching with scores of other patriotic uniformed men across the desert."

Henri shook his head. "I think you watch very bad films, old ones."

I enjoyed hearing his deep laugh. It made a change from him being serious. "What did you do before coming here then?" I waved my hands in the air theatrically, accidentally knocking against my full glass and sending my drink all over my shorts. "Bugger."

Henri went to stand. "I will bring you a wet towel."

Guiltily, I realized this could be my chance to see what he was hiding from me. I shook my head and motioned for him to sit. "No. It was my clumsiness, and anyway, I might have to take these off to rinse them out. You refill my glass; I won't be long."

I hurried inside and took off my shorts, running them under the tap and ringing them out. I glanced out of the window to check he was still sitting out on the porch probably too polite to come inside and disturb me. I hurried over to the table and lifted the tea towel to peek underneath; careful not to move anything. Peering at old newspaper cuttings I noted that they seemed to be about the disappearance of a man who hadn't been heard of for fourteen years. There was something familiar about him, but I couldn't think what.

"Sera?" Henri called.

"I'm on my way now," I said, carefully lowering the cloth once again to cover the paperwork. I pulled my shorts back on and joined him outside. Sitting down I grimaced as my wet shorts connected with the wooden seat, relieved for once that it was such a hot day. Wracking my brains to work out why the missing man seemed so familiar, I said. "You were about to tell me what you did before coming to live on this farm."

"I want to be honest with you, Sera." He looked down at his hands. "I was a detective. I was, how you say, pensioned off, after I did something terrible and a woman I know was killed."

"Tell me." I felt disgusted with myself for nosing through his things. I needed to make amends and helping him share something that was an obvious burden to him would be a start. "Please."

"We knew each other for many years," he hesitated. "Her life had gone very badly. I tried to help her a little by paying for information on suspects and cases that I was working on." He stopped. I took one of his hands in mine and waited silently for him to continue. "I was warned by her brother not to involve her, but she insisted she needed the money and wanted to keep helping me." His voice cracked with emotion and he gave me a pleading look. I wasn't sure if he was trying to persuade me or himself. "I should have known better." He pulled his hand from my grasp.

"Was she the reason you were burnt?"

He nodded slowly. "They set fire to her home. I went into her house to rescue her, but I was too late. She died on the way to hospital." He cleared his throat. "I failed her, Sera, I let her down."

"You nearly killed yourself in the process though, Henri. I can't see how you could have done more."

He shook his head. "I should have listened and left her out of it."

"Well I think you were very brave to put your life at risk."

"No. I didn't listen, and a good woman died."

Trying to take his focus away from the events that obviously traumatised him still, I asked, "So that's why you're retired?"

"Retired? You make it sound as if I am an old man." He stared at the burnt ruins of the barn for a while. Old man, the words echoed in my head. Slowly, as if through an early morning mist, an image appeared in my memory.

"Oh my God," I said, horrified at the prospect of what I was about to say. "That newspaper cutting. The missing man." I watched as his expression changed to one of shock as he realized what I must have done. "He's Pierre, isn't he? Hazel's boyfriend. He lived here with her."

Henri clenched his teeth. I could see the muscle working on his jaw and that he was fighting the urge to be angry with me. "I covered the table for a reason," he snapped. "If I wanted you to see, I'd have shown them to you."

"I know," I said, ashamed at my uncharacteristic behaviour. "It was unforgivable of me, but, oh I don't know… there are too many secrets in my life and I wanted my relationship with you to be without secrets."

He closed his eyes briefly and groaned. Lifting the bottle, he went to refill our glasses.

"No more Calvados for me, thanks," I said. "I don't understand though, why hide them from me?" I asked, confused. "Are they the reason you've come to live on this particular farm?"

He stared at me thoughtfully, then lifting his glass, downed his drink in one.

Intrigued, I wondered why Pierre had gone missing. Leo and Dee hadn't mentioned anything about it, so it must have been after he and Hazel split up, sometime after they had disappeared from the farm in nineteen eighty-nine. I leant back in my chair, crossing my legs thoughtfully, I leant forward, desperate to understand the scenario. I was missing something, but what?

"Why would you be interested in Pierre? Had he done something?" Maybe them leaving hadn't been anything to do with my mum's letter after all. Could Pierre be the reason they left so mysteriously?

Henri sighed heavily. "Pierre was my father, Sera."

"What?" I tried to make sense of it all. "I hadn't realized he had a son."

"He left my mother when I was twelve," he said quietly. "Theirs was never a peaceful relationship, but I missed him. He never forgot my birthday or Christmas. On occasion he would turn up at Maman's house to see me, usually with a gift. They fought, and he left. When I didn't receive a birthday card or any contact from him on my twenty-first birthday, I realized something was wrong."

"Henri, that's horrible."

"The urge to trace him built over the years. I became a detective and never gave up my search for a trace of him."

I tried to put this into the context of Hazel's life. A thought occurred to me. "When were you twenty-one?" I asked, not sure how much I wanted to hear the answer. If he said what I was dreading to hear, then I was about to open a Pandora's box of chaos that could change everything I'd ever imagined about my past.

"Twenty-second of September." He waited for me to take this in.

I could barely catch my breath. I didn't want to face what he was telling me here and wished now that I hadn't looked at the newspaper cuttings. "A month after Hazel went missing with Dee and Leo."

"Yes." He sighed, studying my face for a few seconds before continuing. "He never forgot my birthday, especially an important one. I was certain something must be wrong, but didn't know where to look for him." He stared across the yard at the remains of the barn again.

I followed his gaze and we sat watching the burnt-out shell of the building in silent contemplation. A horrific thought came to me and it dawned on me what he must have discovered. I turned to him. "You think… you think that the body in the barn was your father?"

He kept staring straight ahead. "I know it," he said with conviction.

Startled, I followed his line of vision, picturing Pierre singing and swinging Hazel round in his arms at the last party she'd held. My heart pounded in shock as I tried to take in this information. They were incredibly passionate about each other. Could that passion have led to him being killed? The notion was too dreadful to contemplate.

"But Hazel would never… I mean." I couldn't imagine Hazel being capable of hurting anyone, least of all the man she loved so deeply. "Not Hazel." I looked at him. There was something else. What was he so nervous to tell me? "Henri?" I squeezed his arm when he didn't look at me. "Henri, I know Hazel could never have killed your father. She wouldn't have it in her to do something violent." He still didn't say anything. "Maybe you've got this wrong." Panic rose through me. "Or it could have been someone else? Have you thought of that?"

He glanced at his hands then back at me, his dark eyes filled with unshed tears. I wanted to comfort him, but sensed he hadn't finished confiding in me. He gave a shuddering sigh.

"Go on," I said, terrified to hear what he was about to say, but needing to know everything. Something nagged at my brain. "Wait, if you didn't know where he was, how did you manage to trace him here?"

He reached out and took one of my hands in his, resting them on the table in between us. His actions made me nervous. The tables had turned somehow.

"Promise me you'll listen to everything I have to tell you before making judgement," he pleaded, his eyes boring into me, willing me to agree.

I frowned. "Okay."

He didn't seem convinced by my reply and studied my face momentarily before speaking. "My mother told me my father was living with a singer from London. She knew her name was Hazel." He hesitated and narrowed his eyes. He was waiting for me to react, but I wasn't sure why. He continued, "I spent years researching the records for this woman. I travelled to London and discovered that in the summer of seventy-six Hazel shared a flat with an actress... called Mo."

His words echoed in my head. I stared at him, but it was as if we were in a bubble and I was waiting for it to explode all around me.

"Mo?" I felt sick. Was he about to fill in some of my mother's mysterious history? "Go on," I said, barely able to breathe my heart was pounding so hard in my chest.

"They went missing."

"Missing?" I wanted to cry, but desperate not to give him an excuse to stop, swallowed the lump constricting my throat. "Who did?"

He stared at me massaging his temple with his free hand. "I do not have to continue, if it upsets you."

I wanted to scream at him. "You can't stop now," I snapped. "You have to tell me everything."

He gave my hand a squeeze. "On or around seventeenth of May nineteen seventy-six, Hazel, Mo and a man called Vincent Black travelled to Paris with a group of people. Others who were members at a club where Mo worked also went on the trip, as well as an agent called Jack Collins. I think he represented Mo."

I'd never heard her mention any of these names before, but not wishing him to stop kept quiet waiting for him to continue.

"They flew to Paris to attend a David Bowie concert."

I tried to recollect something clawing at my brain. "The one from the Thin White Duke poster in your study? Wasn't that in nineteen seventy-six?" Why was he going this far back when his father disappeared in eighty-nine?

He nodded. Opening his mouth to continue, he hesitated before carrying on. "The two women and Monsieur Black never returned to London."

I shivered. He wasn't making any sense. "They didn't?"

"*Non.* As you can imagine, I was intrigued. I decided to look further into their lives."

I had always known my mother was an actress and that she worked in London for a short time before moving to Epernay to have me. I'd always suspected there was something in England she'd run away from, not here in France.

"I picked up that she and Hazel must have known each other years ago," I confided. "But I had no idea they were ever close." The revelation stunned me. "Please, carry on."

It was strange hearing him refer to her as Mo. I'd only ever heard Mum referred to as Maureen, except for Katie calling her Nana Mo, and that had been Mum's suggestion. I had assumed it was something she'd come up with as an affectionate name between herself and Katie, not a link to her past.

"The trail went cold," Henri added, raising a shoulder in a lazy shrug. "I could not find anything further about these women for several years. I thought my search was over. Until I was put to work on a cold case. Although it did not involve my father's disappearance, something a colleague said alerted me to this farm." He stared at me intently before carrying on. "The family disappeared from here one night. The woman's name on the lease was Hazel."

I sensed that what he was about to say would answer some of my own questions about what had happened to the family. "Go on, I need to know."

"Hazel isn't a common name," he said. "Also, back then an English woman living in a French town was not as usual as it is now. The connection was clear to me, so I travelled here and discovered that the elderly tenants who came after Hazel had died leaving the farm vacant for some years. I enquired about leasing it." He looked concerned by my silence.

"Sounds sensible," I said, forcing myself to appear calm. My stomach churned. I had to concentrate on hiding my panic. It would be too upsetting to get this far for him to clam up and refuse to tell me every detail.

"I thought if I could move in to where my father's last known address maybe I'd discover what happened to him."

No wonder he kept himself and his business private, I decided. If anyone around here suspected he was investigating their lives, or those of their neighbours, they would consider it snooping and he'd be even more unpopular than he was already.

I studied my nails as the enormity of what he'd confided in me took root. "As sorry as I am about your father's disappearance, Henri…" I said closing my eyes to try and regulate my rising temper. "Why wait this long to tell me about investigating my mother's past."

"Sera?" he began, closing his eyes and shaking his head. "*Merde*, I am a fool for telling you."

I held my hand up to stop him. "No, you should have

told me before," I said hurt that he couldn't confide in me. "I don't understand why it had to be such a secret?"

He rose slowly, wincing as he straightened his leg. "I had to know what happened to my father. I wanted to investigate without anyone becoming suspicious. People are rarely open if they suspect you are trying to find out information. You must surely understand this?"

I probably would have if one of the people he had been researching hadn't been Mum. "You've been tracking my mum like she's some sort of villain. She's an actress, not an escaped convict." I shivered despite the heat. "She might have known Hazel in the seventies," I said, still finding this nugget of information they were ever remotely close a bit of a strain. "Big deal. I can't imagine they were never as close as you're making out though, I would have known."

"Sera." He went to comfort me.

"No," I pushed him away. "I'm going. My mother was right about you and I stupidly thought we could be friends." He grabbed my arm as I turned to leave, holding me back. "Let me go."

"*Non*. You will listen to me, or I will come to your house and tell you."

"No, you won't." I snatched my arm away from him and ran to the car, knowing he couldn't catch up with me before I managed to get inside.

"Sera, please stop."

I ignored his pleas. If anyone was going to tell me what happened, it was going to be Mum. I'd had enough of his revelations, and her secrets. I needed to confront her and find out what really happened all those years ago.

# Chapter Sixteen

17 May 1976 – Paris

## Mo

I couldn't help being a bit disappointed about the venue for Bowie's concert. "Pavilion de Paris sounds so grand," I said to Vinnie as we made our way inside the vast space. "But this isn't what I expected at all."

"That's because this area used to be the meat-packing district and this building was a slaughterhouse," he said, amused at my grimace.

He stroked my arm. "Hey, it isn't now. Anyway, you're here to watch Bowie and listen to the best music in the world, not be concerned with the building."

I recalled a comment Jean-Paul had made when he'd dropped us off. "Is that why he called it Les Abattoirs?"

Vinnie's eyes glinted in amusement. "Yes."

"Oh, I see," I said.

I felt confident and good enough to be seen with Vinnie and his sophisticated associates. I loved my expensive new jade, wide-legged culottes and cream crocheted top that he had treated me to before we'd left London. I still couldn't believe I was here in the 9th Arrondissement in Paris, about to see my hero, David Bowie. Even Hazel's and my state of the art bedroom at the hotel was like something I'd only ever seen before in magazines, with its bright orange decor and designer bedroom suite and light fittings. This was the life I had envisaged for myself.

"I can't believe we're actually here," I giggled, hugging Vinnie tightly.

He looked slick in his tailored suit with his hair brushed back similar to the star we'd all travelled here to watch. He beamed at me and patted my bottom. I spotted him nod at someone at the side of the room. Without saying anything, Vinnie grabbed hold of my right hand and began pulling me with him towards a door. "Come along," he said. "There's someone I want you to meet."

I wasn't in the mood to meet any of his cronies, but didn't think I had the right to complain after he'd treated me to the concert. We walked through a door, past groups of people who looked like musicians and several glamorous women, their shiny long hair and low-cut tops making them stand out among the others in the hallway. I was certain they must be models. I realised they were looking at us and it made me proud to think other people assumed I was Vinnie's girlfriend.

He stopped to chat to a woman, kissing her on her cheek and laughing about something. I looked away, not wishing either of them to see my jealousy. What was this place? Everyone was busy chatting and people barking orders. I glanced into a room where several guitarists were strumming and singing before being led on again behind Vinnie.

"Here," he said, smiling at me. He looked so proud that I panicked in case I'd missed something he'd been telling me. He was staring at me and waiting for me to say something.

"Sorry?"

He shook his head as if he thought I was a hopeless fool. "This way."

The door opened and the woman he'd just been speaking to smiled at me and stepped back allowing us inside. I wished I could be let in on their mutual secret and felt a little uncomfortable at their obvious amusement with me. I stepped inside the room, looked up and into a fantasy.

I think my heart almost stopped for a second. I know my mouth fell open and I couldn't think of a single intelligent thing to say because there, sitting at a table smoking a cigarette, was my idol. David Bowie. In the same room as me. He looked like a god from another planet with his pale skin, orangey hair and more style than any other human could dream of possessing. I couldn't think, let alone speak.

"You must be Mo," he said in his beautiful unique voice that affected his fans so deeply.

I heard Vinnie laugh as he nudged me forward making me stumble when my legs refused to work properly. "I think she's a little overawed."

Bowie's mouth drew back in a smile. "You okay?"

I nodded. "Um." I cleared my throat as it dawned on me that if I didn't hurry up and get a grip, my only chance of speaking to him would be missed. I stepped forward, trembling and breathless. "Yes."

"Vinnie tells me you're from London."

"Yes." I sounded so stupid even to my own ears.

"Maybe we'll bump into each other again when I'm next there," he said before taking a long, deep drag of his cigarette.

"Oh, yes." Why wasn't my brain working properly?

He stood up and coming over to me, glanced in Vinnie's direction. "You were right, Vinnie, she is very pretty." Then turning his attention to me, added, "He assures me that you're going to be a very famous actress one of these days." Taking my hand he raised it to his lips. "Maybe we'll meet up again sometime."

"Thank you," I stuttered.

He smiled. "I hope you enjoy the concert."

"I will," I breathed, not sure if I could manage to move again. "Thank you."

I gave him a shaky smile that I suspected came out as more of a grimace and let Vinnie lead me out of the room. I don't remember walking back to join the rest of the audience, or if Vinnie spoke to me. The shock of what he'd made happen for me was too overwhelming and I promised myself that I'd be forever grateful to him.

He pushed a way for us into the crowd so that we could stand in front of the stage. Vinnie stood behind me wrapping his arms around me.

"Happy?" he shouted into my ear.

I nodded, turning and snuggling close to him, happier

than I'd ever been before. I stood on tiptoes to speak to him. "I can't believe what happened back there. Thank you for doing that for me."

He lowered his head, smiling, and kissed me hard on the lips. "Your reaction was worth it. Seeing you overwhelmed was lovely. It's not often I get to see pure sweetness."

The band walked on to the stage and I turned to face them. Vinnie had made this dream happen for me and I couldn't have loved anyone more than I loved him at that moment.

"I wonder where's Hazel got to?" he shouted. I looked up to see him peering through the crowds looking for her.

I pulled on his hand. "She'll be fine," I said lifting my head, so he could hear me. "She'll be trying to get to know the musicians in here." I thought back to the couple of hours Hazel and I had endured of each other's company in the twin-room Vinnie had booked for us at our hotel in Marne-la-Vallée. "She's desperate to get a gig."

"She's going to go far," he said proudly.

I was unable to think about Hazel's success when I'd failed to achieve anything more than two nights acting in a small part. And that only happened when the understudy for the lead actresses was promoted when she went down with a stomach bug. It wasn't much to boast about, but for a couple of days I wrongly believed my luck had finally changed and I was on my way to stardom.

"She's a fantastic singer," I admitted, squeezing his hand where it rested against my stomach. I'd finally managed to get time with Vinnie without Hazel fawning over him and I was going to make the most of it.

He pulled me closer to him, pointing up to the stage. "Not long now, sweetheart. He'll soon be up there."

The lights dimmed in the smoky atmosphere and the background music stopped. There was a second of silence, before excited voices began chanting Bowie's name. The tension mounted. I was so excited I could barely breathe. I was in my own vision of heaven relishing having Vinnie close behind me. The next second the sound of a chugging train blasted out of the speakers and the early strains of 'Station to Station' played. There was a unified gasp. Bowie strode onto the stage. The crowd roared their appreciation and the beat of the instruments began one by one.

My breath caught in my throat. I couldn't believe only minutes before I'd been in the same room as my hero. I pressed the back of my hand to my lips, it was the closest I'd ever get to kissing Bowie. I'd listened to this music time and again. Nothing prepared me for hearing it played live.

He began to sing, that unique beautiful voice. Standing tall, proud and magnificent in his crisp white shirt and dark waistcoat, holding his microphone ready to thrill his audience. Forgetting everything else, especially my determination to remain cool and contained, I screamed my delight, singing along with everyone else to the rest of the song, then to 'Suffragette City', 'Fame', 'Word on a Wing' and on and on, lost in the magic of the atmosphere.

I could feel Vinnie tapping along. "He's brilliant, isn't he?" he shouted over the amplified music.

"I'm going to meet him again one day," I promised myself.

Tonight was perfect. Soaking up his charisma and brilliance, I knew I'd remember this night forever.

I sang myself hoarse to 'Young Americans', danced to 'Golden Years 'and cried when he finished, angrily wiping away tears blurring my vision of him, not caring about my make-up. The concert finished far too soon. I wasn't ready to leave.

"I love him, don't you?" Hazel said catching up with us as we queued to leave the ugly building.

"Oh, yes," I said, my mind in a whirl, forgetting our earlier differences. "He's magnificent."

"Where have you been?" Vinnie demanded glaring at Hazel, the barely contained irritation in his voice dissipating the excitement from a few minutes earlier. "You should have been with us."

She did that annoying thing I hated of pouting like she was a little girl. I peered at Vinnie surreptitiously willing him not to be taken in by it, irritated when I could see that he had been.

"I'm sorry, Vinnie," she said, looking like a puppy terrified it might be put out in to the dark. "I could see where you were, but I couldn't get past everyone to get to you."

"You might have got lost in those crowds." His voice softened.

I couldn't take any more. "She's a big girl, Vinnie," I said. "I'm sure Hazel doesn't need you looking out for her."

He jerked his head around to face me. "Don't tell me what to do." He squeezed my arm hard.

I winced and glared at him, pulled my arm out of his

grasp, rubbing where I could already feel it bruising.

"You need to be taught a few manners," he said, lowering his mouth so that I could feel his lips moving against my ear.

I couldn't understand how his mood had changed so completely. "I only meant…"

He pulled me to a stop. "Enough. Don't speak." Then ignoring me, he took hold of Hazel's wrist and dragged her along with him, leaving me to follow in their wake.

Confused by this turnaround in his mood, I swallowed the tears that were threatening to choke me. My perfect evening had been ruined by Hazel and her thoughtless antics. Why couldn't she just stay away? I ran to keep up with him as he marched her down the road, terrified he'd leave me to find my own way back to the hotel. I caught up with them as we reached Jean-Paul leaning against the car smoking his usual Gauloises.

He took one last drag of his cigarette, threw it over his shoulder and stood up. "Good time?"

"Take us back to the hotel," Vinnie demanded, grabbing the front door of the car, tapping his foot impatiently as he waited for me to get inside.

"I thought I'd be sitting next to you." I could hear the whine in my voice but couldn't hide my disappointment.

"You thought wrong," he said, not looking at me, his disappointment in my behaviour clear. "Now get in before I push you in."

"Bastard," I hissed under my breath as I stepped in and sat down.

He stood completely still for a few moments, then taking

a deep breath, bent down, his face almost touching mine. "What did you just say?" he asked, each word like a separate sentence.

I might be upset, jealous even, but I wasn't crazy enough to answer him honestly. I'd stupidly forgotten he wasn't one of the lads from back home who could be bossed around.

"Nothing, Vinnie," I said in my sweetest voice. "Why, what did you think I said?"

He narrowed his eyes and studied my face. I silently thanked God for giving me the gift of being able to keep my expression relaxed, despite my terror at that moment as I waited for him to back away. He eventually stood up and slammed the front door shut. I breathed out, unaware until that point that I'd been holding my breath.

I heard him get in the back seat. I daren't be so obvious as to pull down the visor and look at them through the mirror. I could see out of the corner of my eye that Hazel wasn't sitting behind the driver, but in the middle of the seat. There was so much bloody room left on the back seat two of me could have fitted in there next to them. She had chosen to sit close to him. I thought back over the past few minutes. No, he had decided she would. Despite my adoration of him, I sensed she was frightened. I didn't blame her.

"We're going home tomorrow," he said to us, eventually. "With any luck I might have a few things lined up for you both. That is, if you learn to behave yourself."

Forgetting my earlier set-to with him, I turned around in my seat, kneeling on the warm leather and smiled hopefully at him. "Really?" I ignored Hazel's wide-eyed nervousness.

"I said so, didn't I?"

I put my hand over the back of the chair and reached out to him. "I'm sorry I annoyed you earlier, Vinnie," I said, willing him to forgive me. "I didn't mean to, especially after you've brought us to Paris and arranged for me to meet Bowie."

I gazed at him and his expression gradually softened. He smiled at me taking my hand in both of his. "It's fine, baby. It gives me pleasure to treat you; I just get a bit mad if one of you gives me cause to worry. All is forgiven now."

I believed him, and then I noticed him giving Hazel a sideways glance. She turned away and gazed out of the window closest to her as we sped through the Paris streets and out of the city.

The drive took longer than I'd expected. "Why are we going to this village for the night rather than stay in Paris?" I asked, my curiosity overcoming my fear of irritating him.

"Because I have business there."

Jean-Paul pulled up outside the front of the modern hotel and got out to open the doors for Hazel and me. I stepped out and waited for the other two to do the same. The forty-minute drive had been tedious, especially as I couldn't sleep now that the adrenaline from meeting my hero was still pumping through my veins.

I realised Vinnie was still speaking to Hazel in the car, I couldn't make out what he was saying but she didn't look happy. In fact, she looked frightened. I waited silently, not daring to interrupt him. Jean-Paul avoided my gaze focusing his attention on the entrance to the hotel. Eventually, they stepped out of the car.

"You two go and get some kip," Vinnie said, getting into the front seat. He seemed preoccupied. Jean-Paul closed the door behind him and went to get into the driver's side.

"Jean-Paul has to travel to see his family tomorrow, but I'll ask him to drop me back here later after I've finished my meeting."

Without waiting for us to reply, they drove off. Hazel and I stood watching the car's red tail lights disappearing into the distance.

"I wonder where they're going?" she said, her voice quavering.

"You all right?" I asked, curious to know what Vinnie had been saying to her.

She shrugged. "Come on, let's go to bed. We don't want him coming back for some reason and finding us still standing out here when he's told us to go in."

I followed her inside and waited while Hazel went to the Reception desk to ask for our key.

Our room was typical of a modern hotel bedroom with nothing much to get excited about. Everything was cream or orange. The two orange, moulded plastic chairs set either side of the circular white table by the window looked very uninviting. I changed out of the long culottes and crocheted top and got into bed.

"Why did you upset Vinnie earlier?" I asked Hazel as she cleaned her teeth in the small bathroom.

She finished what she was doing and turning off the

fluorescent light, came into our bedroom and got into bed. I noticed she was wearing a baby doll nightie.

"Bought that especially for him, did you?" I sneered, envious that I hadn't thought to do the same.

She ignored me and turned on her side. "Vinnie bought this for me," she said eventually.

I felt sick. Had he already replaced me in his affections? I couldn't bear the thought. "You fancy yourself as Alice's replacement, don't you?"

She sat up and looked at me. "Don't you?"

I glared at her. "So, what if I do?" My heart raced. "I love him though, Hazel," I admitted willing her to feel guilty for vying for his attention. "He arranged for me to meet Bowie before the concert, did you know that?"

She pursed her lips. "You're not the only one he wants to help, you know."

I recalled her scared expression when he was talking to her earlier. I couldn't stand it. I needed to assert my claim on him, for what it was. "We've been sleeping together," I admitted, enjoying her surprise at this unexpected revelation.

She frowned, obviously hating me at that second. I thought she'd been oblivious about how close Vinnie and I had become. Her reaction proved to me that I'd been right. "Good night, Mo." She turned her back to me, but I could tell by her breathing she was feigning sleep.

I stared at my beautiful outfit hanging up in the wardrobe next to the emerald green cocktail dress Vinnie had persuaded Greta to lend me for the trip. I hoped to wear it to accompany him to his business meeting tonight, but could see I wasn't going to get the chance to wear it now. All the dreams I'd harboured for this trip with Vinnie were evaporating.

I closed my eyes willing myself to sleep away my disappointment. Tonight, had begun so well. Meeting Bowie and the coolness of his hand against mine in his dressing room now seemed like nothing more than a dream.

I must have dozed off eventually because when I opened my eyes it was pitch black. I kicked off the sheet in the hot, stuffy room and walked over to the window to open it further. Then I pulled back the curtains, allowing the moon's brightness to flood in cutting the room in two. I turned to go back to bed and that's when I noticed Hazel's bed was empty.

# Chapter Seventeen
## 2003 – Hautvillers, Near Epernay

### Sera

"Sera," Henri shouted from the doorway of the farmhouse. "Let me explain."

Ignoring Henri's pleads for me to listen to reason, I turned the key in the ignition and as soon as the engine spluttered into life, pressed my foot down on the accelerator and drove away as fast as I could. Not stopping at the end of his drive, I held my breath when a huge tractor and trailer raced past, narrowly avoiding crushing my car. I could hear the farmer screaming abuse at me, and held my hand up by way of an apology as I put my foot down hard on the accelerator and sped off towards home.

Unable to hold back any longer, I gave into the tears that almost choked me. Damn Henri. How could he expect me to react favourably after admitting he'd been tracking Mum across two countries for so many years? I reached out, unclipping the small cupboard on the passenger's side of the car and rummaged around until my hand met a tissue.

"Bastard," I sniffed, blowing my nose as well as I could manage with only one hand.

I parked the car outside the house, not bothering to find somewhere shady in a nearby street to leave it. Wiping my eyes with my fingers, I composed myself as much as possible. I didn't want to scare Katie by letting her see me in a dishevelled state. Opening the front door, I walked through to the living room, but it was empty. Hearing voices coming from the kitchen, I followed them and Mum must have recognised the echo of my footsteps in the high-ceilinged hall because she began speaking to me before I'd even reached the kitchen door.

"I was listening to the news on the car radio, when I collected Katie earlier," she said washing her hands. "They've given warnings about fires breaking out around here. You know how frightened I am of those things," she said without waiting for me to reply. "Apparently, the temperatures we're experiencing now are the hottest for nearly five hundred years. They're estimating that almost 14,000 people have died in France already due to the intensity of the heat."

I watched her drying her hands, waiting for her to stop talking so I could ask her to sit down and listen to what I had to say.

"They're even having problems trying to find places cool enough to store the bod…" She stopped mid-sentence when she noticed me standing in the doorway and frowned. "What's the matter?" She waved for me to sit down.

I peered out of the back door. Spotting Katie going down the steps to the garden I realised, with relief, that she mustn't have heard me come in. I sat down and blew my nose once again, lowering my head into my hands to try and gather my senses.

"It's fine," Mum said. "She can't hear us." She pushed the back door until it was almost closed and sat down facing me. "What's happened? Tell me."

I could see the concern on her beautifully made up face and didn't want to worry her any longer than I had already. I explained about my visit to Henri's and repeated everything he'd told me. I expected Mum to laugh it off and tell me not to be so sensitive, which would have been her usual quip for something like this. Instead she sat back in her chair, wide-eyed and silent. All the colour in her face draining away, and for the second time in as many days she looked as if she was about to pass out.

I leant forward, resting my hands on her knees. "Mum? What is it?"

Her breathing came in short bursts and she closed her eyes. I ran to the sink and poured her a glass of water. "Take a sip if this," I said, my voice shaking with fear. I watched her do as I'd asked, and she seemed to calm down a little.

This reaction was completely different to the one I'd imagined. "Mum," I asked quietly, when I thought she had regained a little colour in her cheeks. "Who was Vincent?"

She stood up, but before she could take a step, tried to grab the table, missed, and fell in a heap. I reached out to her, unable to stop her from hitting her head against the table on her way down but managing to stop her from landing too heavily on the tiled floor.

"Mum?" I shrieked, trying not to panic. My tough mother, always so cynical and ballsy had collapsed. I struggled to recollect any first aid and grabbed one of the cushions from the nearest chair, lifting her head carefully to slide it underneath. Then, making sure she was on her side in the recovery position, I ran to the back door for help.

"Leo." I couldn't find him and for a second wasn't sure what to do next. Grabbing a clean tea towel from a drawer, I wet it under the tap, squeezing out the excess water as I returned to sit next to her on the floor.

"Mum?" I said, stroking her clammy forehead, dabbing the broken skin near her temple where her head had connected with the table. "It's okay. Everything's fine."

I tapped her cheek lightly with my fingers and relief poured through me when I noticed her lashes moving slightly. Her eyes flickered once and then opened wide. She went to sit up. I held the damp tea towel against the side of her head with one hand and grabbed hold of her shoulder with the other to slow her down a little.

"Take it easy," I soothed, desperate to keep the panic from my voice. "You've had a bit of a fall."

"What happened?"

I helped her to sit up slowly and passed her the drink. She took a few sips and I could see she was trying to recall what had happened immediately prior to her collapse.

"Oh no," she gasped, covering her mouth with her free hand. She looked at me, her face taut with fear.

I took the glass from her, placing it out of the way on the table. "Let me help you up," I suggested, taking her arm and wanting to get her sitting more comfortably.

She reached up and took hold of the side of the table and together we managed to get her to her feet. "I don't want to be in here if Katie comes in," she said.

"Okay, let's go through to the living room?"

I helped her walk down through the hallway. She sat down on one side of the large yellow sofa and I placed a cushion behind her back. "Thank you, darling," she said, her voice quaking.

I opened my mouth to speak, but before I managed to utter a word the doorbell rang. "I hope it's not the gendarmes again," I groaned, shocked when I noticed Mum tense and move to get up. "No, you stay there, I'll tell them to come back another time."

I walked down the hallway and pulled the front door open, a scowl on my face, ready to give them a mouthful for coming back again so soon.

"Sera," Henri said. He looked miserable and for a second I almost forgot what he had done. "I must speak with you."

I glared at him. "Seriously?" I shook my head. "You can't honestly believe we've got anything to say to each other now." I sighed heavily. "You've been snooping in my mother's past, Henri."

"You 'ave to listen to me." He stopped, appealing for me to listen to him.

"No." I held my hand up to stop him coming any closer. "I've told Mum what you've been doing." I could feel tears welling inside me. "Hell, Henri, she bloody collapsed. I don't know what you think you've discovered about her, but whatever it is, she's very frightened, and I'm not having anyone do that to her. Do you understand me?"

He looked as if he hated me at that second, or maybe it was my mother his anger was directed towards, I wasn't sure. "I am French, Sera, not stupid, of course I understand you. But there are things I must tell you."

"I said, no." I had no intention of him coming to this house and causing more disruption.

He moved to leave, then stopped and looking at me over his shoulder said, "If you wished to confide in me, I would always believe you. Why can you not trust me?"

I did trust him that was the problem. How could I admit to him that my problem wasn't his honesty, but my shock at discovering my only parent had a secret that traumatised her so utterly? I stepped out to the doorstep and held the door closed behind me, so that Mum couldn't hear me speaking to him.

"My mother is the strongest, bravest woman I know, Henri. When she reacted so dramatically to what you'd told me, I knew she'd hidden something she believed was too huge to share." He looked forlorn. Every part of me wanted to forgive him and forget what I'd discovered. "You have your quest to find out what happened to your father and I have to make sure Mum is okay," I said trying to sound reasonable. "We might not like it, but it appears we're on opposing sides of something huge from our parents' pasts."

He reached out and rested the palm of his hand against my cheek. "I understand," he hesitated. "I will go and leave you to care for her."

I watched him walk away, his shoulders stooped, and I wanted to follow him. Henri disappeared around the corner at the end of the street and I went back inside to join Mum.

I crouched down in front of her and as I did so I spotted a cigarette end in the fireplace. Mum hated smoking and forbade anyone doing it in her house. I had never seen Dee or Leo smoking, so assumed it must have been someone else, but who? She squeezed my hand to get my attention. I looked at her, forcing a smile. "Yes, Mum?"

She stared at me without speaking and looked as if she was about to cry. I moved a little closer to her. I had never seen her cry before apart from when she was acting in a part, and it unnerved me that something I'd said caused such a drastic change in her usual calm persona.

She exhaled sharply. "Sera, there's something I must tell you."

"What is it?" I wasn't sure I was ready for her to confide in me.

"Years ago," she began. Her voice cracked. She cleared her throat. She seemed to reconsider how to tell me this news. "There was this man." She took her hand from mine and covered her eyes. "I'm sorry, I can't think straight."

I smiled at her to reassure her. "It's fine. Whatever it is, you can tell me."

She parted her hands, placing one hand either side of her face, trying to weigh up my reaction.

"I love you," I said. "I don't care what you tell me, nothing will ever change that."

She sighed, almost in physical pain. I wondered if the cut

on her head was as painful as it looked. "Will you though, Seraphina? I'm not so sure."

"Yes, I will."

"You're such a lovely, trusting girl," she said miserably. "You have no idea how devious people can be, or how cruel."

I was intrigued. "So, tell me." Now I needed to hear whatever it was. Although she'd always been stern with me, up until Katie's arrival, it had always been just me and her, apart from the few short years I was with Marcus. "Stop fretting and spit it out."

"This man," she said. "Your father."

I widened my eyes. She had never mentioned my father before. Oh, she had given me some flimsy tale about an actor she enjoyed an affair with when she was very young. He had been married, or so she said, and after their tour had returned to his wife not knowing she was expecting me. Other than that snippet, she never offered any further details about him, despite my pleading when I was a teenager. Eventually, I gave up asking. This was the first time she had been the one to start a conversation about him.

"I should have told you about him years ago," she said, sighing heavily. "He died."

I couldn't help being disappointed. "That's it?"

She shook her head, taking the cloth from her head and inspecting the ruby blood that had seeped into the pristine cloth. "I was there when he died."

I thought I heard footsteps coming down the stairs, but was desperate for her to continue. "And?"

"Hazel was, too."

Before I could say anything further, I heard a cry and tumbling down the stairs. My heart plummeting, I leapt up, motioning for Mum to stay seated. I ran out to the hallway. Dee was crumpled on the floor at the bottom of the stairs. Shocked, I ran to help her.

"Dee, bloody hell."

She looked up at me then up the stairs, her eyes wide with fright.

"Are you okay to stand?" I asked, helping her get up very slowly. I took her hands in mine to check her wrists were okay and then glanced down at her legs. She was in shorts, so it was easy to see without making a fuss. She seemed fine, apart from a nasty bruise rapidly discolouring her right knee.

Leo ran from his room and stopped at the top of the stairs. "What happened?"

"Dee fell down the stairs," I said. "Not the top though by the sound of it."

He ran down to join us. "Are you okay?"

She nodded wincing in pain. "It was only about five steps up, but it hurts."

It was a relief to have him to take care of her. "Sorry, Leo," I said, wondering how he had managed to hear Dee falling but not my call for help from him minutes earlier. "Mum's had a bit of a drama too, so I'd better get back to her. I'll leave Dee with you, if that's okay?"

He looked worried. "Is Maureen okay?"

"Yes, she's fine, thanks," I said, willing him to go so that I could return to Mum before she changed her mind about confiding in me. I watched him put his arm around Dee's shoulders and lead her out towards the garden.

"Okay, Mum," I said, desperate to hear more as I joined her in the living room. "Tell me everything."

She smiled at me, back to her usual reserved demeanour that I was used to. "No, darling, I was being silly. Really, it was nothing."

"Too bad," I said, irritated that she'd done exactly what I'd been afraid of. "I'm sick of people fobbing me off. Something happened in your past with you and Hazel and I want to know about it, right now." I repeated everything Henri had said to me, watching the colour drain from her face once again, but this time not caring that she didn't like what she was hearing.

"So, this detective, Henri. I always said there was something shady about him," she sneered. "He's seen fit to poke his nose into my affairs?"

"Well, Hazel's affairs, if we're being precise."

"How dare he come to you with gossip about me?" She sat up straighter, more like her old self, which I admit made me feel much better. "He knows where to find me and come here to discuss this with me, not you."

I didn't mind her getting angry, I'd probably react the same as she was if I was in her place. I wanted to know what made her keep secrets from me for all these years. "What have you been hiding from me, Mum?"

She sighed heavily. "Your father." She stuck her perfect chin out defiantly.

"Yes, who was he?" I concentrated on hiding my excitement that I might finally discover his identity.

"Hazel and I... Well, we killed him."

I stared open mouthed at her. Stunned by the brutal way she'd delivered her admission. Before I gathered my senses enough to process this mind-numbing information, Leo ran into the room, crashing the door back against the wall.

"Have you seen Dee? I only left her for a moment to get her a drink. She's gone."

I was still staring at Mum trying to take in what she'd told me in this latest drama.

"There have been updates on the radio about fires moving in this direction," he added.

I recalled hearing something earlier on the radio about the devastation the fires were leaving in their wake and couldn't bear the thought of losing my home and the precious memories my belongings held for me.

"Have you checked her room?" Mum asked, unable to keep her irritation in check.

"Yes," he replied, his right hand clenched so tightly into a fist that the bones of his knuckles looked as if they were about to burst through his skin. "That's not all though. I can't find Ashley either."

# Chapter Eighteen
## 1989 – Hautvillers, Near Epernay

## Young Sera

I woke the following morning the memory of Hazel insisting I leave her house the previous night still stung. I couldn't imagine why she needed to speak to Dee, Leo and Pierre without me there. She'd always insisted I was part of her family, but this only reminded me that I wasn't however much I liked to imagine it. My eyes were puffy and felt bruised after crying myself to sleep while listening to my Tracy Chapman tape.

As hurt as I felt, I dressed to go to the farm, but Mum had planned a day out for us in Paris and I had no choice but to go with her. We didn't arrive home until after ten that evening, so I went to bed determined to see Dee the following day.

Before Mum was up the next morning, I dressed and ran over to the farm, not caring that it was barely past seven in the morning and no one would probably be up yet. I'd sit on their porch and wait for one of them to stir. I couldn't stand the thought of pacing around my bedroom willing the hands to move on my alarm clock. As expected, no one else was up, so I made myself comfortable on the shabby wooden armchair outside their back door. It had been there for as long as I could remember. Dee and I always fought about whose turn it was to sit in it.

The farm was peaceful, which was unusual. It was a little too quiet for my liking, but not wishing to annoy Hazel, I stayed where I was and stared at her terracotta pots filled with the blooming scarlet geraniums she loved to display at either side of each step.

I must have dozed off, because when I checked my watch again it was almost ten o'clock. I listened for voices, but the place was unnervingly silent. The only noise came from the chickens running freely, clucking to each other, busy pecking at the ground at one end of the yard near the barn. I rubbed my eyes and sat up. There didn't seem to be anyone moving in the house, so I opened the back door that no one ever locked and nervously walked in through the hall to the kitchen.

Plates and cups littered the sides. A box half-filled with newspaper encased plates stood by an opened cupboard door. Strange, I couldn't understand why Hazel would pack away her plates. I returned to the hallway and stopped at the bottom of the stairs. "Dee?" I called, wanting to be heard, but hoping not to disturb anyone.

When my friend didn't answer, I forgot about making a noise and ran up the stairs to her bedroom. The door was wide open, and her favourite jeans lay across her bed. She'd strung the leather belt we'd argued over through the denim loops. I thought that she must have changed her mind about wearing them because of the uncharacteristic heat today. Unusually though, her bed was made, though somewhat hastily. I listened for any movement again, but there wasn't any. Feeling a little uneasy, I decided to try looking in Leo's bedroom, this time knocking before I entered. I was met with another untidy room; his wardrobe doors open and empty hangers along the wooden rail.

Unable to ignore the sense that something was terribly wrong, I hurried across to Hazel's room. Her unmade bed had the bedclothes half pulled onto the floor. Her wardrobe doors were wide open displaying mostly empty hangers and a few scarves on the floor nearby.

I tried not to panic and ran down the stairs, out to the barn and opened the door to check if I'd made a mistake and maybe they had held an impromptu party and were still in there asleep. Painfully aware I was kidding myself, I pushed away the image of the empty wardrobes, certain there could be an alternative explanation than the obvious one. Just because I didn't know what had happened, didn't mean I should imagine the worst, or so I told myself time and time again as I looked for any sign of the family.

Nothing, only the usual mess and detritus from their day-to-day living and partying. Apart from the wardrobes, an evil imp in my brain kept reminding me. I spotted another half-packed box. They wouldn't have packed their things to leave them behind, surely? Boosted by this thought, I took a deep breath, shouting for Dee as loudly as I could.

My heart pounded in the effort of waiting for the answer that I suspected by now would not be coming.

"Dee, please answer me."

Where were they? They hadn't mentioned going on holiday. I tried to think of the last holiday the family had taken. There hadn't been one, not that I recalled anyway. I retraced my steps back to Dee's room and taking a deep breath, pulled open her wardrobe doors to discover that all her clothes were missing. I cried out. They had gone. They had left me behind and by the look of their home they had no intention of ever coming back. I flopped down on Dee's bed and howled.

Exhausted from hysteria, I pushed myself up sitting on the edge of the bed as I dried my eyes with the bottom of my T-shirt. I needed to do something to delay the acceptance of what I'd discovered, so began tidying up. Closing windows, making Hazel's bed, shutting the wardrobe doors until I was satisfied that order had been partially restored. I wanted everything to be ready for them when they did come back home.

Refusing to believe they'd moved out, I unpacked the box of plates and crumpled up the old newspaper, throwing it and other bits of rubbish into the box. Then taking it outside to the bin area behind the barn I hid it out of the way. I washed the dishes and straightened the chairs, pushing them under the table neatly. Remembering the chickens, I went to check if they had enough food and water.

Realising I hadn't seen their dog anywhere, I wandered around the farmyard calling for him, checking the smaller outbuildings to ensure he hadn't been shut in anywhere by mistake. Satisfied they must have taken him with them, I took the key to the front door, left the house, closing and locking the door behind me.

They might have gone, but I was going to make sure no one came here uninvited. I'd heard what happened at these remote places when they thought no one was around. I looked to try and find somewhere clever where I could hide my key. Recalling a hole high up in the trunk of the apple tree in the middle of the yard, where years before a branch had broken off, I grabbed an old bucket and turning it upside down, stood on it and raised my arm, dropping the key into the small space. No one would think to look for it there, I thought, satisfied with my choice of hiding place.

Unable to think what else I could do to keep busy, I began walking home. I was halfway across the hot, dusty field when it dawned on me that maybe something my mother had written in her letter might have been the catalyst that had set this unexpected exodus in motion. I broke into a run and didn't stop until I reached our garden gate.

Breathless, but determined to discover what she had said, I hurried inside, searching each room until I found my mother in the attic. "Mum."

She dropped the lid of the suitcase she'd been rummaging about in and stared at me, startled to see me standing there. "What are you doing in here?"

"I want to know what you put in your letter to Hazel."

She sat back on her haunches. "I beg your pardon?" She glared at me, her initial shock morphing into fury. "How dare you storm in here and demand to know my business? What I choose to say to Hazel is private."

"But, Mum," I went to argue.

"No, Sera. If I wanted to share that information with you I'd have done so already. Now get out of here."

I stood my ground. "No," I argued, shocking her further. If there was one thing I knew not to do it was to defy my mother. "They've gone, and I want to know why."

"Gone? Hazel?" She looked stunned.

"Yes, Hazel; all of them have gone. No note, nothing," I yelled. "What did you say to her to make her run away like that in the middle of the night?"

She sat down heavily on the threadbare rug underneath her and exhaled sharply. "That bloody woman never reacted how I expected her to."

I didn't know what was more surprising, hearing my mother swear or her admission that she'd known Hazel better than she'd ever let on. "What did you say? Please tell me."

She stood up, her composure regained. "I didn't tell her anything that would make her run away, Sera. Hazel's flighty, that's all." She waved me out of the room, following and locking the door after her. "You can't blame me for what's happened at the farm."

I stood aside and watched her go downstairs, head high, deportment perfect. Nothing ever got under her skin. How could she be so unfeeling? I went to my room and sat on the bed trying to think of what might have happened to make them all leave in such of a hurry. Dee hadn't even thought to leave me a note.

The note

Hope swelling through my veins, I ran down the stairs, back outside, through the garden gate, not stopping until I'd reached the farm. I was out of breath, determined to find my mother's note to Hazel. If she wouldn't tell me what was in it, I'd find out for myself. I retrieved the key with a bit more difficulty than I'd anticipated and let myself into the house. Stopping in the hall, I tried to recollect the events of the evening before when I'd delivered it to Hazel. I hadn't thought to go into the living room earlier, so went to see if I could find what I was looking for in there. Standing inside the door, I scanned the room.

"Yes," I cheered, punching the air in triumph. There it was, lying on the top of the desk, a half-crumpled mass. I smoothed it out against the coffee table with the heels my palms. Mum's immaculate script creased, but still decipherable.

*Remember that night after the concert when we went to Marne-la-Vallée? Of course, you do. I wasn't sure if you knew, but they've been digging up the land in that area for a theme park. They've discovered a body, but so far, the identity remains unknown. Don't panic. Keep calm and everything will be fine. M*

"Marne-la-Vallée?" I murmured. Where was that? The name sounded vaguely familiar, but I couldn't think why. I folded up my mother's cream vellum notepaper and pushed it into my shorts pocket. This wasn't something I wanted to leave lying around. Whatever she'd meant by it and how ever upset I was with her right now, I didn't want this falling into the wrong hands. I would rather keep it locked safely away in my safe place.

I returned to the farm every day for the next few weeks, hope dying more each time I arrived to find that nothing had moved since my previous visit, apart from the chickens. They, at least, were happy to see me, welcoming me by clucking and running towards me. I fed and watered them then unlocked the front door and went inside. I'd long since cleared out the fridge and thrown vases of dying wildflowers out onto the compost heap, but hadn't stripped the beds or moved anything else in the house.

It was during one of these visits that I spotted Pierre's hoard of old newspapers he kept for wrapping rubbish, or light fires. I wondered if maybe I could find some information about Marne-la-Vallée and sat cross-legged on the dusty wooden floorboards and began skimming through the first pile. An hour and a half later, almost giving up the idea as a foolish waste of time, I'd turned a page before the name registered in my mind.

Quickly pulling it open again, I rested the large paper on the floor and bent down, reading through the article. So, the place they were too frightened to recall was where they were now building the new theme park. Why that would be terrifying enough to cause Hazel to run away with Pierre, Dee and Leo, I couldn't imagine. It seemed such an extreme reaction to me.

I checked my post box every day hoping Dee would send me a postcard, or any indication to let me know she was okay, and kept feeding the chickens until one day I arrived and stopped in my tracks to see two removal vans parked in the yard. I hid behind the apple tree and watched them for a while. Unable to resist, I crept inside the house and waited for someone to come to the hallway.

"What are you doing 'ere?" a skinny man carrying a sealed box asked, as I stepped back to let him pass me.

"Why are you packing up the house?"

"What business is it of yours?" another man asked, coming through from the living room carrying a box. He stopped. "Are you the one who's been feeding the chickens?" I nodded. "Do you know where the family's gone?"

"No," I answered miserably. "I just came here one morning, and they'd left."

"When was that, do you remember?"

Of course, I remembered. I wasn't sure I wanted to confide in them though. "What's it to you?" I sniffed.

He smiled. "You're a cool little character, aren't you?" He looked at the door as the other man stepped back inside. "What are you, sixteen?"

"Fourteen. Why?"

He pulled a face. "No reason. I just heard they had a daughter your age living here. I think she went to school with my son."

Ordinarily I would have been polite and asked the son's name. If he went to Dee's school, then he would also be a schoolmate of mine, but I wasn't interested in anyone else, only this family. I wasn't going to go behind my friend's back and add to the local gossip mill.

"You don't know where they've moved to then?" I asked willing him to give me a positive answer.

"*Non*. Vanished, it seems."

I pointed at the box he was carrying. "Where are you taking all this?"

"Storage." The other guy replied, walking through the hall and into the living room. "We've been sent 'ere to pack up the place. If they don't settle the outstanding mortgage payments to the bank in three months we will auction it off." He pulled a face. "Not that much of this junk is worth anything."

I gasped. "You can't sell these things; they belong to Hazel and her family."

He bent his head closer to mine. "She should 'ave thought about that before running away, shouldn't she?"

I couldn't move. The only connection I had to my life here had been the objects left behind.

"You'd better get on now," the nicer one said. "We'll be leaving the chickens 'ere for the next tenants." He lowered his voice. "They'll be moving in tomorrow, so I would not return if I were you. You don't want to be caught trespassing, do you?"

I shook my head.

"Good. Now, go."

They watched me leave and determined not to go without something of Dee's, I pretended to start walking down the drive. Checking they weren't still watching me, I dashed behind one of the outbuildings and double-backed to the other side of the house before creeping in through the back door. I waited to hear footsteps to be sure they weren't anywhere near me and once I was certain both men were near the van outside, I ran up the stairs and into Dee's room.

Glancing round to try and spot anything precious to her that she might have left behind, I spotted a small photo album. I picked it up and put it on the bed, slowly opening her dressing table drawer to check inside there. I scooped up two bangles, a necklace with a daisy pendant and a silver ring with an enamel bluebird I recalled her mum buying her for a birthday. I threw everything down next to the album. The jeans were her favourites and she knew how much I loved them. I swallowed back tears when I realised her leaving them on the bed had been her goodbye message to me. So, she had thought of me, after all. I smiled at the notion.

Hearing a thump downstairs, I hurriedly rolled up the jeans and pushed them into Dee's old school satchel I'd spotted lying at the bottom of her wardrobe. I lifted the leather strap over my head, so it lay across my chest and put the rest of Dee's possessions from her bed inside it. As an afterthought, I peeled several photos of us both taken the previous summers and Christmases, slipping them deep into the bag.

I tiptoed into Hazel's room forgetting only to step on floorboards that didn't creak. Hearing the groan underfoot as my weight rested on one near the bedroom door I stopped, holding my breath until I was certain they hadn't heard me and entered her room. Dust motes danced in the sunrays casting long golden shafts across the familiar room. How many lazy days had I spent in this house daydreaming and relishing being part of their family? I took a deep shuddering breath to push away such thoughts and attempt to calm my nerves. It didn't work.

Unable to resist, I took hold of several colourful silk scarves that reminded me so much of Hazel. Lifting them to my nose, I breathed in the familiar patchouli and sandalwood mixture and remembered how she used to joke about being my second mum. I scrunched the material in my hands, pushing them into the bag before grabbing her silver-backed hairbrush, comb and mirror she'd left behind for whatever reason on her walnut dressing table.

My heart ached as I looked at the small silver frame surrounding a picture of Pierre hugging her from behind. Hazel was laughing, her head thrown back as she looked up at him. The sheer joy of that moment captured forever behind glass made me want to cry. I wasn't leaving this behind for some faceless auctioneer to give away to the highest bidder. One of these days, I promised myself, I would give these possessions back to Hazel and Dee.

The men's voices drifted upstairs. They'd finished packing up the living room and kitchen and were arguing about whether to start upstairs in the bedrooms, or clear out the book-filled study first. I wasn't sure if I dare chance crossing the landing again to go to Leo's room. I hesitated. Hearing footsteps coming down the hallway towards the bottom of the stairs, I quickly made for Dee's room and her bedroom window.

Taking a deep breath, I lifted the window frame, trying my best not to make it squeak and stepped carefully out onto her narrow window ledge. Thank heavens I had worn plimsolls; I dreaded to think how difficult it would be to perch on the side of a building wearing sandals. I placed one hand over the other, holding tightly onto the sill as I turned to face the old apple tree. I braced myself before launching forward, only just grabbing the branch and making it to the middle of the tree. I swung my leg up and over the largest branch, restricted only slightly by the bag hanging across my chest, and waited there for a few minutes until my heart stopped hammering so violently in my chest.

I could hear one of the men entering Dee's room. He came over to the window and peered out. Remembering what Pierre had told us earlier that summer when we were out looking for rabbits about keeping perfectly still if we wanted to appear invisible, I barely breathed. Hoping I was as camouflaged as I needed to be behind the leaves I waited. He stared out at the yard and, sensing my presence, looked directly at me. My heart almost stopped with fright, until I realised he was looking past me, through the leaves to the barn.

He withdrew back into her room, and as soon as I heard his footsteps on the stairs, I climbed down my legs shaking. Sighing with relief when my feet were firmly on the ground, I was about to race home, when I spotted one of Dee's red flip-flops near the water butt. She loved them, rarely wearing anything else if she could get away with it.

She wouldn't intentionally leave them behind and I knew then without a doubt that whatever had happened to make them run away it must have been something truly terrible. A well of despair built up inside me. I covered my mouth with my hand, unable to stop the tears from coursing down my face.

Desperate to get away from there, I ran as fast as I could across the fields, not keeping to my usual path, or caring that my legs were being stung by nettles as I raced home. Finally, breathless and in the safety of my bedroom, I quietly locked the door and slumped onto my bed. My legs itched and burnt, but I barely felt the pain. I angrily brushed away tears and unbuckled the two straps holding the satchel closed, tipping the contents onto my eiderdown.

It dawned on me that this was all that was left of a precious period in my life. A time that had been so much of an everyday experience and which until now I'd never realised how valuable it was to me. The dreams Dee and I held of a future studying at the same university would come to nothing. We wouldn't be travelling through Asia, or moving into a flat together in Paris, or London. Our dreams had been obliterated by their disappearance.

I picked up the scarves and wrapped them loosely around my neck, comforted by the scent. Despite the searing heat of the day I pulled on Dee's jeans, doing the belt up and smiling when it closed on the same hole she used. I wondered how long it would take me to get used to being without them, because it was obvious, even to me, that they didn't intend coming back. I hoped one day to be able to remember the happy times I'd spent with them at the farm without it stinging so painfully.

I cried for a bit longer, then blew my nose and glanced out of the window, staring into the sun until my eyes watered. Where was she? How could my best friend leave me behind?

A distant roll of thunder disturbed my thoughts. I held up the most recent photo I'd saved of me and Dee having fun. Our tanned faces beaming cheekily at the camera trying not to giggle. I recalled the evening; another impromptu party at Hazel's. We danced and for once Dee and I joined in with Hazel's singing, laughing with her friends around a large bonfire in the field. I looked carefree, never imagining that this way of life would end abruptly.

I picked up my Walkman and hooked the earphones into my ears needing to escape my thoughts. Pressing play, I went outside holding my hand out palm upwards when I felt the first drops of rain. I walked out of the garden gate and out into the field needing to be away from Mum's house. The rain fell harder and the strains of our favourite Tracy Chapman song, 'Baby Can I Hold You', began playing. I started to sing and then cry, and in the end, I didn't know if my face was wet from the rain or my tears.

# Chapter Nineteen

## 2003 – Hautvillers, Near Epernay

## Sera

Dee had run away, again. Only this time, for a fleeting second, I was relieved.

"Where do think she's gone?" Mum asked Leo.

I was distracted by whimpering coming from the landing and ran upstairs to find Katie sobbing into her teddy. I picked her up and hugged her tightly as she gulped great sobs into my shoulder. "She... she took her, Mummy. Dee took Ashley away," she stuttered.

"It's okay, darling," I soothed. "Dee's a little upset, that's all. We'll find her and bring Ashley back home."

I was following Leo and carrying Katie through the back gate to go and look for Dee and Ashley when Mum bellowed from an upstairs window for us to stop.

"I can't wait for you, Sera," Leo shouted over his shoulder as he broke into a run and hurtled across the field in the direction of the wood beyond Henri's farm.

"What, Mum?" I called, surprised to see she had gone

upstairs and irritated with her for holding me back. "I've got to help Leo find them."

Seconds later she ran outside, bearing down on me, arms open wide. "You're not taking that baby with you. There are reports on the radio of a huge fire on the other side of the hill. It's out of control and the wind is blowing it in this direction. We should stay here in case they come to evacuate everyone from their houses."

I hesitated and stared at Mum. She never usually told me what to do with Katie, especially not with such force and I knew she was right.

"I'm nearly five, Nanna Mo," Katie whined indignant to have been referred to as a baby.

Mum smiled at the angry little girl in my arms. "I know, darling, but I forgot for a moment." She tapped me on the shoulder and pointed towards the woods. "I know the fires are a distance away, but it wouldn't take much for them to reach the village. What if we have to leave at a moment's notice?"

I understood her concerns. "Mum, I have to go. You can keep Katie here and pack a few essentials for us, just in case."

The anguish on her face made me feel guilty about my determination to go.

"Sera, the foliage is tinder dry and this hot wind is aggravating conditions. You can't go in to the woods, it isn't safe."

I turned sharply, squinting through the open gate. I could see Leo almost at the edge of the wood, and darker skies in the distance I'd assumed to be the threat of rain.

Now, as I concentrated a little harder, it was obvious what I was looking at was smoke. Forest fires terrified me, but I couldn't in all honesty stay at home and not go and look for Dee and her little girl.

"I'd rather stay here," I admitted, pulling an apologetic face at her. "I can't though, not when Dee's oblivious to the danger and especially as she's got Ashley with her." I handed Katie to my mum's outstretched arms.

Katie screamed in fury and began to cry. "Katie find Ashley," she insisted, kicking out and throwing her teddy down onto the ground.

"No, sweetheart," Mum said, holding her tightly. "Mummy won't be long. We'll stay here and look out for her."

I lowered my voice. "Mum, if you need to take her to a friend's on the other side of town, do. I'll find you later. I promise I won't do anything reckless, but I know those woods far better than either Leo or Dee and I can't let them get lost out there and do nothing. I'll be fine."

Her eyes welled up with unshed tears. "You'd better be. Now go, if you must, but be back as soon as you can. We'll be waiting for you." She immediately turned away from me and began carrying my screaming child towards the house.

I broke into a run. I wanted to get this over with. Dried grasses broke underfoot as I stepped on them. It hadn't rained for so long I wasn't surprised a few fires had broken out. It was hot and I soon became breathless. I neared the woods and instead of the shade giving relief from the insistent heat, it struck me that the temperature here was warmer than in the direct sunlight. The fire must be getting closer.

I reasoned that they couldn't have got far and finding them wouldn't take too long. I certainly hoped I was right. Needing to stop for a few seconds, I bent down, resting my hands on my knees to help my breathing recover. I tilted my head listening out for any familiar voices. There wasn't even the usual birdsong. I did my best to quell the panic seeping into my mind and lifted the bottom of my T-shirt to wipe my damp forehead before running further into the woods calling for Dee and Ashley as loudly as I could manage.

I had to concentrate as I ran, narrowly avoiding a smaller branch hidden among the long brittle grass. Where were they? They couldn't have gone far. Dee was too frail to carry Ashley for long and Leo must be close behind them by now, surely. I slowed to a walk, the heat making me a little nauseous, but kept walking further into the woods, trying to keep to the usual track I took when going this way. I was so focused on finding them I hadn't noticed I'd been straying deeper than I would normally go. After a little while I stopped to get my bearings and stood, hands on hips, peering through the thickets and overgrown areas. I heard a distinctive crackling of fire as it devastated the vegetation in the forest.

Fear shot through me and my heart pounded. The fire was closing in and I hadn't found them. I turned around, but in the smoky air I couldn't tell which way I'd come. I tried not to panic and concentrated on the matter in hand. Dare I keep looking for them for a bit longer, or should I do as Mum insisted and hurry home?

I rubbed my dry eyes and tried to think. Every instinct told me to get away from here as fast as possible, but I needed to find these people. I couldn't ignore Mum and Katie worrying about me at home though and it was a relief when I heard bells of distant fire engines. They sounded a little too distant for my liking. It was hard to tell which direction they were coming from and it dawned on me that I was becoming so disorientated I wasn't even certain which was the way home.

A loud crash shocked me as something heavy landed about a hundred metres away. I cried out, trying not to become hysterical when I noticed orange flames dancing an insane tango on the hillside, wending their way at speed towards the woods. I didn't care which way my home happened to be now, my only thought was to get the hell out of here and as far away from this place as possible. The smog thickened. I screamed in terror, running as fast as my tired legs would carry me. A sharp edge of bark tore at my shin as I ran past a broken trunk, but nothing was going to stop me.

"Think about it later," I murmured, the sound of my own voice soothing me slightly. "Keep going." I didn't want to die alone. I couldn't bear the thought of my friend and her little girl being in here somewhere. Sense prevailed, and I pictured Katie's distraught face when I'd left her behind. I had to get out of here, for her and Mum.

My legs got heavier. I began to cry. "Keep going," I whispered, focusing all my attention on placing one foot in front of the other. Breathless and trembling, I reached the edge of the wood. It was a long way from where I'd entered. I couldn't believe how far I had gone in my search for Dee. Where the hell had they got to? Maybe she recovered from her hysteria and returned to the house. I hoped so. I began to hobble out into the sunlit field, when I heard the unmistakable creaking and screaming of falling trees as they gave in to the tremendous heat.

I turned towards the sound, light-headed with fright when I spotted how close the fire was to me. I needed to run, but my legs were like jelly and my muscles strained, I couldn't get them to work properly. I was about to give in to my mounting hysterics when I heard a voice.

"Sera. Sera, where are you?" It was Henri calling for me. He sounded frantic and I didn't think I'd ever be so relieved to hear another person's voice.

I tried to answer him, but could only manage a pathetic sob. I needed him to find me. I took a deep breath and tried again. "Henri," I cried. "I'm over here." My voice sounded tinny and unnatural. I pleaded with God to let Henri hear me.

I heard him shout again, and spotted his red T-shirt moving quickly through the thick branches and trees. He called me again. "Sera, where are you?"

"Henri," I sobbed. I glanced over towards the cracking and spitting of the fire as it kept closing in. "We're going the wrong way."

"Sera. Listen to me."

I could hear the pounding of his footsteps as he came

closer and the occasional swearword as he tripped, or bashed into something. "Run, this way," he insisted.

I ran a few steps but the thought of running towards the fire seemed like madness, so I stopped.

"Run to me."

I had to trust him. I had no choice. I broke in to a run of sorts and as the shadows of the wood enveloped me, he almost bowled me over. Slamming into me, he grabbed hold of me pulling me tight against his pounding chest. "I thought I'd lost you."

It didn't even occur to me to be taken aback by his words, I simply clung to him, my hands gripping the back of his damp top relieved not to be along any longer.

"I'm so scared. How did you know I was here?"

"I was on my way to warn you about the fire and saw you from across the field as you ran into the woods." Letting go of me, he then grabbed hold of my shoulders. "It will be okay. Be calm." He scanned the area around us. Pointing towards a dip in the bank he shouted for me to take off my shoes.

"What for?"

"They are the closest thing you have for a spade." He grabbed a large stick and clawed the ground.

He wasn't making any sense. "What are you doing?" We needed to run, not mess about in this hell. I stared at him, not sure whether to laugh or cry at the insanity of what he was doing.

"Dig. *Vite*. Hurry." He motioned for me to get on my knees and copy him. Needing to trust him, I did as he insisted. "We cannot outrun this fire," he panted, as we clawed away at the earth beneath us. "We must dig a ditch and cover ourselves with earth." He took a deep, laboured breath in the airless wood. "I am hoping the fire will jump from this ledge and continue over there, missing us."

Fires didn't jump, did they? It didn't seem very plausible to me, but I couldn't see any alternative. My legs had pretty much given up and even I knew I couldn't out run a fire.

"I couldn't find them," I cried, stabbing frantically at the earth, which thankfully was still a little moist from the shade of the trees. I don't know if it was sheer panic, or a will to live, or something else entirely, but I dug like a crazy woman. With his strength and perseverance, we soon had an area big enough for us both to lie back into the crevice under the bank.

"Lie down, as far back as possible," he said, helping me push myself backwards. The cool damp earth soothed my overheated skin and made what was transpiring around me seem like I wasn't completely involved.

"Now you," I said, arms outstretched to take hold of him. He bent down to come to me, when he stopped. Kneeling upright, his head turned slightly, alerted to something.

"What is it? Henri, get in," I screamed, panic-stricken.

"Crying," he said simply, holding up his hand to quieten me. "Do not move. If I am not back in two minutes lift the material of your top over your face and cover yourself with the loose earth. Do not move until you are certain the fire has passed over you."

I couldn't take in what he was saying. "Henri, you're not leaving me here?"

He turned without another word and ran off into the woods. I lay petrified, my mouth opened in a silent scream of terror. He had left me. He was going to die. We both were.

I could feel the thundering crash of the burning trees as the fire fought its way towards me. This wasn't happening. It couldn't be. I strained my eyes to see him, the temptation to run towards the field taking hold of me. Did I still have time to make it? I was kidding myself. I had no choice but to lie here in this dip in the bank and trust him. I owed it to Katie to at least try to survive. So, giving one last look in the direction he'd gone, I grabbed a small branch and scooped a heap of earth towards my feet, my legs and upwards, slowly covering my body.

I'd just reached my waist, when I heard cries and saw Henri making his way through the undergrowth towards me. He was carrying Ashley, his arm clamping her to his chest. I covered my mouth to stop from whimpering with relief. His other hand gripped tightly around Dee's wrist. As he dragged her to my hiding place, she stumbled, tears coursing down her dusty face.

He put Ashley down next to me. We have little time, Sera," he said breathlessly. "Kick away the earth, dig deeper."

I did as he said. "You too," I shouted at Dee. "Bloody help us."

She glanced at me, then following my lead, took off her wooden sandal, handed me one and we both dug frantically.

If this damn bank didn't collapse on us it would be nothing short of a miracle, I realised glancing up at the roots of the tree arcing above us.

"Enough, no more time now. Get in," Henri ordered, the panic obvious in his voice. "You first," he pushed Dee back to lie flat against the dugout wall, then handing Ashley to her, told her to lie still. "Hold her, tight," he said to Dee. He looked at me, his face taught with tension, "Now you."

I wriggled into the dip, getting as close to Dee as I could. "Lift your tops to cover your faces," I said, repeating what he'd told me to do earlier. Dee lifted Ashley's dirty top over the child's wide-eyed expression. "It's going to be all right, Ashley," I said, giving her a promise, I knew I might not be able to keep. "You'll lie between me and Mummy. We'll cuddle you the whole time."

We didn't have much choice. The dip in the bank was only really big enough for two of us, but at a push we should just about manage. I hoped so, anyway. I felt the weight of damp earth being dropped on my feet, my legs, over my hips and then the heat of Henri's hot, damp body against me. He slid one arm under my head and pressed tightly against me, somehow managing to pull earth over us. I covered my face with my top and hugged the trembling child, grateful to have him behind me.

He only just managed to cover us when a roar of heat, crashing debris and smoke rolled over on top of us in a thunderous fiery wave of destruction. We collectively held our breaths. I squeezed poor Ashley so tight against my chest I worried I might hurt her. Henri squashed against me, pushing me against the others and almost crushing Dee against the earth wall of the bank.

The heat and the deafening rage of the fire seemed like it was taking forever to pass over us, but I reasoned that if I could be almost senseless with terror, we must at least still be alive. Henri's plan appeared to be working. I tried to calm my breathing beginning to hope we might survive this horror and pictured Katie's pretty face. I willed her to hear my thoughts telling her how much I loved her.

After an interminable time that probably only lasted a minute or two, Henri's body relaxed slightly. I daren't speak. I waited for him to tell me what to do next, too afraid to move in case I uncovered our bodies.

He backed away slowly from me then pulled me out of the hole. "It is okay. The fire jumped the bank. We can go."

I took Ashley from Dee and lifted her back out of the dip, reaching a hand out to Dee to help her. She lowered her top from her face and I uncovered Ashley's face and forced a smile. "You see, we're fine," I said, my voice husky from the dry air. "We've had a little adventure."

Dee stared at me, then at Henri; she looked as if she'd made a major discovery. "You risked your lives to save ours."

He closed his eyes briefly and I suspected he was trying to hide his irritation with her for getting us all into this mess in the first place. "We must hurry. Come."

He took Ashley in his arms and took my hand. I grabbed Dee's and we followed him, barely able to keep up as he led us out of the smoking wood, past smaller fires and burning branches to the blackened field and in the direction of the town away.

The walk home seemed to take forever, and I breathed a sigh of relief when we reached the garden gate. We stopped and turned in unison to stare silently over the fields to where fire engines dampened the small fires that sprung up seemingly from nowhere closer to the village. Each of us lost in the trauma of what we had experienced.

He lowered Ashley to the ground.

"Thank you," Dee said, bending down to hug Ashley tightly. The little girl stared up at him.

Henri cleared his throat looking a little embarrassed. He moved his weight from one foot to the other. "I must return to my farm." He ruffled Ashley's hair, gently removing a stray leaf and bent down, his face level with hers. "You were very brave, *ma petite*."

Dee looked at Henri questioningly. "How did you know where to find us?"

I suddenly became aware that I was still gripping hold of Henri's hand, so let go. "Please, come inside with us for a drink," I said, my voice croaky from the smoke. "You must be terribly thirsty, I know I am."

He shook his head. "*Non*. I must check my animals." He moved back to give Dee and Ashley space to pass.

I watched them go inside the house, looking for Leo. The enormity of what we'd just survived began to dawn on me and I started to tremble. "Thank you for coming to find me," I said, certain I'd never been as grateful to anyone else.

He stared at me, his expression solemn before taking hold of me and pulling me against him in a hug. I could feel his warm breath on my neck. "I had no choice," he whispered, leaning slightly back to be able to give me a slow, exhausted smile. "I must go."

I leant against the roughness of the warped wooden gate staring at the devastation in the distance and shivered despite the heat at the thought of what could have been had Henri not managed to find the three of us. Where had he learnt those survival techniques? I ran into the garden towards the house.

"They're not here," Dee shouted from the back door. She held up a note and waved it in the air. "They've all been evacuated to the Hotel de Ville in Epernay."

Desperate to hold Katie in my arms, I looked back out towards the wood and couldn't see any further flames. "I think it'll be okay now. The fire can't burn the same area twice, not straight away. I'll go and fetch Mum and Katie, you and Ashley go and shower." Where is Leo?

I hurriedly grabbed my car keys, not letting myself ponder on what could have been. Mum would be out of her mind with panic until she saw I was okay. I drove to fetch them and after hugging Katie who whined that I smelt of 'dirt and smoke', and having to listen to a lengthy lecture from Mum about my foolhardy actions, I brought them and a couple of our neighbours back to the village. We were stopped by a gendarme by the edge of the village who insisted we leave immediately should another fire spring up anywhere near the town. I agreed with everything he said, desperate to get back to the house and shower.

"You go and shower, Sera," Mum said. "I'll find Katie something to eat and then we can have a well-deserved drink."

I smiled at her, aware I'd put her through hell. Remembering Leo's absence, I whispered my concerns about him to Mum.

"But Leo was here when we left, darling," she said. "I'm surprised you didn't see him when you got back."

"He's here?" Dee asked, coming down the stairs, sounding shocked. "Why didn't he come looking for us?"

"I've no idea," Mum said. "Have you tried looking in his bedroom?"

"No, I haven't," Dee snapped, pushing past me to run up to his room.

"That girl." My mother pointed in Dee's direction, then, glancing up at the ceiling and remembering Katie was in the room, lowered her voice. "If it hadn't been for her foolishness, you and that dear little girl of hers could have perished in that horrendous fire."

I went to argue, then noticed the paleness of my mother's face so walked over to her and put an arm around her shoulder to comfort her.

"Sera, you're filthy, go and shower."

I smiled. After everything that had happened, her main concern was me being dirty. "I'll go and clean up." I spotted Dee coming back downstairs. "She's right though, you could have got us all killed out there today. Why did you run off like that?"

Dee glared at me. "You wouldn't understand." She flounced out of the room and I chased after her. I'd had enough of her moods and this was going to stop.

I grabbed hold of her arm stopping her in her tracks. "I'm

taking a shower and then you and I are going to sit down and sort a few things out."

She snatched her arm away from my hand. "Really? You're calling the shots again, I see."

What the hell was wrong with her? "Hey," I said, too emotionally drained to have a full-scale quarrel. "Mum and I have been good to you, putting up with your moods. I think the least you can do is try to clear the air between us. I want to help you if only for Ashley's sake. She must be wondering what the hell is going on right now."

"Ashley is my business, not yours."

"That's where you're wrong, Dee," I said shaking my head. "We're all fond of her and I'm not going to let you fob me off any longer. I don't know what you think, but to the rest of us she looks traumatised and that's heart-breaking." I started walking up the stairs leaving her behind. "I'll catch up with you shortly."

I went into my bedroom and locked the door. Pulling off my clothes, I kicked them into one of the corners on the bathroom floor. I turned on the shower, waiting until it was reasonably warm and stepped in, soaping myself all over. It was bliss to finally be clean. I shampooed my hair thoroughly, spotting leaves and a couple of clumps of earth in the shower tray. I had endured enough of Dee's self-indulgent misery and I didn't know if it was a reaction against what we'd endured earlier, but I wanted answers from her, whether she liked it, or not.

Someone had to stand up for her daughter and I could see Leo was more concerned with Dee's feelings than

Ashley's. I couldn't understand how he didn't appear to notice the little girl's physical frailty, let alone her emotional state. Satisfied I'd rid myself of as much dirt and grime as possible, I turned off the shower and stepping out onto the cool tiled floor, dried myself hurriedly and dressed in an old cotton sundress.

I sat down at my dressing table and began brushing my hair. Catching my reflection in the mirror, it dawned on me how frightened I still looked. My resolve to be strong dissolved and the shock of what we'd experienced smacked me in the chest like a fist punching me. I began to cry, slowly at first. Allowing the first tears to flow was a big mistake. Within seconds I was sobbing. Hulking great, salty tears coursed down my pink cheeks. As fast as I brushed them away, a further torrent followed at the thought of what might have been.

Henri had only just found us in time; the reality chilled me. I tried to push away the image of Katie standing alone by the window with Mum, wondering when I'd return. My little girl could have been an orphan before she was five years old and it would have been my fault making the decision to run off after Dee. Damn Dee for her selfishness and me for chasing after her.

I cursed the day I'd bumped into Leo in the village. Ever since that morning, my life and that of my family had been dictated to by his sister in various ways. Dee's sullen, emotional reactions to everything always ended up affecting the rest of us. I pulled my hair back, twisting it up into a French pleat and attached a hairclip to hold it in place. I blew my nose on a tissue and wiped away the tears, my upset now replaced by fury. I unlocked my bedroom door and braced myself for the onslaught that was about to happen.

"Dee?" I called barely able to contain my rage. I didn't want to frighten the girls, but I wanted to ensure Dee couldn't ignore me. "You've got ten minutes to get yourself down to the kitchen."

I checked my watch. It was early evening and I wasn't going to spend one more night under the same roof as these people without giving them a few home truths. I checked on Katie and Ashley who were now playing quietly in Katie's room. It was cooler on that side of the house and soothed by their innocent playing, I watched them silently for a little while before leaving them. I walked downstairs and poured myself a glass of rosé, taking it out to the garden. The hot breeze cooled the dry air a little, so at least it wasn't as humid as it had been for the past few weeks.

I walked over to the garden gate and pulled it open, glancing in the direction of Henri's farm and then over to the wood. The smoke had almost gone, but the fire engines were still dowsing the area. I hoped we'd seen the last of the fires. At least the wind direction had changed, and we could rest easy, knowing the village was safe from the fire for the time being.

I leant against the wooden frame, staring over towards the farm and took a sip of the cool liquid. I'd been so unutterably furious with Henri for investigating Mum, but after him risking his life for me I didn't think I had the right to criticise him about anything. In fact, I owed him. I was just contemplating inviting him over for Mum to answer a few of his, and to be honest my own questions, when I spotted Leo out of the corner of my eye coming towards me.

"Hi, how's it going?" He seemed a little awkward, which I'm sure I would be too if I'd run off and left my sister and child to be found by a relative stranger.

"Where the hell did you get to?" I asked, bewildered by his disappearance. "I thought you'd gone to find your sister and Ashley, only to discover you'd come back here while Henri and I risked our lives for them."

He frowned. "I did look for her, but I don't know my way around like you do. When I couldn't find them, I assumed Dee had seen the smoke, come to her senses and run back here." He shook his head, his eyes wide as if reliving a nightmare. "I promise you, Sera, after I'd checked the house, I went to go back to the woods, but could see the fire and knew there was nothing I could have done to help anyone at that point."

I was still furious with him, but what he said did make sense. "I'm fed up of keeping my mouth shut. It's about time I spoke to Dee about the way she's behaving."

"Don't you think she's been through enough today?"

I moved away from the gate and stared at him. "I think I probably know what she's gone through today, Leo. I was happy for you both to stay here, but her moods are very disrupting to Mum and Katie." I shrugged. "If I don't get answers, she'll have to make other arrangements. Ashley can stay here until Dee is settled somewhere, but I'm not going to put up with her unsettling this household any longer. I've had enough."

Something caught my eye moving past the coloured glass in the upstairs hall window. Good, Dee was on her way down. Perhaps now I could resolve this mess.

"Please, Sera," Leo lowered his voice. "You don't know what wounds you'll open up if you push for her to tell you everything."

"I don't really care." I waivered for a second, immediately after reminding myself that Katie and Mum's sanity came first in my priorities and not those of someone I'd known years ago.

He shook his head. "Don't say I didn't warn you."

I was sick of these underhand threats of discourse. They'd held me back from speaking out for too long. Nothing was as bad as almost losing my life, and after this afternoon I was determined to drag this house back to some semblance of calm and normalcy, despite his concerns.

Dee looked at us from the open back door before descending the steps and coming to join us. I noticed her hair was still wet. Maybe she was also ready to finally resolve things.

"Shall we go and sit over there," I suggested, gesturing towards the garden furniture.

Dee nodded and accompanied me, but not before I spotted her ignoring the pointed look Leo gave her.

"Right," I said, when we were all seated. Leo folded his arms across his chest looking nervous.

"Go on then," Dee said. "Let's get this over with."

"Look, Leo explained about the dreadful time you suffered at the hands of your ex," I said.

"That's thoughtful of him," she said giving him a sideways glance. "Carry on."

I raised an eyebrow, not certain why she was suddenly in a hurry to speak to me. "I sympathise with you, Dee. We were good friends once and I care about you."

"You do?" She smirked and shook her head. "Do you care for me like you would a sister?"

I didn't know what she was going on about. I went to answer but before I could Mum interrupted me.

"Stop this," she shouted from the bottom of the steps as she marched to join us. She glared at Dee. "You should be ashamed of yourself."

"Why? Because I know your secret and your precious daughter doesn't?"

I glanced at Mum, confused, but she was too busy glaring at Dee to notice.

"Haven't you caused enough chaos today?" Mum bent down, her face almost nose to nose with Dee's. "I told you to stop. If anyone is going to tell Sera, I will, not you."

I stared at the two of them, like two lionesses fighting for seniority. A sense of dread crept up from my gut. "What are you talking about?" I asked aware the tables were about to be turned on me. "What secret?"

Dee smiled. "The secret your mother's been determined to keep from you all these years." She laughed. "Do you want to know what it is?"

# Chapter Twenty

## 1976 – Marne-la-Vallee, Near Paris

## Mo

Why wasn't Hazel asleep? I looked around for her, then heard the loo being flushed in the bathroom. She came back into the room getting a shock when she realised I was staring at her from my bed.

"Sorry, did I wake you?" she asked.

"No," I said, feeling mean about our earlier quarrel. I tried to find the words to encourage her to share what Vinnie had said.

"I know what you're thinking," she said, climbing back into her bed. "He's not as perfect as you'd like him to be, you know?"

I did know, but wasn't quite ready to admit that my dreams of a future with Vinnie were not going to happen. "I'm not as naive as you think."

Hazel sat up slightly, turning to face me she rested on one elbow. "He's a villain, Mo. I know I've got a thing about him, and he's the best-looking guy I've ever seen, but he can be nasty."

I thought back to his shocking change of mood earlier and his rough treatment of her. "Then why do you still like him, if he's so vile to you?"

She groaned. "It's not just me; he's like this to everyone." She hesitated for a while. "You don't seriously believe that garbage about Alice going home to her granddad's funeral, do you?"

I had. "Yes," I admitted, not sure why anyone would lie about such a thing. "Why, where is she?"

Hazel gave a shuddering sigh and hesitated before replying. "She's in a private clinic in the country somewhere."

Intrigued, I sat up, leaning back against the leatherette headboard. "Go on."

"She was beaten up."

I gasped. "Who'd do such a thing?" Poor Alice, I might not like her very much, but I hated to think of anyone attacking her. "Who hurt her? Do you know?"

Hazel lay back down again, resting her head on her hands. "I shouldn't tell you."

"So why are you then?" She was irritating me now. "Look, you can't announce something this horrible and not finish the story. Who beat her up? Tell me." She remained silent, so I softened my approach. "Please."

"I was told in confidence," she whispered.

This was getting a bit scary. "I promise I won't tell a soul," I pleaded. "You obviously need to share this with someone and surely I'm the ideal person."

She murmured something to herself and covering her face with her hands briefly, said, "You have to promise never to tell a soul. Really, if you repeated this to anyone it could put us both in terrible danger."

"I said I promise, and I do." I pushed a stray strand of hair behind my ear and waited nervously for her to tell me the dreadful secret.

"It was Vinnie."

I shook my head and laughed. "Oh, come on." Was she teasing me? "Look, I know he's a bit brooding and his moods can be a little scary at times, but he wouldn't beat up a woman." As I said the words my brain seemed to catch up with my mouth and my conviction in his strength of character began to wane. "She's his girlfriend," I added, to convince myself more than Hazel.

I could see her nodding in the darkened room. "I know."

I considered this terrifying information. "But how do you know this? I mean, who told you?"

"Who do you think?"

"Jean-Paul seems pretty close to him. Do you think he maybe took her to the clinic then?" I felt sick. This couldn't be happening. I loved Vinnie. Did this mean he could be capable of doing something like that to me? The notion was unimaginable.

"No, I think he only uses Jean-Paul as his driver when he comes over to France and anyway he wasn't the one who told me."

"Then who?" I swallowed the nausea rising in my throat.

"Come on, Mo. It was Vinnie, obviously." I could hear the panic in her voice and my breath caught in my throat. "No one else would dare split on him."

"Bloody hell, Hazel," I whispered when I could finally force out the words. Nausea welled up inside me. "What the hell have you got me involved with?" I leaped out of bed and began pacing the room. My heart pounded as I pictured Vinnie. Could he really be capable of something so violent? My instincts told me he could. "What if he turns on us next?"

"Why do you think I'm so frightened?"

She sounded as terrified as I felt. My new and exciting life didn't seem quite so enthralling now. For a moment, I even wished I was back at home in my boring village where nothing much ever happened. "But he was so gentle when I slept with him," I said.

"Me, too," she replied.

I stopped pacing. "What? When?" Despite my newfound fear of him, jealousy coursed through my veins.

Hazel turned away from me, pulling the sheet over her head. "Last week, when you were working at the cocktail bar."

I stared at her shrouded figure noticing she was trembling. All the jealousy I had felt towards her and our competitive fight over this charismatic man dispersed. Shocked to have almost lost my only friend in London because of Vinnie, I was ashamed to have assumed myself clever and sophisticated simply because of a train journey south to the capital. I had to swallow to keep from crying.

"He's played us both for fools, hasn't he?" I murmured, aware all the dreamy words he'd whispered to me were probably a repeat of the same ones he'd used on Hazel, and others. No wonder she'd been so funny with me in the car. "We've been such idiots."

"Yes," she said, her voice muffled by the sheet and, I suspected, tears. "And he's coming back here to the hotel any time now."

I tried to think what we could do next. Nothing came to me and panicking wouldn't help either of us. I got back into bed, cold despite the intense heat. "Look, he doesn't know you've told me anything."

Hazel began to cry. I could see her shaking and hated myself for pushing her to confide in me. We'd both been naive enough to fall into his trap. How often had he done this sort of thing before? "Maybe Alice wasn't the first girlfriend he'd lost his temper with?"

Hazel whimpered. "I'm scared, Mo."

"Me, too," I said. "But I'm an actress, I can act," I said, with more conviction than I felt. "I'll pretend I don't know anything then he'll have no reason to be angry with you."

Hazel sat up, wiping her eyes on her sheet leaving black mascara stains. "Do you think he's told me on purpose to test if I'll confide in you?"

The thought had occurred to me. "It's possible. After all, he seems to have instigated everything else we've done so far."

"Oh God." She began crying more vigorously this time. "He's going to kill us."

I got out of my bed and lay down next to her, holding her in my arms. He would be back at some point and our plan to act as if nothing had happened wasn't going to work if he found her in this state. "You have to calm down," I said, willing her to take control of herself. "Hazel, listen to me. It's going to be fine. I won't let him hurt you."

She sniffed. "How can you stop him?"

I hadn't thought that far. "I don't know, but I'll think of something. Now stop crying, please." I patted her shoulder. "Go to the bathroom, wash your face and get back into bed. We have to act like nothing's happened. He might just be telling you this to test you and see how you react. He must get a kick out of these mind games, so don't give him the satisfaction and show him you're tougher than you look."

"But I'm not."

"I know," I said trying not to panic but aware that I had to do my best to get her to calm down, for both our sakes. "Try to make him think you are."

I waited for her to finish splashing around in the bathroom and settle back down into her bed. The exhaustion of the flight over here, hours of driving and the concert took its toll and I finally drifted off into a nightmare-filled sleep.

Something woke me. I wasn't sure how long I'd been asleep and rubbed my eyes looking across the room to see if Hazel was sleeping. Her bed was empty. I listened to hear if she was in the bathroom again, but couldn't hear her. Concerned she might have panicked and done something stupid, I got up and went to check if she was okay, but she wasn't there. I splashed water on my face to try and wake me up a bit and force my tired brain to start working.

Knowing it was unlikely that she would have chosen to

go off somewhere in the early hours of the morning, I went to dress in my jeans. Then, remembering I was in the hotel, I opened my wardrobe and pulled out the green cocktail dress Vinnie insisted I bring in case he needed to introduce me to anyone important.

I ran a brush through my hair and checked my face. I hadn't bothered to remove my make-up and spat on a tissue, rubbing it under my eyes to make my face passable. I pushed my feet into the satin shoes matching my dress and left the room to look for her. I told myself there was probably a perfectly rational reason for her to go for a walk at nearly three in the morning and ran to the lift pressing the button several times impatiently. When it eventually arrived, I got in and went down to check the bar and restaurant. However, apart from a couple of noisy pilots there wasn't anyone else about.

I wasn't sure where to try next, but as I stood at the lift waiting for it to arrive, I tried to shift the heavy feeling of doom pressing down on me. It dawned on me that I had little choice but to go to Vinnie's room and look for her. I was unaware if he had returned to the hotel, but couldn't turn my back on her now I knew how dangerous he could be. The lift took me up to our floor and I walked quietly towards his bedroom further along the hallway from ours.

Stopping outside, I leaned my head closer to the door and listened. Voices came from inside. If I'd have stood here hearing him in his bedroom with someone else a few hours earlier, I would have been hysterical with jealousy. Now I was just frightened. I knew him a little better now. I heard a muffled cry and recognised it as Hazel's voice. She was pleading with him and sounded terrified.

My heart raced, and I took a deep breath to try and control my rising panic. I placed my hand on the door handle and slowly turned it, relieved, yet horrified, when it moved in my hand and the door opened. Pushing it ajar, I could hear her cries more clearly now.

"Please, Vinnie, I swear I didn't tell her," she cried, her swollen lips distorting her voice. "She loves you, you know she does. No one can ever change that."

Her pleading was lost on him. I bent my head to look around the door and peered inside. He was crouched over her. Her nightie had been torn from her shoulders and now barely concealed her bruised body. She was too busy shielding her face to notice me. Her right eye was swollen shut and her thighs grazed and bruised. Vinnie knelt between her legs.

How could I have thought myself in love with this monster?

Holding her down with one hand around her neck, he bent his arm back. "You're a fucking liar," he hissed, saliva spraying through his gritted teeth. He clenched his fist, getting ready to strike her again.

Desperate to stop him, I glanced around the room and spotted a heavy glass ashtray. I grabbed it lifting it high, just as he turned to face me, shocked to find me there registering on his face. He hesitated. Squealing in revulsion at what I was about to do, I slammed the heavy object as hard as I could against his temple. I watched in dazed horror as it split his skin, shattering into pieces onto the carpet.

He stared at me, momentarily stunned. Then, closing his eyes, he dropped like a slaughtered bull onto the carpet next to Hazel. She pressed her hands over her mouth to stifle her screams. Shocked by what I'd just done, I bent down to lift his leg off her and helped her to stand.

"You killed him," Hazel whispered.

My heart pounded painfully. I let go of the remains of the ashtray still in my hand, and shivered. "What do we do now?" I asked, swallowing a wave of nausea. "We can't leave him here. They'll come for us."

"Did you have to hit him so hard?" Hazel asked, trembling.

"What? You'd rather I make him angry by tapping his head?" I tried not to panic. "He'd have killed us." I pointed at Hazel. "He's already battered you."

Vinnie's warm blood oozed across the rug reaching my feet and making them sticky. I stepped back.

Hazel grabbed Vinnie's dressing gown from the chair and pulled it over her ripped nightdress. Tying the cord belt, she took hold of my shoulders. "You saved my life, Mo," she panted. "We have to get rid of him though."

What did she just say? I stared at Vinnie, humiliated to realise how easily his movie star looks had distracted me from his dark personality. "How? Where?"

Hazel's hands shook, and I wished we could go back twenty-four hours.

"Get a towel," Hazel said. "Put it around his head before he really starts to bleed."

I glanced at a large glass shard embedded in Vinnie's skull, relieved to note it was stemming the blood flow.

"Quickly," Hazel said. "We'll need to get rid of this rug. We don't want blood seeping through to the carpet. We don't have time to clean this place."

My legs trembled, as I walked to the bathroom to find a towel. A terrifying thought occurred to me as I carried it to Hazel to wrap around Vinnie's head. "If he's bleeding, doesn't that mean he's still alive?"

"Only just, by the look of him." Hazel retched as she lifted his head. "Help me."

We struggled to wrap the towel around Vinnie's head. Once done, Hazel sat back on her haunches. "That will have to do for now." She raked her hands through her messy hair. "I'm going to get dressed, wait here."

"You can't leave me alone," I said, horrified at the thought of being left with him.

"If someone comes answer the door, just don't open it." Hazel grimaced as she pulled a handkerchief out of his dressing gown pocket. "If they think he's in here with you, they'll be too scared to insist on coming in. Make some excuse," she hesitated. "Say he's in the bathroom." Hazel winced as she walked to the door. "You'd better wash his blood off your feet."

I did as she said. I couldn't stop crying as the red water ran from my feet and down the sides of the sink. Spotting one of Vinnie's ties, it dawned on me that if we were going to make him disappear, then we needed to make it look as if he'd left of his own volition.

We needed to hide his things, too. Vinnie was too proud of his personal effects to leave them behind. I ran across the room, tiptoeing around his body. I pulled his suitcase from where he'd left it next to the wardrobe. Wrenching his bespoke suits from hangers, I threw them and his underwear from the drawers untidily into the case.

Hurrying into the bathroom, I opened his leather wash bag. I held it above the sink and brushed my shaking arm across the glass shelf, sweeping his toothpaste, aftershave and razor into the bag. Then, taking his toothbrush from the glass, I dropped that in. I pushed away a mental replay of what I had done to him, and hurriedly zipped up the bag, before throwing it into the case.

I scanned the room for anything I might have missed. "Wallet," I whispered, remembering the brown leather wallet he always had crammed with notes and ready to hand to tip someone lavishly. Though I was now sure it was more to show others how successful he was, than generosity. I pulled open the bedside drawer, retrieving his wallet and a pair of gold cufflinks.

The light reflected off his heavy gold watch. Taking a deep breath, I unclasped it, cringing at the touch of his flesh as I removed it from his wrist. "Damn," I groaned, aware that I also needed to pull off his pinkie ring. It was a bit of a struggle and I gritted my teeth forcing myself to complete the grim task. The heavy gold chain around his neck was all that remained for me to take from his body.

Finally, exhausted and sweating, I pushed the last vestiges of Vinnie's possessions into a side pocket in the case.

The door opened. I froze until I spotted Hazel's dark hair.

"What are you doing?" Hazel frowned, spotting the open case. I explained hurriedly. "Good thinking. Make sure we've got everything. Is his wallet in there?" I nodded. "Because we're going to need money. It's our only way of getting out of Paris and back to London."

My trembling hands made it difficult to close the catches on Vinnie's case. "I'll take this to our room," I whispered to Hazel, desperate to get away.

After checking that there was no one else in the hallway, I crept to our bedroom. I couldn't bear the thought of returning to Vinnie's room, but knew I had no choice. I took a few deep breaths to calm myself and got going.

"Do you think it'd be safe for us to go back to London?" I wondered, not ready to leave the city I had fallen in love with. "Everyone at the club knows we came here with Vinnie and his mates. Won't they ask us questions if we go back without him?"

Hazel nodded, thoughtfully. "I suppose they will. We need to get rid of him before we think about running away though. Help me roll him onto his back," she said. "That's it. Now lift his arm over your shoulder and I'll do the same." We groaned with the strain. "It's going to be an effort, but I've done this a few times with my brothers when they're drunk. I'm sure we can manage to get him out of here if we're determined."

He was heavier than I expected. The effort of carrying him in the warm night air was exhausting.

"Where are we going?" I asked, as it dawned on me that we hadn't discussed the next step of our plan.

"This way."

We dragged him along, his head flopping between our bodies. Too late, I wished I had thought to change out of my heels.

"There's a service entrance," Hazel said, indicating the direction with her nod. I noticed that despite our struggle to move him, Hazel's voice appeared stronger. "I checked it when I went to change," she said. "It's late so hopefully we won't be disturbed out here."

We hoisted him up a little further onto our shoulders.

"Shit, he's heavy," Hazel whispered, her voice strained with the effort.

"Where exactly are we going?" I asked as we rounded a corner at the end of the corridor.

Hazel indicated a service lift. "There are some woods out the back."

Once down on the ground floor, we manoeuvred Vinnie outside.

Hazel stopped abruptly. "Shh."

"What?"

"I thought I heard someone."

We waited. When there was no further sound, we moved away from the doorway.

"I'm scared," I admitted, pushing aside the thought of someone discovering us with his body. I wasn't sure I could go through with this.

"Shut up," Hazel whispered. "You were the one who

smashed him over the head, remember?"

The thought that this was my fault frightened me. I choked back tears. I didn't want to end up spending the rest of my life in prison for what I had done. "I was trying to stop him killing you."

"I know." Hazel's voice softened. "But you were the one who killed him, not me. I'm trying to help you hide his body. Now let's get a move on. The sooner we do this the sooner we can get far away from this place."

After almost dropping him, we eventually reached the wooded area. I was grateful for the denseness of the thick leaves overhead. They diminished the pearl whiteness of the moonlight and gave us much needed cover.

A revolting thought occurred to me. "We need to strip him and dump his clothes."

"Good idea," Hazel agreed. "I'm going to find something for us to dig with. They must have a gardener working in the hotel gardens, he should have a spade or two somewhere."

Hazel had run off into the darkness before I had time to stop her. Pushing away my squeamishness, I stripped Vinnie. I kicked his once beautiful bespoke grey suit out of the way, and stood up. This was a living nightmare. I notice Hazel coming back. She was holding up a huge shovel that looked as if it was used for coal rather than soil.

"I also found this smaller spade." She handed the larger one to me. "Quick, we don't have much time."

We dug for what seemed like hours. We needed to hide all traces of him. Even though he was dead, he still had the power to hurt us. The thought was terrifying.

His head moved.

I dropped the spade and covered my mouth to stop from screaming. "He's still alive," I grimaced, swallowing bile rising in my throat.

"Shush." Hazel's controlled was more chilling than the thought of what we were doing. "We have no choice. We must get rid of him. Now, dig."

I slammed the blade of the shovel down into the hard earth with as much force as my exhausted arms could muster. "Surely this is deep enough now?" I whispered a few minutes later, my body trembling with the effort of trying to remain calm.

Vinnie groaned. The sound seemed to echo through the night air.

I was too scared to look at him, even though I could hear him battling to breathe inches from my feet. "He's still alive."

"I can see that," Hazel spat. "Keep going. We'll soon be finished and then we can forget about everything that's happened tonight."

You might be able to, I thought. My shoulders were agony and my blistered hands stung. My heart almost stopped in my chest when Vinnie opened his swollen eyes and slowly drew his gaze up from my feet to stare at my face. I could barely breathe.

"Mo, for fuck's sake stop staring at him. Dig. We're nearly done."

Yearning for the nightmare to end, I frantically continued digging.

"That should do it," Hazel said, eventually. "Right, I'll grab him under his armpits. You take his ankles."

I reached down, recoiling when my palms connected with his hairy flesh. "Do we have to?"

"After what's happened; what do you think? Right, one, two, three…"

He was almost too heavy to lift. His warm blood made his ankles slippery and difficult to hold. We hoisted him barely an inch from the ground, dragging him the few feet towards his makeshift grave. Straining with his weight, we then released our grip on him, dropping him into the muddy hole. He landed with a sickening thud.

"It's not big enough," I panicked, barely able to breathe my heart was pounding so hard. By the look of the stunned expression on Vinnie's battered face, I wasn't the only one who couldn't believe this was happening.

"Shut up!" Hazel snapped, jumping into the hole next to him.

I grimaced as her feet landed heavily next to his tanned stomach, and watched as Hazel's muddied hands grabbed behind his knees. She pulled them up with difficulty until his feet fitted into the shallow grave. "There, now help me out."

Terrified that he might grab Hazel's ankles, I didn't hesitate. I took Hazel's outstretched hand and pulled. Standing upright next to me, she withdrew her hand from mine and wiped my hands vigorously against the skirt of my ruined cocktail dress.

He whimpered quietly. I saw him staring at me, as if he

was imprinting the image of our murderous faces to savour for eternity. We stared in petrified silence as bloody bubbles dribbled from his bruised mouth. I turned away and vomited.

"Don't think about it," Hazel said, elbowing me. I winced from the force of the nudge to my ribs. "We need to cover him up."

I noticed the sky had lightened to a salmon pink. Soon dog walkers could come through the woods for their early morning stroll. It wouldn't do for one of them to sniff our handiwork. I shovelled the heavy soil over his body as quickly as I could manage. Closing my eyes, I willed the image of his final silent plea to disappear from the back of my sore eyelids. The muscles in my neck and back ached. I straightened up with a little difficulty and took a deep breath of the fresh morning air, relieved that we had almost completed our gruesome task.

I opened my mouth to speak, when the earth shifted near my left foot revealing Vinnie's hands and face. I squealed and dropped the spade.

"Keep going; hurry," Hazel cried.

Picking up my spade, I frantically shovelled soil until he was hidden once more. We needed to disguise the freshly dug soil, so Hazel and I dragged a heavy, rotting branch resting it over Vinnie's grave.

"We need leaves, lots of them," Hazel said knowingly, as if she did this sort of thing often.

Sobbing from the trauma of what we were doing, I wiped my eyes with the back of my dirty hands. Then I searched for more camouflage to conceal our handiwork.

Finally, we were done. Hazel and I studied the area, to see if anyone could tell what was there under the branch and leaves. We had done a good job. No one passing by would ever suspect that there was a body buried here.

"We must make a pact never to speak about this to anyone," Hazel said.

I willingly agreed. Who would I tell and why would I tell them?

"Do you promise?"

"Of course I bloody do."

We stared at each other. I wondered if my face had hardened as much as Hazel's appeared to have done since the beginning of our trip to France.

"Where to now?" I asked, glancing across the lawn at the rear of the hotel.

"I've no idea, but we need to go inside and get our things," Hazel said. "And remember, if you hear anyone coming, run for the shadows."

We took a deep breath and ran out of the darkness of the wood, across the dimly lit backyard, and into the staff entrance at the back of the hotel.

# Chapter Twenty-One
## 2003 – Hautvillers, Near Epernay

### Sera

"You and Hazel killed a man." I still couldn't take in what she was telling me. I stared at her. All these years I'd suspected my mother wasn't telling me everything about her past. After all, as far as she was concerned she didn't really have one to share with me. It never dawned on me she could be capable of something like this. I wasn't sure what to say. I stared at her looking for clues I could have missed about this other side to her character that had remained hidden from me until now.

"What the fuck?" Dee raised her hands in the air. "Are you insane?"

She looked anything but insane to me. I thought of the many times she'd become absorbed by a character she was playing in a film. "You are serious, I suppose?"

She nodded. "Who would lie about something like this?"

I didn't know her at all. I took a deep breath to try and stop my heart from pounding so heavily in my chest. I needed to calm down. Rubbing my eyes, I tried to relieve the throbbing headache I could feel starting. This couldn't be happening.

She came to sit next to me and rested her hand on my back. I looked sideways at her. She looked the same and sounded the same. How could I have not known about this? I opened my mouth to ask the identity of the man, gasping when a thought occurred to me that was so horrendous I had to close my eyes to speak.

"Please," I whispered, my voice barely audible even to me. "Tell me you didn't kill Pierre."

She frowned. "Who?"

"Mum's boyfriend," Leo said, his face pale and tense.

She stared at me her mouth open in confusion. "Hazel's... No, of course I didn't kill Hazel's boyfriend. What do you take me for?"

After what she had just dropped on us, the irony of her question wasn't lost on me. I stood up and glared at her. How did she manage to retain that cool veneer of control about her? The nerve of her being angry with my reply made me want to shake her.

"Mum, you've just announced you killed a man. If he wasn't Henri's father, then who the hell was he?"

She stared at me as if the name of her mysterious victim refused to part from her lips.

"Vincent Black?" Leo murmured eventually, nervously looking from me to Dee. "It must have been him, I suppose?"

Where had I heard that name before? I wondered. I realised Mum was crying. "Was it him?"

She closed her eyes. Incredible that with these revelations being thrown about her only reaction was to allow a few tears to fall. She nodded. "I once stupidly thought I was in love with him," she said, her voice quiet as if it was the first time she was allowing herself to hear this nugget of information.

I walked away from the three of them, desperate for enough space to be able to think more clearly. My world was falling apart and I wasn't sure how much more I could take. I bent to pick a head of lavender, lifting it up to my nose to breathe in the calming, familiar scent. She was my mother and the only other person I'd trusted since Marcus' death. She might be able to play the part of a convincing enough killer in a television movie, but for her to do something as outrageous as physically end another person's life, there had to be a good reason, surely.

"What did he do to you?" I asked, walking back to join them. "You must have been terrified of him to kill him." I looked at her tall, fine frame. She didn't have the strength to fight a man, so this can't have been something she had chosen to do lightly.

"I need a moment to think." She leant her head back and stared up at the blue sky. "I hadn't thought I'd ever tell you." She gave Dee a pointed glare. "I'd give anything to have kept this from you." She recounted her story, her usually loud voice quiet and the look in her eyes haunted. I watched her pick away the skin from beside her perfectly manicured nails and wished I could put my arm around her to comfort her a little but knew that any interruption could cause her to stop speaking, so didn't move as she finished explaining who he was.

"This is ridiculous," Dee shouted. She stood up, knocking over my glass.

I bent to pick it up before she stood on it. The thought of broken glass in the grass under the children's bare feet wasn't something I could cope with right now. "You knew?" I asked irritated she was overreacting yet again.

Dee shook her head frantically. "No. I didn't know anything about this man, or his murder." She almost spat the last word as she jerked her head around to glare at my mother. "You're trying to tell me that my crazy, pisshead of a mother helped you bury a man you were both in love with?" She sat down heavily, burying her face in her hands. "You're completely mad."

"Dee, that's enough." My mother's booming voice shocked us all. Dee looked across at her, hate filling her eyes.

I wished for someone to tell me it was a sick joke. I thought back to what Dee had said to start off this whole sorry confession and realised there was more to come. "If you weren't going to tell me about the murder, what was the big secret you were so determined to share?"

Mum grabbed hold of my hand and squeezed, patting it with the other hand. I could feel her trembling, but to look at her face with her tears dabbed away by the ever-present handkerchief in her sleeve it was impossible to know she was even remotely tense. "Dee was going to tell you that Vinnie was your father."

I frowned, confused. "Sorry?"

"And mine," Dee said, her mouth slowly drawing back into a sardonic smile.

When I'd decided to get to the bottom of what was bothering Dee, I could never have dreamt I would hear anything this surreal. "What?" I repeated, unable to force my brain into a cohesive thought.

"I asked you a question earlier," Dee smirked. "Would you care for me like a sister?"

Mum nodded. "She's right," she said quietly. When I didn't move, she turned her attention to Dee. "When did Hazel tell you?"

My new-found sister and I stared at each other. All these years, I'd had a sibling, and no one had thought to tell me.

"Why didn't you tell us we were sisters when we were little?" I asked, my words sounding as if they were muffled behind a cushion somewhere. "We'd have been delighted back then."

"It might have changed many things, don't you think?" Dee asked.

I agreed. "Mum? Why didn't you or Hazel tell us this before now?"

Mum sighed heavily. "Because we knew you'd probably ask awkward questions." When we didn't say anything to this, she continued. "You were both such inquisitive children, do you imagine for a second neither of you would have wanted to go and look for him?"

She was right, we would have done. Both of us loved any excuse for an adventure and those were sorely lacking where we lived. This news would have come as an exciting change in our pleasant, but mostly uneventful lives.

"We were trying to hide the fact that we'd killed a man,"

she continued. "Don't forget we had to be as inconspicuous as possible."

I needed to glean as much information from her while she was opening up to us. "But you lived so near to each other, yet let us believe you weren't friends, why?"

"We didn't want anyone to see us together. We were scared Vinnie's cronies were looking for the two of us, and…" she hesitated. "Also, it was complicated between Hazel and me. That night scarred us both. Every time I saw her I was reminded about what we'd done. It was easier to keep away from her."

It sounded plausible. "But why end up in Epernay and Hautvillers?" I asked.

"We didn't plan it this way," she admitted. "We just wanted to get away from the hotel and took several trains until we ran out of money. Then the woman who eventually took us in had properties here and we've never left. We continued living near each other to tip the other one off should anyone come sniffing around looking for us." She closed her eyes briefly. "It's hard knowing that at any moment your secret could be discovered. Neither of us had any other family we trusted enough to care for our children if one of us ever did have to go away."

Leo cleared his throat. He'd been very quiet. I'd almost forgotten he was there. "Obviously he couldn't have been my father?"

Mum shook her head. "No, he died three years before you were born, Leo. Sorry. I've no idea who your father is, I would tell you now if I did."

"This is madness," Dee interrupted. "How can you expect us to believe that you, an actress who's spent decades on television and in French films has been hiding from anyone who might have known you back then? Didn't you think someone would recognise you?"

Mum nodded. "There was a possibility, but I was very young when this happened, my make-up was different. It was easy enough to change how I looked." She seemed almost proud of her achievement. "Even subtle changes to your appearance with colours, contouring and hairstyles can make a difference."

I supposed if the police had been looking for Vinnie they must have been searching for two English girls. I suggested this to her.

"Yes, and I never accepted any English-speaking parts. As far as my publicity people and the papers were concerned, I was a mid-list French actress. I reverted to being called Maureen. It was relatively simple, but it worked. Hazel and I took false surnames and came to live on the outskirts of Epernay." She seemed lost in her thoughts for a bit. "It's easier to hide in plain sight sometimes, you know. People tend to look hardest at a distant point and fail to see what's right under their noses."

"Well, none of us had a clue this had happened, so you must be right," Dee said sarcastically. "I'd like to know which one of you killed our father?"

"Yes," interrupted Leo. "Are you, or is Mum his murderer?"

Her face contorted with what I assumed must be revulsion at the memory of what she had done. I recalled her giving a similar expression in a television movie a couple of years before when she had played a murderer then. Was she acting this part too, I wondered?

"As I said, I was the one to hit Vinnie over the head," Mum said quietly. "But Hazel insisted we bury him and that's ultimately what must have killed him."

"How do you know?" Dee snapped. "Why does all this have to be Mum's fault?"

Mum shifted in her seat and cleared her throat. "He was still alive when we buried him," she said.

The three of us stared at her in stunned silence. Every part of me was trying to push this experience away. My life couldn't possibly be the same again.

"Why, Mum? Why did you do it?" Discovering my father was some low-life creep who beat up women was one thing, but finding out that my mother had buried someone alive was another entirely. I went to ask her more, but as much as I needed to know the rest of the story, I could see she was flagging. Something else troubled her. My head ached with shock and concern for her. She seemed to have aged ten years in as many minutes.

Each of us stared at her, lost in our own troubled thoughts. Something niggled in my mind. "Let me get this straight," I said. "The message you asked me to deliver to Hazel the day before she disappeared with Leo and Dee, what did it mean?"

"I'd discovered they were digging up the woods near Marne-la-Valleé, which is where we'd buried Vinnie. We were both always frightened a farmer might find his body, but as the years went by and nothing happened I began to relax. Then, when I realised the area was being turned into a massive building site, I knew I had to tip her off. I wanted her to be careful and keep her mouth shut."

Leo stood up and walked around to the back of Mum's chair. "Instead, Mum panicked and ran away with us."

I could understand Hazel wanting to take her children as far away from the threat of her crime being discovered. "But what's that got to do with Pierre?" I still couldn't believe the fun-loving, occasionally possessive Frenchman had been Henri's dad. It occurred to me that neither of them knew this yet. "Pierre was Henri's dad," I said as matter-of-factly as I could manage.

They looked more stunned by this news than that of our mother's joint murder of Vinnie. There was a stilled silence as Leo and Dee took in this nugget of information and gazed at each other.

"He was Henri's father?" Leo raised his eyebrows.

"Yes," Mum said. "And the reason Henri's leasing the farm is because his father disappeared in the summer of eighty-nine and he wants to find out what happened to him." She studied each of them in turn. Was she paying them back for forcing her to confess to everything today? "You wouldn't know anything about that, I don't suppose?"

"Mum, of course they wouldn't." Why was she trying to shift the focus on to them? She was covering something, but what? I could see by the granite hard glint in her blue eyes that she was relishing telling them this news. She didn't take her eyes off them, and for once I could imagine her being capable of doing something far worse than I'd ever considered before.

"Well?" she asked. "I've been honest with you two, it's your turn to pay back the compliment don't you think?"

Leo looked over at me. His face paled even more as I watched him, and his normally straight shoulders slumped. "She's right, Sera. We do know more about Pierre than we're letting on."

"He's dead," Dee said, matter-of-factly. "Killed that night before we left."

"No. I'm not listening to this anymore." I stood up. I heard movement on the other side of the neighbour's wall. Someone could have been listening to everything we had been discussing. I put my finger up to my mouth to shush them.

My heart pounded as I crept up to the garden wall adjoining the neighbour's property. Their fat ginger tabby landed on the apex of the wall. I exhaled sharply, covering my mouth to stop from screeching.

"What?" Leo shouted.

I shivered. "Nothing, it was a cat." This was too much for me to take in. I didn't want to hear any more about Pierre, not yet. I had enough of my own past to process before I took this devastating news over to the farm to give to Henri. "I'm going to check on the girls and hope they haven't heard any of this. Then later, when they're asleep…" I didn't add, 'and when my brain has caught up with this insanity', "I want you to tell me everything you know about Pierre. I'm going to have to tell Henri what happened to his father."

Leo shook his head. "You're not telling him anything."

I went to argue with him but something about his manner stopped me. "Fine then, I won't," I lied. Henri had a right to know, but with all the talk of violence I didn't like the way Leo was looking at me and wasn't going to tempt fate by challenging him. Not yet, anyway.

I heard Katie's voice shouting from the upstairs window for me and made an excuse to leave them and go to her. I didn't feel safe and could sense the evening ahead of us was going to reveal more secrets yet. I had no intention of keeping Katie here in case things turned nasty and decided to take her to a guest house for a few days. Somewhere away from here until everything was sorted out. I ran up the stairs to find her, guilt flooding my veins. I would give anything not to have to leave Ashley in this house tonight, but she wasn't my child to take.

"What is it, darling?" My faith in human nature healed slightly when I looked down at my little girl's cherubic face, her arms outstretched for me to pick her up. I bent down to lift her, hugging her tightly. "I think it's time you went to bed, don't you?"

"But I haven't had my bath, Maman." She gave me a hopeful grin and I nodded.

"You can go to bed without one tonight, just this once though." She giggled. "Come along, let's give your face a quick wash and clean your teeth, you do have to do that. Where's Ashley?"

"Sleeping," she whispered.

That was a relief. I gave her a quick wash and changed

her, settling her in her bed. I needed time to pack some of her things. As soon as she began to drift off, I took a change of clothes, her swimming costume and a cardigan, packed her toothbrush and favourite teddy that had dropped from her arms and snuck down the stairs and out of the front door to put them in the car.

I stepped back inside the house and turned to close the door as silently as possible.

"Where do you think you're going?" Leo barked from behind me.

My heart jolted. I yelped. "Bloody hell, Leo, did you have to nearly give me a heart attack? What's wrong with you?"

"You didn't answer my question." He stood close to me, not taken in by my bravado.

I refused to let him see how much he frightened me though. "Firstly," I said pointing my finger at him and stepping back slightly to make space between us. "This is my house and you're a guest. You don't have to stay here if you don't like how I behave. Secondly, and most importantly," I lowered my voice to give it as much gravitas as possible, "I don't need to ask permission from you, or anyone else. Got it?"

He lowered his head and moved in closer to me again. "Sera, I have a feeling you think you're addressing someone else. Probably that bloody Frenchman."

I swallowed to moisten my throat, which for some reason had gone incredibly dry. If Leo thought he was going to intimidate me when my child was sleeping upstairs, he was the one who'd got his bearings wrong.

"Leo," I said, very slowly. "Don't you dare think you can boss me around, I'm not Dee and I don't need you for anything. Now, move out of my way." I put my arm out to push past him and hid my relief when he moved. I didn't want to give him any ideas about my plan to take Katie out of the house, so marched out to the garden to find Mum.

"She's gone to bed," Dee said. "Told us she couldn't talk about this anymore, and left. I can't say I'm sorry."

I looked at my half-sister and tried to imagine how different things could have been between us if her family hadn't left when they did, or if we'd been brought up knowing our connection. Or, I thought, if Pierre hadn't been killed that night in eighty-nine.

"What did happen to Pierre, Dee?" I asked unable to hide the tremor in my voice from my confrontation with Leo.

"That night changed all our lives," she said, her voice distant as her thoughts drifted off elsewhere.

It was then I realised that the trauma of what she'd been forced to live with all these years had altered her beyond ever having a chance of recovery. She wasn't the girl I knew and loved back when we were teenagers. She'd died that night, along with Pierre, and if Leo's story about her getting involved with drugs was true, I could understand her need for something to help her forget everything she'd been through.

"Can you tell me how he died?" I asked wanting to find out as much as possible for Henri. I doubted Leo intended letting her tell me anything more than what I already knew.

She nodded, staring into space at some unseen horror.

"He didn't want us to go. Mum refused to tell him why she was so insistent on leaving, so he thought she was just being ridiculous. They argued." She took a deep breath. "When he refused to help her put things in the car she became hysterical. He slapped her." She looked at me. "I saw it all, but Leo was out by the car packing everything into it and only came back into the room when Mum fell over with the force of Pierre's slap. She hit her side on a table and cried out."

I wrapped my arms around me in an effort to stop the trembling building up inside. I wanted her to hurry up and tell me everything, aware I didn't have long before Leo came back outside to shut her up.

"Leo charged at Pierre. He grabbed Leo, who was only skinny then, if you remember, and slapped him. I think Mum falling had shocked Pierre and he was almost demented with her hysteria and Leo having a go at him." She looked at me. "Thinking back, I don't think Pierre meant to hurt Mum, but it was incredibly hot and her reaction to Maureen's letter and her fight with Pierre pushed the atmosphere to breaking point. Mum was desperate to leave. I was frightened and not sure what was going on. I panicked because she refused to give me enough time to run and tell you we were going. Leo was desperate to protect us." She stopped talking and took a shuddering breath.

I walked over to her and crouched in front of her, resting my hands on her knees. "Go on, what happened?" I asked, my voice as soothing as I could make it.

She stared at her hands. "I'm not completely certain, but

one minute I was in the living room crying, the next I was in the kitchen grabbing a steak knife from a dinner plate one of us had used earlier. I ran back to Mum. I don't know what I thought I'd do with it when I got to her, but Pierre turned to leave the room, just as I was going back in." She flinched and closed her eyes.

"Oh, Dee," I whispered, hugging her. Wishing I could comfort that teenage girl who had altered her life forever in a single second of miss-timed madness.

"I'll never forget the look on his face," she cried, large tears dripping down from her chin. "He looked so shocked. We stared at each other; time seemed temporarily frozen. Then Pierre dropped to the floor, clutching his chest, blood seeping through the gaps in his fingers."

"Are you happy now?" Leo bellowed from the doorway. "You had to know, didn't you?"

"She's told me," I said as cockily as I could manage. "So, what? It was years ago. Comfort your sister while I check on Mum."

I hurried away from them to the house, turning to watch Leo and Dee whispering animatedly to each other before stepping inside. Why did he mind Dee admitting she'd killed Pierre? I asked Mum the same question when I went to sit on her bed unable to stop from trembling.

Despite everything she was sitting at her dressing table, as she did every night before going to bed, removing her make-up and applying her night cream to her face and neck. "I'm not sure," she murmured, staring at her reflection in the mirror to ensure she'd rubbed every bit in to her youthful skin. Satisfied, she came over to the bed and pulling back her summer duvet, stepped in and settled down against the large, downy pillows. "Maybe he's being clever."

"How so?" I asked watching her and wondering if I'd ever really known her.

"If neither of them confessed to killing Pierre they could blame it on their mother." She stared out of the window. "As much as Hazel annoyed me, I don't like the way they described her earlier. We must try and find out how she is."

It was odd hearing her talking about Hazel in a caring way.

"She could be steely tough when you least expected it, but as you know, she had a timid side to her, too," Mum said thoughtfully. "If, as they say, Pierre's murder was an unfortunate accident though, they shouldn't have run away. Henri must have gone through hell all these years wondering what happened to his father."

I nodded. "True." A thought occurred to me, and as much as I tried to oppress it, I couldn't help asking, "Don't you ever think about Vincent Black's family and what they must have gone through?" When she didn't react, I added, "Wouldn't they have wondered why he didn't return from Paris?"

She took a jar of hand cream from her bedside table and silently unscrewed the large silver lid, dipping two finger tips into the white cream, she handed the jar to me to reseal and began working the cream into her fingers, around her nails and then over her hands to her wrists. It was almost as if she was covering them from the blood that had once soaked her hands.

"I think about them every day," she admitted. "I did a terrible thing. I can't blame Hazel for it. We were both involved in his death." Her voice faltered at the last word in the sentence and she stopped what she was doing and looked directly at me. "Do you see me any differently now you know this about me?"

I wanted to lie, but she knew me far too well for me to get away with doing so. "Yes." She flinched, so I added, "but only because you've always been a nurturer to me and Katie." I laughed. "And to some of your younger boyfriends."

She didn't smile at my stupid attempt at lightening the mood. "I don't want Katie to ever learn about this." She swallowed and cleared her throat. "I want her to always think of me as kindly Nana Mo who buys her pretty dresses and ice creams."

I smiled at her. "I can't promise not to tell her, Mum. I've resented your secrets my entire life. I will do my best to make sure she doesn't judge you though. I'm sure she'll always love you. I do."

"Good." She took both my hands in hers. "None of us ever knows what we're capable of until we're faced with a situation. I can't tell you how terrified I was that night." She studied my expression. "And the hundreds of nights afterwards when I waited for someone to discover his body and come looking for me and Hazel."

"And now Henri has done that."

She nodded. "Yes, the man who saved your life today, the one to whom I'll always be grateful, is probably going to be the one who sees me answer for my crime."

I had to speak to him. I gave her hands a squeeze. "I don't think he's going to do that, Mum."

"He's a detective, Sera. His life has been about tracking people down and making them pay for crimes they've committed. Why shouldn't he want the same result for Vinnie?"

I wasn't certain, but thinking back to what he'd assured me, I said, "No, I truly believe he's here to discover what happened to his father and now he has. He can tell his family what became of Pierre and put it all to rest."

She looked sad and suddenly so fragile; almost not like my mother at all. "He'll want Hazel's children to pay for what they did though."

"Yes, we can't expect him not to want them to answer for killing his father." I rubbed my tired eyes. "I want to go and see him," I admitted, glancing at the door and lowering my voice, just in case Leo was standing outside listening. "Hang on a sec." I stood up and crept over to the window, peeking down at the garden. It was empty. I had to presume Leo and Dee must be inside somewhere. I returned to Mum's bed and bent down to whisper to her. "I put a few things in the car earlier, in case I needed to get Katie away from here."

"From me?" She looked horrified.

I shook my head. "No, of course not from you."

I explained about Leo waiting for me in the hallway when I came in and his determination not to let me go anywhere. "I think he suspects Henri would be my first stopping point if I left here."

She sat up a little straighter. "Why would you take Katie

there, you barely know the man?"

She was right. "I'm sure I can trust him to look after her for me. I'm not so sure I'm happy having her here with Leo and Dee though, and I don't think it's going to be easy getting them to leave."

# Chapter Twenty-Two
## 1976 – Outside Paris

### Mo

"Why are we going north and what are we going to do when we get there?" Hazel's terrified whisper woke me from a disturbed sleep. "We've got barely any money and they'll probably come looking for us."

I yawned and stretched my aching legs as far as the space in front of the train seats would allow. This was our second train journey. We had dumped some of Vinnie's belongings in several bins around the initial station and loading stones into the case, dropped it into a river nearby with the rest of his things before catching an antiquated bus for a brief trip to a different village to get on another train. We were hot and sticky, and I just hoped we were getting sufficiently distant from the hotel in Marne-la-Vallée.

"Because the first train we could catch was going in this direction," I whispered when she asked me for a second time. "We'll have to do whatever we can with any opportunities that come our way." I didn't hold out much hope but was simply happy to be distancing myself away from Vinnie's dead body more each second. I stared out at the fields as our train passed them by.

"I was thinking you need to dye your hair and I'll cut mine." She pulled miserably at her long dark curly tresses she'd always been so proud of.

"No," I said. "I'll cut mine. I've always wanted to see what it looked like shorter. You can dye yours red and cut it into a different style." I gave her a soothing smile. "We'll be fine."

"You're sure?"

I wasn't, but I couldn't let her carry on getting into more of a state than she was already. I nodded. "How are you?" I asked, unable to forget the sight of her bruised thighs and other areas Vinnie had abused so cruelly. That bastard, how could I have thought myself in love with him?

She groaned. "Sore." She picked at the skin next to one of her thumbnails. "Ashamed."

I put my arm around her trembling shoulders. "You've got nothing to be ashamed of and don't you bloody forget it. Neither of us could have known what he'd do." I thought back to my times alone with him and shivered. "We both thought he was perfect."

She began to cry. "I can't believe what we did to him?"

Neither could I. "Shush, you don't want to alert the other passengers, we have to stay as incognito as possible." I was concerned one of them might read the papers the next day, assuming Vinnie's disappearance would be in the papers, and connect us to him.

"Were we right to," she murmured, leaned slightly forward and glancing around at nearby passengers. "You know, what we did?"

"I don't know," I said honestly. "It's too late to do anything about it now though, isn't it?"

She huddled up, bringing her slim legs up and hugging them. "I need to sleep."

I was relieved. I didn't know how to soothe her. I was grateful for the time I'd spent practising make-up techniques. They had come in handy when I needed to camouflage her bruises earlier, so we could go to the station.

It was slightly alarming that Hazel, after her bravado at Vinnie's grave, had now dissolved into a frightened girl again. I wasn't sure I had the strength for both of us. I stared out of the train window seeing Hazel's sleeping reflection and my own pale expression looking back at me. I would give anything to turn back the clock and find a way to change things. I felt so alone and for the first time in my life, truly frightened. The one thing I did know was that Hazel and I could never return to our parents' homes again. If the police were looking for Vinnie they would probably try and find us there first. I might have been desperate to leave home, but it never occurred to me when I left that I was seeing my family for the last time.

The soothing monotony of the metal train wheels against the rails must have sent me to sleep because when I woke, it was morning and this time when I looked out of the window it was at miles and miles of golden corn-covered fields. The sunrise shone on the thin mist shrouding the town. It would soon burn off and as I looked up to the perfect, cloudless sky, it was hard to fit this picturesque scene with the horror of the previous night. I tried to clear my mind and wake up slowly, gazing at the perfection outside the window.

We needed to concentrate on making new lives for ourselves and somehow disappear in the vast French countryside. I wasn't sure how we were going to manage it though. At least, I mused, the very worst we had to deal with was over now.

\*\*\*\*

"Psst, come here," Hazel waved me over at the café where we had both been working for the past two months since our money ran out and we'd ended up in a small town on the outskirts of Epernay.

We hadn't spent much time getting to know the town, mainly because we didn't have any of Vinnie's money left after buying train tickets and paying for a room for a few nights. We knew nothing much about the area and had only chosen to come here in the first place because Hazel said she had read somewhere about the impressive cathedral in Reims not too far from Epernay.

I looked over at the river seeing one of the boats meandering lazily along carrying tourists being served delicious meals as they gazed out of the window at the surrounding countryside. I walked along this riverbank after work in the evenings and envied the people on the boats with their carefree existences and money to take a holiday and wished I was one of them.

Another reason for choosing this place was its location on the other side of Paris to where we'd buried Vinnie and hopefully far enough away for us to build a new life. Hazel liked to tease me that as Epernay was the champagne capital of France, I should fit in very well with my upper-class aspirations. Personally, I liked it here because it was a pretty town surrounded by vineyards, sunflower-filled fields, and it had happened to be the first place someone offered us a live-in job.

"What?" I said when she called me again. I carried on wiping the outside metal tables and emptying the filled plastic ashtrays into the disgusting bucket I had to carry around with me for this task. "I want to finish early, I've got an audition."

She came closer and began straightening chairs when the *patron* walked past us from his daily visit to the nearby *marchand de tabac* carrying one packet of Gitanes and pocketing another two. I glanced down at the stinking bucket waving away a waft of dank, wet ash with my hand and wondered if most of it was from him.

"I think I'm pregnant," she whispered.

I stopped what I was doing, nearly dropping the bucket I'd just picked up. "Are you sure?"

She nodded, her eyes wide with fear.

I thought back at the sickness I'd been experiencing in the mornings for the past few weeks. "Me, too," I admitted, not only to her but to myself for the first time.

"So, Vinnie lives on."

Nausea welled up from my chest, into my throat. I

covered my mouth with both hands and ran inside to the lavatory, only just managing to reach the bowl in time when I threw up violently.

The door banged open behind me moments later. "What are we going to do?"

I retched again, but this time only saliva came up. Resting my forearms on the black plastic loo seat I swallowed and tried to bring my body back into some sort of order. "I'm glad I cleaned in here earlier," I said, recalling how disgusting it had been beforehand.

I stood up and washed my mouth out with water, ensuring to spit every bit out because we didn't know how clean it was and splashed cool water over my face. It was another hot day and feeling sick didn't help lift my spirits.

"What are we going to do?" Hazel asked again. I could see her standing behind me through our reflection in the mirror, she looked almost accusatory.

I spun around, irritated by her tone. "Are you having a go at me?"

She tilted her head, clenched hands resting on her hips. "Well, you did choose to sleep with that bastard, I didn't have any choice."

I couldn't believe what I was hearing. "Hazel, you were only too keen to sleep with him, don't forget." She went to argue. "I don't mean that last night, but before then. We both had a crush on him, so don't you try and make me out to be the villain here."

She let her hands drop to her sides. "Sorry, I'm just panicking. If we're both pregnant how are we going to get by? One of us needs to work, surely?" We decided to discuss it after we'd finished work for the day.

Later, upstairs in our tiny attic bedroom, I pulled the worn brown curtains back and pushed open the tiny window to let in as much air as possible. We sat on opposite beds, legs crossed, wearing nothing but our knickers and bras in a vain effort to cope with the stifling heat as we talked through our options.

"That's it?" she said, rubbing her forehead with her palm. "We carry on working for as long as possible? Then what?"

"How should I know? We'll need to start making a few friends, make some contacts and maybe one of them might help us."

"Do what?"

I shook my head. "I've no idea. Give us somewhere to live? We can't carry on here when we're both huge."

Hazel lay down on her bed and covered her eyes with the back of one hand. "So much for making the big time as a singer," she sighed.

I stared out of the tiny window wishing there was more of a breeze. I was sick of being sweaty all the time. "You could always, you know."

She opened her eyes and turned to face me. "Get rid of it, you mean?"

I nodded. "I wouldn't blame you if you chose to do that."

Hazel narrowed her eyes. "I hope you're saying this because you're worried that one day this baby might find out how I became pregnant, and not because you want me to keep working and pay our rent when you're heavily pregnant and won't be able to."

"You bitch." I couldn't believe she was being so nasty. "I was trying to be supportive." Her accusation stung. "I'm going for a walk." I stood up, pulled on my black work skirt and a T-shirt and slipped my feet into my worn shoes. "Do what you like."

I missed my footing on one of the narrow stairs out of the building and stumbled, only just managing to save myself from falling. Maybe I should have just gone with it, I thought, as I walked along the pavement before crossing the village square. It would have been the answer to my own personal dilemma if I was to lose this baby. I tucked my short hair behind my ears, relieved to have cut it and surprised after a lifetime of long hair, how quickly I'd got used to seeing myself this way. It was also perfect in this endless heat.

I nodded a hello to the mayor, a portly man who came to the café on a daily basis for three espressos, and a gossip with our boss, Monsieur La Motte. Then I walked down towards the river where I found a quiet spot to sit. I took off my shoes and let my feet dangle in the cool water, lying back, resting an arm across my eyes to shield them from the brightness of the sun.

So much for my audition earlier, I thought. A tiny production that would pay barely enough to buy food and would mean months travelling around the countryside. Not something I could very well do in my condition. I rested my free hand on my stomach, stunned to feel a slight bulge. Vinnie had been dead a little over two months and I'd been sleeping with him a couple of weeks before that, I calculated I must be almost three months pregnant. How could I have been so careless? It served me right for being blinded by his charm when I should have been finding acting work.

I hated having to face the prospect of motherhood. I had managed to persuade myself that my missed periods were due to the trauma of his death and struggling to find somewhere to work and live. Hazel and I had been so certain Vinnie would never be able to hurt us again. We were desperate to put that night behind us and move on with our lives. Discovering he had left behind two very distinct reminders of him was something I wasn't sure I could bear.

I opened my eyes and sat up slightly, resting on my elbows. The water coursed past my feet, pushing them sideways. All I had to do was walk in and the current would take care of the rest. I was never going to be an actress now. The only thing I had left to look forward to, was enduring the pain of childbirth, and a lifetime with a child who reminded me what Hazel and I had done that night. I had nothing left to look forward to. My mind raced. I became light-headed with panic. I couldn't face the next few months. Being a mother wasn't a life. I only ever planned to be an actress and now it was never going to happen. My mother was right, I was destined to be a failure. I *was* a failure.

Staring at the rushing water, I pictured my mother's mocking expression when I'd admitted my ambitions to her. I stood up and without thinking stepped forward dropping into the fast-running river. I heard a scream. The shock of the icy water enveloping me made me gasp involuntarily. Water filled my mouth and nose, forcing itself into my lungs as the current tipped me over crashing the side of my head against a boulder. My last thought was wondering if it hurt Vinnie this much when I smashed the ashtray into his head, and then blackness.

A force kept pressing against my chest. It stopped, and I vomited. I struggled to open my eyes as someone turned me on my side and I vomited again, and again. Choking, I tried to catch my breath but couldn't. People were chattering. Someone barked orders. I didn't understand everything they were saying, but caught the occasional word.

"You're safe now." A gentle, female voice finally soothed. I think it belonged to the hand stroking my forehead. "The doctor, he is coming. Your head is cut."

"I didn't..." I tried to tell her it hadn't been an accident. I didn't want her sympathy. I didn't want to be here at all.

"Shhh, *ma petite*," she said. "I will care for you."

I coughed a few more times, hearing more instructions I couldn't make out.

"You will come to my house. Do not worry."

I opened my eyes to see an elderly lady with eyes so blue it dawned on me she must have been incredibly beautiful when she was young. "I don't know you," I said, wondering how this tiny bird of a person could refer to me as 'little one'.

"Do not concern yourself." She smiled at me. "*Dépêchez-vous.*" Hands lifted me by my shoulders and my ankles and I was carried to a large black car.

"Wait; my friend," I pleaded. I couldn't let them take me without Hazel knowing where I was going. She might be a cow, but she was the only friend I had. "She's upstairs in the café."

"Stop right there," I heard Hazel shout as she ran towards me. "Where do you think you're going with her?"

The old lady explained she was going to look after me at her home for a few days as some men placed me carefully across the back seat of a car.

"Well, you're not going without me," Hazel shouted.

"You shall come also," the lady told her. She thanked the people who helped me and the only thing I picked up from her chatter was for someone to send the doctor to her house. She got in her car and closed the door. "We will go now."

I put my hand up to my head, wincing as I felt a huge wet bump. I checked my fingers and saw blood. I tried to sit up but the world around me swam until I closed my eyes.

"Lie back," she said, her voice authoritative but soothing.

"But I'm bleeding on your leather seats," I said, mortified. Who was this lady and why was she helping us?

"Pfft, it is of no matter. Lie down. We will soon arrive."

I did as I was told. Hazel leaned towards me resting her arm on the back of the passenger seat. "What were you doing?" she asked, looking decidedly unsympathetic with my plight.

I opened my eyes to glare at her, closing them when I realised how much it hurt.

The car slowed soon after and I surmised we couldn't be much more than a mile out of the village. I sat up slowly and peered out of the window as the lady drove slowly down a short stony drive, pulling in through two gateposts and stopping in a yard under the shade of a large apple tree. I squinted, or was it a lilac tree? I asked her.

"It is both," she smiled, getting out of the car. "They grew together, how you say, entangled?"

I nodded, wincing when the gentle action sent pain stabbing into the side of my head. "Ouch, my head."

"Well, if you will go falling into rivers," Hazel said putting emphasis on the word 'falling'.

Cow.

"You can walk?" The lady got out of the car and opened my door waiting for me to react.

I nodded, getting tentatively out of the car and following the old lady up the steps to the porch of her stone farmhouse. I wondered if the shock of what had happened might induce me to miscarry, but kept this thought to myself.

"It's very beautiful here," Hazel said, walking over to a clump of colourful wildflowers next to a barn. "I'd love to live in a place like this someday."

The lady waved us into the cool air of her kitchen and poured us each a glass of her homemade lemonade. The icy liquid was tart, but it was a relief to have something clearing the back of my throat. I was sure it must be grazed by the force of the water that had been forced into my mouth. She motioned for us to take a seat and introduced herself telling us her name was Madame Moreau and she had been a widow for almost thirty years.

"I saw you fall into the river and want to help you," she explained. "You are both strangers to Epernay, *oui*?"

I nodded. Hazel nudged me.

"I do not wish to ask you anything further. We each of us have our secrets and reasons for keeping them. For a young woman to do what you did earlier, I think she needs help."

I wanted to trust this woman, but couldn't imagine why she was so interested in helping us. "Why?" I asked.

She gave us a knowing smile that didn't hide a haunted look in her eyes. "I was young once and I believe I too felt as you do now."

Hazel took a sip of her drink, blinking rapidly as the sharp taste slid down her throat. She coughed. "You don't know us though." I could tell Hazel felt confused by what had happened to me and with us ending up in this stranger's home.

The woman sat opposite us. "No. I was lucky, someone helped me when I needed it most, and for you I would like to do the same."

What choice did we have but to trust her and at least this tiny woman was no fearful opponent like Vinnie had been. We soon discovered Madame Moreau was well thought of in the town, despite distancing herself from the locals. She loved her farm and although I was a little concerned about moving away from the town and in with someone we didn't know, Hazel was so enthralled by the farmhouse she persuaded me, rightly it turned out, that this was pretty much our only option and a good one at that.

It didn't take long for us to want to confide in the old lady about our pregnancies, but she put us at ease straight away.

"I noticed this about you that day by the river, Maureen. It is why I wanted so much to bring you here."

She employed labourers to help in the fields when she needed it, but Hazel and I helped around the farm in whatever way we could to pay our way. We felt at home very quickly and both loved our guardian angel very much. What we couldn't have known at the time was that Madame Moreau was dying. She had no one to leave her farm and a town house to since her son had been killed in the closing months of the Great War.

One evening several months later, she told us about her only other child surviving to adulthood only to die in a car crash. I couldn't help thinking how unfair it was for someone as generous as Madame Moreau to suffer so cruelly and lose both her children.

"I was pregnant with my oldest son, when I met Alfred Moreau," she explained that night. Hazel and I listened to her as we sat, uncomfortable from our large stomachs, filled with a mixture of fear and excitement about having our babies. "He brought me here as his bride. He was kind and now it is my turn to pass on that gift."

We assumed she was referring to us living in her farmhouse. It was only when she died, thankfully having lived long enough to be present at the births of both our daughters that Hazel and I learnt we had been gifted her two properties.

I wasn't sure how to react to the news that she'd chosen Hazel to inherit her farm. I didn't want to leave this idyllic place with my small baby. However, when I visited the town house she'd bequeathed to me, I was overwhelmed by its grandeur and understood much better why she thought it would suit me more than Hazel. As soon as I could I moved with my baby, who I'd named Seraphina, in to our new home. Our babies were almost six months old and Hazel and I were relieved not to have to put up with each other anymore. It was time to move on with our lives and find a way to bury the memory of what we'd done to Vinnie.

# Chapter Twenty-Three

## 2003 – Hautvillers, Near Epernay

### Sera

"Why didn't you tell me this before now?" I asked when Mum had finished speaking.

"How could I," Mum smiled. "You'd have only wanted to know why we were in France and ask more questions about your father, why he wasn't there for me, that sort of thing."

"So, you both struggled alone. Mum, that's awful." I hated to think of two girls younger than me looking for a way to cope with such a frightening situation.

Dee was ashen; she stared at me for so long it was unnerving. I wished she would say something.

"So, Sera," she said finally. "Yet again you come out on top of things."

I frowned. "How do you work that out? Your mother was given a farm."

"I meant about our father."

Not this again. "We're both his children, Dee."

"Yes, but you're the result of a romantic, if not a little

sleazy, fling. I'm the product of rape. Brilliant, not something to boast about to the grandchildren, isn't it?"

"Stop it!" Mum shouted. "How dare you. Your mother loved you regardless of how she became pregnant. In fact," she said looking like she wanted to slap Dee, "she probably over compensated you for what happened."

"Rubbish." Dee slammed her palm down on the table making the plates we'd used earlier rattle. "Just because she didn't try to kill herself like you did, doesn't mean she can look at my face without seeing the man who raped her."

"That's not Mum's fault," Leo said. "She always favoured you over me, and you know it."

I pictured Dee's room with the pretty decorations and little touches making it so much better than any of her friends'. "They're right, Dee," I said. "Whatever you choose to believe, Hazel did adore you and was always trying to show you in small ways." I wasn't sure why I was trying to be so nice to her; after all it was my mother who had tried to end it all, not hers. I decided to try a different approach. "Surely the point we should both remember, is that our mums could have chosen to get rid of us."

I gave Mum a sideways glance. I was saying this for her benefit as much as Dee's. "I'm sure it would have been much easier for them to make new lives for themselves if they hadn't had babies to consider." She didn't argue, so I added, "Hazel managed to give you a magical childhood, at least up to that summer when it all changed. Maybe you should focus on that aspect of your life rather than the negatives that happened afterwards."

We stared at each other. Sisters; enemies.

"Maybe," she said her tone almost threatening. "But you have no idea what happened after that night, do you?"

No, I didn't. "I know about your ex, but no, not about anything else." I didn't bother to remind her that my life hadn't been so perfect either, but this wasn't a competition to see who had dealt with the most misery. "Look, do what you want, but don't bring your nastiness to this house."

"Or you'll what?" Leo said, standing slowly until he reached his full six feet plus. He loomed over the table. I went to retaliate, too drained to care what he might do to me if I did stand up to him. Before I uttered a word, the doorbell rang.

Leo looked at his watch. "Who the hell is that, it's nearly nine p.m.?"

Making the most of his distraction, I leapt up and ran through the hallway, with him thundering after me. "Leave that fucking door closed," he bellowed.

My heart raced. I reached out grabbing the doorknob with one hand and the key with the other, turning both simultaneously, pulling the door back. "Henri!" I almost wept with relief.

His eyes widened to see me as I almost catapulted myself into him. He wrapped his arms protectively around me, looked over my shoulder at the furious man bearing down on him. "It's okay, Sera. I'm here," he whispered, like a soothing kiss. He turned with me, so that he was between me and Leo. "So, you bully women?"

Leo stood inches in front of Henri, glaring at him, his

breathing heavy, more in temper I thought than in exerted effort to catch me. "Get out of this house, this has nothing to do with you."

"*Non*. This I will not do, unless Sera or her mother instructs it of me."

Leo laughed, hands on his hips head thrown back. "Seriously? You think you can tell me what to do? You're a pathetic excuse for a man." He pushed Henri's damaged right shoulder, hard. "You're only half a man, look at you."

My instincts told me that to defend Henri would be the worst thing I could do, so I said nothing.

Henri tensed. "This half-man, as you say, will knock you down if you push me one more time." Henri reached back with one hand and found mine giving me a brief squeeze to assure me everything was fine. I didn't know how much of this was bravado, I'd seen Henri struggle to run some days, but he was fit, and working on that farm must have gone some way to build his strength back up since his accident.

Mum came out to the hallway, closely followed by Dee. "Henri," she said, relief filling her voice. "I want you to take Sera and Katie to your farm for tonight while I sort things out with Dee and Leo. I'm afraid there's been a few misunderstandings."

"She's not going anywhere," Leo said. "Sera, get back into this house."

My blood coursed through my veins, not with fright, but with fury. "Shut up, Leo. I don't know who you think you are, but in my house, you're nobody. Take your sister and that poor unfortunate little girl, or better still please leave her behind. I don't mind keeping her here, but you two need to leave tonight. Go and sort through your issues somewhere else."

"Or you'll do what, exactly?" He sneered at me and I couldn't help likening myself to Mum and how she must have been fooled into believing she was in love with Vinnie all those years ago. It was incredible how blind someone could be when they subconsciously chose to ignore another's true character. I'd been stupid enough to think that something of the shy little boy Leo had once been remained in this tall, handsome physique. But thankfully I didn't even like Leo, despite what I'd fooled myself into believing when he'd first arrived at my home.

"The chances of them finding any body at Marne-la-Vallée now are almost nil, I should imagine. The entire area has been built up for years. I'll call the gendarmes without hesitation," I said. He went to say something, but I held my hand up to stop him. "No, don't think you can threaten Mum with anything, she'll deny it."

"She's right, you know," Mum said, looking relieved at the thought.

Boosted by him wavering, I added, "You, on the other hand, have a confession to make to Henri."

"*Quoi?*" Henri looked at me, surprise registering on his face that I might be referring to his father's disappearance.

I nodded, placing a hand on his shoulder. "Yes, we know what happened to your father."

I addressed Leo again. "Pierre's body can be identified through forensics, if it hasn't been already. He was killed at your family home and missed from the date you, your sister and Hazel vanished. I think there's too much against you for you to even think you can get away with this."

"You mean you won't inform the gendarmes of our involvement if we leave now?" Dee asked eyes wide with hope.

I patted Henri's shoulder. "That's up to you," I said. "You have every right to call them, if you choose."

He put his arm back and sliding it around my waist pulled me forward to stand by his side. "I will decide when I have listened to what they tell me about my father's death."

"Fair enough," Dee said. "You deserve to know the truth. I only wish we'd been honest years ago."

I realised I'd been right and she had been haunted by what she'd done that night in eighty-nine.

"*Moi, aussi*," Henri said. I could only imagine how much of his life had been taken up looking for and wondering where his father could be. All that frustration and confusion would never have happened if these two had told the truth about Pierre's death.

I looked at Dee. "I'd have loved for us to become close again, but I can't see that happening any time now. Go with Leo, leave Ashley here with me, at least until you've sorted out a new life somewhere." She opened her mouth to argue. "I promise I'll take care of her for you," I said. "I'm her auntie, after all."

"You want me to leave her here?"

"Why not?" I said. "She'll be perfectly safe. You can come and get her any time. You and Leo need to sort things out quietly, you can't do that with a child accompanying you."

She didn't look convinced. I caught movement out of the corner of my eye and spotted Katie and Ashley holding hands at the top of the stairs, both with muzzled bed hair and eyes puffy from sleep.

"Maman, why is everyone cross?" Katie asked.

"It's nothing. Go back to bed, sweetie, I'll come and tuck you in soon."

"Ashley's scared," she said.

I opened my mouth to speak, but Dee stepped forward to the bottom of the stairs and looked up at the two sleepy little girls, so like her and me when we were small.

"Ashley, would you like to stay with Auntie Sera for a few weeks while Mummy finds us somewhere new to live?"

I felt a pang to my heart at her use of the words 'Auntie Sera' and waited for the little girl to reply. She looked terrified, then nodded slowly.

"Okay, then. You go off to bed with Katie and I'll come up and see you in a bit."

I took hold of Henri's hand and led him forward, past Leo, now quiet and deflated, and through to the kitchen. It was soothing to feel his calloused hand in mine and I gave it an appreciative squeeze. I heard them follow us into the room and motioned for Henri to sit. Mum sat down next to him. I noticed they were on the side closest to the door, so Leo and Dee had no choice but to walk around the table to get past us if they wanted to leave.

"Right, you two have the chance to put your case to Henri." I let go of his hand as he sat down and stood behind him, both my hands resting on his broad shoulders. I studied my childhood friends for a while, a part of me feeling pity for what they'd gone through. "I'll go and check on the children and leave you four to chat."

I hurried up to the girls' bedrooms, checking on Ashley first. "You okay?" I asked, stroking her cheek. She nodded. "Katie is going to love having you to stay with her."

She smiled. It was the first time I recalled seeing her so relaxed and childlike. "It'll be fine," I soothed. "You mustn't worry about anything."

She didn't take her eyes off my face while I straightened her pillows. "Then will my mummy come and get me?"

I nodded. "She will, as soon as she and Uncle Leo have found you a new home."

Her smile faltered. "No, my mummy."

"Sorry, what?" I asked, thrown by her odd question. "What do you mean?"

She sat up and pulling me down, curved her hand next to her mouth and whispered. "My mummy, at home."

My brain froze. She lay back down again, an expectant expression on her face, waiting for me to answer her. Her chin began to wobble. I assumed she was being open with me because she'd seen me stand up to Leo. Her face crumbled. I could see she was frightened now and didn't know what to do.

"Hey," I whispered. "I promise I won't tell anyone what you've asked me. I'll do my best to find your mummy for you, okay?"

Her panic receded a little. She nodded.

I put my finger up to my mouth when I heard someone coming up the stairs. "Don't say anything. Leave it to me."

She closed her eyes. By the time Dee reached the bedroom door, I was leaving. "She's fast asleep," I said quietly, willing her to leave the child alone.

She glanced in the room and I had to hold back a sigh of relief when she retraced her steps back down to join the others.

I went into Katie's room and sat on the edge of her bed trying desperately to gain some sense of my jumbled thoughts. What the hell was going on here? All I knew was this little girl, whoever she might be, trusted me and I needed to ensure she was returned to her real mother. Who was this kid?

The first thing I needed to do now Dee and Leo had agreed to let Ashley stay with me was to get them to leave. After that I could find a way to track down the little girl's mum. I went to the hallway outside her room. I opened the bedroom door and with my heart pounding, strained to hear any sound coming up from the kitchen. There didn't seem to be any raised voices. I calmed down a little, willing my vague seed of a plan to work.

I needed to re-join them before they became suspicious by my absence. I listened at the kitchen door to get the gist of what was being said, when I heard Leo's voice saying, "I don't see any reason for us not to leave first thing in the morning."

I checked my watch; it was almost nine-thirty.

"No, you will leave tonight. If, as you say, my father's

death was an accident," I heard Henri say, "And you didn't intend to kill him, then I will allow you to leave, but only tonight. If you go now, I will take you to the station. There are a couple of trains leaving Epernay through the night. If you insist on staying, then I will call the gendarmes and have you arrested. It is your only choice"

I could have kissed Henri for giving them very little option but to leave straight away.

"You want us to leave now?" Dee asked.

I stepped forward and entered the room. "Why wait?" I said, determined to see the back of them before Henri changed his mind, or they changed theirs. I sat down next to Henri.

Leo watched me. Did he realize that I'd discovered the truth about Ashley and now knew that he had only brought Dee here to hide her and Ashley away from whoever might be looking for them? He looked like he was mulling over his next move. I didn't catch his eye, but forced a smile in Dee's direction.

"You don't have to, of course." I hoped the reverse psychology Mum always used on me would work for her. "But it's not as if you've ever been happy in this house. I'd have thought you'd want to get as far away from here and the farm as soon as you could."

The reminder of the farm seemed to do the trick. Dee grabbed hold of Leo's sleeve. "She's right, I hate it here. I have to go tonight, and if you care anything about me at all you'll come with me."

"But what about Ashley?" he asked, glancing at me. I

kept my expression neutral and patted Mum's hand for something to do.

"The child will be perfectly fine here," Mum said. "She has Katie to play with and you can come and get her when you're settled elsewhere." She caught my eye. I could see she'd picked up that I was trying to hide something. "Why don't I come and help you pack, Dee. Who knows, the change of scenery could be exactly what you need."

Dee nodded. "You're right. Leo, we're going."

He didn't argue, but got up and followed Dee and Mum out of the kitchen, stopping at the door to give Henri and me a brief look. The heat of Henri's leg against mine was comforting and I was deeply grateful for his return to the house. Neither of us spoke. He placed his hand over mine and kept it there until we heard Leo speaking from the first-floor landing.

"He is a dangerous man, Sera."

I nodded. "I realise that now. I'm so relieved you came here tonight. Do you mind not informing the gendarmes about what happened to your father?"

He shook his head. "It is in the past and they were children. I have been able to solve the mystery of my father's disappearance, and for me, right now, this is enough."

I heard footsteps coming down the stairs. "Thank you," I whispered.

"Thank me when they have gone." He hesitated, staring at me intently. "Sera, what is wrong?"

I pointed towards the open doorway. "I'll tell you later."

I went to the kitchen and waited while Henri joined

Mum and the others. She said her brief goodbyes to Dee and Leo mainly to witness their exit before hurriedly closing the front door and locking it behind them.

"I thought they'd never leave," she said, coming back into the kitchen and resting against the worktop. She looked drained, her shoulders drooping. "Henri is a good man, Sera, I misjudged him terribly."

"All I care about right now is that they've gone, Mum. I hope he makes sure they get on to a train, any damn train and leave Epernay for good."

She stifled a yawn with the back of her hand. "Would you mind if I went to bed now?"

"No, of course not. I'll stay down here for a bit."

She closed her eyes for a moment. "You should try and rest if you can," she said. "Henri told me he'd come back in the morning. He said you should get some sleep." She sighed. "Who knows what we'll have to deal with tomorrow."

I dreaded to think. "I'm shattered too." I walked up to her and gave her a hug. "I'm sorry for inviting them into our home."

"You didn't know what would happen, darling." She linked arms with me and leading me out of the kitchen stopped to wait while I switched off the light. "I can't believe they've actually left."

"Nor can I," I said hoping I didn't wake up and discover this was all a misleading dream. I decided to wait until the morning to tell her what I'd discovered about Ashley; she had coped with enough shocks for one day. It wasn't as if I could do anything much tonight anyway, I reasoned. I checked the house doors were locked and we went upstairs.

I was about to get into bed when I remembered the small photo I'd taken from Hazel's room of her and Pierre in eighty-nine. I walked over to the corner of the room and knelt. Dragging back the edge of the carpet I lifted the small end of the floorboard to reveal my childhood hiding place where I stored all my secret bits. I rummaged around with my hand until I came across the silver frame and pulled it out. Wiping the dust from the glass against my pyjama shorts, I lifted the picture and studied it. Would it be the right thing to do to offer this to Henri? Or should I take the picture out and cut Hazel's body from the photo? Unsure what to do, I decided to leave it and let him decide.

\*\*\*\*

I barely slept and was washed and dressed by the time Henri rang the doorbell at eight-thirty the following morning. Mum took the girls out to the shops so that we could chat about him dropping Leo and Dee off at the station.

"Where should they be now?" I asked willing him to say Outer Mongolia, or better still, Mars.

"South, they said. I do not know if they disembarked at the next stop, or any after that," he said looking as exhausted as I felt.

I would have loved proof of their destination, but that wasn't going to happen. Eventually Mum came back with the girls and after handing them some sweets left them to go upstairs to play in Katie's room. She joined us and I finally told them what Ashley had said to me the night before.

Neither of them spoke for a while and I waited until they'd contemplated this latest piece of information.

"She's an odd child, Sera," Mum said. "Are you certain she wasn't just messing with you?"

"Mum, she's five, supposedly," I shook my head realising quite how little I knew about the little girl with my daughter. "How would she think up something so weird?"

"Henri," Mum said. "What do you think? Should be take this allegation seriously?"

He looked surprised at her question. "*Mais, oui*. If it is not true then we have lost nothing, but if it is, this child must be returned to her parents immediately." He rubbed his stubbly chin. "I contact my ex-colleagues. Maybe they can find information about a missing child. Do you recognize her accent?"

"I suppose it could help narrow down the search for her family," I said. "I'm not sure I recognize it though."

Mum and I looked at each other. We'd both lived in France for so long, I wasn't sure we could determine much from the little Ashley had said to us during her stay.

"By the lilt of her voice," I said hoping I wasn't making a stupid mistake. "She sounded as if she's had contact with someone from Edinburgh way. I don't think she's Scottish, but she has a slight tinge of an accent in the way she says some of her words, don't you think, Mum?"

"Possibly," she agreed, looking upset that she couldn't add anything more useful.

"Good, well done." He gave me a reassuring smile. "I'll find out everything I can for you. We must act immediately, before they return and try to reclaim her."

Mum looked horrified by this comment. "Thank you, Henri," she said. "I'm incredibly grateful to you for this and for being so generous about not pressing charges against Leo and Dee. I don't think I could stand them being here for a moment longer than necessary."

He didn't look as pleased as Mum about the situation, but tilted his head in a half nod and left. I spent several hours catching up with my work. I had forgotten it was my day to have a stall at the market and decided that even though I was hours late starting, it would still be better to spend some time there than none. Mum was happy to have the children saying it was too hot for her to go out anywhere.

Despite the humidity of the continued heatwave, I also needed something to take my mind off everything that had transpired over the past twenty-four hours. I fervently hoped Ashley was playing a silly game and that Dee was her mum. The alternative was too horrible to contemplate. I took the photo of Hazel and Pierre with me, pushing it carefully into my back pocket, so I could drop it off with Henri on my way home from the market and went to set up my stall.

I usually preferred to be somewhere in the middle, but had missed the opportunity by being so late to arrive at the town square, so ended up being at the far end of the market. "Ahh, Sera, we thought you weren't coming to join us today," the elderly lady with the fruit stall said, as I gave the change to my first customer of the day."

I laughed. "I forgot what day it was," I admitted, which was partially true.

The heat was unbearable and because I'd only got the last stall in the market, the covering was slightly damaged and didn't shade me as much as I would have liked. I drank some water from a bottle and fanned my face with one of the booklets I gave away with each of my sales to advertise the rest of the stock.

It was surprisingly busy for such a hot day. The locals were used to coping with high temperatures during the summer, but this was hot even by their standards and having spent several years in Edinburgh I'd still not managed to acclimatize to the days when the humidity was especially high, like it was today. I tipped a little bit of water into my hand and wiped it over my face and the back of my neck.

"These would be perfect for our beach house, honey," a tourist said, waving her husband over to come and have a look at my signs. "Could you post these to the States for us?"

I nodded. "Yes, of course."

"Charlie, come here and look what I've found." She worked her way slowly through each sign checking them thoroughly, putting several of the more damaged older signs to one side. "Look, aren't they gorgeous?"

Charlie didn't look nearly as impressed as his wife, but smiled dutifully, and agreed with her each time she held one up and declared it to be her favourite. I kept smiling, happy to let her carry on and hoped she would eventually end up buying at least one of the enamelled signs.

"Okay, I'd like these here," she said pointing to ten of the better signs. She certainly knew what she was looking for. "How much will it cost to buy and ship them?"

I picked up the small set of hanging scales from my basket and weighed each of the signs, noting everything down in a notebook. Then taking out my small calculator, I began working through her choices, writing everything down in my invoice pad for her. "This will be the cost of the signs, and this," I pointed to a second total, "is how much it will be to send them to you in the States."

"Charlie?" She nudged her bored husband. "Are you listening to the girl?"

He took off his peaked cap and wiped the sweat from his heavy brow with the back of his hand before replacing it. "Honey, I'm happy if you are."

She grabbed him and kissed his cheek. "I knew you'd love 'em as much as me." I wasn't sure he even cared what they looked like. "Pay the girl, will you?"

Without waiting for his agreement, she thanked me and moved on to the next stall.

"I'm afraid I only take cash," I said. I'd been caught out before my people I didn't know and this was a larger sale than most. I waited nervously, hoping this wouldn't put him off. It didn't. He paid me and I took down their name and address, handing him a receipt barely able to keep the smile from my face.

I lifted the signs down, wrapping each one carefully and placing them in my 'sold' box ready to take home and prepare for sending. When I stood up again I spotted Henri moving slowly through the crowds milling around the marketplace.

"Henri," I shouted standing on my tiptoes to wave at him. "Over here."

He stopped and held his hand up, moving as quickly as he could towards my stall.

"Any news?"

He nodded. "It is not good." His tanned face was strained. "I am sorry."

"Are you saying Ashley was telling the truth?" I could tell by his distress that he was. "What do we do now?"

He came around to my side of the stall. "I've spoken with your mother. She has packed up Ashley's belongings and is taking the girls to playgroup for the morning. She is getting them away from the house in case Dee and Leo return. The group leader has been informed and they will keep the children there with your mother until the gendarmes arrive."

"I can't believe it." I stared at him, stunned at how low Dee had sunk in my estimation. "We have to go."

He helped me pack my signs into the back of my car. "We must not go to your house, not until this has been sorted. We have no way of knowing if Leo and Dee will be there and I cannot take the chance of them following us and finding the girl." He was so in control and I realised what a loss he must have been to the police service.

"Okay. I'll drop these off at the studio. You follow me there and then I'll come to the school with you."

On the way to the school he filled me in on the rest of what had happened since I last saw him. It was hard to imagine that only three hours had passed since then.

"Her real name is Sophie." He barely contained his emotions as he explained more of what he'd discovered. "Her parents moved to Scotland a year ago, so didn't know many people there. Dee was a volunteer at the school; she helped the little ones with their reading."

"So that's how she got to know Ashley, um Sophie," I said almost to myself.

"Her mother recently started a new job, I am told. She worked long hours, sometimes arriving late to collect her daughter. Dee always offered to stay with the child. One day, the mother arrived late to collect her and she had gone."

I pictured the horror on that poor mother's face discovering her child missing. "Poor woman."

"*Oui.*"

An icy tingle ran down my spine making me shiver. "How didn't we know about her being missing? Wasn't the story reported in the international papers? I suppose it's been reported in the Scottish papers?"

"Yes, in the Scottish papers where Sophie is from. All the papers there and in England have been printing stories about the case. The French newspapers though, have been filled with the horrors of the heatwave and the fires breaking out. No one was looking in Hautvillers for a kidnapped child. It's not your fault you didn't know."

"What happens when we get to the school?"

"Her mother is on a flight. Because of the English press involvement, it was easy to prove to the gendarmes that she was Sophie's mother. A UK benefactor is flying her in his private jet to the nearest airport and she arrives within one hour." He put his foot down harder on the accelerator.

\*\*\*\*

I held Katie in my arms as we watched Sophie clinging to her mother's neck being carried to a waiting car. This little girl looked completely different to the one who had stayed at my home for the past few weeks. Her mother turned and mouthed a thank you to me. I could see how like her Sophie was. She shouted her thanks to us once again. Sophie waved with one hand, holding tightly onto the teddy Katie had given her with the other. I didn't care that tears were running down my face as we waited for them to get into the car and drive away.

Henri went to speak to two of his ex-colleagues who had arrived with the gendarmes. I hugged Katie, unsure how I would ever be brave enough to leave her at playgroup again.

"She's fine, darling," Mum said, reading my thoughts and stroking my arm. "And so is Sophie, now she's back with her own mother."

"I can't believe Dee could do such a thing," I swallowed the lump forming in my throat.

"Or Leo, he covered for her all this time," Mum said.

I nodded. "We've been harbouring two fugitives and a kidnapped child." I choked on the last words. Thinking I was going to be sick, I handed Katie to Mum and I ran inside to the bathroom. I leant over the sink resting my forehead on the cool tiles behind it trying to come to terms with the fact that I'd inadvertently helped keep Sophie from her mother.

"Sera, Sera," Henri called from the hallway. He must have heard me because the next thing I knew he was in the Ladies with me, hugging me tightly. "It's all okay now.

Sophie is back with her maman, she will be home soon."

"But we held that child at our house. I should have realised something was wrong. I knew she was withdrawn and unhappy, it just never occurred to me it could be because of something this horrendous."

He held me close to him. "*Cherie*, you looked after her. Katie was her friend and you discovered the truth in the end. The child trusted you enough to confide in you, that is a good thing."

I sniffed. "Her poor mother." He handed me a tissue and I blew my nose. "What about Dee and Leo?"

"They are looking for them now. The police believe Dee became obsessed with the little girl after her own baby died."

"I can't believe she did such a thing."

"Maybe their past is what caused them to be this way." He placed a finger under my chin and lifted it slightly. "I will be prosecuting them now for what they did to my father, Sera."

"I know." I didn't blame him at all.

"Before, I assumed Papa's death had been a tragic accident. These two people have proved how cruel they can be by taking the little girl, so now I am happy to press charges against them. The authorities are also checking out my theory that Leo started the fire at the barn."

I couldn't believe it. "But why would he do something like that?"

Henri shook his head. "I believe he started the fire to cover up any tracks left behind when they killed my father. He needed to hide Dee and Sophie at your home, but couldn't be near to the farm knowing the body might be discovered at any time."

"And in the process ended up causing Pierre's body to be discovered," I added thoughtfully.

"*Oui.*"

Did I ever know Leo at all? I wondered. "Do you think he meant for me to see him that day I drove through town?"

Henri nodded. "Do you take the same route each time?"

"Yes, several times a week, and usually at the same time, too." I thought about the plans Leo must have made to cover up what his sister had done, all the lies. "I'm pleased you're prosecuting them for your father's death," I said honestly. "Which reminds me." He watched silently as I pushed my hand into my back pocket to retrieve the picture. "I didn't know whether to cut Hazel from this, or not, but your dad looks very happy and I didn't want to ruin the picture. I thought I'd leave it up to you to decide."

He took it from me as if I was handing him the most delicate trinket and stared silently at his father's image. "Thank you, Sera," he whispered, looking down at the photo cupped in his hands.

"I took it from Hazel's house after they disappeared," I admitted. "It's been hidden in my room since then."

He smiled at me. "We have many of the answers now."

"Yes," I said. "Answers to questions we didn't know we should be asking." It was all too surreal. "It's going to take a long time for me to trust my instincts again. I thought I knew those people." I didn't add I'd also thought I'd known my mother, but she'd turned out to be capable of far worse than anything I ever imagined. "How can we ever be certain we truly know the people closest to us?"

Henri hugged me tightly. Placing his right hand behind my head, he kissed me. My upset and fear caused by everything that had happened instantly dispersed. I kissed him back, confident that with him in my life everything was going to be all right.

He moved back slightly. "To answer your question, we can't ever be sure who to trust," he said. "But we need to trust people. I promise you can trust me." He kissed me again as if to reassure me further. "Don't let what happened change you, Sera. You have me. I will not let anything bad happen to you ever again. Be brave, *cherie*. Enjoy your life and the people in it."

"You know what, Henri?" I said, finally free from my past. "I think I will."

# Also by Green Shutter Books

Broken Faces

## The Boardwalk by the Sea Series:

Summer Sundaes, book 1

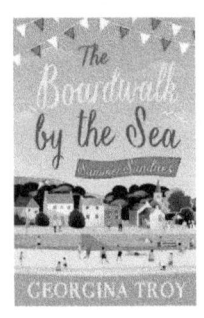

Shadow of the Marula Tree

# THANK YOU FOR READING RUN FOR THE SHADOWS!

Ella Drummond is a pseudonym of author Deborah Carr.

Her next book, WHILE I SLEPT,
is available now

You can join Ella's Readers' Group for FREE and receive the occasional book update, insider news, subscriber treats, here: http://www.deborahcarr.org/ella-drummond/

If you've enjoyed Run for the Shadows, please consider leaving a short review at Amazon.com, and Amazon.co.uk

CPSIA information can be obtained
at www.ICGtesting.com
Printed in the USA
BVHW030938250319
543619BV00001B/79/P

9 781720 979685